THE COLTONS

Meet the Coltons—
a California dynasty with a legacy of privilege and power. Family legend has it that when an heirloom diamond-and-sapphire necklace is placed on the right Colton bride, the sapphires—symbols of truth, sincerity and faithfulness—glow a clear azure blue. And with this gift, each jaded bachelor gets a second chance and discovers a love far more precious than the rare gem!

Harrison Colton: *The vengeful tycoon.* When the sister of his ex-fiancé shows up begging for his help, he discovers that the steel wall surrounding his heart isn't as impenetrable as he'd thought.

William Colton: *The playboy earl.* Rather than succumb to a loveless union, he'd willfully chosen poverty over prestige. But now he must convince the beautiful, destitute widow living next door of the sincerity of his love....

Jason Colton: *The determined doctor.* When this hardworking M.D. rushes to aid a pregnant woman, her secrecy suggests she's cut from the same cloth as his former bride-to-be. Now she must persuade him that their meeting was more than mere chance—but destiny!

KASEY MICHAELS is a *New York Times* and *USA Today* bestselling author of more than sixty books that range from contemporary to historical romance. Recipient of the Romance Writers of America RITA Award and Career Achievement Award from *Romantic Times Magazine,* in addition to writing for Silhouette, Kasey is currently writing single-title contemporary fiction and Regency historical romances. When asked about her work for the Colton series, she said that she has rarely felt so involved in a project, one with such scope and diversity of plot and characters.

RUTH LANGAN, award-winning, bestselling author of more than sixty books, both contemporary and historical, has been described by *Romantic Times Magazine* as "a true master at involving your emotions, be they laughter or tears." Ruth has given dozens of print, radio and TV interviews, including *Good Morning America* and *CNN News,* as well as such diverse publications as the *Wall Street Journal, Cosmopolitan* and the *Detroit Free Press.* It should be obvious to all her readers that Ruth Langan loves her work and lives to please her readers. "Colton's Bride" is a story that truly touched her heart. She hopes it touches all of yours, as well.

CAROLYN ZANE loves to write stories about pregnancy, as she is one of those hateful women who feels her best when she's expecting. While other women might have languished with morning sickness, Carolyn devoured barbecue beef sandwiches and chocolate cake with ice cream. Or anything that was not nailed down...with ice cream. Her husband, Matt, being the supportive sort, joined her in her ice cream habit. Had Carolyn known how wonderful the whole pregnancy thing really was, she most likely would not have waited sixteen years into her marriage to try it and would have well over a dozen children by now. As it is, she is kept more than busy with her two beautiful little daughters, Madeline and Olivia, and her adopted son, golden retriever Bob Barker.

THE COLTONS

Brides of Privilege

KASEY MICHAELS
RUTH LANGAN
CAROLYN ZANE

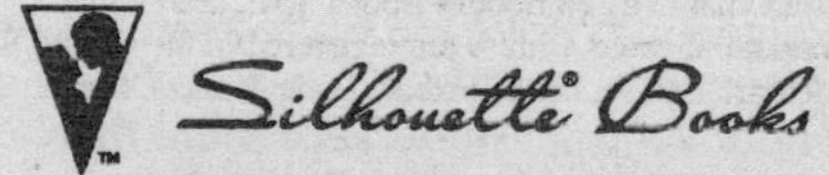

Silhouette® Books
Published by Silhouette Books
America's Publisher of Contemporary Romance

If you purchased this book without a cover you should be aware that this book is stolen property. It was reported as "unsold and destroyed" to the publisher, and neither the author nor the publisher has received any payment for this "stripped book."

Special thanks and acknowledgment are given to Kasey Michaels, Ruth Langan and Carolyn Zane for their contributions to THE COLTONS: BRIDES OF PRIVILEGE.

SILHOUETTE BOOKS

THE COLTONS: BRIDES OF PRIVILEGE

Copyright © 2001 by Harlequin Books S.A.

ISBN 0-373-48444-5

The publisher acknowledges the copyright holders of the individual works as follows:

SAPPHIRE BRIDE
Copyright © 2001 by Harlequin Books S.A.

COLTON'S BRIDE
Copyright © 2001 by Harlequin Books S.A.

DESTINY'S BRIDE
Copyright © 2001 by Harlequin Books S.A.

All rights reserved. Except for use in any review, the reproduction or utilization of this work in whole or in part in any form by any electronic, mechanical or other means, now known or hereafter invented, including xerography, photocopying and recording, or in any information storage or retrieval system, is forbidden without the written permission of the editorial office, Silhouette Books, 300 East 42nd Street, New York, NY 10017 U.S.A.

All characters in this book have no existence outside the imagination of the author and have no relation whatsoever to anyone bearing the same name or names. They are not even distantly inspired by any individual known or unknown to the author, and all incidents are pure invention.

This edition published by arrangement with Harlequin Books S.A.

® and TM are trademarks of Harlequin Books S.A., used under license. Trademarks indicated with ® are registered in the United States Patent and Trademark Office, the Canadian Trade Marks Office and in other countries.

Visit Silhouette at www.eHarlequin.com

Printed In U.S.A.

CONTENTS

THE COLTONS: BRIDES OF PRIVILEGE

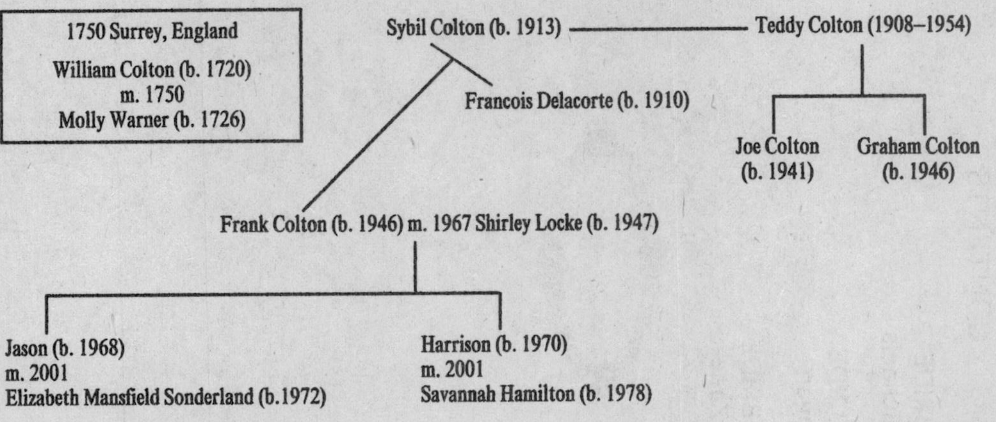

SAPPHIRE BRIDE
by Kasey Michaels

Chapter 1

Lorraine Nealy stuck small yellow arrows on the neatly typed pages. "Here, here and here," she said rather unnecessarily as she then placed each page on the desktop. The paper arrows that said without words "Sign here, bozo" were also redundant, but Harrison Colton didn't say anything; he just signed on each indicated line. Break Lorraine's stride and she unfailingly started over from the beginning. Harrison was just about done signing the papers and the idea of going back to Go wasn't part of his plan.

"Lorraine," he said at last, as his personal assistant—she'd made it very clear she was *not* a secretary—gathered up the contracts, "whatever would I do without you?"

"You'd wither and die, Mr. Colton. The whole place would fall down around your ears. It wouldn't be pretty, trust me,'' Lorraine responded without missing a beat.

In her middle fifties, Lorraine had been at Colton Media Holdings for thirty years and had convinced herself that she was the linchpin that held CMH together. She'd been Frank Colton's personal assistant until Harrison's father had let go of the reins enough to let his younger son take over, and now she ran CMH through Harrison, as she'd tell anyone who asked. Even if they didn't ask.

Harrison smiled, stood up, reached for the navy-blue sport coat he'd hung on the back of his chair. ''In that case, I'm probably safe in leaving early today, with CMH in such reliable hands. Unless you've got more papers for me to sign?''

''Nope, all done. Your collar's crooked,'' Lorraine added, and Harrison quickly reached up and straightened it, slipping the Windsor knot on his maroon-and-navy striped tie back into place as well. At thirty-one, he had yet to adopt CMH's own policy of casual Fridays, although he had heartily subscribed to the optional work-at-home Fridays. He had only come into the office to sign the contracts, and was more than ready to get an early start on his weekend.

Smoothing down his collar, he then ran a hand over his jet-black hair before Lorraine could tell him that he looked like he'd been ''rode hard and put away wet,'' and picked up his briefcase. ''I am excused, aren't I, Lorraine?'' he asked, already heading for the door.

''Actually...'' Lorraine began, and Harrison

stopped halfway across the wide expanse of beige Berber carpeting, turned to look at her, his green eyes narrowed. "No, never mind. I'll get rid of her. Just go out the side door."

"Her?" Harrison, intrigued in spite of himself, shot a quick look toward the closed door that led to Lorraine's office and the reception area. "Her who?"

Lorraine clasped the contracts to her rather flat chest and rolled her watery blue eyes. "Her who has been sitting in my office for the past hour, obviously unable to take a hint and go away. That her."

"No appointment? No, of course not. I don't make appointments for Friday afternoons. But she didn't leave? Wow. Lorraine, you must be losing your edge. When you say no, strong men cringe. I know I do."

"I told her maybe," Lorraine said so quietly that Harrison had to step closer in order to hear her.

"You said maybe," Harrison repeated, sincerely impressed. "You never say maybe, Lorraine. Yes, no, not in your wildest dreams. But never maybe. What does this woman want? Is she collecting for homeless poodles and hit your one soft spot?"

"There are rarely homeless poodles, Mr. Colton," she replied tightly. "Poodles are eminently lovable, and almost always find homes."

"Yeah," Harrison said, grinning. "With you. What are you up to, at last count? Ten?"

"Six, with all of them expecting me home in the next hour to feed them, so if you're done dragging your feet, please leave by the side door so that I can go back out there and truthfully tell this Hamilton woman that you've gone for the day.''

''Whoa,'' Harrison said, holding out an arm, blocking Lorraine's exit. ''Did you say Hamilton? *Annette* Hamilton? No, that couldn't be. She's Annette O'Meara now.''

Lorraine pulled a small piece of notepaper out of her pocket and checked it before saying, ''Not Annette. This is a Ms. Savannah Hamilton. I'll tell her you've gone. Would you like me to set up an appointment sometime next month?''

No, he didn't want Lorraine to make an appointment for Ms. Savannah Hamilton for next month. What he'd like is for Lorraine to arrange for Ms. Savannah Hamilton to be on the next space launch headed for Mars. And definitely with the trip being a real family vacation, so that Sam and Annette went with her.

Harrison rubbed at his jaw as he walked back to the desk and laid down his briefcase. ''What does she want?''

''What do any of them want?'' Lorraine said. ''A job. They think they can do an end run around the personnel department, bat their big baby blues at you, and have their byline on a story within six months, their Pulitzer within the year. Like I said, I'll get rid of her. I should have gotten rid of her an hour ago.''

''Why didn't you?''

Lorraine shrugged her thin shoulders. ''I think you're right. She does have a sort of stray-dog or wounded-puppy look to her. All dressed up and nowhere to go. And she seemed to be more unhappy about being here than I was to look up and see her standing in front of my desk. Maybe, I thought, she isn't looking for a job. Maybe she's looking for something else. I thought I could get her to tell me what she wanted, but she said it was a personal matter and I couldn't get her to say anything else. Even my homemade peanut butter cookies couldn't get her to talk."

"Wow," Harrison said, slipping off his sport coat and walking behind the desk. Trying to keep it light, so that Lorraine didn't suspect anything, he continued, "When the peanut butter cookies don't work, there's nothing else left. Thumbscrews, the rack—none of them are more potent than your peanut butter cookies. I'm surprised you didn't call Security and have Ms. Hamilton tossed out on her rear."

"Me, too," Lorraine said, her hand on the doorknob. "I take it I can relax now and Ms. Savannah Hamilton's personal matter doesn't have anything to do with an unexpected Colton cooking in the oven, because you seem truly surprised to see her, and because I know you're a good boy. Sometimes. So, you'll see her?"

Harrison lowered his six-foot-two-inch frame into the chair behind the desk. He ignored the first part of Lorraine's little speech because he was too used to her to object. "But you can go home once you've shown her in. And don't worry. I took three karate lessons when Jason and I were kids, so I don't think she'll be able to overpower me."

"Your father was never flippant," Lorraine reminded him. "He would never have made that crack, or the one about my peanut butter cookies."

"True. But you love me. You even worry about me, and I'm probably crazy, because I like it," Harrison said, wondering if he wanted to keep Lorraine here, and talking, or if he wanted her out of the room now, and Savannah Hamilton in it. "Give me five minutes, then send her in, okay?"

He needed five minutes, to think about Savannah Hamilton, to beat down the anger that automatically surfaced whenever he heard the Hamilton name. He needed time to remind himself that this wasn't six years ago, he wasn't a gullible idiot anymore, and he could handle whatever Savannah was going to say without either going ballistic or allowing some unexpected scabs to come off what he most sincerely hoped were healed wounds.

Six years. That was a long time, but maybe not long enough, because he still could remember everything with shameful clarity.

What a naive idiot he'd been back then. Straight out of graduate school and ready to take on the world, but on his terms. He'd refused his dad's offer of a job with CMH and had set out to make it big on his own, without family help. And he'd done it, too, and only joined CMH when he'd already proved himself. He'd done just fine, except for that early speed bump with the Hamiltons.

An employment speed bump, and an emotional one, both of them damn painful. Harrison steepled his fingers in front of his nose and allowed the memories to overtake him, just for a few moments.

He'd joined Sam Hamilton's company with high hopes, and when he'd met and quickly fallen in love with Sam's older daughter, Annette, it seemed like a fairy tale straight out of the storybooks.

That probably should have been his first warning.

Sam Hamilton had welcomed him as a son, given his blessing to the engagement, and begun planning a huge society wedding. So far so good. Harrison had liked the affable Sam, loved the beautiful, dark-haired Annette, and gotten a huge kick out of her rather solemn and serious younger sister, Savannah.

Harrison smiled now as he remembered Savannah. Nice kid, a really nice kid. The baby sister he'd never had. He'd felt a little sorry for her, a motherless child whose father made no secret of the fact that he believed Annette had gotten the looks and Savannah the brains—and Sam Hamilton believed brains in a woman were about as out of place as suspenders on a bikini.

How old had Savannah been? Seventeen? Yeah, about that. She'd still been at boarding school, and Harrison had visited her there several times because she was homesick and because the school was close to the highway that led to his parents' home in Prosperino, California. He'd visited her, dropped off things from home that she wanted, and somehow got involved in helping her with a school project.

He wondered how that had worked out, if she'd gotten a good grade. Not that he'd ask her, because that was ancient history, just like his job at Hamilton's and his engagement to Annette were ancient history.

''Bastard,'' Harrison grumbled, thinking about Sam Hamilton, thinking about the day Sam had asked him to come into his study for a small talk. Small talk? Like hell. Sam had passed some legal papers across the desk to Harrison, telling him he'd made up a prenuptial agreement that included giving Sam a stake in CMH. As if Harrison would ask his father to do any such thing!

Harrison sighed, shook his head. ''And then there was one,'' he said to himself, remembering how he'd stormed out of Sam's study, grabbed Annette by the hand and taken her outside to tell her it looked like they had a problem. Would she consider eloping with him? They could hop in the car and be in Reno by nightfall, be married by morning.

''Idiot. Stupid, stupid idiot,'' Harrison grumbled, picking up the pen he'd just used and winging it across the room. No way was Annette going to elope. In fact, unless he agreed to sign the prenuptial agreement, no way was she going to marry him. She didn't even pretend to really love him, didn't bother to lie. She saw their union as advantageous to her father, financially, and to herself, socially. Without a stake in CMH, without Harrison waking up, going home, and taking a cushy job at CMH, suddenly *he* was about as useless as suspenders on a bikini.

Oh, yeah. He wanted a Hamilton in his office. Sure he did.

Still, this was Savannah. She'd never done anything to him, right? She'd been as young and innocent as he'd been stupid and gullible. It wasn't her fault her father was a son of a bitch and her sister a heartless gold digger.

Harrison leaned forward and hit the button on the intercom. "Send her in please, Lorraine, and then you can call it a day."

He stood, not bothering to slip on his sport coat, and stepped from behind the desk, planning to meet Savannah halfway. It was the least he could do.

The door opened and Lorraine stepped halfway through the opening, putting her back against the door as she waved for the visitor to enter. "Ms. Savannah Hamilton to see you, sir. And I'm outta here. Don't do anything I wouldn't do."

"Thank you, Lorraine," Harrison said, wondering how old he'd have to be, with how many titles, and after proving himself how many times, before Lorraine treated him like a grown-up. He probably couldn't hope to get that old.

And then there was no more time for thinking, because Savannah Hamilton was in the room.

She hadn't grown at all, was still probably about an inch over five feet five, which made her a full three inches taller than Annette. Her hair was still the same ash blond in an almost startling contrast to Annette's coal-black hair, although Savannah now wore hers in a tight French twist, instead of the ponytail he remembered.

Her slim body was also pretty much the same. Long straight legs, narrow waist and hips, shoulders just a little too wide. Eyes as blue as the California sky, and still with that faintly startled, nervous look to them; eyes she used to look at him for the count of three, then averted to inspect the Berber carpet.

Creamy white skin. He remembered that she'd done a paper on the dangerous effects of the sun—and gotten an A. Obviously she remembered as well, because the scattering of freckles over cheeks and nose he could recall seeing were nowhere in evidence. Then he noticed the lipstick and the blusher and the eye shadow. She looked good, he imagined, but she didn't look like Savannah. She looked like Savannah trying to look like Annette.

That made him angry.

"Hello, Savannah," he said when she didn't speak. "What an unexpected pleasure."

She lifted her head, looked at him squarely, and then smiled. "Oh, I sincerely doubt that, Harry," she said in that slightly husky voice that had always pleased him, then seemed to remember that she was here for something important, at which time the smile disappeared like the sun behind a cloud.

"Harry," Harrison repeated. "Man, I haven't heard that in a long time. You're the only person who's ever called me Harry."

She looked up again, and as he was getting pretty tired of trying to make eye contact with her for more than three seconds, he quickly led her to the small grouping of chairs he used for informal meetings, and motioned for her to sit down. "I shouldn't call you Harry," she said as she tucked her purse between herself and the arm of the chair. "I'm sorry."

"Don't be, Savannah. I like it. And at least then nobody's disappointed when I come into the room and they realize I'm not Harrison Ford.'' Harrison sat down in a facing chair, across the low cocktail table because he had the feeling that if he sat any closer Savannah might bolt, run out, and he'd never know why she'd come here in the first place. ''So, how have you been?''

''I—I just completed grad school,'' she told him as she twisted her hands in her lap.

''And probably graduated with honors. You were always a great student.'' Damn, but she was nervous. Was he really so intimidating?

She nodded. ''How about you, Harry? I read in the papers about how your dad has handed most of the reins over to you. Your own company doing well, and now this? In the article I read, the reporter called you a tycoon and a genius.''

''Don't believe everything you read in the papers, Savannah,'' Harrison said, shifting slightly in his chair. The last thing he wanted was a discussion with any Hamilton about his finances. ''So, how's the family?''

He watched as a rather becoming light-pink flush ran into Savannah's cheeks, much more natural than the blusher she wore, in his opinion. ''Annette filed for divorce last week,'' she told him, then quite clearly watched for his reaction.

''Is that so?'' he said, happily surprised to realize that he didn't give a damn what Annette was doing. ''Too bad.''

''I think she's sorry, Harry,'' Savannah said, and he remembered that Savannah had always had this way of trying to explain her sister, make excuses for her. Even six years ago. "I know that she broke off her engagement to you because she'd met Robert, but I also know she knew she'd made a mistake almost from the beginning. Robert O'Meara isn't exactly...well, let's just say that I don't think he and Annette had much in common."

"Robert O'Meara must be sixty years old, Savannah. How could Annette have expected them to have anything in common? The man was as old as Sam." Then Harrison held out his hands, signaling that he shouldn't have said what he'd said, and that he didn't want to pursue the subject. Still, he had to know. "So that's what they told you? That Annette met O'Meara, then dumped me, gave back the ring, told me she's sorry but please take a hike?"

"It's not true?" Savannah asked, her eyes wide. "I always just assumed—"

"No, no, of course it's true," Harrison said quickly. "I did the gentlemanly thing and stepped aside. I'm only sorry I never stopped by your school to say goodbye. So, did you get a good grade on that paper we worked on together?"

"An A, yes. Thank you."

"I didn't do much more than find some research materials for you," Harrison said, moving to the small bar to pour himself a glass of water, and one for Savannah. His throat was dry, and tight, and he felt angry with Savannah for coming here, for bringing back memories he'd carefully buried. Still, he might as well get it over with. "And your father? How's Sam?"

She bit her bottom lip, turned away from him.

That wasn't good. That wasn't good at all.

"Savannah? What's wrong? Is Sam ill?"

She shook her head. "No. Not ill."

"But he's not good?"

Another shake of her head.

"Savannah, we could be here all day, playing twenty questions, but I think you're here to talk about Sam. So let's talk about Sam, okay? Did he send you here?"

That brought her head up. "No! I mean, no, of course not. He has no idea I'm here. Nobody knows I'm here. I don't think *I* know why I'm here, but I can see now that it was a mistake." She put down her glass, picked up her purse and stood. "Goodbye, Harry. It—it really was good seeing you again."

He let her take about three steps before he said, "Sit down, Savannah. Now."

Savannah sat down once more, put down her purse. But she still didn't look at him.

He let her dig in her purse for a handkerchief, dab at her eyes, blow her nose, and then he leaned forward in his chair and asked her bluntly, "Are you going to tell me your problem, or am I going to have to refuse to take you out for pizza?"

His references to the few times he'd stopped at her school and rescued her from cafeteria food seemed to calm Savannah, and she took a deep breath, gave him a watery smile. "And you won't let me have pepperoni on the pizza you won't buy me, right?"

"You hit that one right on the button," he said, wondering if he should tell her that her mascara had run, so that she looked like a blond raccoon. No, he'd better not. Her self-confidence seemed pretty shaken as it was, without letting her know her war paint had slipped. "Now, tell me why you're here. Please?"

She played with the clasp of her purse for a few moments, snapping and unsnapping it, then stood up, began to pace. "I'm not trying to make a break for it, Harry. But I can't say this and stay still, okay?"

"Okay," Harrison said, trying to keep his tone neutral. He felt this insane urge to go to her, hug her close, tell her everything was going to be all right, just fine and dandy. But he doubted that she'd let him hug her, for one, and he was pretty sure hugging a Hamilton, any Hamilton, would be a lose-lose situation for him. "Anytime you're ready, Savannah. And I promise not to interrupt."

She stopped pacing, turned and smiled at him. "Oh, please, interrupt whenever you want. I'm sure you'll want to."

She bent to pick up her glass of water, drained it. "Here goes," she said, pacing once more. "Dad's company is in trouble," she began, then went on quickly, "I mean, really in trouble."

"That's too bad, Savannah," Harrison said, mentally doing handsprings. He was itching to hop on the internet, find out just how badly Sam's business was doing, and at the same time wondering what he could do to help that business tumble over the last cliff toward bankruptcy.

"Dad's at the end of his rope," she continued,

picking up a small paperweight and passing it from hand to hand. ''It's Robert's fault, of course.''

''Of course,'' Harrison repeated. ''*How* is it Annette's husband's fault?''

Savannah put down the paperweight and returned to sit in the chair across from Harrison. ''Well, I'm not sure of all of this, but Annette said that Robert had promised to invest a considerable amount of money in Dad's company, plus give Dad stock options or something in his own company. Sort of a wedding present, you understand.''

''Oh, yeah,'' Harrison said, barely able to keep the bitterness out of his voice. ''I understand. So? What went wrong?''

''What went *wrong* is that Robert never bothered to mention to Dad that he was highly leveraged or that the Internal Revenue Service had about a dozen liens on his company, on Robert as an individual.''

''In plain English,'' Harrison said, ''good old Robert was not only broke, he was in debt up to his eyeballs. Is that it?''

Savannah nodded. ''Dad's lawyers and Robert's lawyers kept everything quiet for several years, and out of the courts, but now both companies are in trouble.''

''So Annette filed for divorce. Nothing like a loyal wife, I always say.''

''Oh, no, no. Annette felt duty bound to hold true to her vows. She told me so. But then he— Well, he's been unfaithful. She can't forgive that, and I don't blame her.''

Harrison fought the urge to ask Savannah if she

wanted another glass of water, to make it easier for her to swallow the pack of lies her sister had handed her. But he was a nice guy, he told himself, and Savannah didn't need him telling her that her father was a bastard and her sister had all but whored herself for money. Except that whores get paid.

Then it hit him. "Savannah, you aren't here running interference for Annette, are you?"

"Running interference, Harry? What's that?"

"Forget it," Harrison said, hoping he'd been wrong, and Savannah wasn't here to talk him into meeting with Annette, listening to Annette tell him that she'd made a mistake, that she loved him and wanted him—and his money—back. He was pretty sure his stomach wasn't strong enough to listen to that. Besides, from everything Savannah had said, and from what she hadn't said, he'd realized that she hadn't a clue as to why the engagement had been broken off six years ago. Not a single clue. "I'm just getting paranoid in my old age, I guess."

"Oh," Savannah said, and went back to nervously rubbing her hands together, so that clearly she had more to say. Maybe she hoped if she rubbed her hands together long enough a genie would appear and say the words for her.

But, coming from Savannah or a genie, Harrison was pretty sure he didn't want to hear any of it. Which didn't explain why he opened his mouth and said, "Come on, Savannah. Tell me everything. I want to help. Really."

"I don't know why I thought this would be easier than it is," she said, almost to herself, then looked at Harrison. ''All right, Harry. I'm going to say this fast, because otherwise I'll lose my nerve. Dad has this idea in his head that I should marry James Vaughn. Do you know him?''

Why had Harrison thought that nothing Savannah could say would make him think any worse of Sam Hamilton? Why had he believed that Sam Hamilton was already about as much bad news as he could be, and couldn't sink any lower?

''Jimmy Vaughn?'' he asked, trying to imagine the loudmouthed, oily man with Savannah. Kissing her. Touching her. Taking her so obvious innocence and crushing it. The thought sickened him. ''The guy's been married about six times, for crying out loud. Your father shouldn't let you within fifty miles of him.''

''Five times,'' Savannah said quietly, ''and Dad has made it very clear to me that James would be able to save us from financial ruin if I agree to the marriage. Dad...Dad says it's my duty to marry money.''

''Sam Hamilton should ride a hot poker straight to hell,'' Harrison said, heading for the bar again, this time to splash some Scotch in his glass. ''You're not going to do it, are you, Savannah?''

''I don't want to,'' she told him, swiveling in her chair to talk to him. ''That's why I'm here.''

Harrison looked at Savannah for long moments, then redirected his attention to the glass he held. He poured another inch of Scotch into the glass. ''Go on,'' he said, the words *déjà vu all over again* running through his brain.

"I know it's a lot to ask, Harry. Too much. Definitely. But we could consider it as a sort of loan, you know? And you'd get a piece of Dad's company. I know James is supposed to get forty percent of it when—*if* he marries me. And we wouldn't have to marry. I mean, that wouldn't really be necessary, right? It could just be a business deal. You help out Dad, he signs part of the business over to you. I know you still acquire companies, Harry, aside from running CMH. I read that in the article I told you about. If anyone could turn around Dad's business, make it profitable, it's you. The tycoon with the golden touch, just like I read in that article."

She stopped talking and stopped wringing her hands in her lap. She looked up at Harrison, her expression part determination, part terror, her huge blue eyes awash now in both ruined mascara and brilliant tears. "I know I have no right to ask this of you. I know that, truly. But I can't marry James Vaughn, Harry. I just can't."

"So walk away, Savannah," Harrison said, knowing he sounded cruel. "You're a grown woman now, not a child anymore. Walk away. And if you want to tell Sam to go to hell before you leave, you have my blessing."

"I can't do that either, Harry," Savannah said, gathering up her purse once more, getting to her feet. "He told me something last week, something I never knew, never wanted to know. I—I owe him."

"Excuse me? You *owe* him. How? For sending you to school? For putting a roof over your head?

Give me a break, Savannah. Parents don't tell their children they *owe* them. Not good parents."

"He's not my father," Savannah said, closing her eyes. "He told me last week, Harry. He's not really my father. My mother confessed an infidelity right before she died, and told him that Annette's his, but I'm not. My mother died when I was five. Dad—Sam's known all this time. I'd—I'd always wondered why Annette and I look so little alike. Now I know. Now I know a lot of things."

Harrison felt as if he'd just been punched in the gut. He quickly poured some Scotch into a small glass, pressed it on Savannah as he took her purse and led her back to the chair. "Are you all right?"

She took a sip of the Scotch, made a face. "I'm not sure, Harry. I'm still pretty numb, to tell you the truth."

"And now you think you *owe* Sam. What do you owe him for, Savannah? For telling you this pile of—"

"He was telling the truth, Harry. He even showed me a letter from my real father that he found in my mother's things. He was an air force colonel, and he died in a plane crash overseas before I was born. The—the letter was all about how he'd be home from Spain in three weeks, and he and my mother would run off together." She took another small sip of Scotch. "So you see, it's all quite true. I'm really not a Hamilton at all."

"Look hard enough and there's a silver lining in every cloud," Harrison muttered, then mentally smacked himself. Savannah was torn apart, an idiot could see that. And only a real bastard, like Sam Hamilton, would have deliberately torn her apart after all these years of keeping a secret of such gravity. Only a real bastard, like Sam Hamilton, would save up that secret, to use it when he needed to use it, needed a hammer to hold over Savannah's head.

"Can you help me, Harry?" she asked when Harrison didn't say anything else. "I know it's kind of crazy, but I feel that if I can help Dad save his company, I'll have paid him back a little for what my mother did to him, how she hurt him. But—but I just can't face marrying James Vaughn. And I hate Dad for asking me to, even as I feel I owe him something. I know that someone who comes in and puts fresh money into a business, saves it, is called a white knight. I rather liked that terminology."

She hesitated a moment, then gifted him with a watery smile. "I've thought about this long and hard since last week, and you're the only white knight I know, Harry. You always were."

"Give me a minute," Harrison said, seriously in need of clearing his head before he could say anything else. He'd forgotten, until that moment, that he'd suspected that the teenage Savannah had a crush on him. But it hadn't occurred to him that she might still see him in the role of hero. It was a decidedly uncomfortable role.

He knew that Savannah had no clue that her sister—half sister, he corrected—had been a very willing participant in Sam's first stab at marrying his daughters off in exchange for money. Not a single clue. As far as Savannah knew, Annette had simply fallen in love with Robert O'Meara and jilted him.

And yet, without knowing any of this, here was Savannah, coming to call on her old friend, her sister's former fiancé—her white knight—to ask his help in bailing out that same father financially.

Definitely déjà vu all over again.

Except that Savannah had been offered to James Vaughn, not to Harrison, and she had magnanimously said that Harrison didn't have to marry her. Would he just please help her save Sam Hamilton, a man he'd be more than happy to hand an anchor if the guy was drowning.

"What happens if I help Sam?" Harrison asked at last. "You wouldn't marry Vaughn, I've already figured that out. But what then, Savannah? What will you do then?"

"You mean what will I do about my...about Sam? That is what you're asking, isn't it?"

"That's why you graduated at the top of your class, which I'm betting you did," Harrison said. "So tell me. Are you going to stick around, wait for the next time and end up bailing out Sam again?"

"The next time? You think there would be a next time?" She shook her head. "No, I'm not. I love Dad, I think, but I'm not blind to his faults. I'm not blind to Annette's, either, although I wouldn't want to speak badly of her, especially to you. But I've spent a lot of years being the odd man out, and now I know why. I've had a lot of questions answered in this past week. But I can't just walk away, Harry. In a way, I do owe him. That doesn't mean I'm not moving out of the house if I can find another way to help him. I'll go off on my own, and probably without looking back.''

Harrison nodded. ''All grown-up, aren't you, Savannah?'' he asked, taking her hand, helping her to her feet. An idea had begun to form in his head, and he needed time for it to percolate. ''We'll talk some more, but first let's go get some pizza.''

Chapter 2

Savannah stood in front of the mirror in the rest room of Sal's Pizza Parlor, wondering why Harry hadn't told her that her mascara had run. She looked all smudged and out of focus, almost wounded.

"Waterproof," she grumbled as she wet a paper towel and rubbed at the smudges. "What a crock."

A middle-aged woman exited the single stall in the small rest room and Savannah stepped aside, to allow her access to the sink. "Thanks," the woman said, soaping her hands. "Are you all right?"

Savannah took an involuntary step backward. Was it that obvious? "Yes, thank you," she said. "I'm fine."

"That's good," the woman said. "I thought maybe you'd been crying. Waterproof, smudge proof, possibly even hurricane proof, but I've yet to meet the mascara that can hold its own through tears." She turned off the taps and dried her hands on a paper towel Savannah handed her. "I carry a small bottle of baby oil in my purse, along with the kitchen sink and any other essentials, as my husband would say. It works wonders on those smudges."

Before she knew it, the woman had rummaged through a truly impressive large purse and produced the bottle, as well as a travel pack of tissues. "Here you go," she said, dripping a few drops of oil on the tissue, then handing it to Savannah. "Oh," she added as she walked to the door, "and whoever he is, he's not worth it. None of them are, trust me."

Savannah watched the woman go, then turned back to the mirror and wiped the tissue over her left eye. It worked, almost too well, as now the tissue held not only the smudged mascara, but the eye shadow, as well. There was no choice now except to clean off the entire right eye, too, which she did.

"I don't know how, but that looks even worse," she told her reflection. "Oh, the hell with it," she said, turning on the taps and reaching for the soap.

The next time she looked at her reflection, while dabbing at her wet skin with even more paper towels, the Savannah Hamilton she had known all her life was looking back at her. "There goes well over one hundred dollars of makeup and makeover down the drain," she said, and realized she wasn't sorry.

It had seemed like such a good idea, stopping at a local department store, having the woman at the makeup counter do her face for her, then buying some of the cosmetics.

She'd wanted to look more professional, more *finished,* before she faced Harry. And, to be honest with herself, she'd also wanted to sort of hide behind the makeup. She thought she'd feel more confident. She'd ended up looking ridiculous.

Not that she'd expected Harry to take one look at her and jump her bones—as Elizabeth Mansfield, her roommate at the private school and all through college had once so delicately put it—then say, "Why, Savannah, I have the perfect solution. You're beautiful, you're here, and I think I'm nuts about you. Let's get married!"

No, she hadn't thought that would happen. Not in her wildest dreams.

Well, maybe in her wildest dreams.

"Okay, back to reality, Savannah," she said, rummaging in her purse for a tube of lipstick, usually her only makeup. "He might help you, he might not, but he's going to be sending out a search party soon if you don't get out of here and back to the table."

Taking just another moment to push an errant lock of ash-blond hair behind her ear, check over her beige slacks and matching blouse and hip-length sweater vest, and pick a bit of damp paper toweling from the gold chain around her neck, she declared herself to be as ready as she was ever going to be, and left the rest room.

She located Harry at a scarred wooden table in front of the window that overlooked the rest of the small strip mall located only three blocks from the building housing CMH. They'd walked here, under a wonderfully warm early spring sun, and Savannah was pretty sure that if she just had an hour or so to sit, she could walk back in her new high heels without wincing too much.

Harry saw her and half rose from his chair until she sat down across from him. He looked at her, and then he smiled. "Now there's the Savannah I know and love. Complete with freckles."

"Is that your way of saying I still look seventeen?" she asked him. "How depressing. And I'd hoped I'd grown up."

Harry looked nonplussed for a moment, then said, "Oh, you've grown up, Savannah. Definitely. I ordered the large pie, half plain, half pepperoni. Okay?"

"Okay," she said, nodding, pulling the soda he must have ordered closer to her, taking a sip from the straw. That felt better, and maybe would even keep her tongue from cleaving to the roof of her mouth.

How long had she had this silly crush on Harrison Colton? From the first day she'd come home from boarding school to see him standing beside the pool in their backyard, laughing at something Annette had just said to him? Probably.

So tall, so extraordinarily well constructed, his jet-black hair wet and shiny from the water, his eyes so green they seemed to be made of precious emeralds. Those long, straight legs sprinkled with dark hair. That smile that could lure angels from the heavens.

Her friend Elizabeth, who had come home with

her for the weekend, had stood there with her mouth hanging open, then finally said jokingly, "If we play our cards right, Savannah, we can lock your sister in the pool house and have him all to ourselves. What do you think, is that a plan?" She and Elizabeth had both been rather shy, but they'd had an active imaginary life.

Savannah smiled at the memory, although in a way it was bittersweet, because Annette and Harry had announced their engagement that same night, just as Savannah was pretty sure she'd lost her heart to him, for now, for forever.

"You're smiling," Harry said now, interrupting Savannah's thoughts. "What are you smiling about?"

"Hmmm?" she said, then snapped back to reality. "Oh, nothing. I was just remembering the first day I met you. You threw me in the pool."

"Only after watching you take twenty minutes to slowly inch your way in," he reminded her. "And you were already pretty wet. You had a friend with you, didn't you? The three of us spent the afternoon pretty much trying to drown each other, as I recall. What was her name?"

"Elizabeth Mansfield, and she'd be amazed that you remember her. She got married right after college last year, but I don't think things are going well for her right now. Well, actually, I know they're not. Otherwise, I might have gone off to cry on her shoulder and you wouldn't have had to hear any of this."

"That's too bad about your friend, but I'm glad

you came to me, Savannah. We did have fun that day, though—you, your friend Elizabeth, and me. Annette didn't join us in the pool," Harry said, obviously caught up in his own memories. "She'd just had her hair done for the party that night and didn't want to ruin it. But, you know, now that I think about it, I don't think she ever went in the pool."

"She can't swim," Savannah said, then shook her head. "No, that's not true. Annette can swim. She just doesn't like getting wet, ruining her hair and makeup. Funny. I don't have to be within fifty miles of a pool to ruin my makeup."

"And I'm very glad you did, Savannah," Harry told her, sitting back as the waitress set down a large metal tray holding their pizza, two plates and a very thick wad of paper napkins. "No, seriously," he added as Savannah made a face, "I've always thought you were very much what the magazines call an All-American girl. Very natural."

"And I always wondered why I didn't look as sleek, petite and sophisticated as my sister," Savannah said, picking a thin slice of pepperoni off a slice of pizza, then popping it into her mouth. "Now I know why. Life is just chock-full of little surprises, isn't it, Harry?"

"You're hurting, aren't you?" Harry reached across the table and squeezed her hand. "And I don't blame you, Savannah, not one bit. You've had a hell of a shock, and more than one." He sat back again, and she saw a slight tic working along his smooth jaw. "I'd like to punch Sam Hamilton into the middle of next week."

Savannah gave him a weak smile. ''I guess that answers my question then, doesn't it? You're not going to invest in Dad's company, bail him out. I can't say I blame you, or that I'm surprised. I knew it was a long shot, at best.''

''Eat your pizza, Savannah,'' Harry said as his cell phone began to ring. ''I've been waiting for a call-back after phoning a source I know. Let me take this outside.'' He stood, flipped open the phone, and Savannah could hear him saying as he walked away, ''Talk to me. Did you get it?''

Did the ''source'' get *what,* Savannah wondered, watching through the window as Harrison paced the pavement, alternately talking and listening.

He looked very much the tycoon at that moment. Tailor-made slacks and jacket, hand-sewn shoes, his posture straight and rather commanding. He was definitely Harrison Colton now. So very different from the Harry Colton she remembered, had played badminton and water polo with, had shared pizza with, had told her silly, teenage dreams to.

Savannah picked at her pizza, eating the pepperoni first, as she had always done, and finally tackling her second slice, all the time pretending not to watch as Harrison talked and paced and listened.

The woman who had helped her in the rest room stopped beside the table, her husband in tow, the man still finishing a slice of pizza. Gesturing with a toss of her head, to indicate Harry on the other side of the window, she winked and said, ''I stand corrected, sweetheart. *That* one might just be worth it.

Good luck! Come on, Bill. Shove the rest of that in your mouth and let's get going or we'll be late."

Savannah smiled at Bill, who just lifted his free hand and, fingers held straight and tight together, began opening and closing his hand against his thumb. "Talks your ear off, the woman does," he said, then quickly took off after his wife, who clearly was used to leading the way.

Savannah laughed as Bill followed his wife. She relaxed a little, until she remembered that Harry was hearing information right now that deeply affected her life. She pretended not to look at him, but kept looking at him every three seconds.

Finally, Harry snapped the cell phone closed and came back inside the restaurant, slipping back into his chair. He picked up a slice of pizza and took a healthy bite.

"Well?" she asked, watching him chew. "What did your source have to say? Because that was about Dad, wasn't it? You were checking him out. Maybe even checking my story, making sure I wasn't making this all up."

Harry swallowed, then took a drink of soda. "I knew you weren't making it up, Savannah. Trust me, I know Sam Hamilton enough to believe that everything you told me is most definitely true, and very much his style. Oh, and just between you and me, it looks like Annette is getting out while the getting is good. Word on the street is that her soon-to-be ex-husband is going to be indicted for tax fraud next week. Lovely family you've pretty much no longer got, Savannah. Just lovely."

"And you want no part of them," Savannah said, nodding her head. "I don't blame you. Coming here today was a bad idea, all the way around. You're probably still angry with Annette for breaking the engagement, on top of everything else. I know how much you loved her."

Some strange sort of shadow seemed to pass over Harry's face, and Savannah suddenly found herself slightly frightened. "Harry? I'm sorry, I shouldn't have said that. Really."

Harry sat back in his chair, looked at her levelly. "No. No, that's all right, Savannah. It's all water under the bridge, and all that baloney. I really can't blame Annette. I mean, looking back on all of it now, and taking everything I know into consideration, I'd say she did the right thing. It never would have worked out between us."

"You're very generous," Savannah said, looking at him intently. "And you're lying. Why are you lying, Harry? Don't I have the story straight? Was there more to everything than I've been told?"

Harry pulled a couple of bills from his wallet, laid them on the table and stood, holding out his hand to Savannah. "Being such a good student all these years, don't you think that right now you should be cramming for your final on current events, rather than worrying about a six-year-old course in ancient history?"

"Current Events," Savannah repeated, wincing. "Meaning Dad's failing business, James Vaughn, and what I should be doing about both of them. Yes,

I suppose so. It's just that I want to apologize for bringing Annette's name into this so much."

"And yet you just did it again," Harry told her as they walked back to his office building. "I'm going to have to dock you a nickel every time you do that from here on in, you know. How else do you think I got to be a tycoon, if I didn't grab for every nickel I could get?"

"Now you're teasing me," Savannah said as he slipped his arm around her waist and she did her best to ignore how good it felt to have him touch her that way, so easily, as if the six years they'd been apart meant nothing to him.

"Me? Teasing you? Savannah, shame on you. When have I ever teased you?"

She looked up at him as she swept that same damn errant lock of hair out of her eyes. "When? How about *how?* As in, let me count the ways. By the way, where are we going? Shouldn't we have turned left at that last corner?"

"If we were heading back to my office, yes. But as we're not, I think we're going the right way."

"Where are we going? Does it have anything to do with that phone call?"

Harry, still with his arm around her waist, walked her toward a wooden bench in a small sidewalk park. Savannah sat down, watching as he joined her, and wondered why she felt like her life was about to make yet another huge turn in a little over a week. "Harry? You've done something, haven't you? You have the same look on your face as you did the day you saw I was about to land on Boardwalk and you had three hotels sitting there."

He smiled, tugged at the lock of hair that she was once again trying to tuck behind her ear. "Leave it, I like it that way," he said. "But you're probably right, and I do look about the same as the day I bankrupted you in Monopoly. It's that killer instinct in me coming out. All the best tycoons have it, or so I'm told."

"Oh, great, and I'm in the line of fire, aren't I?"

"Only indirectly," he assured her. "Right now I've got my sights on Sam's company. It's a real mess, by the way. Big-time mess. Luckily, and probably quite by accident, Sam did manage to keep the company separate from O'Meara's, so the federal government isn't after him. Of course, they're about the only ones who aren't after him but, hey, you can't have everything."

"I wish you'd stop smiling as you tell me this, Harry," Savannah said, belatedly realizing that the Harry she'd known six years ago and the Harry sitting next to her now were two very distinctly different people. She was also beginning to believe she may have just made the biggest mistake of her life in coming to him for help.

"Sorry," Harry said, no longer smiling. "I know this isn't funny. As a matter of fact, it's a damn shame, because Hamilton, Inc., used to be a pretty good company. I know, because I researched it before taking a job there. Before I realized that Sam Hamilton has what we in the business world call a fatal flaw."

"What fatal flaw?"

"He's greedy, Savannah," Harry told her frankly. "He had a nice company, a nice income, a real safe haven. But, like so many others, he overextended himself in a booming economy, tried to grow too fast, counted on money not yet in his pocket. Money he believed to be in other people's pockets."

"Robert O'Meara's money," Savannah said, believing she understood. "He counted on Robert's money, didn't he?"

"He definitely counted on money from his son-in-law," Harry answered, and again Savannah saw that shadow pass over his face and again she wondered. "But the company is still a good one, the product still a good one, so I think that, yes, it is worth investing in, worth owning."

"Owning?" Savannah sat up very straight. "I didn't say anything about Dad—about Sam *selling* the business. He just wants a major investor."

"And a rich husband for the woman he raised as his own daughter. He probably listed your school fees as part of his business expenses. Sell one daughter, pretty much blackmail the other one. That's our Sam—a real prince," Harry told her, and she looked away, no longer able to meet his eyes. "Think about it, Savannah. You can only tap an investor once, twice if you're lucky, but a rich son-in-law is more like a bottomless pit, isn't he? Okay, so Annette's husband was pretty much a dry well. But Vaughn's financially solid, if morally bankrupt. Not that Sam cares about that last part. I've got to hand it to the guy. I mean, if at first you don't succeed, try, try again."

Savannah stood, looked at a spot just left of Harry's head. "I'd like to go back to my car now, Harry. We are through here, aren't we?"

"Not quite, Savannah," he told her, also rising, and once more slipping his arm around her waist as he headed down the street once more. "I've already got my legal department drawing up papers that will be on Sam's desk by Monday morning. Papers outlining my plan to ride in like the white knight you've hoped I'd be, settling all his debts in exchange for an interest in his company. Fifty-one percent interest."

"Fifty-one percent?" Savannah dug in her heels, so that Harry had no choice but to stop. "Sam will never go for you having controlling interest in the company."

"I'm betting he will, especially when we wire him that we've just eloped, pretty much cutting off his options with James Vaughn. Once we're married, Savannah, it will be my way or the highway, and Sam is going to know that. Frankly, I *need* him to know that."

"But—but, you don't want to *marry* me. I know that was the plan with James Vaughn, but I certainly didn't come here today to beg you to marry me, save me. I wanted a white knight, Harry, not a bridegroom."

"Then you want me to call off my lawyers?" he asked her, turning on the sidewalk to face her, his hands on her shoulders. "Cancel the offer? Stand back and watch you sacrifice yourself to James Vaughn because of some twisted idea you've got that you can't walk away from Sam and Annette without first giving them some great big farewell gift of solvency?"

"You know I don't want to marry James Vaughn," Savannah said. "But marry you? Is that really necessary?"

"It is if I'm going to get Sam to see the light, realize that James Vaughn can't do for him what I can do for him. Vaughn won't have any incentive to help Sam anyway, Savannah, not once the main prize is gone."

"Me? I'm the main prize? The company is the main prize. Don't be ridiculous, Harry."

"You always did underestimate yourself, Savannah. I don't know why, but for a very smart girl, you've never really been able to see yourself very well. I blame Sam for that, as well, always happy to tell everyone that Annette got the looks and you got the brains, and making it sound like you lost on both counts. You're lovely, Savannah, and always have been, in your own way. Believe me, James Vaughn is having some pretty wild dreams about having a young, beautiful virgin in his bed."

Savannah looked down at her too tight shoes. Harry was embarrassing her, hurting her, and at the same time making her feel wonderful. "Who says I'm a virgin?"

For the first time since she'd walked into Harry's office and felt her life turn upside down for the second time in days, Savannah heard him laugh out loud, definitely in very real amusement.

"I was *not* trying to be funny!" she said, breaking away from him, blindly walking down the street, still heading in the direction Harry had been taking her.

He caught up to her, slipped his arm around her waist once more. Like he owned her. Like he had the right.

She didn't pull away, remind him that he had *no* rights where she was concerned.

"Savannah, don't you want to know where we're heading?" Harry asked after he'd steered her around yet another corner.

"I couldn't care less," she responded, lifting her chin, wondering if it was possible to walk straight out of Prosperino and into oblivion, already knowing that, if it were possible, it wasn't likely—at least not in these shoes.

"Okay, but I'll tell you anyway," he said, pulling her to a stop, "because we're here."

Savannah looked up, saw that they were standing directly in front of the Prosperino City Hall. "Oh, God," she said, her voice barely a whisper.

He took her hand and led her inside the cool building with the marble walls. They stopped in front of the building directory and Harry announced, "There it is. Marriage licenses, third floor."

"You go ahead, I'll meet you there," Savannah said, already heading toward the front doors, and sanity.

"Savannah Hamilton!" Harry called after her,

loudly enough for heads to turn. "You have to marry me. Think about the baby!"

"Oh, dear," Savannah heard an elderly lady say to her equally gray-haired friend. "It's like I've been telling you, Maude. The whole country is going to hell in a handbasket."

Her cheeks flaming, her hands drawn up into fists, Savannah turned to confront Harry, who was standing at the elevator, holding the door open for her, and looking about as innocent as he had the day he'd shown up at her boarding school with a faked note from her father stating that she was to be allowed to leave the grounds with "my trusted representative." That trusted representative had then taken her for her first clandestine, off-campus pizza.

Strange. Until this very moment Savannah had not realized that, for all his smiles and flippancy, Harry had become a much more—the word that entered her head was *intense*—person than he had been six years ago.

Not that she'd expected him to have lived inside some bubble, rather the way she had done, and not have changed at all.

Savannah wondered just how much Annette had to do with the changes she saw in Harry.

"On or off, lady?" an older man standing at the back of the elevator asked. "Not that I'm in any big hurry to get to jury duty, but I don't think they want me to be late."

"Oh. Sorry," Savannah said, glaring at Harry as he waggled his eyebrows at her and grinned yet again. Now this Harry was the Harry she remembered. The Harry she'd fallen for like a ton of bricks, and with all the intensity a seventeen-year-old could come up with—and that was a lot of intensity.

"Come on, Savannah," Harry urged, thankfully more quietly. "You want to leave home but said you had nowhere to go. Now you do. Besides, do you really want to keep the name Hamilton?"

"I can get a job, and the name Hamilton hasn't hurt me yet," she told him, playing for time, wishing there were a big computer screen somewhere that would flash the right answers to her, tell her what to do.

No. No, she didn't want anyone to tell her what to do. She was tired of people telling her what to do.

"You know what? I don't think I like being a pawn. Sam's or yours. Goodbye, Harry. Thanks so much, but no thanks," she said, and then she turned and ran.

"If you don't mind my saying so," the man in the elevator said, "you really blew that one, son."

"Not yet, I haven't," Harrison responded, letting go of the door. "Happy jury duty, sir, and sorry for holding up the elevator."

"Yeah, I'm hoping for a murder trial. Better than sitting home, watching the soaps and listening to my wife tell me to take out the garbage. Never retire, son. It's a living hell, and they call you for jury duty every time you turn around, I swear it."

Harrison smiled, thanked the man for his advice, then trotted after Savannah, who couldn't exactly outrun him in those ridiculous high heels she was wearing.

Although he did realize that he rather enjoyed watching her try, admiring the way her hips swayed side to side as she half-walked, half ran down the street.

He caught up to her at the corner, taking her arm and leading her into a patch of shade next to one of the buildings.

"Savannah, I'm sorry," he said quickly, noticing that her big blue eyes were unnaturally bright with unshed tears. "I'm as much of an ass as Sam, and if you want to kick me in the shin and leave me here, I won't blame you. But first, please listen to what I have to say."

"We have nothing to say to each other, Harry," she told him. "Nothing."

"You're wrong, Savannah. I owe you the truth. Do you want to hear it, or are you going to deliver that kick and then make another break for it?"

She tipped her head and looked at him with some curiosity. That lock of hair had broken free again, and he found that he'd developed a considerable affection for the way it seemed to frame her perfectly oval face, skimming past her cheek, curling into her chin. "Five minutes, Harry. I'll give you five minutes."

"Great, but not here. Let's go back to the office."

She walked with him, stepping to one side when he tried to put his arm around her waist, and Harrison knew he'd let old hurts blind him to the new hurts he'd learned about from Savannah, inflicted himself with his clumsy, full-steam-ahead plans.

He used his key to get into the locked building, and they rode the elevator in silence, walked through the hallways of middle management in silence, entered his executive suite in silence.

"Hello," Lorraine said happily from behind her desk. "I've been expecting you."

"Really," Harrison said, wondering if his executive assistant would like an all-expenses-paid trip to Outer Mongolia. One way, of course.

"Yes, really. They always return to the scene of the crime," Lorraine said, looking at Savannah. "Are you all right, honey?"

"Yes, I'm fine, thank you," Savannah said, shooting Harrison a look that probably could have frozen fire, then pushing open the door to his office and stepping inside.

"Listening at keyholes, Lorraine?" Harrison asked, glaring at the woman.

"In your father's day, yes. Now I just leave the intercom switched on, considering that you've never quite figured the thing out." She sat back, spread her hands. "Hey, she could have been a terrorist or something. You didn't really think I'd desert you, not with everyone else leaving at noon. Although I will say I only expected you to come back so you could fill me in on everything that's happened. Which is why I quickly hid in the closet when I heard the two of you were about to leave. So, are you going to bail out the company and save that poor girl? Wait, I've got a bigger question: Are you going to tell her the truth about what happened six years ago?''

''How would you know what happened six years ago?'' Harrison asked, then waved his hand. ''Scratch that. You know everything that happens around here. It's why I can't fire you. You'd just go to some rival media company and spill your guts, right?''

Lorraine's smile disappeared. ''I would *never*—''

Harrison stepped around the desk and dropped a kiss on Lorraine's thin cheek. ''I know, Lorraine. I'm sorry. But I'm under a little stress here.''

''Just don't hurt her, Mr. Colton,'' Lorraine said, gathering up her purse and one of her always present paperback mystery novels. ''There's something, I don't know, vulnerable about her.''

Harrison nodded, then headed for the office, walking straight to the desk and pulling the plug on the intercom. Ten seconds later, the outer office door closed as Lorraine left.

''She's a very nice woman,'' Savannah said, uttering her first direct statement to him in more than ten minutes.

''She's a terror and a tartar, and I don't know what would happen to this place without her,'' Harrison said, pouring them each a cold soda. ''Okay,'' he said, handing one glass to Savannah and taking the other with him as he sat down, both of them in the same seats they'd occupied earlier. ''Truth time.''

''*Whole* truth time?'' she asked, her face so pale,

he believed he might be able to count every freckle on her cheeks and nose.

"Whole truth time," he agreed. "But to do that, we have to go back six years, which isn't going to be comfortable for me. We have to go all the way back so that I can tell you that this is the second time around for Sam when it comes to what he considers the best way to increase his bottom line. The only difference is that, unlike you, Annette was a willing coconspirator."

"I don't understand," Savannah said quickly, then frowned. "No, that's not true. I do understand. Harry, are you telling me that Annette agreed to marry you because Dad was hoping you'd bail him out of some business problem he had back then? But that's silly. You were working for him. You didn't have any money."

"Keep going, Savannah. I think you'll figure it out," Harry said, watching her closely.

"You didn't have any money," Savannah repeated, looking around the rather opulent office. "You didn't, but your father did. Is that it? Sam wanted you to get your father to invest in Hamilton, Inc.?"

"Oh, better than that, Savannah. He wanted us to invest with him *and* he wanted a piece of CMH, as a sort of gift to him for allowing me to marry his daughter. When I told him to go to hell, Annette finished the one-two punch by telling me that if I didn't agree she wouldn't marry me, that she'd only agreed to marry me because I was rich, could help her father and give her the life she deserved."

"So *you* called off the wedding," Savannah said. "Not Annette? And it had nothing to do with Annette falling in love with Robert?"

"So far so good," Harrison said, knowing he could count on Savannah's quick mind to fill in the rest of it, which would probably end with her at last kicking him in the shins. "Now here comes the part that doesn't make me look so good, the part I didn't want you to figure out quite so fast."

"You must have been so angry. And so hurt. You loved her, Harry. I know you loved her. How could she have been so cruel? And so stupid! Didn't she realize how lucky she was that you— Well, never mind about that right now."

Savannah put down her glass, got up and walked to the window overlooking the street. "Six years later, I show up here, pretty much telling you the same sort of story, except that it's a little different this time because I'm not a willing participant. Still, the end result would be pretty much the same, except that I'd switch grooms, right back to Dad's first choice—you."

She turned to face him. "Is that irony, Harry? My major may have been environmental studies, but I'm pretty sure that's irony. Anyway, Dad would be bailed out and, if you're serious about marrying me, he'd have his bottomless pit of money to draw on. Except he wouldn't, would he? Not if you demand fifty-one percent."

"No, Savannah, he wouldn't. I'd have controlling interest in Sam's company, he wouldn't get squat from CMH or any of my holdings, and because I was married to his last remaining asset, he'd have to grin and bear it. Unless Annette wants to go tycoon hunting, that is. How do she and James get along?''

''Like oil and water,'' Savannah said, rubbing at the side of her neck, obviously deep in thought. ''This would work out very well for you, wouldn't it, Harry? Revenge on Dad, waving me in front of Annette...all that good stuff. But what's in it for me?''

''A lot, if you were anything like your sister,'' Harrison said, quickly adding, ''if you thought marrying for money was a good idea. A little less, if you're just looking for a way to free yourself from Sam and start a life of your own. But I won't bail Sam out unless we do the whole thing. Otherwise, all I've got is a company I have to pour some big bucks into to get it back on its feet, and you're still out there, with Sam laying a guilt trip on you for what your mother did, and James Vaughn is still in the picture.''

''How long?''

''How long would we stay married? That is what you're asking, isn't it?''

''I think it's a good question, and about the most reasonable one yet,'' Savannah said, tipping up her chin. ''And, of course, it would be strictly a marriage of convenience, both yours and mine. A business agreement. Nothing more.''

Harrison looked at her, saw all that vulnerability Lorraine had seen, and nodded. ''A business agreement. All right. I agree. We'll even set a time limit.

How does two years sound to you? I get my revenge, because I'd be lying if I said that doesn't have some appeal, and you get out from under Sam's boot. At the end of two years, you have your freedom again, and no worries about Sam. I'd say we both win."

"I'm a winner, Harry? Then why don't I feel like celebrating?" Savannah asked, heading for the door. "Come on, we'd better get back to city hall before it closes for the weekend."

Chapter 3

Harrison came into the office on Saturday, to clear the decks for what he thought would most probably be a full week, once Sam Hamilton found out, hopefully by Monday afternoon, that—to use the technical term for it—his goose had just been plucked and cooked.

He'd sent Savannah back to her "father's" house late Friday afternoon after warning her that she wasn't to say anything to the man about the small civil marriage ceremony planned for Monday morning. Not a word. He'd also gotten her promise that she'd meet him at his house on Sunday evening, her bags packed, and they'd proceed from there.

Where the hell they were going, where they'd "proceed" to, he hadn't the faintest idea. He only knew that he was already having second thoughts about this marriage-in-name-only stuff.

It had seemed like a good idea at the time and, he knew, he would have agreed to most any condition at first, when his need for revenge overcame his own personal code of ethics, but Lorraine had been right. Savannah Hamilton was vulnerable. And young. Beautiful. Desirable.

He hadn't noticed that at first, or had tried not to notice it, concentrating on remembering her as she'd been six years ago, and not as she was now. All grown-up.

Definitely all grown-up.

He could still call it off, call it all off. And he probably should. He was using Savannah, plain and simple, to get some of his own back on Sam Hamilton.

Sam Hamilton. Truly a world-class bad guy. A throwback to the bad old days where daughters had been seen as little more than a marketable commodity.

"And that's why I can't call it off," Harrison told himself as he paced the carpet in front of his desk. "He's got Savannah on such a guilt trip because of her mother's supposed sin, that he'd still have her married to a creep like Vaughn within a week."

Just as it had the night before, when he'd sat at home in the dark, sipping Scotch, the thought of James Vaughn having any sort of association with Savannah tied his gut in a knot.

He'd tried, for most of the evening, to tell himself it was because Vaughn was a womanizer, because Savannah would be devastated by the man's lifestyle. There were so many reasons, so many very valid reasons, why Savannah could not be allowed to sacrifice herself in a marriage with James Vaughn.

What he tried not to tell himself was that he couldn't get past the nauseating thought of Vaughn touching her, that *he* wanted to be the one who kissed her, touched her, awakened her.

Yes, he'd always liked Savannah. Right from the start, from the first day he'd met her, when he was twenty-five and she had been just seventeen. He'd liked her as a sister, admired her bright mind, enjoyed her shy smiles. Even enjoyed the way he used to catch her looking at him when she thought he hadn't noticed.

But that had been six years ago, when he'd been young and dumb and easily flattered by a young girl's very obvious crush on him. He could laugh at the whole idea, because he was engaged to Savannah's sister, in love with Savannah's sister.

Who hadn't been in love with him.

Harrison walked to the window, the same window Savannah had looked out yesterday. He thought about Annette, something he hadn't allowed himself to do for a long time.

She had been so beautiful. Milk-white skin, midnight hair, huge violet eyes. So perfect. Maybe too perfect.

Or maybe he'd been too blinded by her beauty to see the imperfections. The way she refused to do much more than sit herself down and look beautiful, dismissing any notion that she should go in the swimming pool, play badminton in the hot sun, eat anywhere other than the best restaurants, and always, always keep him at arm's length when he tried to move beyond kisses.

He'd thought of her as some sort of fragile fairy princess, and had treated her accordingly. He had, he realized now, concocted a dream around Annette, allowing her beauty to conjure up other attributes, such as kindness, and a loving heart.

It had been Savannah who'd been kind and loving. Happy to be alive, willing to get down on the floor and play board games, not at all upset to be dunked in the swimming pool.

It had been Savannah who had been *real.* Annette had been a dream.

But Savannah also had been seventeen years old.

"She's not seventeen anymore," Harrison reminded himself as he closed the blinds on the afternoon sun, on his thoughts that had very little to do with anything called a marriage of convenience. A loveless marriage. An unconsummated marriage. A marriage meant only as the perfect revenge.

"That's it," he said, heading for the phone on his desk. "I can't do this. Not to Savannah. It wouldn't be fair, not to either of us."

But before he could pick up the phone, his private line rang, and he swore under his breath before answering it. "Colton here," he barked out, wondering which one of the few people who had his private number had taken the time to track him down at the office on a Saturday afternoon.

"'Colton here,'" a singsong voice came right

back at him. "My goodness, Harrison, there's no need to bite my head off."

"Gran," Harrison said, subsiding into his desk chair, a reluctant smile slipping across his face. "How's the arthritis?"

"Still knocking on the door, but I won't let it in, thanks for asking."

Harrison smiled at the old joke. He asked her every time they spoke, and every time she had a different answer. The whole family indulged in the game. "Well, that's good. What are you up to? Last time you called this line it was to ask me if I had Prince Albert in a can, then told me to let him out. Did it ever occur to you that women of a certain age don't make prank phone calls? Especially trans-Atlantic prank phone calls."

"Not lately, no," Sybil Colton said, her voice clear as it made its way across the miles, all the way from Paris. "And when did I become a woman of a certain age?" she asked, and he could hear her blowing out cigarette smoke. He could picture her sitting at her ease on one of her overstuffed couches, a martini at her elbow, a cigarette stuck into an ivory holder. "I'm old, Harrison. That's the only certain thing about me."

Harrison glanced at the clock on his desktop. "You're also up past your bedtime, Gran," he said, feeling himself relax. There were few pleasures in this world greater than having his eighty-eight-year-old grandmother phone him from her home in Paris. "I'd have thought you'd be getting your beauty sleep."

"I'll get more than I need of that soon enough, Harrison," she returned. "Besides, I couldn't sleep. I've got something on my mind, and I wanted to talk to you about it. Your brother is so oblivious to anything that doesn't have to do with gall bladders or horrid skin rashes, and whatever else excites doctors these days, and Frank and Shirley are still on vacation. Nobody takes more vacations than my Frank. Is that son of mine taking advantage of your good nature, Harrison? Is he working you into an early grave?"

"I'm hanging in there, Gran," he said, then mentally backtracked, to get the main point of Sybil's rambling. "Is something wrong? Why did you feel the need to talk to someone tonight? And why did you mention Jason first? Aren't you well? You didn't go out dancing and fall, break a hip?"

"Darling, who *are* you talking to? Some dotty old woman? Certainly not to me," Sybil told him, and he could hear her taking another drag on her almost always present cigarette. She called it living dangerously, and reminded anyone who tried to talk her into quitting that, at eighty-eight, there wasn't too much she *could* do that was dangerous. "Can't I just call to see how my grandson is doing? Is this a crime?"

"You called just to ask how I'm doing," Harrison said as he picked up the paperweight Savannah had held yesterday, turning it in his hands as he held the phone tucked between his head and shoulder. "Okay, old lady, who are you and what did you do with my real grandmother?"

Sybil's husky laugh made Harrison smile.

"Oh, all right. So perhaps I did have a reason to call. But that doesn't mean I can't ask how you're doing, now does it? So, Harrison, how are you doing? Take over any companies lately? Seduce any beautiful women? You know, both Frank and Shirley are champing at the bit for some grandchildren. The least you could do is accommodate them."

"Translation," Harrison said, "why can't you find a nice woman, get married and settle down. Gran, are you sure you're not psychic?"

"Psychic? Why? Harrison! Are you getting married? Oh, my goodness, a scoop! I've got a scoop, haven't I? Hah! Frank will be livid. Here he is, the media mogul, and here I am, that old babe six thousand miles away, and I've just scooped him. Who is it, Harrison? Please tell me it isn't one of those anorexic super models you rich men seem to find attractive."

"Down, girl," Harrison said, already regretting having said anything at all to his grandmother, who wasn't above placing a conference call to his parents, his brother and three dozen of her closest friends to tell them all that little Harrison was finally getting hitched, and wasn't it about time. "I'm *thinking* about getting married. That's all. Just thinking about it."

There was a slight hesitation at the other end, and then Sybil said, "Gun-shy, huh? I'd still like to pull that girl's hair out by the roots, you know. Her and her father both. I swear to you, Harrison, if I never hear the name Hamilton again, I'll die a happy woman. Unless it's to tell me that Sam Hamilton and his little gold digger have finally gotten their comeuppance.''

This was *not* going well, Harrison decided, walking with the cordless phone still tucked under his chin, reaching down to pluck a bottle of water out of the small refrigerator designed to look like just another end table.

He wondered what his grandmother would think if he were to tell her that she was going to hear the name Hamilton again, because he was most probably going to be married to Savannah Hamilton by noon Monday.

He decided not to chance it. His grandmother was much too smart a lady to not smell a rat. He couldn't chance that. Not when he was most likely to be cast in the role of head rat.

''Gran,'' he said, figuring a lie was probably his safest bet at the moment, ''I'm expecting an important call, which is why I'm here at the office instead of on the golf course. So, much as I'd love to hear about the many ways you've figured out to twist Sam Hamilton into a pretzel, maybe it's time you told me what's on your mind.''

''Back off? That is what you're saying, isn't it, Harrison?'' Sybil asked. ''Oh, very well. Especially because I really do need to talk to you about something. Did you get Meredith's invitation to Joe's sixtieth birthday party?''

Harrison did a quick shifting of mental gears at his grandmother's mention of his uncle Joe. Where Harrison's father, Frank, had always been more of a city boy—if Prosperino could be called a city, and it couldn't, at least it was nowhere near the size of Los Angeles or San Francisco—his cousin Joe had chosen to spend most of his time on his very successful ranch some miles outside the city.

Not that Joe was a rancher, at least not primarily. Joe Colton, the original self-made man, owned mining properties, oil wells, a large shipping company, and had interests in many other businesses. In fact, it was Joe Colton that Harrison used as a model for his own career, the one he had so successfully melded with his position at CMH.

Harrison used to go out to the ranch often, enjoying Joe's company, enjoying the company of his cousins and the foster children and adopted children Meredith and Joe raised with such love. The Colton ranch was a happy place.

Or it had been, until about ten years ago, when Meredith and one of their adopted children, Emily, had nearly been killed in a freak automobile accident.

That accident had changed Meredith in ways Harrison had never fully understood. And, by the tone of his grandmother's voice as she'd mentioned Meredith's name, he wasn't the only one who thought so.

"Harrison? Are you still there?"

"What? Oh, sorry, Gran. I was trying to remember. And yes, I got the invitation. Sounds like quite the bash, doesn't it? Are you flying over?"

"Yes, I'm coming over, or at least I hope to. But I'm not planning on enjoying myself."

"Ah, ever the optimist," Harrison said, going back to his desk and sitting down. "What's the matter, Gran? Don't you have anything to wear? That's hard to believe, considering the Paris dressmakers weep with joy each time you drop in to see their new collections."

"Oh, yes, Harrison, just what I want to wear in California. A ball gown. Admit it, Harrison, this isn't like Meredith at all. A gala? Meredith hates galas, all that spit and polish and the rest. Used to be, Meredith's idea of a good time was everyone showing up for a huge family picnic. I don't get this black tie and gown business, damn if I don't. And I can't understand why Joe is sitting still for it."

"It is his sixtieth birthday, Gran," Harrison pointed out. "Maybe he wants something more formal?"

"Joe? Hardly, Harrison. It's just not Joe. And it used to not be Meredith. I'm telling you, Harrison, something fishy is going on out there, and has been for a long time. I can smell it, all the way from Paris."

Harrison pinched the bridge of his nose with thumb and forefinger. "Now, Gran—"

"Don't you 'now Gran' me! I was just there last year, remember? Meredith treated me like a *guest! Me!* Meredith never treated me like a guest, much less an unwelcome one. And then there's Emily, the girl who was in the accident with her."

"What about Emily? She recovered just fine, didn't she?" Harrison asked, pulling a paper from the fax machine, recognizing it as a quickly thrown together report on Sam Hamilton's finances. His fax didn't print in color, but if it did, there would have been a lot of red ink. He wanted to get off the phone, look at this page, and at the pages that kept spitting out of the machine.

"Did she, Harrison?" Sybil asked, then waited for her grandson to pick up on her mysterious, doubting tone.

He decided not to disappoint her, because he knew his grandmother, and she was going to tell him what she thought whether he wanted to hear it or not. Trying to put on the brakes would only prolong the agony. "Okay, Gran, spill your guts. You have my attention."

"Well, finally! Your father thinks I'm losing my grip, you know. But I knew I could count on you."

"I'm a real prince," Harrison said wryly, pulling another two sheets of paper from the fax and scanning them. Sam Hamilton needed a large infusion of cash, and he needed it soon, or else the company was heading straight to bankruptcy court. James Vaughn needed that headache like he needed another hair weave. No, Vaughn wanted Savannah. Young, innocent Savannah. And Sam was more than happy to act as pimp and procurer. Harrison threw the papers onto the desktop, cursing under his breath. Maybe he wasn't a prince, but he knew he was a damn sight better than James Vaughn!

"I've always said you were my prince, darling," Sybil said, then went on with her story. "Here's the skinny. Emily was knocked out in the crash, and when she woke up she said she saw *two* Merediths looking at her. Did you hear that, Harrison? Two Merediths.''

Harrison nodded. ''I know, Gran, I've heard that story, too. Two Merediths, one sweet and smiling, one mean and evil. Emily was just a kid, Gran, and she'd just been knocked out, concussed. I'm surprised she didn't see six Merediths, a pink elephant and a clown in a top hat.''

''Oh, really?'' Sybil said, and Harrison could tell that he'd upset her. ''Then explain to me why Meredith isn't Meredith anymore, Harrison. Explain that!''

''I can't explain that, Gran, because it's not true. Okay, so she's a little different now, more distant, less involved in the day-to-day happenings at the ranch, unwilling to take on any more foster children. Did it ever occur to you that she considered the car accident her fault and that she blames herself for Emily's injuries? That she might not want any more children at the ranch because of that guilt, and the pain she felt when Emily was injured? Remember, Gran, Joe and Meredith's son Michael was hit by a car and killed. That's a lot of tragedy for one woman.''

''Maybe,'' Sybil said, her tone mellowing a bit. ''But I still say there's something fishy going on, Harrison, and I want you to go out there and take a look around, see if I'm right.''

''Go out there? Gran, I can't. I've got— Well, I've got a takeover in the works, Dad is away, and I've got CMH to run. It's impossible. I'm sorry.''

''It's the girl, isn't it?'' Sybil asked, and Harrison

winced. "Come on, come on, you dropped a hint or two, but I can tell that there's more. Well, don't you forget, Harrison. Don't you forget the test."

"The test?" Harrison was nearing the home stretch on this phone call, he could feel it, but now his grandmother had led him off on another tangent. "What test?"

"The Colton necklace test, Harrison. It hasn't been wrong yet," Sybil said, and he swore he could see her rolling her eyes at his question. "And now I've got to go, as you're obviously trying to be thick and won't listen to me. Perhaps I'll call your brother, Jason, one of these days, if he still remembers me. That boy works too hard, and so do you, I suppose. Besides, I don't know why I let you keep me on the phone so long, these calls cost the earth. Damn phone companies. Good night, darling."

Harrison was left looking at the phone, hearing the dial tone. "Batty old woman," he said, grinning as he put down the phone and reached for the rest of the small stack of papers waiting for him in the fax machine. "I can't wait to see her again."

It was Saturday night, and Harrison couldn't believe he was sitting alone in his empty house, the ball game on television, a can of soda on the table next to him, and a sapphire necklace in his hands.

This was all his grandmother's fault, bringing up the necklace, especially at a time like this.

He knew the history of the necklace, had heard the story numerous times over the years, and it had always struck him as fanciful, highly romantic and rather nice.

Right now, however, he was eyeing the necklace as if it might come to life at any moment, and bite him.

The original necklace had been given to the earl of Redbridge by none other than Queen Elizabeth I. Beautiful sapphires, in a heavy, fairly garish diamond setting, the necklace had been handed down to the oldest son of each succeeding generation, until it came into the hands of one William Colton, the third earl of Redbridge.

William had been a very bad boy. Duty called William, as it had called all the Coltons, but duty never kept a man warm at night. Still, because he knew he must somehow replenish the Colton's fairly empty coffers—now there was a bit of irony, considering what was going on now—he became betrothed to Katherine Mansfield, whose family had little consequence. But the Mansfields did have money—as Sybil Colton had once said it—out the wazoo.

Harrison took a deep drink of soda, not quite liking the comparisons he was seeing between the long-ago Coltons and Sam Hamilton. Still, that had been another time, another age, another set of right and wrong.

And besides, William had come through at the end, although it had been a close-run thing.

It had been on the eve of the wedding of William and Katherine that good old Willie had brought the legend-wrapped sapphire-and-diamond necklace to his betrothed, as a bridal gift. Why he'd waited so long to give it to her, nobody knew, but his timing hadn't been exactly great.

Maybe it had been the legend attached to the necklace that had kept him from placing it around Katherine's throat. Maybe William had been pretty sure what would happen, and he hadn't wanted to know, hadn't wanted to take the chance that his marriage of convenience was cursed by that damn necklace.

As the story went, Harrison remembered, the beautiful sapphires were capable of doing the eighteenth century version of "two thumbs up" or "two thumbs down" when it came to the suitability of Colton brides.

Clasp the necklace around the wrong neck, and the stones turned muddy. Murky. Dim.

Drape those same stones around the right throat, and the sapphires winked, the diamonds danced, and all was right with the world.

Harrison didn't believe in that sort of fairy tale.

But William had believed it, and when Katherine took the necklace from his hands and fit it around her neck, William had watched, aghast, as the sapphires turned dull and lifeless, almost ugly.

Surely the necklace, if not the fates, had spoken. Either that, or William had been looking for just such an excuse, because he called off the wedding ceremony.

That sort of thing just wasn't done in those days, and many believed a betrothed couple to be legally married even before the vows were said in church.

Even the law believed it. A guy could get thrown in the slammer for deserting his betrothed hours before the wedding. A guy could get sued. Hell, if the bride-to-be had brothers, a guy could get challenged to a duel and end up being very dead.

Somehow, William had escaped any of those fates, although a feud worthy of the Hatfields and the McCoys had sprung up between the Mansfields and the Coltons, so that England wasn't a very comfortable place for William—especially once he found his true love, slapped the necklace on her to make sure, and watched as those sapphires did their twinkle-twinkle thing that was their blessing on the union.

Harrison watched the last Dodger strike out in the bottom of the ninth in a losing effort, and flicked the remote. The television screen went dark as he thought about the rest of the old story.

William, so the story went, had had enough of jolly old England, and the feud with the Mansfields, and he and his bride hopped a ship headed for the New World, which is how his particular branch of the Colton family had made the leap from England to America.

Over time, William and his heirs made and lost several fortunes, one of their down-turns forcing a later Colton to sell the necklace.

"But Dad found you, didn't he?" Harrison said, holding up the necklace and glaring at it. His father, Frank, had made a fortune in media holdings, heard about the necklace being offered in an auction, and had brought it home, happy as a clam to have rescued this family treasure. ''He found it, he had it cut into two small chokers, one for Jason's bride and one for mine. And now here you are. Gee,'' he grumbled sarcastically, drinking down the last of the soda. ''Lucky me.''

The phone rang and Harrison let the machine take it, only jumping up to lift the receiver when he heard Savannah's voice. ''Savannah?'' he said quickly, before she could hang up. ''Is everything all right? It's late.''

''Oh, no, no, Harry, everything's fine.'' She hesitated a moment. ''Well, it's as fine as it can be. Sam told Annette. Told her he's not my father. He promised he wouldn't say anything, but he did. She confronted me tonight, came to my room to tell me she knows. Now Annette's after me as well, telling me it's my duty to marry James.''

''And...?'' Harrison said, sensing that there was more coming, as if he hadn't already heard enough to banish any lingering misgivings he might have as to whether he was doing the right thing in pretty much forcing Savannah into this marriage of convenience. As a matter of fact, it would probably take everything in him not to hop in the car and go get her now, get her out of that house, away from those people.

''Well...I hadn't planned to say anything,'' Savannah went on hesitantly. ''Really, I hadn't. I know you said I shouldn't, that you wanted everything to be a surprise on Monday...''

''You told her,'' Harrison said, closing his eyes.

Yeah, well, so much for best-laid plans. "Then what happened?"

"You're right. I told her. It was stupid of me, Harry. Stupid and juvenile, and I even think I said something like 'Oh, yeah, well let me tell *you* something.' I shouldn't have done it. As to what happened next? She—she didn't take it well," Savannah said, and Harrison actually smiled. He hadn't known Savannah to be a master of understatement.

"How didn't she take it well?"

"She said some fairly ugly things, about you, about me, about my mother. She was Annette's mother, too, Harry, and Annette's older, knew Mother better than I could, since she died when I was only five. Oh, Harry, she called her a whore, and called me an ungrateful bastard. It was terrible."

"I'll bet it was. And, Sam? Does he know?"

"Not yet," Savannah said. "He's in Las Vegas for the weekend, with James. Celebrating. He won't be back until tomorrow night. There's no way of reaching him because he didn't tell us where he's staying."

Celebrating. Celebrating the sale of the daughter he'd raised as his own. If Harrison had felt less than a prince a while ago, Sam Hamilton was something lower than human. "Okay," he said, shoving the necklace back into its velvet box, dropping it into the drawer in the table beside his chair, then immediately forgetting it. "You stay there. You stay right there, and I'll come get you."

"That isn't necessary, Harry," Savannah told him.

His temper, barely held in check, suddenly flared. "Like hell it isn't! If you think I'm going to leave you there alone with Annette, you're crazy. Just stay there and—"

"Harry, I'm outside, in my car, using my cell phone," Savannah said, interrupting him. "I—I just wanted to be sure you were home, and awake. It's midnight, Harry. I didn't just want to come ringing your bell."

Harrison was already half running down the hallway from the study that was in the rear of the house, hitting light switches as he went. "I'll be right there," he said, hanging up the phone, tossing the cordless instrument on the foyer table before opening the door and heading out to the circular driveway.

It was only as Savannah stepped from the car, and he took her in his arms, to comfort her—that was all, just to comfort her—that Harrison realized just how very glad he was to see her, that she had come to him.

Still holding her close against him, feeling her tremble, they walked back inside the house. He led her straight to his study, told her to sit down, and he went into the kitchen to put a kettle on the stove. Hot tea. That was what his mother had always served in times of stress, swearing that there was nothing like hot, sweet tea to banish the cold, warm the heart and calm the nerves.

He stood next to the stove, impatiently waiting for the kettle to boil, then made up a tray with two cups, a bowl of sugar and a small pitcher of milk. He carried it back to the study.

Savannah was standing at the fireplace, her back turned to him.

"Come on, Savannah. Come over here and sit down. Drink this while it's hot."

She stayed where she was for several moments, time for him to look at her, dressed in old blue jeans and a black pullover, her long, slim body graceful even as she stood still. She wore her hair down tonight, the sweep of it brushing against her shoulders, obscuring her features as she finally turned to him, keeping her head down, her eyes averted from his.

She looked nervous. She looked hesitant as she moved toward the couch and the low table where he'd placed the tray. But she didn't look like the Savannah of his memory. She looked like the Savannah of yesterday afternoon: fully grown, beautiful and able to arouse him in ways that had absolutely nothing to do with old memories.

"Savannah?" he asked, sitting down beside her, frowning as she flinched when he reached out a hand to push her hair away from her face. "What's wrong? You're not afraid of me. You wouldn't be here if you were afraid of me."

She raised her hand to the side of her face as she turned toward him. "Of course I'm not afraid of you, Harry. I—I just had a little accident. That's all."

Harrison took hold of her hand, gently lowered it, turned her chin so that she was facing the light. "She did this?" he asked through clenched teeth, taking in the livid bruise on Savannah's cheek, the small cut near her eye that had to have been caused by one of the many rings Annette always wore.

Savannah nodded, then pressed her palm to her face once more. "She called me a few choice names, too," she said, then gave him a watery smile. "Oh, and did you know I'm getting secondhand goods? Annette's leavings?"

"Is that right?" Harrison said, spooning two sugars into Savannah's teacup, trying to control himself.

"Yes, that's right," Savannah told him, accepting the cup. "But, before you think I'm some spineless, battered idiot, I think I should tell you I punched her when she said that. After she hit me. I'm pretty sure she's going to have one hell of a shiner."

Harrison picked up Savannah's right hand after she'd replaced the cup on the tray, and noticed some redness and puffiness around her knuckles. "Did it feel good? Hitting her back?"

"Oh, yeah," Savannah said, and now her smile reached her eyes. Her dry eyes, with no sign of tears in them. "It felt *really* good."

And then they laughed. They laid their heads back against the sofa cushions, looked at each other and laughed like loons.

Chapter 4

Savannah woke slowly, stretching beneath the sheets, turning onto to her side to snuggle into the pillow—and winced when her injured cheek pained her.

Rolling onto her back once more, she blinked several times, slowly remembering how she'd gotten there in the first place.

She'd been laughing. She and Harrison had both been laughing. Silly. Overreacting, probably.

And then, she remembered, squeezing her eyes shut on the memory, she had begun to cry.

Too much. It had all just been too much. She'd been walking on eggshells ever since her father—no, not her father, Sam—had sat her down and told her about her mother's infidelity, about how he had done the right thing and raised Savannah as his own.

Told her that she *owed* him for her mother's lies, that the time had come to pay that debt.

She'd cried when he told her, Savannah remembered, but perhaps she hadn't cried enough, hadn't gotten it all out of her system. Or, perhaps, it had been Sam's command that she marry James Vaughn and thereby rescue Hamilton, Inc., that had dried her tears and sent her into a state of near numbness that had paralyzed her for days.

During every one of those days, Sam had come to her, told her that her time was limited, that she had to make up her mind, or else they'd all be out on the street, the company lost, everything he'd worked so hard for destroyed. He was counting on her. Annette's future depended on her. And she owed them. By God she *owed* them.

Savannah turned back the sheets and left the bed, heading for the shower in the connected bathroom.

She owed them? When had she begun to question that statement? Was it during her bouts of tears, when she remembered that Sam had always treated her so differently from Annette? All those years of hearing how beautiful Annette was, how highly polished. What a good and obedient child she had been, what a lovely and loving daughter, and how even now her father always came first for her, even after her marriage.

But she, Savannah, had always been a disappointment. Always the tomboy, climbing trees, skinning her knees, collecting bugs and bringing them into the house. And she wasn't pretty, didn't even *try* to be pretty, or help Annette with her hostess duties when business associates came to dinner. Not that she'd been invited back to any of those business dinners, not after she'd argued environmental issues with the president of a company that was busily cutting down every tree in the Northwest that he could lay a chain saw to, without a thought to future generations.

"Too damn smart, and smart-mouthed, for your own good," Sam had told her. Upon reflection, he might have been right, considering that Savannah recalled that she had only been fourteen at the time. Sam had sent her to boarding school the week after that incident, and she had only come home on weekends or for holidays. That removal from the house had pretty much sent the message to Savannah that her father couldn't stand the sight of her.

Annette treated her like the ugly duckling younger sister, when she noticed her at all, and Sam was hardly ever around when she came home.

But then Harrison had come into the picture, when she was seventeen. He'd been nice to her, frolicked in the pool with her, talked to her, listened to her. He'd visited her school, bringing her magazine articles on the environment his father's company had printed, helping her with her year-end project, taking her out for pizza.

When, during that terrible week, had Savannah's thoughts turned from the shocking news she'd learned, from the future Sam had planned for her, to Harry and how he had seemed to care about her?

Did it matter? All that mattered now was that

she'd acted on impulse, come to see Harry, and now it would appear that she was going to marry Harry.

"For all the wrong reasons," she told herself as she stepped out of the shower and wrapped a large white bath sheet around herself as she hunted for a smaller towel to dry her hair. "Of course, that's all off now, now that you opened your big mouth and told Annette."

The thought of her sister had Savannah turning to the mirror, leaning close to inspect the mark on her cheek. The redness had gone, leaving only a slight swelling and some discomfort, along with a quarter-inch superficial cut near her eye. Man, that woman packed a wallop—although Savannah felt sure she'd given as good as she got.

She might even be proud of herself, having stood up for herself that way, except that she shouldn't have been caught up in the argument in the first place. But Annette had come to her room, goaded her, baited her, and she'd finally fought back with the only weapon she had. Harry.

And Harry had laughed. Oh, he'd been upset, but then he'd laughed. They'd both laughed, right up until the moment Savannah had felt her chin begin to tremble, until the moment a wave of grief that was nearly physical had swept over her, until the moment Harry had taken her in his arms while she bawled like a baby. For her mother. For the father she'd never known. For the childhood she'd missed. For the mess she was in now. For...well, just for everything.

Harry had held her, tried to comfort her and finally carried her up to this room, told her to wait while he got her suitcases from the car so that she could change into her pajamas.

She'd tried to tell him no, that she'd go to a hotel, but her heart hadn't been in that protest, and Harry had known it. He'd put her suitcase on the bed, opened it, then kissed her cheek and left her alone, telling her to get a good night's rest. Everything, he'd promised, would look better in the morning.

So here she was. Sleeping under the same roof as Harry, irrevocably alienated from her family, such as it was. It was morning now, and she'd cried, and she'd slept, but she still had no clear idea as to what came next.

She only knew two things. The first was that her teenage crush on Harry had never gone away, and had now matured into love. The second thing she knew was that there was no way she could marry him.

Harrison had started the bacon when he'd heard the shower go on in the guest bedroom, and his timing had been perfect, because he was just spooning scrambled eggs onto two plates as Savannah entered the kitchen.

He hoped this excellent timing was an indication of how well the rest of the day would go, but one look at Savannah's expression told him he'd probably been too optimistic.

"Sleep well?" he asked as she went to the coffeemaker, poured the hot, fragrant liquid into two cups she then carried to the table.

"Yes, thank you, Harry," she told him, sitting down, picking up her fork. "I slept really well. You?"

"Like the dead," he said, lying through his teeth. He'd been up until nearly three, pacing his study, wondering how deep and hot the hell he'd be sent to would be if he gave in to impulse, climbed the stairs and knocked on Savannah's door. If he went inside and offered her comfort. Offered her more than comfort.

He hadn't done that, of course. He was too much the gentleman. He'd been raised too well. And he knew that, if he did, Savannah would be right in seeing him as just one more person trying to take advantage of her.

But there was another problem, and he was pretty sure Savannah had already gotten to the heart of it. He was more than sure she'd be pointing it out to him before they finished breakfast.

He'd been up since six, trying to figure out how he could dance out of her conclusions, turn them around, convince her that this marriage they'd agreed to was still a viable option.

"You're a very good cook," Savannah said as she ate. "I was never allowed in the kitchen, but I did take an elective home economics class at school. I thought they'd teach us how to cook, but all they taught us was how to pick a quality caterer. Private schools sort of exist in their own little worlds, don't they? But when I lived in an apartment during grad school, I did learn to make a mean microwave pizza. Still," she said, attacking the hash browns he'd made from scratch, "I never tried tackling anything like this."

"Bachelor living, Savannah," Harrison told her, finishing up his own breakfast, then carrying the plate to the sink. "It's either learn to love frozen dinners or learn to cook. I decided to learn. My mother suggested I hire live-in help, but I'm rarely home for more than breakfast, so I decided against it."

Was that enough small talk? Harrison was pretty sure it was. The next time Savannah opened her mouth, she was bound to tell him "thank you very much, but the marriage is off."

"Harry—" she began, swiveling on her chair, to look at him.

"Want to hear something wild?" he interrupted quickly, grabbing at the first conversational gambit that popped into his mind.

She looked at him, sighed, then brought her empty plate to the sink. "Okay, Harry. Tell me something wild. Lord knows I haven't heard anything wild in at least, oh, ten or twelve hours."

"We'll leave these until later," he said, running water over both plates, then taking Savannah's hand and leading her into his study, then coming back to the kitchen to pour each of them another cup of coffee.

"Open that drawer, the one right beside the chair you're sitting in," he told her as he carried the cups back into the room. "See that blue velvet box? Take it out, Savannah. Open it."

She looked at the box, tipped her head slightly

and looked at him. "Open it? Why?" she asked, obviously with a lame attempt at humor. "Is it full of some miniature version of those exploding paper snakes?"

"Something like that," Harrison said, as her comment came a little too close to home for comfort. "Go on, Savannah, open it."

She did as he asked, slowly opening the six-inch-square, thin box, then opened her mouth in a silent *O!*

"Something else, isn't it?"

"Is it...is it *real?*" she asked, touching her fingertip to the center stone of the sapphire-and-diamond choker. "God, Harry, it's real, isn't it? What are you doing leaving something this valuable just sitting around here, where anyone could find it, steal it?"

"Are you going to steal it, Savannah?" he teased, then laughed as she made a face at him. "Now, do you want to hear the something wild? It's about the necklace."

Still holding the box, but not taking the necklace from its white satin bed, Savannah curled up on the chair, her legs tucked up as she signaled that she was ready to hear his story.

Now that he had her attention, and had diverted her from whatever it was she wanted to say to him, Harrison realized that he'd probably just dug himself another hole. Talking about suitable Colton brides wasn't exactly a topic he wanted to explore this morning.

Still, he'd opened his mouth, so there was nothing

else to do but tell the old story, then wait for Savannah's response. It wasn't long in coming.

"Did Annette ever try on the necklace? How did it look on her? Did it sparkle?" she asked, still holding the box, but no longer running her fingertip over the stones of the choker.

"Annette? No, as a matter of fact, I think I'd forgotten about the necklace, until my grandmother brought it up yesterday. That's when I got it out of the wall safe." When Savannah shot him a quick, questioning look, he continued, "Okay, so I almost told her we were getting married. I didn't, but I almost did, and that's when she mentioned the necklace, and the story around it. But my grandmother is in Paris. She wasn't standing right in front of me, making rotten remarks. So, if you're worried about spilling the beans—"

"Blowing the deal," Savannah interrupted, giving the thing her own spin. "Throwing a monkey wrench into the works. Eliminating the element of surprise."

"Exactly, all that stuff," Harrison agreed. "If you're worried about any of it, don't. Nothing's changed."

"Oh, well, Harry, that's not true," Savannah told him, shutting the box and placing it on the table beside her. "Annette knows now, so Sam is going to know by tonight. The element of surprise is gone, and he'll know what you're up to before your people put the offer on the table. I don't want to get into a lot of old sayings, but forewarned *is* forearmed, right?"

Harrison drank the last of his coffee, stood up. "And I'm telling you it's no big deal. I still make the offer, Sam still can't refuse."

"Harry, sit down. I can't watch you when you pace, and that's what you're about to do, isn't it?"

Harrison sat down and began tapping a hand against his knee. Realizing what he was doing, he stopped.

"When I came to your office on Friday, Harry, I was a mess, and still believed that I had some responsibility to bail Sam out of a problem he created all on his own. I was confused and hurt—I'm still hurt, I won't lie about that—and I dumped it all in your lap."

"I'm not complaining," Harrison countered, knowing he wasn't helping himself.

"No, you aren't, are you? Because, as I know now, Sam and Annette had pretty much tried the same thing with you as they're doing now with James Vaughn. You saw my predicament as the best shot at a fitting revenge you'd ever find. You get control of Sam's company, and you take the one thing Sam has left—bargaining power. Me, if you want to be specific. I mean, at least you were honest about it all. The takeover, the marriage, all of it. But none of it is necessary now, Harry. We both know that."

"Because you've burned your bridges," Harrison said, looking into the bottom of his coffee cup, surprised to find it empty. "After Annette's little display last night, you've decided that both she and

Sam can sink or swim on their own, because you're gone. History. Am I right?''

Savannah touched her cheek. ''You could almost say Annette slapped some sense into me. I don't owe them anything, Harry. Which brings me to my main point. *You* don't owe me anything, either. You can still get your revenge, because now you know how desperate Sam is, how much he needs an investor. This is supposing, of course, that James Vaughn will be out of the picture by tomorrow, when they all figure out that ungrateful little Savannah has taken a powder and isn't coming back.''

She sighed, stood up, looked down at Harrison. ''So that's it, isn't it? Harry, I thank you, I thank you so very much, for everything you've done, everything you've offered.''

''However, you don't need me anymore, so thanks for everything, but you're out of here?'' Harrison said, also standing. ''What about our marriage license?'' he asked, knowing he sounded ridiculous, hoping he didn't sound bitter.

Savannah shrugged, tried not to look at him. ''I suppose you could always frame it, put a caption under it that says something like There but for the Grace of God...''

''Not funny, Savannah,'' he said, putting his hands on her shoulders. ''Where will you go?''

She looked at him, and he saw that her big blue eyes had gone bright with unshed tears. ''Where? I don't know. I've got a small trust fund from my mother that Sam couldn't touch. I can live on that for a while, and I *am* educated, you know. I'll find a job."

"Stay here until you do," Harrison heard himself say. "Please, Savannah. It's a big house. Besides, I don't want you where Sam can get at you. At least not right now. Come on, Savannah. I'm making sense, and you know it."

She lowered her eyes for a moment, then looked up at him again, nodding without saying anything.

"All right," Harrison said, trying to keep the elation out of his voice. "Then it's settled."

"For a week," Savannah said, stepping away from him. "Two at the outside. That should give you enough time to make Sam see reason, get you your revenge. Enough time for me to find employment and an apartment here in Prosperino."

"Whatever," Harrison said, agreeing with her even as he was busily making other plans.

Savannah came into the house through the kitchen Thursday evening, tossed her brand-new briefcase on the table, then—because she'd seen Harrison's BMW in the driveway—sang out, smiling at the silliness of what she was about to say, "Hi, honey, I'm home!"

Ten seconds later, Harry walked into the kitchen, dressed casually in a white knit golf shirt and khakis, holding the evening newspaper. "You're pretty bright and cheerful, Savannah," he said, reaching into the refrigerator and pulling out two cans of soda. "I take it things went better in the trenches today than they did yesterday."

"Yesterday, every other day this week, and all of last week," Savannah corrected, taking the soda can from him, popping the lid, then taking a quick, thirsty gulp. "You are now, sir, looking at one of the gainfully employed."

She waited for his reaction, watching him closely. He stopped in the midst of opening his own soda can, his body going very still for the count of three. Then he smiled, a bright smile. Possibly too bright a smile? Or was she reading too much into a smile? Hoping too much on a smile?

"Savannah, that's terrific!" he said, putting down the soda and coming across the room to wrap her in a bear hug, lifting her completely off the ground. "Just terrific!"

"Yeah, it is, isn't it?" she answered, straightening her suit jacket, then removing it, to lay it across the back of a nearby chair. "You knew that today was my second interview with Boggs, right? Well, I have to tell you, Harry, they *love* me. They positively *adore* me." Her smile grew wider. "I start in two weeks, when they open their new facility. It's ground-floor stuff, Harry, entry level. But I'm *in!*"

"Savannah Hamilton, about to fight the good fight for water waste management. Do you think you'll be able to handle all the romance in that job?"

"Idiot," Savannah said, giving him a playful punch in the arm. "It's an important job, in an important industry. You know that, too, unless you really want another lecture from me on the environment, the lack of unpolluted water, and all that good stuff."

"I'll pass, thanks anyway, although I might let you twist my arm until I ask you to write an article or two for me," Harry said, bending down to give her a kiss on the cheek.

He kissed her on the cheek a lot. Touched her a lot, but never too intimately, never threateningly. For almost two weeks, they'd lived together in this house, eaten their meals together, watched videos together, beaten each other at board games, and sat beside each other late into the evening in the study, just talking.

She felt as comfortable with Harry as she'd ever felt in her entire life, with anyone. And yet each night, as they headed upstairs to bed, as they climbed the stairs together, after Harry kissed her on the cheek and they went to their separate bedrooms, Savannah had felt as unhappy as she'd ever felt in her life.

Unhappy. Unfulfilled. Damn it—*frustrated!*

More than once, after assuring herself that Harry was asleep, she'd padded back down to the study, to take out the necklace, hold it in her hand and stare at it, watching the sapphires and diamonds twinkling in the light.

She'd never taken it out of the box, never tried it on. The temptation was always there, but she was too afraid to give in to it.

She was too afraid that if she tried it on, the stones would go all muddy and dull.

And now she'd be leaving.

"Harry? Should we go out to dinner, to celebrate? My treat."

"*Your* new job, *my* treat," he answered, already heading for the hallway. Then he stopped, turned back. "Oh, I almost forgot. It's a done deal as of this morning at ten o'clock. You're now looking at the new majority owner of Hamilton, Inc."

"You did it," Savannah said, subsiding into a chair, her knees suddenly weak. They'd done lots of talking these past days, but they'd never mentioned Sam, or Annette, or Harry's intention of taking over Sam's company. "Did you see him? Did he ask about me?"

Harry looked at her, slowly shook his head. "I'm sorry, Savannah. No, he didn't ask about you."

"Oh," she said, wondering why that hurt so much. Maybe old habits just died hard, and she'd lived too long hoping to please Sam, wishing for his attention. "Well, I guess I shouldn't have expected him to, right? He probably doesn't even know I'm here."

"He knows, Savannah," Harry said, pulling out another chair, sitting down across from her, taking both her hands in his. "Okay, I'll tell you. But then you've got to let it go, Savannah. You've got a new life, a new job and the whole world in front of you. You have to let it go."

"I know," she said, squeezing his hands, then pulling away from him. "Tell me everything."

"There really isn't that much to tell," he said, picking up his soda can once more. "It was all lawyers and signing papers and business, for the most part. Not that there wasn't a small, rather ugly outburst when Sam finally realized the restructured company will now be called Colton-Hamilton, Inc. That wasn't pretty, but when you have someone over a barrel, Savannah, it's time to take what you can. I took.''

''You really don't like him, do you? How long before you buy him out entirely? That is your plan, isn't it? To get him, and the Hamilton name, totally out of the picture?''

''You think I was vindictive?''

''No, probably not. I think you've waited six long years, bided your time, and then hit him with all you had. They hurt you, Sam and Annette both, and now you've hurt them back, except that they'll still have enough money. It's their pride you were after, because they'd hurt yours.''

''No, Savannah, you're wrong,'' Harry said, looking at her intently. ''I didn't continue with the buy-in because of what happened six years ago. Oh, I started out that way, I won't lie to you about that, but that's not how it ended up. I did it because they made you cry. I did it because of your childhood, the way they'd treated you, the way they'd tried to use you with James Vaughn. I did it, Savannah, because they deserved it.''

Savannah pressed her palm against her mouth and slowly shook her head as she stared at him. ''No,'' she whispered at last, lowering her hand. ''Oh, Harry, no. How could you do that? For *me?* I didn't want this for *me.* I didn't ask for this. Or maybe I did. Maybe, deep down inside, I did want to see Sam grovel. I don't think I want to talk about this anymore.''

She stood, ready to run out of the room, but Harry's next words stopped her. ''Don't you want to know what Sam did say about you, because he did say a few things? And what Annette said? She was there, you know.''

''Annette was there?'' Savannah said, not realizing that she'd lifted her hand to touch her cheek. ''Why on earth was she there?''

Harry stood, smiled as he walked toward her. ''I can't be sure, and I don't want to sound too arrogant, but I think she was there to seduce me.''

''Did it work?'' Savannah asked, backing up a step, feeling pain knife through her, a response too deeply embedded, for too many years, to conquer in a couple short weeks. Because Annette always got everything she wanted. Because Annette had once had Harry.

''Let's put it this way, your sister doesn't take hints very well. But I think she'll figure it out.''

''What did you say to her?'' Savannah asked, caught between a fresh bout of nerves and no little fascination as she watched Harry's expression go from mildly amused to unexpectedly serious.

''I told her,'' he said, taking hold of both her arms, ''that I was flattered, but I'm interested elsewhere.''

Savannah wet her lips, lowered her eyes. ''Oh. Well...well, that should have worked.''

''She wanted to know the lady's name.''

''Did she?'' Savannah said, trying to smile. ''I—I imagine that might interest her. Did you tell her?''

"No. Not until I tell the lady." He rubbed his hands up and down her arms, looked at her with his green eyes turning dark, serious. "Do you want me to tell the lady?"

"I—I—" The clock in the nearby study chimed the hour of six, and Savannah quickly stepped back, took a steadying breath. "We'll never get a reservation if we don't call now. You call, and I'll go upstairs and change, okay?"

Harry leaned a shoulder against the refrigerator, nodding his agreement. "Take your time, and just change into something casual. I've got this sudden hankering for delivered pizza. Unless you really want to go out?"

"No...no, that sounds, um, that sounds good. I'll just go take a shower and...okay. Pizza's good."

Savannah got as far as the stairs before she had to hang on to the newel post to catch her breath.

He'd gone too fast. He'd gone too far.

Two weeks. She'd lived under his roof for almost two weeks. Two weeks during which they'd renewed an old friendship, learned more about each other and left a lot of things unsaid.

Two weeks during which he'd learned that yes, he was attracted to Savannah.

Two weeks during which he'd learned that attraction and love were two very different things. Because he now loved her. Loved her with all his heart.

Two weeks during which he'd settled an old score, not for himself, as he'd believed, but because Sam Hamilton had hurt Savannah, and he'd crush anyone who ever hurt her.

But now he was pushing it. Going too fast. Savannah had just come out of her cocoon, just begun to spread her wings. She'd extricated herself from a really bad home life, had just been offered her first job, and her whole world was in front of her, ready to be lived.

Did he really believe she would want to marry him, live here with him? Love him?

Gratitude. That was what she felt for him, and that was to be expected. Gratitude, and possibly a little fear, as he had shown her he was more than Harry, the guy who had befriended a lonely teenager. He was also Harrison Colton, businessman. Sometimes ruthless businessman.

In time, she'd understand that, no matter what his motives, he had done what was best for Hamilton, Inc. Fifteen hundred employees would keep their jobs. The company, with his money and expertise, would flourish, grow. The people he'd worked with for eight months six years ago, the friends he had made, were mostly still there, and they'd been overjoyed to hear the news when he'd gathered them in the company cafeteria and made his announcement.

So he'd done a good thing. For some good, and some not so good reasons. He was a businessman, and he could live with that. He did, however, wonder if Savannah could live with that. He believed, hoped, that in time she could.

It had been pretty low of him to tell Savannah about Annette, but Savannah had a good heart, a forgiving heart, and he could tell that she was still feeling at least slightly sympathetic toward Sam and her sister. Trying to reestablish contact with either of them would be a mistake—much like trying to pet a shark.

"Which doesn't mean she wants *you* running her life now," Harrison reminded himself as the doorbell rang and he headed down the hallway. "And you don't want to run her life. You just want to be a part of it. So don't screw this up!"

The delivery boy left a few moments later, still grinning at the size of his tip, and Harry went back to the study, putting the pizza down on the coffee table, where he'd already assembled plates, napkins and two bowls holding a premixed tossed salad he'd poured ready-to-serve out of a plastic bag.

A bottle of wine was open, and breathing, and he had two glasses chilling in the freezer. He walked around the room, turning off the two table lamps he'd switched on, then lit the candles that sat waiting in their holders.

Everything was ready. He'd had time to run upstairs and pack a suitcase, enough time to book two seats on the noon flight to Reno. The stage was set. His hopes were high.

And the damn necklace was in the drawer, where he planned to keep it until at least ten years after their wedding.

The only thing that could go wrong now was that he'd come to the wrong conclusion, that Savannah liked him, was grateful to him, but didn't love him.

He heard her coming down the hallway and went to meet her, nervous as a schoolboy.

Chapter 5

Savannah walked through the downstairs hallway as though in a dream. A lovely dream, a fairy tale that showed all the signs of leading to a happy ending.

She'd tossed her suit on the bed, raced through her shower, then had taken the time to smooth on body lotion before slipping into a pair of soft pink velour shorts with a matching pullover top. Her hair was in a ponytail, she had lipstick on, but no other makeup. Her nose was shiny and her feet were bare. She'd sprayed Obsession between her breasts.

And she felt nothing like a gangly teenager.

"Don't you look comfortable?" Harry said to her as she entered the study and sat herself down at the opposite end of the blue-and-green-plaid couch. "Hungry?"

"Famished," she said as he lifted the lid on the box, exposing a large pizza. Half plain, half pepperoni. "Do you think we're in a rut?" she asked, accepting the slice he'd slid onto a plate. "We could try mushrooms. Bacon. Anchovies."

"Not in this lifetime. I'm a purist when it comes to my pizza, thank you. Let me get the wineglasses."

She watched as he went to the kitchen, feeling her heart beat faster as he came back, holding two frosted glasses, smiling at her in a way that quickly had her taking a bite of pizza, then wondering how on earth she'd ever planned to swallow it.

"My grandmother phoned again today," Harry said, pouring the wine. "Sometimes I don't hear from her for weeks, but she's really got a bee in her bonnet right now. I'm willing to bet she'll be calling Jason any day now and driving him up the wall with her suspicions."

"Suspicions?" Savannah asked, happy to have something to talk about. *Anything* to talk about. Although, she quickly realized, if his grandmother had phoned back because Harry had nearly "slipped" and told the woman about his supposed upcoming marriage, she might be more willing to have a rousing discussion on the always volatile state of West Coast weather instead. "What's she suspicious about, Harry?"

"It's a long story, concerning another branch of the Colton family here in California. My uncle's family. Are you sure you want to hear it?"

"Definitely," she answered, relaxing slightly. She

didn't know if she was merely delaying the inevitable or was afraid that there *wasn't* any inevitable; that she and Harry would share a dinner, talk and then once more go upstairs to their separate bedrooms. "Does this story have anything to do with the necklace?" She looked over at the table beside the deep-blue corduroy chair. "You know, you really should put that thing in a safe. Although I can't wait to tell the story to my friend Elizabeth. Elizabeth Mansfield, that is. Not that there's any chance her long-ago relatives were the Mansfields your ancestors had all that trouble with. Now please put that necklace away."

"How did you know I haven't put it back in the safe?" Harry asked, putting down his pizza and going over to retrieve the necklace, putting it down on the coffee table, where it sat, glaring at her. She moved the pizza box, so that the lid fell back over the case, hiding it from view. "But you're right. I'll put it there after dinner, okay?"

"And after you tell me the story about your relatives. I've read about Joe Colton, his businesses, his charities, but I really don't know much about him. Is that who this story is about? Joe Colton?"

"Yes, Uncle Joe, although I haven't called him that in years on his orders, now that, as he told me, I'm all grown-up and everything," Harry said, grinning as he picked up his pizza once more. "Plus, he's always been more of a friend to me, rather than just an uncle. He's really a great guy, Savannah. A great guy."

Savannah looked at the pizza box lid, knowing

what was under it, her attention still not completely on Joe Colton. "You said your brother has a matching necklace because your father had the original necklace cut up and reset. Does Joe Colton have one, too?"

"No, just me and Jason. Lucky us. Anyway, the reason Gran keeps phoning is because Meredith, Joe's wife, is supposedly planning a real all-out bash for Joe's sixtieth birthday. Black tie, huge orchestra, the whole nine yards."

"What's so suspicious about that?"

"Nothing, if you're not Gran. I think she shares my assistant's love of mystery novels. That, and she probably has too much time on her hands. I suggested she take a lover, and she told me to mind my own business—and who said she doesn't *have* a lover."

"That's hysterical! I'd love to meet your grandmother. And I already like Lorraine."

"Don't ever tell her," Harry said, grinning. "She likes to believe she has the power to strike fear into the hearts of all us lesser mortals. Fairly often, she does. Anyway..."

"Yes, anyway," Savannah said, polishing off her wine and holding out the glass for a refill. She needed Harry to keep talking, and felt that *he* needed to keep talking. They were both, obviously, afraid of something. She only wondered if he was afraid of the same thing she was afraid of—that this would be their last night together.

"Anyway," he continued, "I don't go out to the Colton ranch all that often anymore. First it was college, then work. And, frankly, they're such a huge bunch—Joe and Meredith's own kids, the ones they've adopted, the foster children who live with them—that, well, I guess that was just a bit more noise and happiness than I was interested in there for a while."

"They asked you why you and Annette had broken your engagement?" Savannah said, pretty sure she was right.

"They did, yes. And then I found myself being set up every time I went there, another smiling young woman sitting next to me at almost every meal. So I call, but I don't often visit. That's probably why I don't notice whatever it is Gran is so sure she notices. That, and the fact that Gran is a conspiracy freak. She's got every book ever published on both Kennedy assassinations, on the Lincoln conspiracy, the Martin Luther King conspiracy—even who killed Cock Robin. Not that I don't agree with her, on some of it, but there's nothing suspicious going on at the Colton Ranch. It's impossible."

Savannah put down her plate, wiped her fingers on a napkin. "You do know that you've lost me, don't you? Right about at the Cock Robin part, I think."

Harry smiled. "Gran's nearly ninety years old. She smokes, she drinks, she isn't above cussing, and she's got a mind as sharp as a tack. I can't wait till you meet her, Savannah."

"Except for when it comes to her suspicions about something going on at the Colton ranch?"

Meet her? Harry expected her to meet his grandmother? Savannah felt the small hope, already inside her, begin to grow.

Harry's smile faded, and he looked at Savannah for some moments, his eyelids narrowed. "That doesn't compute, does it? But her reasoning on this is just too off the wall, Savannah. Something about one of Joe's adopted kids, Emily, waking from the car crash she was in with Meredith about ten years ago and saying she saw *two* Merediths. One sweet and smiling, one—get ready for this one, Savannah—one mean and evil."

Savannah rubbed her hands on her arms. "Spooky. How old was this Emily at the time?"

"I'm not sure. Maybe ten, twelve. Something like that. And she'd been pretty badly injured. She still has nightmares about the accident, Gran says. Anyway, also according to Gran, Meredith hasn't been quite the same since the accident, and she's using this huge party to point out one of the ways Meredith is supposed to have changed."

"Why?"

"Because Meredith and Joe, for all their money, for all the lifestyle they could have, have always been very down-home. Very natural. Meredith's idea of a great party, as I remember it, is a barbecue, nine million kids underfoot, and maybe even a sing-along. Anyway, Gran phoned me again today, realizing I hadn't bought into her suspicions, to give me new evidence."

"What was it?" Savannah asked, pulling her legs up under her as she listened.

"She phoned Meredith to personally reply to the invitation, and Meredith didn't ask about Gran's arthritis."

Savannah raised one eyebrow as she looked at him for a few moments, then said, "Well, damn, Harry, that just about nails it, doesn't it? Meredith must have hit her head in the crash—a crash obviously caused by alien body snatchers, because we have more than our share of those here in California—and then morphed from nice down-home lady to evil party-throwing monster, right in front of Emily's eyes. It's the only explanation. I'm surprised neither you nor your grandmother has considered it."

Harry made a face at her. "I can see I'm not going to be able to let you and Gran alone together. Except that it is strange that Meredith wouldn't ask Gran about her arthritis. The fact that she's nearly ninety and still spry as a teenager—with *no* arthritis—is sort of a running gag in our family. The only one who doesn't start off each conversation with a question about Gran's arthritis is Jason, but that's because he's a doctor, and Gran said she made it a policy years ago never to answer health questions from a doctor."

Savannah laughed, shook her head and finished her wine, realizing that she might have finished it too quickly, because her head felt sort of light, and her limbs had loosened. "You'll be going out to the ranch for the party, won't you?"

"I will if you'll go with me," Harry said, using his foot to push the coffee table farther away from the couch. "You already said you want to meet Gran. My parents will be there, and Jason—if we can all tear him away from his hospital."

Savannah realized that she was twisting her hands together in her lap and immediately stopped. "Do you...do you really want to show up at the ranch with another Hamilton? I wouldn't think so."

Harry's grin answered her question, most of her questions. His next statement answered the rest. "I really hadn't thought about that, Savannah. However, now that you mention it, I'd much rather show up with Savannah Colton than Savannah Hamilton. But not for any other reason than that I happen to love you very much and want you to marry me."

"You love me?" Savannah asked, beginning to tremble, as if a cold wind had somehow invaded the room. "Are you sure about that, Harry?"

He moved even closer to her, and she was warmed by his heat, could feel her tremors easing as she looked into his emerald eyes, saw a softness in them that, wonderfully, was directed straight at her. "Savannah, I think I've been in love with you ever since you walked into my office, and back into my life. And if I wasn't completely convinced in that first moment, I was completely convinced when you walked toward me at the pizza place, your face all clean and shiny as it is now. Savannah, you're the most honest, most unaffected and natural, the most completely wonderful and unselfish woman I've ever known. And that ponytail of yours is sexy as all hell."

"I'll bet you say that to all the girls," she said, feeling more than slightly dizzy.

"Don't interrupt, because now I'm going to talk about me." He cupped his hand around the back of her neck as he slowly drew her toward him. "I think I've earned some sort of award these past two weeks, because I wanted to give you some time. Time to get past what Sam said to you, time to realize that I wanted one whole hell of a lot more from you than any ridiculous chance for revenge—before I told you how I feel, possibly scared you away. Have I waited long enough, Savannah? Do you believe me? Believe that I love you?"

"Oh, yes, Harry," Savannah said. "I have to believe you, because I love you so much. I think I must have loved you forever."

He took her fully into his arms then, looking at her, seeming to devour her with his eyes even as he waited, without words. Waited, she felt sure, for her smile, for her to raise her own arms, slide them around him. Waited for her silent "yes" to the question he hadn't asked. To all the questions he'd yet to ask. Her answer would be yes, to all of them.

So she took the initiative, wrapping both hands behind his neck, and pulling him even closer, close enough for their mouths to meet, for their breaths to mingle. Close enough that there was no longer anything between them; not the past, not Annette, not Sam, not even their future. There was only the now, the moment, and she willingly, eagerly, gave herself up to it.

As he had just two weeks ago, Harry lifted her

into his arms, carried her up the stairs. But at the top of the landing, he turned left, heading to his own room. Taking her with him, carrying her, kissing her, mumbling words like *love* and *gentle* and *always.*

The California sun had set, and Harry's bedroom was in shadow, not that Savannah was in any mood for a tour. She only knew that his bed was wonderfully soft, the sheets on that bed cool and welcoming, his body warm as, their clothing now somehow gone, he held her close to his heat.

He kissed her. He kissed her gently, then with passion. Coaxingly. With his fires burning hot, and then softly, sweetly, until she didn't know her name, where she was, how she'd gotten there. All she knew was that Harry held her, Harry touched her, Harry loved her.

His hands skimmed her body, made it sing, brought her alive in ways unknown to her, awakening her to what it meant to be a woman, a woman loved by a man.

Her breasts tingled, and he touched them. With his hands, with his mouth. Her body yearned, and he stroked it to the point of bursting with the need growing inside her.

She held him, ran her hands over his back, kissed his neck, his shoulder, tried to get closer. Ever closer. There was no fear, and the pain she felt came and went so quickly that she barely had time to register it.

Because Harry loved her. Because Harry was loving her.

And she was loving him right back. Moving beneath him now, instinctively raising her legs, wrapping herself around him, opening to him, drawing him inside the very heart of her.

"Open your eyes," Harry whispered near her ear and, with tremendous effort, she did as he said. She saw his face above hers, looking down at her with a wonder in his eyes that gave her the power, the strength, the wholehearted belief to return that look, open her heart and mind to him, give herself to him and yet take from him as well.

"Forever," she breathed against his mouth. "Forever, Harry."

"Forever, Savannah," he promised, and then he crushed his mouth against hers, his tongue mimicking the thrusts of his strong body. Moving with her, moving in her, their bodies saying as much or more than their words. Making a promise. The promise of forever.

Harrison woke slowly, looked over at the illuminated face of his bedside digital clock, and couldn't believe it was only eight o'clock. Then, his mind clearing, he realized that light poured in through the draperies, and grinned. Eight o'clock in the morning.

Well, that explained things.

He moved his arm slightly, as it had fallen asleep, just as Savannah had fallen asleep against his shoulder, wrapped close to him.

He bent his head slightly, kissed her fall of ash-blond hair, pressed another kiss against her smooth forehead. But Savannah only sighed, smiled in her sleep and wrapped her arm more tightly across his bare stomach.

How he loved her. They'd talked half the night, made love the rest of it. Yes, they'd be married. Immediately. Not using the "tainted" marriage license they'd gotten, but after flying to Reno. His family would probably insist on a large reception later, possibly even another ceremony, and that was all right with him, all right with Savannah. But they wanted, needed, to be married now.

Harrison rolled his eyes, as something about the thought of "married now" and "Reno" and the printout of his digital clock bothered him.

He'd booked them on the noon flight to Reno! How in hell could he have forgotten that?

Carefully disengaging himself from Savannah, pressing one last kiss on her slightly pouting lips, Harrison gathered clothing from drawers and closet and headed for the shower. He'd already packed last night, so that was no problem, and if Savannah didn't have time to pack he'd buy her anything she needed in Reno. He'd buy her the world if she wanted it.

The beauty of Savannah was that she didn't want the world. She just wanted him. Loved him.

His hair still damp from the shower, he bent over the bed, running a fingertip down Savannah's cheek. "Savannah. Oh, Mrs. Colton, time to wake up."

Savannah's deep blue eyes looked up at him a moment later, and she turned onto her back and smiled. "Mrs. Colton. I think I could get used to that."

"You'd better, because you're going to be hearing it for the next fifty years, at least. Now, do you want to get showered and dressed, so we can get to the airport and make it official?"

"What—what time is it?" she asked, then turned her head, looking for a clock. "Oh, Lord! Eight-thirty?" She pulled Harrison down on the bed, poked his chest. "Why didn't you wake me earlier? I have to shower, I have to get dressed. My hair is probably a mess. I have to *pack!* Harry! How could you have let me oversleep?"

Her bare breasts had nearly come free of the sheets, and Harry nuzzled between them, laughing against her warm skin as she now beat on his shoulders, saying something about not having anything decent to wear to a wedding.

"You won't have to worry about that in a minute, Savannah," he told her, "especially if you keep wiggling around like that, because I won't let you out of this bed until next week."

He looked at her and laughed at the sudden shock on her face, shock that was quickly followed by a wide grin. "Are you saying I'm irresistible, Harry? I think I like that."

"Naw," he teased, slowly pulling down the sheet. "You're not irresistible. I'm just insatiable. It's a curse." He cupped one bare breast in his hand, ran his thumb lightly over her nipple. "But I'm a brave man. I'll learn to live with it. Unless you mind?"

Her answer was more than satisfactory.

An hour later, Harrison was in the kitchen, washing the dishes from last night's untouched salads, when the doorbell rang. He walked toward the door, smiling as he heard the shower running upstairs. The sound stopped just as he opened the door.

"Yes?" he said, not looking at whoever was at the door, because his mind, and his heart, were both still upstairs.

"Good morning, Harrison," Annette Hamilton O'Meara said, stepping inside the foyer before he could react and slam the door in her beautiful, smiling face.

Annette was shorter than Savannah, more rounded, and the sort of woman who almost always wore dresses and always looked great in them. Her thick mass of black hair was done in a casual, upswept style, her makeup was perfect, and her violet eyes danced with mischief. Once, just looking at Annette had turned a younger Harrison's insides to jelly. Now all he wanted was to throw her out on her rounded rear end and slam the door.

"We have some unfinished business, I believe," she said, walking farther into the foyer, looking around. Appraising the contents, Harrison decided. She spun around on her three-inch heels and looked at him, those violet eyes narrowed. "Or did you really think I believed you yesterday? You hinted that you and my sister were *involved.* Harrison, really. If you thought that would make me jealous, obviously you don't know me very well. I mean, Savannah? You couldn't be attracted to *her.*"

"Go away, Annette," he said, pointing toward the open door. "Please. Go far, far away. I don't want Savannah to see you."

The moment he'd said the words, Harrison knew he'd made a mistake.

"She's *here?* Daddy said it, but I didn't believe it. Oh, Harrison, that's so sick! You couldn't have me, so now you're sleeping with second best? It's more than sick. It's pitiful. Wasn't it enough to hurt Daddy the way you did? Did you have to rub my nose in it as well, bedding that tomboy? You owe me an apology, Harrison!"

Harrison looked at Annette for some moments, seeing absolutely no resemblance to Savannah. Realizing that Annette might have superficial beauty, but that Savannah—his Savannah—was beautiful inside and out.

"You know, Annette," he said, walking toward the study, because he still had to clean up the pizza box and the wineglasses, "you're right. I do owe you something, but it's not an apology. What I owe you is my thanks, for showing me, six years ago and again now, that I've made the right choice. You're not a nice person, Annette. Sam may have had something to do with that, but you're also a grown woman now, and not a nice one. That's your fault. And your loss, because Savannah cared for you at one time. She won't make that mistake again, believe me."

"Ooo, I'm just shaking, Harry, you scare me so much," Annette said sarcastically. She had followed after him, throwing her purse down on the couch, looking at the pizza box, the wineglasses. "What's this, Harrison? Leftovers from your celebratory dinner after humiliating my father yesterday? The scene of the great seduction? Both?''

''I think we're done here, Annette,'' Harrison said, knowing he wasn't above grabbing her by the elbow and physically throwing her out. He didn't want Savannah to know she was here. He didn't want Savannah subjected to Annette's vicious tongue, her insulting remarks.

''I'm not going anywhere until I see my sister,'' Annette said, sitting herself down on the couch, crossing her legs and looking very much like a woman who would not be moved. ''I need to warn her about you. Because you're using her, aren't you, Harrison? You used her to find out about Daddy's business, and you hid her away from us so that we couldn't talk to her, explain things to her.''

''Oh, I think you explained things to her really well, both of you,'' Harrison said, flipping the lid of the pizza box closed, then picking up the box and heading for the kitchen. ''By the way, it was your left eye, wasn't it? I can still see the bruising.''

He actually smiled as one of the wineglasses hit the doorjamb as he walked through to the kitchen. He'd put the dried-out pizza down the disposal, and if Annette wasn't gone by the time he got back to the study, he might put her down the disposal as well. At least figuratively.

But when he returned to the study, it was to see Annette standing in front of the mirror over the fireplace. The blue velvet box, that had been hidden by the lid of the pizza box, was open on the table, and the Colton sapphires were around Annette's neck.

Worse, Savannah was standing just inside the doorway from the hall, looking at her sister, her face so pale, Harrison feared she might faint. He went to her, put his arm around her waist and drew her close. "It's all right, Savannah. I've called the exterminators. She'll be gone shortly."

"Well, well, the gang's all here," Annette said, turning to glare at both of them. "Oh, and I heard that, Harrison, and you are *not* funny. Besides," she said, touching a hand to the choker, "I think I just might have gotten lucky. These aren't real, are they, Harrison? You've given Savannah paste jewels, seduced her with fakes. Why, that's almost hilarious. It certainly has made my day."

Harrison looked at Annette, a woman whose violet eyes should be eminently flattered by the sapphire-and-diamond necklace. Instead, the center sapphires, always so brilliant as they sat against the satin inside the velvet box, looked dull, almost black. Annette's complexion, such a creamy white, looked muddy, and the makeup over the fading bruise around her left eye had a greenish cast to it, so that it looked as if she'd put on her makeup in the dark, and misjudged badly.

Annette undid the clasp of the choker, picked up her purse, then dropped the necklace into Harrison's hand—discarded it like garbage—before stopping in front of Savannah. "He was mine first, you know," she said.

"He was never yours, Annette," Savannah told her quietly, her voice calm. "People don't belong to each other, and they aren't beholden to each other. They don't *owe* each other anything. What we get from each other is equal to what we give to them. Harry's given me his love, and I've given him mine. Freely, without strings, without hoping to gain anything in the exchange. And, Annette? I feel sorry for you, because you just don't get it, do you? And you never will.''

Harrison cocked his head to one side, one eyebrow lifted, as Annette Hamilton, her always-a-lady veneer cracking, snorted her disdain and left the house, her high heels clicking angrily on the parquet floor.

Savannah took a deep breath, let it out slowly, then reached up and kissed Harrison square on the mouth. ''Well, that was interesting. Shall we go now?'' she asked, her blue eyes sparkling, not with tears, but with love.

''Soon, but not yet,'' Harrison said, holding up the necklace. Sunlight streaming in the wall of windows behind him caught at the stones, so that they reflected the light, glittered, winked. ''I want you to try this on.''

She backed away, suddenly frightened. ''Oh, no, Harry. Not me. Not that thing! That thing is scary.''

''The stones looked terrible on her, didn't they?'' Harrison said, taking a step closer to Savannah as she backed up another step. ''Hell, she looked terrible wearing the stones. Interesting, don't you think? Not that I believe that old legend. Do you believe that old legend, Savannah?''

''Harry, we're going to miss our plane,'' Savannah persisted, still looking at the necklace he dangled in front of her.

"You're afraid, Savannah," he said, grinning at her. "You're afraid of these stones."

She wet her lips. Looked at the necklace. Looked at Harrison. Looked at the necklace again. "I—I've come downstairs a few times, after you went to bed, and looked at it. But I'd never try it on." Her gaze shifted to Harrison once more. "Harry, what if it looks horrible on me, the way it did on Annette? What would we do then?"

Harrison shrugged. "Take it out back and bury it under the rosebushes?" he suggested, taking hold of both ends of the necklace and advancing on Savannah once more. "But you know what, darling? I think I believe in the story behind this thing now. I never did before, but I do now. And I'll bet you this necklace is going to be proud to be put around your neck."

"You'd be betting an awful lot, Harry," Savannah warned him, then let her shoulders slump. "Oh, all right. God knows I've done enough wondering about the thing." She turned her back to him and lifted her hair so that he could fasten the choker around her throat.

Harrison hesitated for just a second, wondering if he'd made a mistake, because Savannah definitely seemed to believe in the old story attached to this string of jewels. But then he slid the necklace around her neck, shut the clasp and, with his hands on her shoulders, walked behind her to the fireplace. To the mirror over the fireplace.

Savannah had her eyes closed, he could see in the mirror, and he smiled at the way she had her bottom lip caught between her teeth as she hunted inside herself for the courage to open her eyes.

''Beautiful,'' Harrison said, squeezing her shoulders. ''Absolutely beautiful.''

Savannah half turned her head toward him, her eyes still closed, then opened them, peeked toward the mirror out of the corners of her eyes.

She saw what Harrison saw. She saw the two of them, reflected in the mirror. She saw his hands resting lightly on her shoulders. She saw the love in his eyes, Harrison was sure, because his reflection amazed even him.

But, even more than that, she had to see sapphires such a deep, clear blue that they nearly leapt with light and color.

She had to see how beautiful she looked, even more beautiful than the necklace that had waited so long to shine this way again.

''I love you, Savannah soon-to-be Colton,'' Harrison said, turning her in his arms, drawing her close to him. ''I didn't need that necklace to tell me I'm holding the right bride in my arms, or that I'm the happiest man in the world.''

''But it doesn't hurt, does it?'' Savannah said on a laugh, sliding her arms up and around his neck, drawing him down to her. ''Oh, Harry, how I love you.''

Fortunately, there was another, later plane heading to Reno. Lorraine Nealy made the reservations for them, which was pretty hard to do, as she was fairly well occupied patting herself on the back.

* * * * *

COLTON'S BRIDE
by Ruth Langan

To lovers everywhere.
And to Tom, who knows why.

Prologue

London, England, 1750

"Katherine." William Colton paused in the doorway of the formal parlor of the Mansfield manor house and stared in annoyance at the array of guests. So many people, including his own family, already assembled.

"William." Seeing her proud, handsome husband-to-be, Katherine Mansfield handed her crystal goblet to a maid and walked slowly across the room.

She heard the murmurs of approval from the guests as she moved among them, aware of the pretty picture she madc. Hadn't she and her mother spent endless hours choosing the perfect gown? It had taken two of their most skilled ladies' maids to coif her hair into the upswept nest of curls that best showed off her lovely face.

She paused in front of William and offered her hands to be lifted to his lips, knowing she was the envy of every woman in the room. And why not? He was not only the first son of the earl of Redbridge, but a dashing, arrogant rogue, who'd cut a wide swath through the eligible women of London.

After kissing her fingers, he continued holding her hands in his. "I'd hoped we would be alone, Katherine."

"Why, you naughty thing." Her mouth curved in a smile. "After we speak our vows on the morrow, you can have me all to yourself for a lifetime. But your family and mine wanted to be here to help us celebrate this joyous occasion. After all, it isn't every woman who is given the honor of marrying the son of an earl."

She touched a hand to his chest. Anyone watching would suppose she was placing her hand over his heart. In truth, she could feel the slight bulge of the velvet pouch in which rested the famous Colton sapphires. Her heartbeat sped up. "I can't wait to have everyone see me wearing the necklace, William."

It was, he realized, all he had to give her. That and a title, which the Mansfield family coveted. Though the Mansfields had wealth beyond belief, they were commoners. And in their circle of friends, wealth was never enough. In truth, their union would benefit his family as well, since the Coltons were desperately in need of an infusion of gold. Thankfully, Katherine's father could provide all they desired.

William could see their parents and guests watching and listening and felt a twinge of annoyance. This wasn't going at all as he'd planned. He'd hoped that this, the eve of their wedding, would afford them a private and exceedingly tender moment in which to present the Colton sapphires.

On an impulse he caught Katherine's hand and led her across the room. With every step he heard the whispered speculations about the jewels.

After stepping onto a balcony, he paused to draw the draperies closed behind them.

Katherine's lips were pursed in a pout. "I did so want everyone to see you present me with your family jewels."

"As you said, my darling, they'll have a lifetime to admire them. But this is such a special time for us." At least he was trying to make it so.

They both knew this was no love match. But at least they didn't repel each other. There was mutual respect. And in time, he hoped, friendship might even blossom into love. He'd been raised to understand the importance of duty to family and country. It had never occurred to him to refuse to accept his obligation.

He led her toward the balcony railing and tipped up her face to the moon-washed sky.

But instead of the kiss he'd anticipated, she lay a hand on his chest. "Hurry, William. I can't wait another minute to see the Colton sapphires."

He swallowed his annoyance and reached into his breast pocket, removing the dark velvet cloth.

"I'm sure you've heard of the history of these sapphires and diamonds, Katherine. They were given to the first earl of Redbridge by Queen Elizabeth, and have been worn by every Colton bride since. But they're much more than mere jewels. This necklace is said to be enchanted. We believe it is endowed with special powers.''

''So I've been told. I can't wait to see for myself.''

Curious, Katherine watched as he carefully unrolled the cloth and held the treasure in his hands. The necklace of glittering sapphires and diamonds shone brighter than the stars.

''William. They're absolutely stunning.'' Katherine's voice held a note of reverence in the hushed silence as she lifted a finger to stroke the jewels. ''Oh, I can't wait to show the others.'' She turned away and lowered her head slightly, giving him access to her neck.

William obligingly draped the necklace around her and bent to the clasp.

''Hurry, William.''

He frowned as the clasp refused to close.

She tapped a foot. ''What's wrong? Is it too dark out here? Oh, I knew we should have done this inside, with the others watching.'' Holding the chain to her throat, she turned.

William stared in stunned surprise at the jewels. Minutes ago they'd been dazzling in the moonlight. Now, resting against her skin, they looked dim and murky, as though they'd lost all their luster.

''What is it, William?'' She bent her head to the jewels, and then tilted it upward to see his scowling face. ''Whatever is wrong with you?''

He shook his head and lifted the necklace away from her skin. At once the stones seemed to pulse and gleam like fire, mocking him.

"It's...the clasp. It must be loose." He closed the clasp, then opened it again. It worked perfectly.

Refusing to believe what he'd just seen, he again placed the necklace around her throat, this time keeping her turned toward him, so that he could see the stones.

Almost at once their luster faded, the stones growing dark, almost muddy against her skin. And the clasp, which moments earlier had closed easily, now refused to be fastened.

A feeling of dread snaked along William's spine. It was true. He hadn't imagined what was happening here.

Seeing him hesitate, Katherine put a hand to her throat, but the necklace, like something alive, slipped through her fingers and would have dropped at her feet had William not caught it just in time.

His hands shook as he felt the stones, alive and pulsing, against his palm.

"What are you doing, William?" Katherine frowned as he began hurriedly rolling the jewels into the length of velvet.

"It would seem that we were both about to make a dreadful mistake." He tucked the parcel in his breast pocket and reached for her hand. "I know you can't understand completely, Katherine, and I most humbly apologize for that. But the Colton sapphires have never been wrong. The very fact that the colors of the stones keep changing and growing murky is a clear sign that we were about to do something that would have made us both miserably unhappy for a lifetime."

She snatched her hand away and took a step back. "What are you saying?"

"I'm saying that we can't be wed on the morrow."

"Because of a necklace? You'd risk the wrath of both our fathers, and the scorn of our friends, because of a necklace?" Her eyes narrowed with sudden fury when she saw the determined look on his face. "You can't be serious, William. If you persist in this childish behavior, I'll be humiliated in front of all London."

"The jewels—"

"Are stones. No more—no less." Her voice lifted to near hysteria. "They aren't magic. They don't possess special powers. You're using this as an excuse."

William shook his head. "Try to understand, Katherine."

"I understand this. You need me more than I need you, William. If you walk away now, I may not acquire a title, but you'll have even less. My father will see to that. I'll not suffer alone in this humiliation."

"I realize the consequences of my actions, Katherine. And I beg your forgiveness." His eyes narrowed with fierce determination. "But the stones are never wrong. I cannot in good conscience go through with this."

"Nay! You will not do this to me!" She tore open

the drapes to the balcony and fled weeping into the parlor.

Seeing her tears, the crowd fell silent while Katherine's mother tried to console her. "Whatever has happened, Katherine dear? Tell your father and me. I'm sure we can help."

"You and Father can't make this right. No one can. William Colton, that wicked, wicked fiend, has broken our engagement on the eve of our wedding. And all because of his...hated necklace." She fell into a fit of tears and nearly collapsed before being helped from the room by several of the servants.

In the stunned silence that followed the pronouncement, William was left to face the fury of two very angry and bewildered families.

"A man who would have such a fool for a son," Henry Mansfield shouted, "must surely be a fool himself." His eyes were hot with fury as he jabbed a finger in the chest of the earl of Redbridge. "Your son did not deserve my daughter. Nor do you deserve my friendship. From this day forward, you are unwelcome in my home, and in my circle of friends. I shall live to see you and your progeny destroyed, as you have destroyed my only child." He turned away to support his weeping, trembling wife.

The old earl was beyond fury. He had never before had to suffer such a public humiliation. He shot one glance at the silent, stunned guests before catching his wife's arm and starting toward the door, where a servant stood holding his traveling cloak.

On the threshold he turned to face his son. In front of the entire assembly he shouted, "Mark my words,

William. You have disgraced our good name. You are no longer my son, nor will you inherit my title and estates. All will pass instead to your younger brother. What's more, be warned. If I should see you on the street, I will not acknowledge you. You are dead to me. Dead. Is that understood?''

William saw the tears glistening in his mother's eyes and wished for some way to comfort her. But a line had been crossed. He understood that, with this single act of defiance, he had lost everything that had ever mattered to him. Home. Family. Friends. As well as the title and way of life that had been passed from father to son for hundreds of years. All those who had once loved him would remain not only unforgiving, but also determined to see that he pay for having brought disgrace upon the family name.

And all because he knew in his heart that the sapphire necklace, so long a source of pride to his ancestors, had been warning him. He and Katherine Mansfield would have brought each other only heartache. And now, because of it, he would have to face a different sort of heartache. One that would strip him of pride, of privilege, of dignity and honor.

He stalked down the steps of the Mansfield home. Without a backward glance he leapt onto the back of his stallion and was swallowed up into the darkness, heading into the unknown, alone and friendless. His past destroyed. His future as bleak and bitter as the night that closed in around him.

Chapter 1

Surrey, England, 1755

"Look at him." The tenant farmer leaned on his shovel and watched as a black-clad horseman came into view over the ridge. "I've heard that he's the disinherited son of an earl. And now he's nothing more than his lordship's lackey. No wonder he always looks so arrogant and keeps to himself."

The youth working beside the farmer glanced over and nodded. "There are those who say he's the reason Lord Kent has more than doubled his holdings."

"Aye. And why not? A man with neither heart nor conscience has a way of making servants double their efforts. I've heard that old Duncan and his grandson were tossed off the land their family has worked for a hundred years or more."

The youth looked horrified. "It's true, then?"

"It is." The farmer nodded. "The last I heard they were sleeping in hay barns and begging, in order to survive. And all because of the blackheart, William Colton."

Seeing the object of their fear and loathing drawing near, the farmer and youth bent to the task of turning the soil. As the horseman approached, neither man dared to look up. But as he rode past, both of them spat into the dirt, just to let him know what they really thought of Lord Richard Kent's hated overseer.

"You've been doing a fine job for me, William." Lord Richard Kent leaned heavily on his cane as he crossed the room and eased himself into a chair.

"Thank you, your lordship." William Colton, clad in a dark jacket, his pants tucked into fine black boots, stood in front of the fireplace looking more like the lord of the manor than his employer. It had been bred into him. The way he stood, the way he dressed, even the way he looked. The strong jaw. The proud, some would say arrogant, look in those icy blue eyes. The stiff spine. And the ever present frown. "I've spent the past fortnight visiting your tenant farmers. You'll be pleased to learn that your share of their profits will be more than double that of the previous year."

"What about those who have fallen behind on their payments to me? Have you removed them from the land as I ordered?"

"Aye, your lordship."

"Very good, William. And the deeds I requested for the new parcels of land from Lord Turnberry's widow?"

"They're all here." William stepped forward and presented Lord Kent with a handful of documents.

The old lord's eyes glittered with unconcealed greed. "Excellent. I see that I chose the right man when I hired you to oversee my estates."

"I've made a note of those tenants who appear, either because of age or ill health, to be slacking off. If you'd like me to fetch the ledgers—"

"Leave them, William."

At his words William looked up in surprise. Lord Richard Kent had a habit of going over the ledgers almost daily, tallying his profits and losses. His desire to become the wealthiest landowner in Surrey was no secret.

The old man took a coughing spell and held his handkerchief to his mouth for several minutes, until his breathing returned to normal. "I wish to speak with you about a different matter."

William met the old man's eyes, wondering where this was leading.

"When you came here five years ago, William, I felt that you'd been heaven-sent. As you know, my unfortunate accident left me unable to continue to properly oversee my estates. Without a son, I feared I might soon be taken advantage of by my nephew. But thanks to you, and the excellent tutors who surely taught you in your youth, I've not only managed to keep my estates, but I've actually seen my holdings increase."

He glanced over at the silent young man, aware of the depth of pain at the mention of his youth. In five years, William Colton had never once spoken about himself. Neither his past nor his present, nor his hopes for the future. Still, it was impossible for him to keep his family history a secret. It was known throughout England that William Colton had been disowned by his father, and had been the cause of a long-standing rift between the Mansfields and the Coltons.

Lord Kent considered the Colton family's loss to be his gain. Perhaps because of his earlier humiliation, this young man had acquired a shrewdness, a toughness, that was becoming legend. The tenant farmers, fearful of being ruthlessly tossed off the land they'd worked for generations, were now producing more than ever, filling Lord Kent's coffers until they were brimming with gold.

"As you know, my wife, bless her, could give me no heirs. I have a nephew who will one day lay claim to my holdings." The old man smiled. "Though I'm certain he's the reason I've lived so long. The thought of my estates falling into the hands of young Marcus causes me to shudder. He will surely squander it on wine and women before he is a score and five."

Lord Kent indicated a chair. "Sit, William." He smiled at the look of uncertainty on the younger man's face as William took the chair across from him. "My physician has recommended that I retire to my London town house, where he can better tend to my health. But before I do, I have a business proposition to offer you. If you continue looking out for my estates with the care you've shown in the past five years, and continue increasing my holdings at the same rate, I shall offer you not only what you are now paid, but also a percentage of the profits."

William's head came up sharply. This wasn't at all what he'd been expecting. "Do you realize how much money you're talking about, my lord?"

The old man nodded. "You'll be a wealthy man, William. A man of means." His lips curved into a smile. "But it's only fair, for you have a gift for choosing the finest parcels of land, and seeing that those who work them remain amazingly productive." He found himself wondering what this young man's secret was. Did he beat the tenant farmers into submission? Or were they so cowed by the thought of being tossed off the land of their ancestors by this angry man that they doubled their efforts? Whatever the secret, Lord Kent was grateful.

"I've heard you're a hard man, William. I admire that in a man." Lord Kent stuck out his hand. "Now, to tempt you even further—" he held out a document "—I had my solicitors settle the deed to that piece of land you now live on. It's yours, debt free, if you agree to my offer."

William found himself speechless as he studied the deed. His land, free and clear, which no one could take from him. "How could I not agree to your most generous offer? Thank you, your lordship."

"No. It is I who thank you, William. For your diligence has doubled my holdings, and made it possible for these tired old eyes to watch a sunset instead of being tied to a stuffy ledger.'' He looked over at the younger man. ''Something I'd recommend for you, as well.'' He paused a moment. ''Tell me, William. How long has it been since you've given yourself a moment to appreciate a sunrise or sunset?''

Seeing the young man draw into himself, he realized that he was already being shut out. It would seem that the wall William Colton had built around himself was too high and too thick for anyone or anything to penetrate. As he had so often these past five years, he thought about the tales he'd heard. It would be shameful for the son of an earl to be reduced to overseeing another man's estates. But William Colton had borne his shame with the same arrogance as he'd once worn his wealth and title.

The old man got slowly to his feet and shuffled across the room. ''I'll be leaving for London on the morrow. Now that I'm leaving my holdings in such competent hands, I'm in rather a hurry to begin the next stage of my life.''

The next stage of my life. How well William understood that.

When he was alone William turned to stare out over the vast rolling hills of his employer. Though this land was green and lovely, it couldn't hold a candle to his father's estates. He'd consciously refused to allow himself to go back to that place in his mind, knowing the pain it would cause. And so he'd moved forward. His entire education had been focused on turning his inheritance into even greater wealth. When that had been denied him, he'd had no choice but to use his knowledge for his employer, never dreaming he would be invited to share the wealth.

Now he'd been given the opportunity of a lifetime. The chance to better his own future. Until this moment, he'd been unwilling to think beyond today. He'd seen his future stretching out in endless days of work and endless nights of loneliness and despair. His only friendship the old man and boy he'd taken in, who now shared his home. His only comfort a tankard of ale and an occasional tavern wench.

He'd thought it enough. Until now. Now, for the first time in five years, he could see a glimmer of hope.

He decided to celebrate his good fortune by stopping at the Bubble and Squeak, where they served the finest mutton in all of Surrey.

William stumbled along the darkened lane, cursing the fact that he'd refused the offer of a lantern when leaving the tavern. He couldn't recall the mutton, but the ale had been fine. And flowing frequently, it would seem. He'd lost count after half a dozen tankards. But he was grateful that tomorrow was Sunday. If he had to sit a horse and inspect another holding at first light, he'd surely go blind.

He bumped against the closed gate and tumbled to the ground when it swung inward. He nearly turned the air blue with a few well-chosen oaths before picking himself up and starting forward.

"Just a few more steps," he muttered aloud, "and you can tumble into your own bed."

A good thing he'd refused the offer of a tavern wench to warm it. Not that he hadn't been more than a little tempted. But he was far too addled to make good use of her.

He reached the door and leaned a hip into it. It stuck for a moment, and he cursed the old man who had no doubt latched it before going to his bed. He was forced to shove with all his might before it gave way and he stumbled inside, crashing into a wall with such force he could see stars.

He didn't recall a wall there yesterday. He must be drunker than he thought. Not that it mattered. He deserved to be a little drunk after the good fortune that had come his way this day.

He put a hand to his head and lurched across the room. It was blacker in here than a witch's brew and he stuck his other hand out in front of himself to keep from bumping into anything else. That didn't help him when he stumbled over something on the floor. Though he didn't fall, he came close, and swore again as he stopped and struggled to get his bearings. Everything seemed turned around.

Just then he heard a door open and saw a light coming toward him. The old man, Duncan, he supposed, come to fetch him to his room.

But it wasn't Duncan.

"God in heaven." He stared at the vision, unable to believe his eyes. He must have hit his head harder than he'd realized. "An angel."

She wore something long and gauzy that looked

as though it had been spun from moondust. It skimmed every curve of her body and drifted to the floor, swirling around her bare feet. She didn't so much walk as float.

His gaze moved over her, from the tips of her toes to the top of her head. There were clouds of hair, all soft and burnished gold, tumbling in curls around a face so beautiful, it couldn't possibly belong to a mortal.

He shook his head, hoping to clear his fuzzy brain. "Am I dreaming? Or are you real?"

"Oh, I'm real enough." The voice was low, breathy. And as musical as a harp. "And so is this." The angel lifted her hand and for a moment all he saw was the candle.

But then he caught sight of the dueling pistol in her other hand and started to hastily back up.

"Wait. Stop. Why are you—" He felt the scrape of the wall against his back as she lunged, jamming the pistol against his chest.

"Unless you get out of here this minute, I'll be forced to—"

The rest of what she was about to say was lost as, in one smooth motion, he brought his arm up in an arc, sweeping the pistol from her grasp and sending it falling to the floor. In the next instant he had his arms around her waist, pinning her arms to her sides.

The candle slipped from her nerveless fingers and dropped to the floor where it was snuffed, plunging the room into darkness.

"How dare you..."

There was that angel voice again, sending curls of pleasure through his veins straight to his loins.

"I might ask you the same." His voice was thick with ale, and something else. An unexpected need made his voice gruffer than usual, and prickled just under his skin, warring with common sense. Need won as he fisted a hand in her hair and dragged her face close. His mouth found hers in the darkness and covered it in a quick, hard kiss.

At the first taste of her he reared back as though burned, wondering at the shock that jolted through his system. In his entire life, he'd never felt anything quite like this strange, quaking sensation. Was it his imagination? Or had the entire room just tilted at a crazy angle?

He had to find out. Very deliberately he drew her close and covered her lips with his, drinking from her sweetness until they were both breathless.

"I may be drunk," he muttered against her temple, "but not too drunk to know the difference between an angel and a flesh-and-blood woman." In the blackness he could smell her hair. It smelled of rainwater. And he could feel the press of that soft womanly body against his. He was shocked by the way his body responded. Apparently he wasn't nearly as drunk as he'd thought.

"Now tell me why you greeted me in such a manner, woman, with a dueling pistol to my heart."

"I'll attack any man who dares to break into my house." Her breath, as sweet as a field of wildflowers, was warm against his face. He had to pull himself back from thoughts of kissing her yet again.

Then the meaning of her words registered in his fuzzy brain. "Your house?"

Too late he realized that he'd been so dazzled by the sight of the vision coming toward him, he'd forgotten to take the time to look around. Could it be that he was in the wrong place?

The gate. That was what had confused him. The widow Warner, who owned the small holding down the lane from his, had a fence and gate just like his.

Very slowly he released her and took a step back in the darkness. Then he bent down, feeling in the dark for the candle. When he found it he held a flint to the wick until it caught and flared.

He lifted the candle to study his surroundings.

"I'm...sorry, madam. I thought I was home. I...had a bit of ale."

"More than a bit from the smell of you." She wrinkled her nose and took a step back. "I recognize you now. The gentleman—" she spoke the word with such disdain, he had no doubt what she really thought of the description "—who oversees Lord Kent's estates. You will leave at once, sir." She held out her hand for the candle.

He handed it over, and as their fingers brushed, he felt a rush of heat that startled him. In the light of the candle he caught sight of the greenest eyes he'd ever seen. Watching him the way a doe might watch a hunter who was poised to release an arrow into its heart.

"I most humbly apologize, madam." His voice, rich and cultured, held no hint of warmth. "Though not for that kiss. I'd be a liar if I were to apologize for that. And though I've done many things of which I'm not proud, lying isn't one of them.'' He made a slight bow. ''I bid you good night.''

He turned away and let himself out the door. Before he'd taken two steps he heard the sound of the latch being thrown, and for good measure, a brace being set against the door.

He smiled in the darkness. The widow Warner, it seemed, was taking no chances on having her sleep disturbed again.

At least, he thought as he stumbled down the lane to his own place, he now knew she slept alone. Though, from the heat of that kiss, he couldn't fathom why.

Why had no man snatched up such a treasure? Could this ethereal creature be the same dried-up prune of a widow who'd lived in her father's cottage for the past two years?

He'd seen her from a distance, of course, but had paid her no heed.

Perhaps, in the cold light of morning, he'd discover the flaws that had escaped his attention during this brief encounter. But for now, he had no doubt the image of her, like some beautiful avenging angel, would play through his mind for whatever time was left of this night.

Chapter 2

Molly Warner hurried along the lane, happily struggling under the weight of the heavy basket on her arm. After attending Sunday services, she'd delivered a gown to Mistress Mobley at the parsonage, who had paid her with a dozen eggs. She'd spent many a day and night stitching a fine shirt and waistcoat for the miller, and had been rewarded with a sack of flour. And a nearby farmer's wife, who had commissioned a fancy dress and bonnet for her soon-to-be-wed daughter, had given her a portion of beef from a recent slaughter.

Molly lifted her face to the rare summer sunshine and sighed with pleasure. She felt as though she'd just earned a king's ransom. There was enough food here to last for weeks if she was frugal. She couldn't recall the last time she'd seen such bounty. The endless days and nights of sewing until her fingers grew stiff and her vision blurred had been well rewarded.

Her smile faded slightly as she passed the gate of William Colton. This fine day and the treasure in her basket almost made up for the horrible night she'd been forced to put in. And all because of that drunken lout.

She'd spent the rest of the night tossing and turning, unable to put him out of her mind. It was bad enough that he'd reeked of tobacco and ale, a smell that would forever remind her of her late husband. But the final insult had been that he'd dared to lay his hands upon her person. And kiss her.

Even now, just thinking about it had her shivering. There had been something so dark, so dangerous, so...unnerving about him.

She blamed her response to that kiss on fear and shock. What else would explain the heat that had coursed through her veins, turning her blood to molten lava? How else to make sense of those strange, curling sensations deep inside when he'd trapped her in his arms? In all the years she had been Jared Warner's wife, she'd never known anything to compare.

What annoyed her the most about her response was the character of the man who'd kissed her. She'd heard the whispers. A man who had brought shame to his family, though she knew not why. A man hated by those who were forced to toil under his angry, unforgiving eye. A man given to bouts of drinking and wenching.

She'd had her fill of such a burden.

She unlatched her gate and started up the garden path, lined with hedgerows and primroses. It made her sad to see the way the flowers had gone wild. When her father had been alive, he'd kept everything neatly trimmed. Now vines grew everywhere, choking the life out of some of the bushes, and even climbing up the walls of her cottage and threatening to block the sunlight from the windows as well. But she had neither the strength nor the time to properly see to them. It took all she had, sewing all day and late into the night for others, to keep body and soul together. Had it not been for her skill with needle and thread, and this, her father's small holding here in Surrey, she would be completely destitute.

It had been a humbling experience to return here after Jared's death and admit to her father that her husband's drinking, gambling and wenching had left her with nothing but the clothes on her back. If his debtors could, they would have demanded even those. And one, whose coarse manners had shocked her to the core, had even made a lewd suggestion that he knew of an easy way for her to pay off her husband's debts.

After eight years with Jared Warner, the peace she'd found here in her childhood home was a soothing balm. Even the difficult care of her father in his final days had brought not a single word of complaint from her lips.

And now, after just one nighttime encounter, her peace of mind had been shattered once again. By the monster who lived right next door. Now she would have to be ever more vigilant, to protect her honor and her person.

When she reached her door, she was startled to see the object of her dark thoughts coming around the back of her cottage. He hadn't yet seen her. He was dressed all in black, giving him a dark, satanic look. His head was tipped back, studying the trees that towered over her roof, looking for all the world like a country gentleman surveying his estate. The muscles of his arms strained the sleeves of a white shirt. His long legs, encased in black breeches and shiny black boots, enabled him to move easily through the tall grass.

At his feet was a hound. At her arrival the animal picked up his ears, then gave a low growl of warning.

That had William's attention turning to her.

"Mistress Warner." He wasn't aware of the frown on his face. After the night he'd put in, his head still ached, and his mouth was so dry he could hardly swallow. It would be a long time before he'd have the desire to taste ale again.

Now, this woman's lips were another matter.

"Mr. Colton." She stayed where she was, determined to keep as much space between them as possible.

She looked so different in the daylight. Her gown was plain, the fabric worn and faded. A shawl carefully draped around her shoulders disguised any trace of womanly curves. Her hair was pulled back into a prim knot, and covered by a bonnet. But none of that could erase the memory of the angelic creature who had boldly attacked him with a dueling pistol, and whose lips had been sweeter than May wine.

"I've come to apologize for last night." He walked closer and the dog followed.

In the sunlight his eyes were a brilliant blue. She hadn't expected that. Nor was she prepared for the way he stared at her with an intensity that had her heart leaping to her throat.

She'd felt the strength of her nighttime attacker. Now she could see for herself the width of his shoulders, the muscles of his arms. He was so tall, she had to tip her head back to see his face. A face that was, up close, ruggedly handsome, with a broad forehead, aristocratic nose and a slight cleft in his chin.

"I accept your apology." She tore her gaze from him to glance down at the hound. It seemed safer, somehow. Besides, she had to escape those penetrating eyes. "I didn't know you had a dog, though it might better be called a wolf."

A huge creature, more gray than black, with a great shaggy coat and a face so broad, it could surely break a man's arm with one snap of those powerful jaws. "I don't believe I've ever heard barking coming from your place."

"He rarely barks. And he isn't mine. That is to say, he's been sleeping on my doorstep. He wandered in from the forest, half-starved, and I gave him some food. Now he refuses to leave my side."

"Then I'd say he's yours, Mr. Colton, whether you wish it or not." She turned toward her door, eager to escape. "Now if you'll excuse me, I'll bid you good day."

"Wait." He touched a hand to her arm as she brushed past him. Just a touch, but he drew back at once as if burned, and she found herself wondering if he'd felt the same flash of heat that was already burning its way along her spine.

What nonsense. She could see, by the harsh look in his eyes, that all he felt was arrogance.

"I was wondering if you would be willing to sell your property."

"Sell my—" This was the last thing she'd expected him to ask. She shook her head. "I'm sorry. It isn't for sale."

"I've long thought it would be a fine addition to my own land. And now that we've met, I'd hoped that you might be willing to at least consider my offer."

"This is the home of my father. It's where I spent my childhood." At her words she saw something flash in his eyes. A hint of pain perhaps. But then, just as quickly, he blinked and the look was gone, replaced by a look so dark and dangerous, it had her turning away, determined to be free of him. Over her shoulder she called, "It is not for sale, Mr. Colton. For any price."

She unlatched the door and stepped inside, quickly closing it behind her. Once inside she leaned against it a moment and realized that her legs were actually trembling. She'd had a terrible need to escape that man, though she knew not why.

He made her extremely uncomfortable. The look of him. And especially the touch of him.

She mistrusted handsome men. They thought all females vulnerable to their charms. And once that charm was stripped away, there was nothing left of them but an empty shell. No one knew that better than she. Jared Warner had been a handsome, charming fellow. So charming, he'd talked her father into giving her in marriage when she was but ten and five. Now, almost ten years later, she felt as though her entire girlhood had been spent on a man who'd never given a thought to anyone but himself.

Nay, given a choice, she much preferred a man whose face resembled a mule's. Such a man had to rely on virtue and strength of character. If she ever married again, which seemed highly unlikely, given her age of twenty-four and her circumstances, she would choose kindness and virtue over any other quality. Gold was as easily lost as earned. Good looks had a way of fading with time. But a good heart...ah, now there was the only true treasure.

When she'd composed herself, she deposited her basket on the table and removed her bonnet and shawl. As she made her way to her small bedroom, she caught a glimpse of man and dog through the window.

Instead of returning to his home, she could see her neighbor start off across the meadow toward a distant woods, with the dog running happily beside him.

They were a good fit, she thought. Both man and beast seemed a bit too big, too overpowering, for polite society. And both seemed more than a little wild.

She busied herself preparing a meal. She was determined to put the angry, arrogant William Colton out of her mind for good. Even though, with but a thought, she could still recall the way her blood had heated, and her mind had emptied, at that single, shattering kiss.

William walked through a field sweet with clover and waist-high grass. The dog seemed content to walk beside him, pausing occasionally to poke its nose in the ground, following the scent of a bird or rodent.

When he came to a tall, rounded rock, William paused to lean a hip against it, then pulled a pipe from his pocket and fiddled with tobacco and flint. It was a luxury he'd afforded himself in recent years, to pass the time late at night, when he was too restless to sleep.

In the distance was a flock of sheep grazing on a hillside. There had been sheep at his father's estate. As a boy he'd loved going with the tenant farmers in late afternoon, watching the dogs herd the flock toward the holding areas.

At the memory he felt the pain of loss, as sharp as an arrow through the heart. It always seemed to catch him by surprise. Just as quickly he brushed it aside.

It hadn't always been possible to empty his mind of the memories. But he'd learned over time that it was not only possible, but necessary for his survival.

Without the ability to move beyond the past, he would surely have given in to the pain of such loss and given up on life itself.

For so long now he'd simply gone through the motions of living. He'd found employment, saved his money, settled into this land and cottage. He'd even taken in an old man and boy who had no place to live, and no means of survival, though not so much out of the kindness of his heart, but rather because of guilt. But until now, he'd adamantly refused to allow himself to think beyond the here and now.

For the first time in five years he could think beyond today. Perhaps there truly was a future for him. This land was his now. All his. And no one could take it from him.

It occurred to him that it was time to add some sheep to his holdings. The land could accommodate several hundred. Of course, if he were to add the widow Warner's land, he could double that amount.

The widow Warner.

He drew smoke into his lungs and slowly expelled it. He'd seen her in passing ever since she'd returned to her father's cottage. Near two years he'd seen her. And yet he'd never really noticed her. She'd always struck him as plain, dull and unassuming. Until last night.

That image of a fiery vixen with the face of an angel was burned into his memory. Seared into his very soul.

He'd thought, upon awakening, that he'd imagined it. But seeing her again today, he knew it was no figment of his imagination. For the first time he'd looked beyond that tidy knot of hair and that simple frock to the woman. The reason those green eyes were rarely noticed was because she never looked directly at anyone, choosing to stare at the ground instead. Was she truly shy? he wondered. Or was it all an act, designed to keep others, especially men, away?

Of course. It was the same with her body. She chose to wear shapeless, ill-fitting gowns and bulky shawls to hide those soft, womanly curves.

She was a strange one. Despite the shabby clothes and humble demeanor, he could sense strength in her. When confronted, she didn't back down. And when she'd felt physically threatened, she'd attacked with all the ferocity of a wounded she-bear.

While waiting for her to return from the village, he'd had time to look around her holdings. The gardens were in need of tending. The cottage, at least what little he'd seen, was in need of a great deal of repair. Still, she'd refused his offer to sell. Which said to him that she had no need of money.

Or perhaps it was only *his* money she resisted.

He was intrigued. Was she barely getting by? Or was she merely a skillful actress, playing the part of a penniless widow? Was she the shy, prim woman she showed to the rest of the world, or the bold, beautiful angel he'd seen last night?

He smiled and tamped the last of the tobacco from his pipe before returning it to his pocket.

He intended to make it his business to find out a great deal more about the widow Warner in the days to come.

Chapter 3

Molly set the dough to rise, then picked up her basket of sewing and headed for her favorite spot in the garden. On a bench in the sunlight she set out her precious skein of yarn, spool of thread and needle and began work on her latest project. Camilla Cannon was the wife of one of the wealthiest landowners in Surrey. She had commissioned a gown and matching shawl in palest peach, and had even provided the fabric and the special soft yarn for the shawl, which Molly had promised to crochet. It meant many hours of very precise needlework. But if Mistress Cannon should be pleased with her work, there was no telling how many other fine ladies might pay her to do the same.

Molly loved working here in the garden. In her mind's eye she could see her mother doing much the same, seated at this very bench, her young daughter at her knee, patiently teaching her to make the fine even stitches that were the envy of all the other women in town. Molly was proud of her handwork. And grateful that her mother had provided her with a means of caring for her own needs. She pitied the poor widows and orphans who were often reduced to working in taverns, or worse, in order to survive. Jared may have wagered and lost everything of value before his death, but he couldn't take away her pride in her work.

Out of the corner of her eye she saw movement in her field. She looked up in surprise to see a white-haired man and a boy walking purposefully across her land. Almost as if, she thought, they were counting their paces.

By heaven! They were, she realized, measuring her land.

She stood, dropping the fabric into her basket before lifting her skirts and racing toward them.

"You there." She saw the two stop and turn as she hurried forward. They were trailed by the wolf-like dog she'd seen with William Colton. The sight of him had her drawing back apace.

"Aye, miss." The old man doffed his cap and nudged the boy to do the same.

"What are you doing on my land?"

"Just stepping it off, miss."

"I can see that. But why? Who are you? And what concern is it of yours how much land I own?"

"Begging your pardon, miss." The old man's face was ruddy from a lifetime working the fields.

"My name is Duncan Biddle. And this is my grandson, Tyler. We live over there." He pointed toward the cottage of William Colton.

"I thought I'd recognized his dog." She glanced around and saw that the creature had run off.

"Aye, miss. And this day, before he left for Lord Kent's estate, Mr. Colton asked me to measure his land."

"And mine?" She saw the slight flush on the man's cheeks at her question and decided to press the point. "Did he ask you to measure my land as well?"

"Aye, miss."

"Did he say why?"

Duncan brightened. "Mr. Colton's thinking about raising sheep, miss."

"Sheep." It was difficult to imagine the surly gentleman who lived next door doing anything more challenging than lifting a tankard to his lips. Then she remembered William Colton's offer to purchase her holding. "I suppose with my land, he could raise twice as many."

"I suppose so, miss." The old man took a step back. "But if you object to our being on your land, Tyler and I will go now."

"I do object. Not to your presence, but to Mr. Colton's arrogance at measuring land that isn't his. I hope you will tell him so. Good day to you, Duncan Biddle and young Tyler."

Before she could turn away Molly saw the lad looking beyond her with a puzzled frown.

"What's that in Wolf's mouth?" The boy lifted a hand to shade the sunlight from his eyes.

"Wolf?" Molly turned and caught sight of the dog bounding toward them, holding the skein of precious yarn in his mouth. It had unraveled, leaving a trail of lacy peach strands drifting across the field like lovely pink ivy.

"Oh, no! Not Mistress Cannon's yarn." Molly lifted her skirts and started toward the hound, who saw her coming and darted to one side.

"I'll get him, miss." Tyler raced after the dog, shouting and whistling.

Wolf, caught up in the game, dashed happily about as Molly, Duncan and Tyler chased after him. As he ran this way and that, he left even more yarn in his wake, until there was none left on the skein.

At that very moment William Colton returned home to see three-half-crazed creatures racing across the meadow, filling the air with shouts and whistles. By the time Duncan caught the dog and forcibly removed the skein from his mouth, the entire field was abloom with peach yarn. And sitting in the middle of it all was Molly Warner, her face in her hands, weeping.

"Here now," William shouted. "What's all this about?"

"This is all your fault." Seeing him, Molly lifted her face, streaked with tears of despair. "Look what your horrid dog has done."

"I'm afraid it's my fault." Old Duncan came huffing up, out of breath, eager to explain. "We should have locked Wolf up in the cottage before we came on the lady's property."

"He didn't mean anything by it." Tyler had hold of the dog's neck and was being dragged along as Wolf raced forward, tongue lolling, tail wagging, to greet his master. "He thought he was playing."

Everyone, it seemed, was talking at once. And none of them was making any sense.

"Silence." At William's snarling command, their words died on their lips.

Satisfied, he turned to Molly. "Now, Mistress Warner, you will tell me what has transpired here."

"Your grandfather and son," she began, only to see the three men grinning wildly.

Her temper went up a notch. "You find me amusing?"

"Nay, miss." Duncan shook his head. "It's just that we aren't related to Mr. Colton."

"Not his grandfather? Not his son?"

"Nay, miss."

"You are servants, then?"

At that the man and boy shared another quick grin before William said tiredly, "Duncan and Tyler share my home and help with the chores, Mistress Warner. Now about this—" he lifted a hand to encompass the yarn-covered field "—this pink-frosted landscape."

"Your dog—"

She saw the way he was shaking his head and repeated the phrase with more emphasis. "*Your* dog—" she was not about to allow him to deny responsibility for that animal "—which you claim is not yours at all, got into my sewing basket and ruined an entire skein of yarn."

William nodded toward the boy. "Take the empty skein and retrieve what you can, Tyler." He reached into his pocket and withdrew several coins. "I'll be happy to pay for whatever has been lost, madam."

She glanced at the coins and then up at his scowling face. "This was very special yarn, meant for a very special shawl."

With a huff of impatience he dropped several more coins into her palm before giving a slight bow of his head. "Then I hope you look better in it than your field does, madam." He turned toward the old man. "All the way home I've been thinking of that mutton stew you promised to make, old man. I'm fair starving."

Duncan looked uncomfortable as he replied, "Begging your pardon, sir. I haven't given a thought to supper yet. We've been...otherwise occupied."

William's scowl deepened, and he shot a look at Molly, to let her know he blamed her for this lapse.

"That's it?" She got to her feet, hands on her hips, watching them walk away. "You give me a few coins and a simple apology, and expect me to dismiss this entire incident?"

William turned to face her. "What I expect, madam, is to return to the comfort of my home and fill my belly with—" he glowered at the old man "—yesterday's cold stew."

As the two walked away, with the dog at their heels, Molly stood watching. Then she turned to see Tyler inching his way across the field as he began the daunting task of retrieving the yarn from every blade of grass, every branch, every twig.

With a sigh she turned away and hurried back to her cottage. Once there she was grateful to find that the dog had left the rest of her sewing intact. She bundled it into the cottage, then went about preparing her own meal.

An hour later she heard a soft tap on the door and hurried over to find young Tyler standing there, with a gnarled, twisted, and absolutely filthy skein of yarn in his hands.

"Thank you, lad. I'm grateful." She struggled to put a brightness in her tone she didn't feel, for she couldn't imagine what use she'd find for yarn smudged with grass stains. She feared that no amount of scrubbing would ever make this right. "If you'll come inside I'll give you a biscuit for your trouble."

"Thank you, miss." The boy tore his cap from his head, holding it in front of him while he stared around the tidy room. "It smells good in here." He noted the bundle of lavender drying from the ceiling.

"Thank you." At the table Molly split the biscuit open and slathered it with wild gooseberry jam. The boy's mouth watered as she filled a cup with milk from a crock.

She pointed to a basin of water. "You may wash up over there."

"Wash up, miss?" The boy seemed surprised by the suggestion.

She merely smiled. "You'll find soap and a linen cloth, lad."

He crossed the room and stared at the soap and water, then with a shrug, began to wash the grime from his hands. In an instant the water in the basin turned muddy. He rinsed off the soap and dried, leaving streaks of dirt on the clean linen square.

"Here you go, Tyler." Molly indicated a place at the small, wooden table.

"Thank you, miss." He sat and devoured the biscuit in three quick bites, then drained the glass in loud gulps.

Seeing it, she had a sudden thought. "Are you starving, lad? Does William Colton refuse to feed you?"

"Oh, nay, miss. Nothing of the sort. I've plenty to eat. But not anything as fine as this."

Molly offered him a second biscuit, then sat across the table with a cup of tea. "How long have you and your grandfather worked as servants for Mr. Colton?"

"We're not his servants, miss." The boy's voice held a note of pride. "When we came to live with Mr. Colton, he told us he'd tolerate no servants in his household. And that if we chose to stay, we would eat at his table and sleep under his roof."

"If you chose to stay?" She seemed startled. "What an odd phrase. Why would you choose to stay with him?"

"Because we had nowhere else to live. My grandfather spent a lifetime working as a tenant farmer. But when he could no longer produce enough to please Lord Kent, we were sent away."

It was a cruel fact of life, and one she'd seen so

many times. Life was difficult for everyone, she feared. Her sad story could be repeated all over England. As could the lad's.

"But how did you come to live with Mr. Colton? Have you no family? Where is your father?"

"Nay, miss. And my father is passed." The boy looked down at his hands, avoiding her eyes. "When Mr. Colton learned that we had nowhere to go, and were sleeping in hay barns at night to survive, he invited us to share his home."

"And how did he learn all this about you and your grandfather?"

The lad's face turned several shades of red and he seemed relieved at the sudden knock on her door.

Molly hurried over to open the door, and was surprised to find William Colton, still scowling. Was that all the man knew how to do?

He looked beyond her to Tyler. "There you are, lad. Your grandfather was getting worried. Come along now."

As the boy hurried across the room William asked, "Was he able to retrieve your yarn?"

Molly nodded and plucked the skein from the pocket of her apron.

Seeing the condition of it, William arched a brow. "Do you think you'll be able to clean it?"

"I'll try. But I have my doubts about it."

He studied the tiny tendrils of red-gold hair that had slipped from the neat knot at her nape, and found himself intrigued by the way they curled softly around her cheeks. He had an almost overpowering urge to reach out and touch them. Instead, he closed his hand into a fist at his side.

Tyler paused beside Molly.

She smiled and surprised him by leaning down to brush a kiss over his dirty cheek. "Thank you for fetching my yarn. It must have been a tedious task."

"I didn't mind, miss." The boy gave her a dreamy smile and touched a hand to the kiss, as though to hold it there. "Thank you for the biscuits and jam."

He stepped outside and exclaimed happily when he realized Wolf was there, as well, "Hello, old boy. Have you come to say you're sorry?"

Boy and dog looked at Molly with such sorrow, she couldn't help smiling.

Tyler looked hopeful. "Does that mean he's forgiven, miss?"

Molly nodded. "I suppose he is. After all, he was just behaving like a dog. From now on I'll have to see that my sewing basket is kept away from him, so he won't be tempted to play again."

William's brow arched as he followed the boy outside. He waited until they were some distance from her cottage before clearing his throat.

"Mistress Warner fed you?"

"Aye. Biscuits as light as clouds. And jam so sweet, it reminded me of Christmas morn."

At his description William frowned and lifted a hand to tousle the lad's hair. "You make it sound fine, indeed. If I'd known such a reward was waiting, I'd have fetched the widow Warner's yarn myself."

"Nay." Tyler placed a finger over his cheek, where the warmth of Molly's kiss still lingered. "For then you'd have had her kiss in place of me. And I haven't felt anything as sweet since my mum was alive."

The boy raced ahead toward the lights of the cottage, with the dog at his heels. Leaving William alone with thoughts of the pretty widow Warner.

She'd occupied a great deal more of his time today than he cared to admit.

Always before, he'd been able to lose himself in his work for Lord Kent. But today he'd found himself distracted by an image that flitted through his mind. An image of an angel in a gossamer gown, drifting into his arms and wrapping herself around him, offering him pleasure beyond belief. He'd actually been able to taste her, smell her, feel her body pressed to his.

And could still, if truth be told.

Despite the coolness of the evening air, he found himself sweating. And thinking of things that would make an angel blush.

Chapter 4

Molly stepped inside and latched the door. As she crossed the room she found herself thinking about her neighbor. What a strange man was William Colton. So angry and gruff. And yet, despite all the bluster, it would seem he had room in his heart for strays. Both the human and the animal variety.

Not that it changed anything. He'd had no right sending his serv—Duncan—to measure land that wasn't his.

She glanced at the coins she'd dropped into her sewing basket. At least he'd been enough of a gentleman to make amends for the ruined yarn. Of course it meant that she'd have to walk to town in the morning and replace what had been ruined. But if she worked late into the night, sewing by the light of the fire, she could still deliver the gown and shawl by next Sunday.

She sighed and removed a blackened kettle from the fire. Lifting the lid, she ladled beef and gravy onto a plate and sat down to eat her dinner. Afterward she carried fresh water from a nearby stream and heated it over the fire to wash her dishes. She then used the warm water to wash the skein of yarn, setting the strands to dry in neat rows across the table.

That done she stripped off her dress, chemise and petticoats and washed them as well, for the soap and warm water were too precious to waste. And when everything was hanging by the fire to dry, she used the water to wash her hair, and then herself. Slipping into her night shift, she tossed a shawl over her shoulders and walked out into the garden. There she settled herself on the bench and combed her damp hair until it began to dry.

It was a perfect summer night, with perfumed breezes, a full moon and a sky awash with millions of stars. Molly paused, comb in hand, to watch the path of a shooting star. And though she knew it was childish, she couldn't help squeezing her eyes tightly shut while she made a wish.

"Come along, Wolf." William opened the door to his cottage and the animal slipped outside, eager for a night run.

Already the other room was filled with Duncan's snores and Tyler's soft sighs as sleep overtook them. William was too restless to consider sleeping yet. A long walk was what he needed to clear his head.

He latched the door and followed at a leisurely

pace behind the dog, watching as Wolf stopped every few steps to explore the ground before sniffing the air and racing ahead.

William avoided the road, choosing instead to keep to the fields, climbing steadily upward until he could look down on his land. He sat on a stump and filled his pipe, then held a flint to the bowl and expelled a wreath of smoke while he studied the gentle slope of fields. There was a time when he would have looked upon this humble property as nothing more than a miserable hovel. Anything less than a palace, or a fine manor house, would have been considered beneath him. In his youth it would have never occurred to him to care for all his own needs, from the food on his table to the clothes on his back, without help from others. Worse, he would have looked with disdain on the men and women who saw to his every pleasure, without giving a thought to them as human beings with their own cares and concerns.

His father would never know what a nightmare he'd thrust his son into when he'd ordered him out into the cold dark night with nothing but the clothes on his back.

William drew on the pipe and expelled another cloud of smoke. At the time he'd been so desperately alone and afraid of what the future held. Like Duncan and Tyler, he'd been forced to sleep in a few hay barns before finding a way to provide for his needs. But along the way William had found so many strengths inside himself. Strengths he'd have never uncovered without experiencing the most wrenching of pain. He could never go back to the life he'd once taken for granted. That life of ease as the son of wealth and privilege. Now he could take pride in himself and his accomplishments, instead of merely the accomplishments of his ancestors. Not even the title earl of Redbridge, which had once meant more than anything in the world to him, could tempt him to give up this freedom he'd discovered. A freedom born, not of heredity, but by the sweat of his own labors. With this freedom came another, even more precious. The freedom to choose his friends, not by the coin in their purse, but by the goodness in their hearts. The freedom to wed a woman out of love instead of obligation.

Not that he ever intended to marry.

The woman hadn't been born who would tempt him to give up this hard-earned freedom.

Against his will a vision crept into his mind. More angel than mortal, floating slowly toward him, golden hair tumbling around a face so lovely, it took his breath away.

He turned to look at the darkened outline of the cottage of the widow Warner. An annoying female if ever there was one. In the past few days she'd caused him more trouble than he'd had to deal with in years. And just when his life had taken a turn for the better.

He needed to remember that she wasn't that vision. That had been the ale, creating a fuzzy image that was so far from reality, it was absurd. Reality was a prickly woman in shapeless clothes who found fault with everything, from his dog to his friends, to the way he chose to live his life. He'd be well rid of her when he finally persuaded her to move.

Shaking the tobacco from his pipe, he stuck it in his pocket as he made his way down the hill. From here he could see that her land would be a welcome addition to his. Her tiny cottage would be perfect for Duncan and Tyler, giving him a bit of freedom in his own place. Not that he minded having them underfoot. They'd given back as much as he'd given them. The old man could do almost anything, from tending animals to growing crops. Thanks to Duncan's careful attention the hedges were trimmed, the roof freshly thatched, the stones removed from the fields and piled one on top of the other to form a lovely fence. The lad was every bit as industrious, using all that energy to scrub the hearth, fetch water from the stream and help with the household chores.

William felt a proprietary pride as he drew near the widow's cottage. She'd said she wasn't interested in selling. But he'd seen how distraught she'd been over the mere loss of some yarn, and how eagerly she had accepted the coins he'd offered. That told him her situation was more desperate than she'd let on. He had no doubt that when he placed enough gold in her hands, she'd be unable to resist his offer to buy. He nodded his approval as he approached the overgrown gardens. All this would soon be his, if he remembered to tread with care.

Patience had never been one of his virtues. Perhaps it came from being the son of wealth and privilege. Or perhaps it was just a lack in his character. At any rate, what others saw as arrogance he saw as simple impatience to finish whatever job was at hand.

A flash of movement to one side caught his attention and he paused to look over. What he saw had him stopping in midstride. It was the angel of his dreams, looking, if possible, even more beautiful than he remembered. She wore that same shimmering gown that flowed over her body like water flowing over pebbles in a stream, revealing every line and curve of that lithe young body. And what a body. Tiny, but perfectly proportioned, with high, firm breasts and a waist small enough for his hands to span. Her head was tipped to one side as she ran a comb through the silken strands of her hair. Her face in profile was so perfect, it took his breath away. Those long lashes appeared to be gold-tipped in the moonlight. A tiny upturned nose, high cheeks, and the most perfect mouth. A mouth made for kissing. He smiled at the thought. And a gently rounded chin that she could lift higher than any queen when her anger was aroused, as she surely would be right now if she knew she was being observed in this most intimate ritual.

He decided to keep his presence a secret. After all, why risk that famous temper?

It occurred to him that he would be content to stay here, keeping his silent vigil and gazing at her all through the night if she would but remain.

Just then the dog came bounding up behind him.

Hearing the rustle of footsteps, Molly turned. Her eyes went wide with fear when she spotted the shadowy figure.

To save face, William stepped from the shadows into the patch of moonlight. "Forgive me, Mistress Warner. I didn't mean to startle you. I was out walking Wolf, and had no idea I'd find you in the garden."

She picked up a shawl from the bench and draped it over her shoulders for modesty. "Do you make it a habit to walk your dog in my gardens, Mr. Colton?"

"No, I..." He mentally cursed himself for once again fueling her ire. "Of course not. But Wolf ran and I simply followed."

Just then the dog sidled up to her, tongue lolling, tail wagging. Molly couldn't resist. She bent down and scratched behind the dog's ears.

When she looked up she could see those penetrating blue eyes staring into hers. She had to caution herself not to turn and run, though it was what she wanted to do.

"I'll bid you good night now, Mr. Colton."

He didn't speak. He couldn't. Nor could he look away. She had, quite simply, hypnotized him. All he could do was stare at her standing in a spill of moonlight, which seemed to cast her in a pool of liquid gold.

He knew he ought to leave. To leave her as he'd found her. Alone, with only the soft, perfumed breeze for company. But he couldn't.

"Mr. Colton?" She took a step closer and reached out a hand to him. "Are you feeling unwell?"

He took her hand between both of his. She jerked back, but he tightened his grasp and drew her closer.

"I'm not drunk."

"I didn't accuse you."

"I've been trying to convince myself that what I saw that night in your cottage was caused by the ale. But now I know better."

"Please Mr. Colton—"

He touched a hand to her mouth to silence her. But when he felt the softness of her lips against his fingertips, he kept them there while staring down into her startled eyes. Very slowly he traced his thumb around the outline of her lower lip until he felt it tremble. Tremble? Could it be that she was as moved by this as he?

"I'm going to have to kiss you again, Mistress Warner."

"You mustn't...I forbid..."

Before she could pull away he closed his hands over her upper arms, holding her fast. Then he gathered her close, all the while keeping his eyes steady on hers.

His mouth found hers, touching ever so lightly. Through sheer force of will he managed to keep the kiss gentle as he sipped, tasted, brushed. He absorbed the quick flash of heat, felt the way his blood began to sing. But he was determined to keep it light. He might have succeeded, if he hadn't heard her little sigh. Just a quick intake of breath, but it had all his good intentions crumbling like a house of cards.

"Oh, you taste so good. Like fine wine." With a

groan of desperation he hauled her firmly against him and covered her mouth in a kiss so hot, so hungry, it had the blood throbbing in his temples.

"Mr. Colton, you must stop this." She pulled away, but was hauled back, only to be kissed again, until he stole her very breath from her lungs.

His lips moved over her face, grazing the hair at her temple, then brushing her eyelids, her cheek. Hers was the softest skin he'd ever known. He couldn't seem to get enough of her. If he could, he would devour her.

His hands at her shoulders tightened, drawing her even closer, until he could feel her body imprinting itself on his. All that softness and those lovely curves taunted him until the thought of taking her, lying with her, had desire flooding through him.

Molly's breath caught in her throat. She'd never known such heat. A heat that threatened to melt her bones and sear her flesh. And still he continued kissing her until all fear was gone. In its place was need. A need so wild, so desperate, she thought she might go mad from it.

The fear she'd felt only minutes ago was now becoming excitement. Her arms slowly lifted to curve around his neck. There was no thought of resistance now. Only pleasure. She gave herself up to it and heard his moan as he took the kiss deeper.

He could feel her, soft and pliant in his arms. Desire was swift, all-consuming, and for a moment he tempted himself with the thought of carrying her inside her cottage and ravishing her.

He backed her up, pinning her between the outer

wall of her cottage and his body. She was instantly aware of his arousal. And her own. Her breath was coming hard and fast, burning a path of fire along her throat. Her skin was damp and flushed, her heartbeat drumming painfully at her temples.

William felt a flash of triumph as a little moan escaped her lips. It would seem the very cool widow had been hiding a fiery, passionate heart. The thought of taking her here and now had his own pulse racing.

Then just as quickly he banked the need as reality, like a dash of frigid water, washed over him.

What had he been thinking? This wasn't some tavern wench, offering him a moment of pleasure. This was his neighbor, whose property he hoped to buy. By all accounts a proper young widow who was probably shocked to the core by his bold behavior. What he had read as passion was no doubt anger or fear.

He lifted his head and saw her eyes snap open before they widened in surprise. Her lips were still moist and swollen from his kisses. Lips that even now caused his pulse to stutter. Her hair spilled around her face in a wild tangle of damp curls.

He caught a strand and allowed it to sift through his fingers while he studied her. "I said I wasn't drunk. But that's not entirely true."

"What do you mean?"

He bent and brushed his mouth over hers. "One taste of your lips, Mistress Warner, and I'm hopelessly drunk." He tugged on the lock of her hair. "What is your given name?"

"That's..." She wondered at his ability to speak, to think. Her mind felt frozen. Her voice sounded strange and breathless in her own ears. "That's none of your business."

"I'm making it my business."

"Why?"

He gave her one of those dangerous, icy smiles. "After what we've just shared, I no longer think Mistress Warner and Mr. Colton are appropriate. My given name is William."

"I prefer Mr. Colton."

"As you wish. And your name?"

She swallowed. "Margaret. I'm called Molly."

"Molly." He framed her face with his hands. His smile grew. "Molly Warner. Your name suits you. Sweet. Your kisses are sweet. Sweeter than the finest wine." He tempted himself a moment more, then resisted, lowering his hands to his sides and taking a step back. "I bid you good night, Molly Warner. I'm sure I'll dream of you tonight. And this garden of delights."

He whistled for the dog, then strode off into the darkness, leaving her standing where he'd left her. As motionless as a statue. For she feared if she but moved, she would surely shatter like fine crystal.

Chapter 5

Molly latched her gate behind her and stepped out into the lane that led to town. In her pocket were the coins she intended to use to buy the precious yarn for Camilla Cannon's shawl.

Her movements were slower than usual, for she'd put in another long and sleepless night. All thanks to William Colton.

What was she to do about him? He seemed to bring out the worst in her. Temper, of course, though she was by nature a cheerful soul. But worse than her temper was this...unexpected passion. The mere thought of how she'd behaved had her cheeks flaming. One touch from that man's lips and she became some sort of wanton. Why, even in her marriage bed she'd never felt such a hungry yearning. A desire for things proper ladies wouldn't ever consider dreaming of, let alone doing.

He frightened her. As did these feelings he'd awakened in her. She hoped and prayed that she never had to see him again. For she would surely embarrass herself if she did.

As if the fates were mocking her, she heard the clattering of a horse's hooves and the sound of a familiar deep voice behind her. She paused, only to see the object of her thoughts approaching.

"Good morrow, Molly. On your way to town, are you?"

"Aye." She glanced up at him as he slowed his horse to a walk, then quickly looked away, aware that her face was flaming, when he slid from the saddle to lead his mount while matching his steps to hers.

Oh, how grand he looked, dressed all in black, leading Lord Kent's magnificent stallion. He'd recently washed and his dark hair still bore the droplets of water, glistening in the morning sunlight.

"Are you off to work then?"

He nodded, and she thought how handsome he was when he wasn't frowning. "Aye. With Lord Kent off to London, I'll be working harder than ever."

"Most men would consider slacking off when there's no one around to answer to."

"I'm not like most men."

The vehemence with which he spoke brought a bubble of laughter. "So I've noticed."

"What does that mean?"

She shrugged. "I've heard that you guard his lordship's estates as though they were your own."

"Really? And what else have you heard about me?"

She ducked her head, aware that she was blushing. "That men fear you. And those who don't, respect you."

"Which would you rather have, Molly? The fear of others, or their respect?"

"I should think all people desire respect." She glanced over. "Isn't that what you would choose?"

He shrugged. "I suppose. To that end I've begun teaching young Tyler to read and write and do sums, so that when he's older he might have the respect of others."

"Tyler told me that you invited him and his grandfather to live with you when you found them sleeping in a hay barn. Is that true?"

"In a way." William frowned, remembering. "I'd banished them from Lord Kent's estate."

"Why?"

"Because it was my job. I'd been ordered to see that those tenant farmers who could no longer produce were put off the land."

Her chin came up in anger. "Even though some of those farmers had been on the estate for generations?"

He shrugged. "That wasn't my concern. I had a job. I did it. And when I banished the old man, I thought no more of it until a few days later. I was at the farmers' market in the town square, when I felt a tug on my jacket and realized that someone was trying to pick my pocket. Imagine my surprise when it was a filthy urchin with the face of a cherub."

"Tyler? A pickpocket?"

"Aye. I thought briefly about turning him over to the constable. But—" he stared off into space "—something about him touched my heart."

Molly wondered where he went when that look came into his eyes. He seemed not so much angry as haunted.

He pulled himself back from his bleak thoughts. "So I took him home and fed him, and that's when I learned that he and his grandfather were the very ones I'd sent packing. I persuaded the lad to take me to where his grandfather was hiding, though I had to give him my word as a gentleman that I wouldn't bring the old man harm. And that's when I decided to bring them home to live with me."

She was amazed by what she'd heard. "You hardly knew them, yet you brought them into your home? How did you know they wouldn't kill you in your bed and help themselves to all you had?"

His frown grew. "First of all, I had little of value. Certainly not enough to warrant taking my life. And then, of course, to know Duncan Biddle is to know that he is an honorable man. Besides, I felt responsible for their circumstances. Because of me, they'd lost everything that once mattered to them."

Molly's voice lowered with passion. "Losing everything doesn't necessarily mean we lose our humanity. At least not if we were honorable and decent to begin with."

He turned to face her. "That's what I've begun to learn."

She paused. "That was a most kind and generous thing you did for Duncan and young Tyler."

He looked embarrassed by the unexpected compliment. "They've given me far more than I've given them. They filled a void in my life." His voice lowered. "And perhaps gave me back my humanity, as well."

"And what of your own family?"

The instant the words were out of her mouth she regretted them. The bleak look was back in his eyes. "They are dead to me. As I am to them."

"Then I'm glad you have the old man and his grandson."

William's voice was gruff with emotion. "Duncan has become my tutor. It is he who taught me how to grow my own crops, cook my own food, even wash my own clothes."

"How is it that you didn't learn such things in your youth?"

He shrugged. "My tutoring consisted of languages and sums, art and music and science."

"How fortunate for you. There are few who are given such a privileged education."

"You think so? I would say my world has broadened considerably since leaving my father's—" He looked up at the sound of a horse and cart coming at a fast clip, put a hand to her elbow and helped her to the side of the road. At the mere touch, they both felt the heat and struggled not to react.

As soon as the cart moved past, they stepped apart, aware that the tension was back.

They both seemed relieved that they'd reached the heart of town. But before they could go their separate ways, Molly saw Camilla Cannon stepping out of a shop directly in front of her.

The woman turned a flirtatious smile on William. Like most women of the town, she found the handsome, brooding man with the mysterious past too much of a challenge to ignore. "I've heard that Lord Kent has entrusted his vast estates to your care while taking himself off to London, Mr. Colton."

William nodded. "I'm pleased that he places such trust in me."

"And why not?" Her smile warmed. "I hope you won't be too busy to come to tea when my husband's cousin visits me from the country."

He bowed his head slightly. "I'd be honored."

Pleased, she turned to Molly. "Mistress Warner. How is work progressing on my gown and shawl?"

Molly flushed. "It goes well, Mistress Cannon."

"Will you have it ready by Sunday as you agreed?"

Molly nodded. "Aye. Sunday. As agreed."

The woman smiled. "Don't you adore the peach color? I had to send all the way to London for the yarn."

"Aye, it's lovely, Mistress Cannon. The color will look perfect on you."

The woman gave a haughty nod before bestowing another smile on William. Then she hurried away.

William turned to study Molly, seeing the way

her hands were twisting nervously. "The yarn wasn't yours?"

"Nay."

He put a hand over hers. "Forgive me, Molly. I thought it was mere vanity that had you upset over Wolf's antics. I had no idea."

She swallowed. "My sewing puts food on the table and keeps the roof over my head. Without it, I'd have no way to survive."

She glanced at the row of shops along the main street. "I'd best go now and hope that someone can match the yarn from London."

"Did you try salvaging the yarn Tyler retrieved for you?"

"Aye." She nodded. "I was able to wash off most of the soil and grime. But many of the strands are torn or knotted. I'm afraid there won't be enough to do a proper job of it."

"I wish you luck, Molly."

When she realized he was being sincere, her smile returned. "Thank you."

As she hurried away it occurred to William that she hadn't once called him by name. Progress with the widow Warner, it would seem, was going to be slow and painful. Not that it mattered, he told himself. After all, the only thing he cared about was earning her trust so he could acquire her property.

If there should be any other reason for his sudden interest, he refused to admit it. There were some feelings, much like old wounds, that were buried too deeply to be probed without causing a great deal of pain. He refused to ever again become ensnared in a woman's trap.

Molly trudged along the road in the heat of the late afternoon, weary beyond belief. She'd spent many frustrating hours visiting every shop in Surrey, in the hope of matching the yarn. All to no avail. She would have to make do with what she had, and hope that Camilla Cannon wouldn't be too angry.

The woman could ruin her, Molly thought. With a single word to the other women in town, she could be denied any further employment. If that should happen she would have to accept William Colton's offer to sell her home and land, in order to survive. But where would she go? What could she do with the pittance this place would bring? A year from now, or two years at the most, she could find herself in a strange town, alone and penniless, and reduced to working in a tavern. Or worse. She shivered.

As she unlatched the gate and started up the lane she was startled to hear the sound of an axe biting into wood. Was someone chopping her precious trees?

She rounded the lane and stared in disbelief. Duncan was trimming her hedge, chopping away at the old dead wood. Tyler was busy dragging the branches beside her cottage wall, where she kept her meager supply of firewood.

"What's this?" She stared around in amazement. "Duncan, what are you and the lad doing here?"

"Cleaning up your gardens, miss."

"But why?"

"It was William Colton's suggestion, miss. He said whenever Tyler and I had a bit of time, he wanted us to see to your needs."

"He did, did he? We'll see about this."

All the anger and frustration of the day bubbled up, threatening to choke her as she lifted her skirts and picked her way across the field toward William Colton's cottage. So, he had decided he'd waited long enough. Now he thought he would simply take over her land with or without her permission. Well, he had a thing or two to learn about her. She may be just getting by, but that didn't mean she intended to simply step aside and let him do as he pleased.

She paused on the stoop and gave a sharp rap on his door.

When he opened it and caught sight of her he gave her a long, steady look. "Well, Molly. What a surprise."

"I had a bit of a surprise myself." Her tone lowered with fury. "When I returned from town just now, I found Duncan and Tyler trimming my hedges."

His words were clipped. "What's wrong? Don't tell me they cut down something of value? It isn't like the old man to be careless—"

She held up a hand to stop him. "They haven't damaged anything." It galled her to add, "They're doing a fine job. At least as much as I could see of it."

"Then what—"

Her chin came up in a defiant gesture he had

come to recognize. "And just how am I supposed to pay them for their work?"

"Is that what this visit is about? And here I'd hoped that you were simply paying me a neighborly call." He stepped aside. "Won't you come in, Molly? You look like you could use a cup of tea."

"I've no interest in your tea. I'd like to know how I'm supposed to pay you for this sudden generosity."

He merely gave one of his dark, knowing smiles. "Come in, Molly. We'll talk over tea."

She brushed past him and stared around in surprise as she settled herself at a highly polished wooden table. She'd assumed that three men living without benefit of a woman's touch would have to tolerate a certain amount of dirt. But the cottage was as clean as hers, and in far better shape.

Despite the warmth of the cooking fire, the room was refreshingly cool after the heat of the day. And she was, she realized as she settled herself at the table, exceedingly tired.

"How was your day in town?" William placed a steaming cup in front of her, and poured one for himself as well.

"Fruitless. I checked every shelf in every shop in Surrey. There is no yarn like this." She reached into her pocket and dropped the strand on the table.

"I'm sorry, Molly." William placed a hand over hers and felt the now familiar tingle of heat at even that simple touch.

"Not as sorry as I." She sighed deeply, then lifted

the cup to her lips and drank. "Oh, this is lovely. I was in need of it this very moment."

"Then I'm happy to oblige." He watched as she struggled to relax. "Now about payment for those chores." He saw her frown return and lifted a hand before she could protest. "There are many things Duncan was able to teach me. But one thing we haven't been able to manage is making proper repairs to our clothes." He unrolled his sleeve to show her a frayed cuff. "This was my favorite shirt, but it's now relegated to something I can only wear in the comfort of my own home."

When she remained silent he said, "I thought we might barter services, Molly. You have need of new thatch for your roof, and a bit of pruning in your gardens. Duncan and Tyler and I have need of decent repairs to our clothes. It would be mutually beneficial if we could—" he cleared his throat, hoping she wouldn't be offended by the implication "—see to each other's needs."

Her smile was slow in coming. But when it did, he felt himself begin to relax.

"That's very kind of you, William."

Had she actually spoken his name? He wanted to ask her to say it again, but he didn't want to call attention in case it had been a mere slip of the tongue. To his ear it had sounded so noble, so manly when she'd said it.

"Then you agree?" He offered his hand.

She stared at it a moment before nodding. Then she placed her hand in his. "I do."

For the space of several moments they stared into

each other's eyes as they shook hands. Then William surprised her by lifting her palm to his lips where he pressed a kiss to the center, then kissed each of her fingers as well.

Heat spiraled through her veins and centered deep inside, where it seemed to pulse and tighten. How could it be that the mere touch of him had the power to do this to her?

She pulled her hand away and got to her feet. "I really must go. I haven't a thing ready for my supper."

"You could stay and share our roast goose. I brought two fine geese home today, and Duncan has already set them to cooking."

"Roast goose." She spoke the words on a sigh.

"Aye. And I must admit, Duncan can do things to make a goose taste better than anything. If you're going to stay and sup, you'd best do it when it's Duncan who is cooking. What passes for food when Tyler and I take our turns is often unfit for man or beast."

"You all take turns?"

"It's only fair. For we all do our share of the work."

What a puzzle he was. If the rumors she'd heard were true, William Colton was the son of a titled nobleman. And yet here he was, wearing frayed shirts and sharing household chores with a man and boy he'd rescued from a hay barn.

Molly paused at the door. "I thank you for your generous offer to share your meal, but I really need to get back." After stepping outside she turned. "If you'll bundle together the clothes that need mending, I'll start on them as quickly as possible."

He lifted a hand to a stray curl that kissed her cheek. Again she was forced to endure that rush of heat and that quick flutter of her heartbeat.

"There's no rush, Molly. We've waited this long. We can wait until you finish what you've started for others."

He watched her lift her skirts and start across the field, and realized he'd managed to diffuse that amazing temper of hers.

But what was he going to do about this fickle heart of his? Whenever she got too close, he forgot all those fine promises he'd made himself, about avoiding romantic entanglements.

This was strictly a business arrangement, he reminded himself. The more he earned her trust, the more willing she would be to consider selling him her land.

Now if he could just avoid looking into those green eyes. Or touching those silken tresses. Or getting too close to the very bewitching Molly Warner.

Chapter 6

The sound of a carriage had Wolf rising from his spot in front of the fire and issuing a low growl of warning.

William hurried to the door and greeted the man who stepped down. The two stood in the doorway talking, before William reached into his pocket and paid the man. The two shook hands. Minutes later the man took his leave, and the team and carriage rumbled into the darkness.

William glanced toward Molly's cottage and saw the light in the window. Despite the lateness of the hour, she was still up. Working, he had no doubt.

"Come, Wolf," he called.

The dog slipped outside and began to race across the field, with the man following at a more leisurely pace.

When he reached Molly's door, he knocked and listened to the sound of her footsteps as she approached. The door opened, spilling light into the darkness. He studied the way she looked framed in the doorway. Despite the lateness of the hour she was still dressed. Her hair had tumbled free of its neat knot, with little tendrils spilling around her forehead and cheeks. Her eyes showed the hint of fatigue.

"Don't you ever sleep?" He kept his tone light.

"I could ask you the same thing." She peered beyond him into the darkness. "What are you doing here?"

"I came to see you." He motioned. "May I come inside?" Seeing her hesitation, he added, "Just for a moment."

She opened the door wider and stepped aside.

He brushed past her, aware of the way his body responded to hers. Sometimes, especially late at night when his defenses were weak, he found himself aching for her. An ache that had been costing him a great deal of sleep lately.

He glanced around the tidy room. "How is the gown for Mistress Cannon coming along?"

"Very nicely." She pointed to the length of fabric tossed over the end of the chaise. "It's almost done. Just a few more seams." She sighed. "But I fear the shawl will be a disappointment to her."

"Perhaps this will help." He reached into his pocket and retrieved a skein of pale-peach yarn.

Molly's eyes widened. She clapped her hands over her mouth and simply stared. When she could find her voice, she managed to whisper, "Wherever did you find that?"

"When I learned that one of Lord Kent's solicitors had to travel up to London, I asked him to buy this for me."

She shook her head in disbelief. "But how could he have possibly known the exact color?"

"I gave him the strand you'd left on my table."

"The strand...?" To her utter astonishment, tears filled her eyes and she was helpless to stop them as they spilled over and trailed down her cheeks.

Mortified, she turned away to hide them. But it was too late. William had seen. He was so touched, he reached for her and turned her into his arms.

"Oh, William." She wrapped her arms around his neck and felt a sob catch in her throat. "No one has ever shown me such a kindness before."

"Then I'm doubly pleased. Pleased that I could be the first and pleased that I had the opportunity to make up for my dog's despicable behavior."

"So now he's your dog?"

"It would seem so." He could feel the dampness of her tears against the front of his shirt, could feel the little tremors she was struggling to hide. With his lips to her temple he murmured, "Does this mean that Wolf and I are forgiven?"

"More than forgiven." She lifted her head and smiled through her tears. " I am in your debt, William. I don't know how I'll repay you."

He framed her face with his hands, wiping her tears with his thumbs. "You already have, Molly.

Just seeing your smile is all the payment I'll ever need."

For the space of a heartbeat he stared down into her eyes, feeling such a welling of tenderness, his heart seemed too big for his chest. He was afraid to breathe. Afraid to speak, for fear of spoiling the moment.

Instead of words, he lowered his mouth to hers and kissed her. Just the merest touch of lips to lips. As gentle as a raindrop falling on a flower petal. But he could feel her heart thudding, as wildly as his own. And for some unexplained reason, he felt wildly ecstatic. Oh, he wanted to shout. To swing her around and around until they were both dizzy. And he wanted, more than anything, to kiss her again. And then again.

It occurred to him that in her overwrought state, it might be an easy matter to take this further. But he knew he had no right to take advantage of her vulnerability.

Instead he drew a little away and lifted her chin with his thumb and finger. "Promise me something, Molly."

"What?"

His voice was unusually gruff. "Promise me that you'll put aside your worries now and take yourself off to bed. There's time enough tomorrow to deal with Camilla Cannon's shawl."

Her smile came through, quick and bright, warming his heart as nothing else could. "Aye. I promise. Thanks to you, William, my sleep will be undisturbed by fears of what might have been."

"That's my girl." He brushed his mouth over hers, and felt himself actually tremble before forcing himself to walk to the door. The sooner he was out in the fresh night air, the safer they would both be.

"Good night, Molly."

She stayed where she was, as if sensing that they were walking a fine line that could still be crossed at any moment. "Good night, William."

He pulled the door firmly shut. All the way back to his cottage he cursed and called himself every kind of fool. He could have had what he most wanted, without any effort. For years now he'd prided himself on taking what he wanted. But this was different. Though the ache for her was stronger than ever, he knew he'd done the honorable thing. He didn't want her to confuse gratitude with something entirely different.

Love? he wondered.

What utter nonsense. The need building inside him was nothing more than lust. A perfectly reasonable emotion, considering his situation. He'd been a long time without a woman.

Perhaps it would be better for both of them if he took himself off to the tavern tomorrow night. The women there had no illusions about their emotions. The only thing they lusted over was gold.

But as he drew near his own cottage, he knew he could never be satisfied with a tavern wench now that he'd tasted the sweetness of the beautiful widow Warner. It was Molly he wanted. No one else could come close.

* * *

"Good afternoon, Duncan. Tyler." Molly carried a tray to the garden bench and uncovered it to reveal thin slices of tender beef and a plate of biscuits, as well as a dish of jam and a pot of tea.

Almost at once the two lay down their tools and hurried over.

It had become a ritual. Whenever they found time to work at her place, she would insist that they stop at midday to eat. The man and boy, accustomed to simple fare, had begun raving to William about the widow Warner's fine cooking. Nobody, it seemed, made biscuits as light as hers. And nobody in all of England had ever cooked beef to such perfection. The simplest tea and jam drew such compliments, William had finally lifted his hands in exasperation.

"Soon," he'd cried, "you'll tell me even her water is heaven-sent."

"That could be," Duncan had replied with a grin. "For it tastes cooler when she serves it on that pretty little tray out in her garden."

They'd brought home more than compliments and a basket of freshly mended clothes. Gradually they'd learned, over those midday lunches, from bits and pieces of things she'd let slip, that her husband had been a wastrel. That he'd died far too young, leaving his young widow destitute. That she had returned to Surrey to nurse her father through a long, painful illness, and that he'd left her nothing of value except his land and small cottage.

"Do you think she'd be willing to sell it, Duncan?"

The old man glanced across the table and frowned. "If she did, where would she go?"

William shrugged. "Is there no family?"

"None that she's spoken of."

"Perhaps you could ask the next time you're having one of your lovely tea parties."

At his tone of sarcasm he saw the old man's head come up. Both Duncan and Tyler had become extremely protective toward the widow Warner. In fact, like Wolf, who had taken to lying at her feet, begging for the touch of her hand on his head, or a scratch of her fingers behind his ears, they all seemed to have become almost territorial where Molly Warner was concerned.

"Perhaps you'd like to ask her yourself, William."

"And when would I have time to do that?"

"Tomorrow. We're putting new thatch on her roof. We could use another hand."

William shrugged. "I'll give it some thought. I suppose I could miss a few hours at Lord Kent's estate."

The old man smiled as he walked away.

In the morning the three trudged across the field to the neighboring cottage to begin the task of removing the old thatch and replacing it with new. They surprised Molly, who was just returning from the field with a basket of blueberries.

She looked so bright and pretty, it took William a full minute to find his voice. While Duncan and Tyler carried on a running conversation like old friends, he merely stood and stared. The breeze tugged at her hair and caught her skirts, flattening them against her legs. Her eyes fairly sparkled in the morning sunlight. And her face. How was it possible, he wondered, for one little female to look so fresh, so lovely, without any effort at all?

What had happened to make her so beautiful in his eyes? Her frock was the same shabby one she wore every day, though it probably required washing every night, since it was always spotless. Her shoes were dull and worn. Her apron was little more than a few remnants of fabric cleverly stitched together to form several deep pockets. But there was nothing dull or worn about her smile. It rivaled the sun.

"Good morning, William." She turned that smile on him now as she made ready to step through the doorway. "How is it that you're here today, instead of overseeing Lord Kent's estate?"

"I thought I'd give Duncan and Tyler a hand. It's time I learned a thing or two about thatch."

"And no one better to teach you, I'd wager." She turned that brilliant smile on the old man. "Duncan constantly amazes me with all the things he can do."

"Aye," Tyler called as he began catching the old rushes which Duncan was already tossing from the roof. "There's no finer tutor in all of England than my grandfather."

William tore himself away from Molly to join the old man. Under Duncan's tutelage he began removing the old thatch and tossing it to the ground, where

Tyler gathered it up to be bundled for burning in Molly's fireplace over the long winter.

When the roof was bare of old thatch, the two men climbed down and began tying the fresh rushes into bundles, and hauling them to the roof. This was a much more difficult task, and one which required a great deal of patience, for the rushes had to be secured against wind and rain and all manner of rough weather.

While they worked, they were aware of the most tantalizing fragrances wafting from inside the cottage. By the time the church bells sounded the midday Angelus, the door opened and Molly carried a linen-covered tray to the bench in the garden.

"I hope you're hungry," she called, "for I've made..." Her voice trailed off when she caught sight of William up on the roof.

In the heat of the day he'd removed his shirt. Muscles rippled across wide shoulders and a broad back that was slick with sweat. When he jumped down from the roof and turned to face her, she saw a mat of dark hair on his chest that trailed his flat stomach and disappeared beneath the narrow waist of his pants. The sight of him stole her breath away. She'd never seen a more perfect body.

He flashed her a smile. "What's this?"

"I've...brought a basin of cool water for washing."

"Ah." He bent to it, soaping his arms, then splashing water over his face and head. Not wanting to soil the clean linen she'd set beside the basin, he picked up his shirt and mopped himself dry before slipping it on. "Something smells wonderful."

"Pot pies." She couldn't seem to look away. She stared, fascinated, as he buttoned his shirt and tucked it into his waist. The damp fabric clung to his chest, clearly revealing the outline of muscles. "One for each of you, for I saw the way you were working, and knew you'd all three be ravenous."

"Bless you, miss." Duncan, who'd been watching her as she stared at his young friend, washed, then stepped aside so that his grandson could follow suit. "I'm sure I speak for the lad when I say we've come to look forward to your meals."

"Not nearly as much as I've come to look forward to all the help you've given me, Duncan." She indicated the steaming pies, each one big enough to be a complete meal.

While the men dug in, she poured water from a pitcher and handed around three goblets.

"Oh, miss." Duncan closed his eyes as he bit into the pastry filled with beef and summer vegetables in a thick gravy. "How will I ever be able to enjoy heaven one day unless the angels can top this?"

Molly's laughter rang on the air. "Why, Duncan Biddle, I do believe you're trying to charm me."

"Nay, miss. I speak the truth. This may be the finest meat pie I've ever tasted." He turned to his grandson. "What say you, lad?"

The boy was so busy shoveling food into his mouth, he couldn't speak. When he'd finally managed to swallow, he nodded. "Aye, Grandfather.

I've never tasted anything so fine. If I finish all this, I'll be as fat as Mistress Sloan's sow."

Molly laughed again. "Then I suppose it would be foolish of me to bring out slices of that blueberry pie I baked."

The boy's eyes went wide. "Truly? A blueberry pie?"

She nodded. "Do you think you could manage a tiny sliver, Tyler?"

"Aye, miss. I believe I could."

The lad watched as she returned to her cottage and came back carrying a tray with three of the biggest slices of pie he'd ever seen, as well as a pot of tea.

"I'm worried that we're depleting all your food, miss." Duncan helped himself to a cup of tea and leaned his back against the trunk of a gnarled tree and he slowly savored the dessert.

"Nonsense. Don't you worry about my food. What you've given me is far more important." Molly filled William's cup and felt the heat rise to her cheeks at the way he was staring at her.

He looked so natural, so right, sitting in the grass of her garden, one arm wrapped around his bent knee, the other holding a cup of tea, while sunlight played over his face, casting him in light and shadow.

She pulled herself back from her thoughts. "My roof has been leaking for years now. And I couldn't afford to hire anyone from town to replace my thatch. Without the generosity of the three of you, I'd surely be facing a very bleak winter."

"It's hard to think of winter when the weather is this gentle." Duncan glanced from William to Molly, wondering if either was aware of what was in their eyes. It would seem his young friend was reaching a milestone in his life. Though for now, he probably wasn't even aware of it.

The old man drained his cup and scrambled to his feet. "It's time we got back to our work, men."

Reluctantly William followed suit.

While he worked, he found himself thinking about the way he'd teased Duncan and Tyler about the widow Warner's tea parties. Now that he'd experienced one for himself, he had to admit that Duncan was right. Her food did indeed rival the angels. And despite the heat of the day and the challenging work, he was having the time of his life.

Molly Warner, it would seem, had the rare ability to make even the most tedious task on the most ordinary day seem like a slice of heaven.

Chapter 7

"What's this, old man?" William looked up from the table, where he was neatly writing in a column of figures in one of Lord Kent's ledgers.

Duncan was standing behind him, holding out his dark coat, which looked as clean as when it was new. "I hung this on the branch of a tree and brushed it. I figured you'd want to be looking your best today."

"Looking my best? Whatever for?"

The old man merely smiled. "The lass has to walk all the way to town this morning for Sunday services, carrying that heavy basket on her arm."

William gave him a suspicious look. "I suppose you volunteered my services."

"Not in so many words. But I—" the old man had the good manners to look ashamed "—I did suggest that you might be willing to lend a hand."

"If you're so concerned, why didn't you offer to go yourself?"

Duncan rubbed his knee. "I would but all these extra chores I've taken on have made the old joints a bit stiff."

"I see. Very well." William allowed himself to be helped into his coat. He gave a last lingering look at the ledgers, then turned away. At the door he paused to see the boy and man watching him. "If you hear that the church collapsed on the entire congregation, you'll know why. I'm not sure the town of Surrey is ready for this."

"You'll do just fine, sir." Duncan limped to the door and stood watching as William started across the field toward Molly's cottage. When he closed the door, his limp was suddenly forgotten. He turned to his grandson. "Come, lad. Let's take Wolf for a nice long walk through the forest. Maybe we'll take a basket along in case we spy any blueberries."

"William." Molly couldn't hide her surprise when she found him standing on her stoop. "I was just about to leave for town."

He took the basket from her arm. "I thought I'd walk along." He glanced up at the sunlight spilling over the edges of high, ruffled clouds. "It looks like a grand day for a walk."

She latched the door, and was even more surprised when he offered his arm. Her own smile widened as she linked her arm with his. "It does indeed."

He studied the parcels inside the basket, wrapped

in plain white linen to shield them from the dust of the road. "Are you pleased with the gown and shawl?"

"Oh, aye. More than pleased. I only hope Mistress Cannon will be, as well."

"And how can she not?" He closed a hand over hers. "Tell me. Can any other woman in Surrey sew as fine a seam as you?"

"Nay. I had a fine teacher. But I've learned that in this life, success doesn't always come to the one who does the best job, but rather to the one who wields the most influence."

He'd know something about that. Because of his father's wrathful edict, he'd found many doors closed to him. There were many in England who believed that the disinherited son of an earl must be a scoundrel.

He nudged aside such thoughts, keeping his tone cheerful. "You wield a bit of influence yourself, Mistress Warner. Look at how Duncan and Tyler sing your praises. Not to mention Wolf, who, I'm told, has now become your lapdog." He bent close. "A woman who can tame both man and beast does truly inspire awe, my lady."

"Oh, William, if only I had your confidence." She gave a delighted laugh. "When I'm with you, I almost believe such fantasies."

"Then believe, dear lady. The proof is in the man you see beside you. Do you think I would be willing to idle away my morning in church for anyone but you?"

The two were still sharing a laugh when they

reached the home of Camilla Cannon. It was one of the finest in all of Surrey.

Though it had been William's intention to remain outside the gates, he couldn't seem to tear himself away from Molly for even a brief time. And so he accompanied her along the pathway and up the steps. A manservant invited them inside and led them into a grand room where they sat until the lady of the house could be summoned.

Camilla Canon came dancing lightly down the stairs and into the parlor, completely ignoring Molly when she caught sight of William.

"I hope this means you accept my invitation to tea next week."

He managed to keep his smile in place, though in truth, it took a bit of work, for he'd forgotten all about it. "I'd be honored. What day will your cousin be arriving?"

"My husband and I will be fetching her up from the country by midweek." She glanced in puzzlement toward Molly. "Did the two of you come together?"

Molly flushed. "In a manner of speaking. I was on my way to town when my neighbor happened by."

Accepting the explanation, Camilla stared hopefully at the basket. "Is this my gown and shawl, Molly?"

"Aye, Mistress Cannon." Molly unwrapped the gown first and held it up for her inspection.

William could see, by the woman's eyes, that she

was delighted as she examined the workmanship before handing it over to a maid.

"And the shawl?"

Molly proudly unwrapped the second parcel. Even William's jaw dropped at the beauty of her work.

"Oh, my." Camilla Cannon put a hand to the soft, delicate shawl that could have been spun by angels. Each tiny stitch was perfection. "Molly, this is exquisite." She reached into her pocket and removed several coins, which she gave to Molly. "I can't wait for everyone to see me in this. I do hope you'll agree to make me more."

"Aye. I'd be happy to, Mistress Cannon, if you but say the word."

"You'll be hearing from me soon, Molly." She looked beyond the young widow to the man standing behind her. "As for you, William Colton, I'll send one of my servants with the time and day of tea."

He nodded.

Camilla Cannon was still examining her fine goods when the butler escorted William and Molly to the door.

When they were safely away, he saw Molly staring at the coins in her hand. She looked up to see him grinning broadly.

"Didn't I tell you she'd love your work?"

She nodded. "But I didn't believe you."

He paused and caught her hands between both of his. "Now do you believe?"

"Aye." She closed her eyes a moment, allowing

the relief to wash over her. For another fortnight or so, she would have food in her larder and would manage to keep the roof over her head. And soon she would have enough saved to pay off her father's debts.

Gradually they were swallowed up by the crowd of men and women hurrying toward the chapel.

William leaned close to whisper, "If you'd like to celebrate, we could skip the service and find a cozy inn where we could break our fast."

"Oh, William." She looked scandalized. "After this fine blessing, I do believe I have to attend Sunday service before I celebrate my good fortune."

"What's this?" He pressed his lips to her temple. "Afraid it might be snatched from you?"

She flushed. "I suppose that's part of it."

He felt a wave of regret at his light banter. After all, she'd known a great deal of grief in her young life.

"But I also feel the need to give thanks for this, William."

"All right." He turned toward the chapel, keeping her hand tucked in his. "We'll pray first. Then we'll drink a bit of tea to celebrate your good fortune."

"You don't like your tea?" William closed a hand over Molly's, concerned by the way she was staring into the cup, as though looking for something in its depths.

She looked up, startled. "Oh, it's fine. It's better than fine." She lifted the cup to her lips and drank.

"It warms me clear to my toes." The way his touch did, though she couldn't possibly say that aloud.

"You seem troubled."

She shook her head. "I was just trying to recall the last time I'd eaten food I hadn't had to cook myself. I think it was when I was ten and three, and I was with my father. I felt very special, and very grown-up." She smiled. "I'm feeling the same way now."

"You are special, Molly."

She flushed at his compliment.

"And this is a special day."

"How so?"

His smile matched hers. "If the look on Camilla Cannon's face was any indication of the way she feels about your handiwork, I'd say she's about to spread the word far and wide that Molly Warner is the finest seamstress in all of Surrey. Perhaps in all of England. Women will be flocking to your door, eager to show off for their friends and neighbors."

"Such a pretty dream." She looked over at him. "I'll just settle for what I have. For with these coins added to what I've saved, I'll soon have enough to pay my father's debts, and I'll not have to fear the constable ordering me from my home."

"What are you talking about?"

She flushed and looked away. She hadn't meant to let that slip.

He touched a hand to her cheek. "Tell me, Molly. Why would the constable order you from your own home?"

She sighed and ran a finger around the edge of

the cup, avoiding his eyes. "When my father grew ill, there was no way to care for him and earn my keep as well. When his meager savings were gone, I was forced to go to Lord Bowers, who owns the land adjoining mine to the south. He loaned me the money to settle my father's debts, with the understanding that I would repay the loan within the year, or he would lay claim to my property."

"How much longer do you have to repay the debt?"

"It's overdue. But he's a kind man. He's given me a grace period. Lord Bowers said, as long as no one else steps up to pay the debt and lay claim to the land, he'll give me whatever time I need." She touched a hand to the coins in her pocket. "I've been forced to live a frugal existence, and will for many more years to come, but at least I've been able to hold on to my legacy, small though it is."

"Then this is indeed a celebration." He signaled the serving wench and ordered ale.

Molly shook her head but he ignored her protest. When the wench had retreated, he touched his glass to Molly's. Looking into her eyes, he whispered, "To your legacy."

They drank.

"Tell me, Molly." He leaned closer. "If you were to make any dream come true, what would it be?"

She looked away a moment, until he caught her face and turned it toward him.

"You'll laugh," she said softly.

"Nay. And to prove it, if you tell me yours, I'll tell you mine."

She looked into his blue eyes and saw herself reflected there. There was something about him that inspired her trust. And she found herself telling him what she'd never told another soul.

"If I could have but one dream, it would be to travel to the New World."

His eyes widened. "You would risk all and go to America?"

She nodded. "I know it's a foolish dream. But I've heard it said that even those of lowly birth can attain great things there. The citizens of that far-off land care nothing for nobility. Even those who arrive in disgrace have the freedom to begin life anew." Her eyes glistened, and without realizing it, she reached a hand to his. "Think of it, William. A place where each person is judged, not by past glories or mistakes, but by how they choose to live their lives from the moment they set foot on that hallowed ground."

He gave her a gentle smile. "You think America is a holy place?"

"What else would you call the soil of freedom?" She blushed and looked down at the table. "You must surely think me addled."

"Nay." He closed his hand over hers and was rewarded with her look of pure surprise. "I must admit, Molly, that I've given little thought to that strange land across the sea. These past few years have been spent trying to prove that my life counts for something."

"Every life counts for something, William."

He felt the warmth of her touch spreading along his arm, and singing through his veins, and realized that he had no need of ale when he was with her.

As voices swirled around them in the crowded room, he heard only hers, trilling with laughter. As faces moved past his line of vision, he saw only hers, so lovely it took his breath away. It occurred to William that he was having a wonderful time.

How long had it been since he'd felt so carefree? Since he'd sat at a fine table and laughed with a beautiful woman, and shared the secrets of his heart?

When their goblets were empty, he walked her home, amazed that it was already late afternoon.

"Where has the day gone?"

Molly seemed equally surprised. "I don't know, William. It has passed much too quickly."

"Aye." Because of the company, he realized. He suddenly released her hand. "Stay here."

She stared in openmouthed surprise as he left her by the side of the road and dashed through the field, picking an armload of wildflowers. When he could carry no more, he returned to press them into her arms.

"Oh, William. You did this for me?"

The look on her face was priceless. For the space of several seconds she merely stared at them. Then, to hide the tears that threatened, she buried her face in them, breathing in their perfume.

He couldn't recall when his heart had ever felt this light. At her door he dragged her close, crushing the flowers between them to kiss her full on the mouth.

"William!" Her face flamed. "It's broad daylight. People might see us."

"Let them." He kissed her again for good measure, loving the way her eyes warmed and her lips softened under his. If he could, he would stand here like this until day turned into evening, and evening into night, holding her, kissing her, wanting her. Aye, wanting her with an ache that had no cure.

"Good day to you, Molly."

"Good day to you, William."

He strode away, feeling as though he could leap over fences. Over trees. And all the while, the fragrance of wildflowers filled his lungs. The taste of Molly's lips, as sweet, as clean as a forest stream, remained on his.

When he returned to his cottage, he found Duncan and Tyler, hands and mouths stained blue from their trek in the woods.

"How was your day with the lass?" Duncan got up to toss another log under the kettle of stew.

It occurred to William that the old man's limp had miraculously disappeared. But he decided to say nothing about it. He was in far too fine a mood.

"The day was grand." William removed his coat and rolled up his sleeves, having decided that the evening would best be spent working on Lord Kent's ledgers. Otherwise, he might give in to the temptation to walk back to Molly's cottage and taste those lips again.

If he did, there would be no stopping him. Not until he'd tasted every lovely inch of her. And allowed himself to give in to this need that was threatening to slowly drive him mad.

Chapter 8

William closed the ledger and snuffed the candle. He felt a measure of satisfaction that he'd managed to concentrate, despite the distracting thoughts of Molly that had plagued him throughout the evening. At least now he understood why her clothes were so shabby, despite the fact that she was such a fine seamstress. Even the simplest fabric would have drained her precious savings. Every coin she earned was necessary to pay her debt.

Then he realized something else. By sending Duncan and Tyler to help with her chores, he'd actually cost her more money. Her pride wouldn't allow her to accept their help without some sort of payment. And so she'd let other work go to mend their clothes quickly. And had probably gone without food herself in order to feed them.

Foolish female. His hands clenched at his sides. What else was she suffering in order to hold on to that relic of her childhood? How many nights must she go without sleep, just to pay the debt of a dead man?

It was pride that drove her. He knew something about that. He'd had far too much in his youth. But he now realized that much of what he considered pride was actually arrogance. It had taken the loss of everything he'd once considered important before he'd begun to realize what was truly important in this life. Respect for self. And the love of a few good friends.

He smiled as he heard the sound of snoring from the other room. Duncan and young Tyler had retired to their beds shortly after dark. Those two had added so much to his life. They were, he realized, his family now. He'd thought he was saving them from a life of abject poverty. But they'd given him so much more than he'd given them. They'd brought him out of his own misery to appreciate the sound of other voices in his home. Laughter. Teasing. A reason to get up each morning. A reason to return to his own home each night.

And this was home now, thanks to them. But he wanted more.

He wanted Molly.

If he could just lie with her, for a single night, this aching need would be satisfied. Then he could enjoy his newfound wealth and success, and move on with his life.

He stopped pacing and strode to the door. Just

thinking about Molly, about the way she tasted, the way she felt in his arms, had the need rising once more.

He turned away, counting the steps to the table, then back to the door. But it was impossible to get her out of his mind.

With a muttered oath he yanked opened the door and stepped outside. Wolf raced out behind him, then paused and lifted a nose to sniff the air.

William glanced toward Molly's cottage, actually hoping it would be in darkness. Then he could talk himself out of this madness.

He felt a wave of annoyance at the flickering light he could see in her window. Why couldn't she have just this once done the sensible thing and retired at a reasonable hour? Now the temptation would eat at him during his night walk with his dog.

Just as he was turning away, Wolf began barking frantically and started racing across the field.

More annoyed than puzzled, William started after him.

"Damnable creature," he muttered. "He'll have the entire town of Surrey awake if he keeps this up."

The dog disappeared in the darkness, his barking growing more distant, and William stopped to look around in annoyance. Had Wolf run all the way to Molly's?

He looked up and saw what appeared to be a strange darkened haze rising from her roof. A trick of the eye, he thought. It was a mist of some sort.

But as he continued to stare, he felt his heart stop. That was no mist. It was smoke.

"Fire," he shouted, then louder, "Fire! Duncan! Tyler!"

His heart in his throat, he dashed across the field, all the while shouting for the old man and boy to wake up.

When he reached Molly's door, the air was thick with the smell of burning wood. He leaned a shoulder to her door and forced it open. At once Wolf dashed past him and raced to her side.

At first she appeared to be surrounded by flames. But as William's eyes adjusted, he realized that it was the rug at her feet that was burning. She was attempting to put out the flames with a blanket. But each time she would beat back the fire in one spot, another would burst into flame.

"Here. That's not enough." William raced across the room and pushed her aside, then began hauling the burning rug out the door, unmindful of the flames that singed his flesh and licked at his shirt. Once he'd tossed the burning rug aside, he hurried back inside to help beat back the fire that had begun climbing up the curtains at the window and along one wall.

"Flee, Molly," he ordered. "Go outside where you'll be safe."

"Nay. I can't." She picked up a bucket of water and tossed it at the flaming curtain.

Just then Duncan and Tyler arrived, still pulling on their clothes.

Without a word the two joined in. Duncan

grabbed a burning blanket from the end of the chaise and beat out the flames, then used it to beat a thin line of fire that was inching along the wall.

"We need more water, Tyler," Molly shouted.

The lad caught up an empty bucket and hurried out, returning shortly with water sloshing over the rim. He handed it to Molly, who gave it a quick desperate toss.

They did this over and over until there was no sign of fire anywhere in the room. They stared around in dismay. The walls and ceiling of the little cottage were charred. The curtains, the little wooden table, the rocking chair, all burned beyond repair.

They stumbled outside, choking and coughing, to sit in the grass.

"How did this happen, lass?" Duncan asked between gasps of breath.

"I fell asleep sewing. The gown in my hand must have brushed against the candle."

"God in heaven." William caught her hand. "You could have died."

She gave him a weak smile. "I'm fine, William. Thanks to all of you." Just then she looked down at his hands. Despite the black soot that covered them, she could see that they'd been burned and were beginning to blister. "Oh, no. You've been hurt."

"It's nothing." He snatched his hands away and got to his feet. "You can't stay here tonight. You'll have to come back to my cottage."

She shook her head as he helped her up. "Nay, William. I can't leave now."

"And why can't you?" He looked toward Duncan and Tyler for support. "We've plenty of room."

"Aye, lass," the old man said. "We'll see that you have the privacy you require."

She gave him a gentle smile. "I know you would. And I thank you. But this is my home. I need to be here, to satisfy myself that the fire is truly out. If I were to leave, I wouldn't be able to sleep. I'd feel a need to stand vigil at the window all night long, watching for smoke."

"If you won't leave here," William said firmly, "then I'm staying with you."

"There's no need, William."

"Aye. There is. I'll not have you here alone." William turned to Duncan. "You and the lad may as well go off to bed. As for me, I'd be no good at my place. Like Molly, I'd be forced to stand vigil at my window all night long."

The old man nodded. "I quite agree. This way, we can all rest better, knowing the lass is safe."

"Safe." Molly smiled before touching a hand to the dog that hadn't left her side since he'd first arrived on the scene. "When I heard Wolf's barking, and saw William in the doorway, I knew I would be safe." She walked to the old man to press a kiss to his cheek, then kissed his grandson, as well. "Thank you both for coming to my rescue."

"How could we not? You've come to mean so much to us. Good night, lass," the old man called.

He wrapped an arm around Tyler's shoulders, and the two started across the field toward their beds.

Molly turned to William. "Sit on the bench in the

garden and I'll fetch some water to bathe your hands."

She was gone before he could utter a word of protest. A short time later she returned with a basin and pitcher. She knelt before him and began to wash his hands. "Do they hurt, William?"

"Nay."

"Oh, William, I was so frightened."

"Not nearly as frightened as I when I saw the smoke."

"But then I saw you there in the doorway." She stunned him by lifting his hands to her lips and pressing a kiss to each palm, sending heat spiraling through his veins. "And I knew I'd be safe."

"Is that what you think?" He stood and drew her up with him. He was watching her with a look of such intense concentration, she found it impossible to look away. "That you're safe with me?"

"Of course." She nodded.

He gave a hiss of annoyance and dropped his hands to his sides as he turned away.

"William?" She touched a hand to his back. "What are you doing?"

"The honorable thing. I'm leaving now, before it's too late."

"I don't understand."

"Don't you?" He shot a glance over his shoulder. His eyes looked as hot and fierce as they had that first night, when he'd stumbled into her cottage and frightened her half to death. "Go inside now, Molly, and latch your door. Then, and only then, will you be safe."

* * *

For the space of several minutes Molly stood in the dark, watching as he walked away. His sudden change of mood puzzled her. Was it something she'd said? She went over every word in her mind.

Safe. She'd told him she felt safe with him. And then he'd changed right before her eyes.

As the realization dawned, she recalled something else. He'd said he was doing the honorable thing. Sweet heaven. He was leaving her alone in order to spare her honor.

"Oh, William." With a hand to her mouth she dashed through the darkness after him. When she caught up to him, she lay a hand on his arm and felt him flinch. "Please don't go, William. I don't want you to leave me alone."

"I have to." His voice was gruff. "If I stay, you will most definitely not be safe."

"I understand now, William." She stepped in front of him and touched a hand to his chest. "I didn't at first, but now I do. And I want you to stay."

He caught her roughly by the upper arms and held her a little away, as if determined to keep her at bay. "I have nothing to offer you, Molly. Nothing. Do you understand? I have been disowned by my own father. Turned away by my family. Whatever wealth and title I might have had has been denied me forever. By associating with me, you will bring nothing but shame upon yourself."

"The choice is mine to make, William. I care not for wealth or title. It's you I want. Only you."

He went very still, hoping to make her see the error of her ways. "I can make you no promises, Molly."

"I'll ask for none."

His eyes narrowed. "If that's true then you're a fool."

She lifted her chin in the way he'd come to recognize. "Perhaps I am. But I want you to stay the night with me. To hold me. And—" her voice trembled just a little "—love me, if just for the night."

He moved his hands slowly up her arms, across her shoulders, drawing her inexorably closer. Against her temple he muttered, "Then God help us, for I haven't the strength to resist."

He crushed her against him and covered her mouth with his in a kiss so hot, so hungry, it seemed to steal all her breath. And still it wasn't enough. He kissed her again, lingering over her lips, drawing out all the sweet clean taste until he could feel it filling him.

His voice was a whisper inside her mouth. "You realize, don't you, that we're both a couple of fools?"

"Aye."

He felt that slender young body imprinting itself on his, and was desperate for more. With a muttered oath he lifted her in his arms and carried her to the cottage. Inside they made it as far as the door to her bedroom, where he paused to kiss her again. A mistake, he realized. The hunger for her was so great, he had to fight a desperate urge to tear her clothes from her and take her right here on the floor.

His tongue tangled with hers, mated, while his

hands moved down her back, igniting fires along her spine.

"I've wanted you, wanted this, since the first time I saw you." The words were whispered against her mouth while his hands moved up her sides until they encountered the swell of her breasts. His thumbs stroked, and he felt her nipples harden.

"I never dreamed. I'd thought no man would ever want me, William. I've been soiled and discarded. Like damaged goods."

Damaged goods. Wasn't that what he himself had been feeling for so long now?

"Oh, my darling." He felt something loosen around his heart. A band that had been there for so long now, squeezing the very life from him.

He lifted a hand to the row of tiny buttons on her faded gown. "I want to undress you."

He kept his gaze fastened on hers as, with easy, unhurried movements, he unbuttoned first one button, then another, until he was able to slip the gown from her shoulders. It slid to the floor, to pool at their feet. Then he untied the ribbons of her chemise and parted the fabric.

"You're even more beautiful than I'd imagined." He whispered the words against her throat, before running wet, nibbling kisses across her collarbone, then lower, to the swell of her breast. "Oh, Molly. Molly. You're so beautiful."

She swallowed, shocked by the desire that rocked her.

"You're trembling." He gathered her into his

arms and pressed his lips to her ear. "Are you cold?"

"Nay. It's—it's the wanting. Though I was wed, I've never...wanted a man before." She looked away, shamed by her admission.

He couldn't imagine anything that would have thrilled him more. He tangled his fingers in her hair and dragged her head back. "Look at me, Molly."

She did. And what she saw stunned her. Those fierce blue eyes that she'd once thought cold and cynical, were burning with heat and desire. "I'm trembling, too. And all because of you, Molly. Just you."

He dragged her against him and plundered her mouth. She felt the heat grow until it was a raging inferno.

She had a desperate need to touch him as he was touching her. Reaching a hand to his shirt, she nearly tore it in her haste. Then she reached for the snaps at his waist until his clothes joined hers on the floor at their feet.

Now, at last, they stood, flesh to flesh, and she thought she would surely die from this wanting that shuddered through her.

He lifted her onto the narrow bed and lay beside her, gathering her close. His kisses were by turn harsh, then gentle, as though he waged a war within himself. His hands moved over her, drawing out hidden pleasures that had her sighing, then gasping with pleasure, and sometimes with shock.

He studied the way she looked, lying in a spill of moonlight, her skin gilded, her eyes gleaming like fire. Her golden hair tumbled over his arm, and he thought about the first time he'd seen her. He'd wanted desperately to touch. Now he could touch, taste, to his heart's content.

His lips moved along the sensitive little hollow of her throat, then lower, to her breast, where he nibbled and suckled while his big clever hands moved over her, weaving a magic of their own.

When her hands fisted in the bed linens, he drove her to the first peak. She shuddered, struggling for air, and arched against him. Before she could recover he took her again, loving the look of stunned surprise in her eyes.

This, he realized, was a place she'd never been before, and he was thrilled to be the one to take her. He could feel her heartbeat thundering in her chest. It matched his own. He was nearly drunk with feelings for this woman. His woman, he thought fiercely. Only his.

He struggled to bank his feelings. To draw out this moment, for it was all he had to give her. But then she touched him as he was touching her, and he knew he was lost.

A single touch from her and all the madness was unleashed. He levered himself above her, whispering her name. He fisted a hand in her hair, loving the way her eyes stayed steady on his.

The need was so great now, clawing to be free. And still he waited, taking them both to the very brink until, desperate, she clutched at his shoulders and wrapped herself around him.

They came together in a firestorm of passion.

This was how he'd wanted her. How he'd dreamed of her. No longer cool, but instead like a wildfire, raging out of control. The last thread of his own control dissolved, and he felt himself being washed along in a tide of desperate passion.

He murmured her name over and over as he climbed with her to the very top of the mountain. He looked into her eyes in that moment before they stepped off the edge, and what he saw shattered him completely. For in that one final instant he saw her heart in her eyes. A heart so pure. So trusting. A heart fairly bursting with love.

It was the last thing he saw before he followed her over the edge.

Chapter 9

Molly awoke and lay very still. She'd never known such a night. It still didn't seem possible that she and William had shared such intimacies. The entire experience had been like a rare and wonderful dream. One she still couldn't quite believe. She had expected, after they had collapsed into each other's arms, that they would simply sleep. Instead, they had loved again and yet again. And each time it had been different. At times they'd been overcome with such sweetness, such tenderness, it made her want to weep. At other times they'd been gripped by a sort of madness that thrust them into the dark side of passion, which excited her even while it shocked her.

She yawned and stretched and reached for the man whose arms had held her all through the night.

Finding the bed empty, she opened her eyes, expecting to find him dressing.

The room was empty.

She washed quickly in a basin of water, then drew on her simple day dress and hurried from the room.

"William?" She opened the bedroom door and stared around at the destruction to her cottage. Seeing that the house was empty, she decided that he must have gone back to his own place, in search of clean clothes.

She felt a quick little flutter of disappointment, but brushed it aside. He had a life of his own to see to. Hadn't he told her he could make her no promises? She couldn't expect him to ignore his work, his obligations, just to be with her.

She stoked the fire and placed the blackened kettle over the hot coals. Afterward she walked to the doorway and stepped outside, breathing in the morning air, still ripe with the acrid stench of charred wood.

She glanced at the cottage across the field and felt a shiver of anticipation. Would William come to her before he left for Lord Kent's estate? But as the minutes passed, and then an hour or more, she realized with a sense of dread that he wasn't coming.

She hurried back inside to her bedroom, where she examined her reflection in a small chipped mirror. Oh, how she wished she could be more beautiful. She tried to see herself as William saw her. But all she saw were fine lines around eyes that appeared troubled, cheekbones a little too defined, and a mouth that was too wide. She stared down at her hands, which bore the effects of the fire. The skin was blistered, the nails torn and ragged. Not a lady's hands, she thought sadly. Not the hands a man would want moving over him in the quiet of the night. And her clothes. So threadbare. So shabby. She wished she could afford to keep the lovely clothes she made for other women. But she'd learned years ago that wishing wouldn't change a thing.

She set aside the looking glass and shook her head. Who was she trying to deceive? Still, she clung to the hope that William would appear in her doorway and dispel the nagging little doubts that were beginning to creep in.

He'd made her no promises.

She poured her cup of tea and sat by the fire, struggling to hold the fear at bay. But the seeds had already been planted. And with each minute that passed, those seeds began to grow.

She suddenly put aside her tea and set herself the task of cleaning up the debris left from the fire. There was work to be done. As she began hauling out the charred remains of her meager belongings, and sweeping out her cottage, she hoped the hard, physical activity would keep her mind too occupied to allow the fear to fester.

Molly knelt in the garden, picking vegetables for her dinner. All day she'd pushed herself to the limit, refusing to stop. For whenever she allowed herself even a moment, the fear was there, snapping at her heels like a mad dog, its vicious little teeth ripping into her heart, ravaging it.

She paused and looked up. What was that sound? She wiped a hand over her forehead, leaving a dirty smudge. There it was again. A rapping sound. A knock. Someone was at her cottage, knocking on her door.

William. He'd come to her.

She snatched up her basket and started along the garden path.

When she stepped around to the front stoop, she saw a man peering in her window.

At her footsteps he turned. "Mistress Warner?"

Her heart stopped when she recognized him. "Constable Eton."

He glanced at her, then away, as though avoiding her eyes. "I've come to tell you that the debt on your property has been settled."

"Settled? But I didn't...I haven't yet..." She paused when she saw him shaking his head.

"The debt was paid to Lord Bowers, who sent me to notify you of that fact. And to give you this." He stepped closer and handed her a legal-looking document, bearing the seal of the landowner.

She could feel her legs trembling, could feel the weakness spreading through her, and she tightened her grasp on the basket in her arms, as though needing to cling to something. Anything. "Are you... telling me I must leave my home?"

She could read the pity in his eyes, which only made it worse.

The constable cleared his throat. "I know not,

Mistress Warner. That will be between you and the gentleman who bought your land."

"And who would that be?"

He motioned with his head. "Your neighbor, Mr. William Colton."

She swallowed. "I see." She took a step closer, then paused to put a hand to the wall to steady herself. "Thank you, Constable Eton."

He left her leaning weakly against the side of her cottage, her face devoid of all color, her eyes staring blindly.

When he was gone, she stumbled toward the front stoop and slumped down, too weak to take another step. At first she couldn't seem to focus. Her mind refused to work. But gradually, as she studied the document deeding the land, her father's land, her land, to William Colton, all the fears that had been swirling in her mind suddenly began to take shape and focus.

Hadn't William made it plain, right from the beginning, that he wanted her land? How many rumors had she ignored? Rumors about Lord Kent's hard-hearted overseer, who did whatever necessary to double his employer's wealth? William Colton was known as a shrewd, ruthless man. When she refused to sell, he'd found a way around her. And she'd been the one to show him how.

Fool, she berated herself. How could she have been such a fool? Hadn't she vowed after Jared to never again allow herself to trust a man? Especially one who was good-looking. And yet, after scant meetings with the handsome, charming William

Colton, she'd tumbled into his arms and had actually invited him into her bed. Only to have him mistreat her, just as Jared had.

Silly, romantic, love-starved fool.

Shame mingled with fury as scalding tears streamed from her eyes. She buried her face in her hands and wept until there were no tears left.

Then, as the tears dried, pity was replaced by a newer, stronger emotion. White-hot fury. Getting to her feet, she took an unsteady step, and then another. William Colton wouldn't get away with this. At least not without a fight.

She lifted her skirts and started across the field just as dusk was beginning to settle over the land. When she reached his door, she rapped a fist against it. From inside she could hear the sound of Wolf's high-barked welcome, followed by the sound of hurried footsteps.

"Ah, Molly." Duncan held the door wide and gave her a bright smile. "Come in, lass."

She paused on the threshold. "I've come to speak with William."

"He isn't home from town yet, but I'm sure he'll be eager to see you." He studied her tight, pinched features. His smile faded. "What is it, lass? Has something happened?"

"Aye." She glanced at Tyler, standing beside his grandfather. Her fight wasn't with these two. "Something...dreadful has happened, Duncan."

He caught her hand and led her inside toward the fire. "I'll fix you some tea, lass, and you'll tell me."

She shook her head. "I can't tell you. It's between Mr. Colton and me.'' Seeing him pouring water into a cup, she held up a hand. ''I can't accept that, Duncan.'' She would steel herself to take nothing from this place. No act of kindness.

She turned away and began to pace while the old man and the boy merely watched in puzzled silence. The dog lay by the fire, his head turning from side to side, watching as she paced.

''I trusted him.'' She was talking more to herself than to them. With the deed still crushed firmly in her hand, she crossed her arms over her chest. Her chin jutted defiantly. With every step, every word, her temper grew. ''My first impression of him was a drunken lout. Had I not let myself believe the word of others, I might never have changed that opinion. Might never have come to this. After all, he was so arrogant, so sure of himself, he actually sent you to measure my land without even a by-your-leave.''

The old man glanced toward the door, then suddenly took a seat by the table and stretched out his legs, enjoying this remarkable display of fireworks. The lad followed suit. They sat in silence, watching and listening.

Molly stopped, stared down at the dog, her hands at her hips. ''All those unexpected kindnesses. The gold to cover the cost of your...romp with my yarn. And then that skein of yarn, the exact shade I needed, all the way from London. And all calculated to earn my trust. Oh...'' She closed her eyes and lifted her face to the ceiling, hissing out a breath of anger. ''How could I have been so blind?''

She glowered at the man and boy. ''I listened to

all your fine tales of William Colton's kindnesses. And gradually I began to believe." She turned away to pace again. "I forgot all the promises I'd made to myself after Jared. I let that horrible, mean, miserable excuse of a man buy me a meal at an inn." Her voice trembled, as she remembered. "I let him fill my arms with wildflowers and my mind with ideas of living again. Loving again. I foolishly believed that he found me pretty. That he...loved me." Her voice trailed off for a moment, and she stared into the flames. Then she looked up, her voice low with passion. "And he made a mockery of that love."

"I am guilty of many things, but not of that." A familiar deep voice said very slowly, "I would never betray you, Molly."

She whirled to find William standing in the doorway. How long had he been there? How much had he heard? From the look on his face, everything. That was fine with her. She wouldn't have to repeat herself. Not that she could. She was beyond anger now. Beyond fury. Almost beyond words.

"Then how do you explain this?" She held up the crumpled document in her fist, shaking it in the air.

"Forgive me, Molly. I had hoped to get home sooner and be the one to tell you. But I was detained."

"You needn't worry yourself." Her tone was filled with self-loathing. "The constable was most kind. He merely informed me that I no longer own my father's land." Her voice rose to near hysteria.

"My land is no longer mine, he said. And if I want to continue to live there, I will have to make arrangements with the new owner, William Colton."

At that Duncan sprang to his feet and lifted a fist, as if to do battle on her behalf.

Before he could speak William held up a hand, cautioning him to remain silent. "It's true that I paid off your debt, Molly. But not for the reason you think."

"Are you telling me you no longer desire my land?"

He shook his head and reached into his pocket. "Here is a copy of the deed, signed by Lord Bowers himself. It's yours, Molly, to do with as you please."

"You—" she stared at the scrolled paper, and then up at his face "—you paid my debt? And yet you do not intend to take my land?"

"Nay. It's as you say. The land is yours, free of debt."

"But why?"

"I realized something when I awoke this morning. Something I've been avoiding until now, because—" he cleared his throat "—because I wasn't ready to accept it. But now I must. It isn't your land I want, Molly. It's you. I want you in my life. Now. Forever."

She couldn't seem to wrap her mind around what he was saying. Even though her anger had evaporated as suddenly as a mist in morning sunlight, her mind refused to work. "You want me?"

"As my wife, if you'll have me."

"Oh, William." She felt a sudden lightness around her heart. A sudden dizziness that had her holding her hands to her head. "This is all happening too quickly. I came here to hate you."

"I don't blame you for hating me, Molly. I've spent years hating myself. But now I feel such love in my heart."

She shook her head. "I don't know what to say."

"Say yes. Say you'll be my wife, Molly."

She swallowed the lump that was threatening to choke her, then nodded, afraid to trust her voice.

"Oh, praise heaven. I was so afraid…" He gathered her into his arms and pressed his lips to her temple. Against her skin he murmured, "I don't deserve you, Molly. I have been scorned and shunned and disowned by my own family. And that will, in turn, bring shame upon you as my wife. But if you'll but love me, I'll do everything in my power to make you happy."

"You already have, William."

Across the room, the old man and the boy were wearing matching looks of amazed delight.

Tyler's eyes were dancing with excitement as he called to William and Molly, "Will you two be getting wed soon?"

William looked down at the woman in his arms, whose eyes were bright and shining with excitement. "Aye, lad. As soon as we can arrange it." He lifted Molly into his arms and started toward the door. "In fact, we'll go to her cottage right now and make our plans."

Tyler started after them. "May Wolf and I come along and help you with the plans?"

William paused in the doorway and winked. "Nay, lad. You have to stay here. I suspect we might need the entire night to...talk through all our plans."

"But I—"

"Not now, lad." With a grin his grandfather put a hand on his arm to stop him. The old man paused in the doorway, his arm around his grandson's shoulders, watching as William started across the field, carrying Molly in his arms.

Halfway there William paused to press a kiss to Molly's sweet lips. He absorbed the familiar jolt to his system and prayed he'd have the strength to make it to her door before kissing her again.

"I love you, Molly Warner."

"And I love you, William Colton. Though I must confess, I'd pretty much convinced myself that I'd lost my heart to a rogue and a scoundrel."

"I'm aware of that." He chuckled against her mouth, sending heat spiraling through her veins. "Even if I hadn't already discovered how much I loved you, I'm quite certain I'd have lost my heart just watching that lovely display of fireworks back there. You were simply amazing." He kissed her again, long and slow and deep, and felt the need rise until it staggered him. "Remind me to always stay on your good side, Molly Warner. For I'd hate to have to face that temper of yours."

She wrapped her arms around his neck and returned his kisses with a fire that nearly brought him to his knees.

Those last few steps to her cottage were the longest of his life. His only comfort was the knowledge that he'd have the rest of his life to kiss her. To love her. To dream with her. For only in Molly Warner's arms could he make all his dreams come true.

Epilogue

"You'd best hurry." Duncan stood in the knave of the church, admiring the way his young friend looked in the fine new shirt and waistcoat Molly had made him. "The church bells have begun to toll. It's time, William."

"The vicar will wait a few minutes longer." William picked up the bouquet of wildflowers he'd gathered early that morning and breathed them in. Then he made his way to a small room where Molly stood waiting.

Once there, Duncan and Tyler remained a few steps back, while William knocked. When she opened the door, all three caught their breath at the sight of her.

Molly felt the color rise to her cheeks at the look in William's eyes. "I wanted to surprise you." She twirled, causing the hem of the gossamer gown to float around her ankles.

She had outdone herself. The sheer white fabric might have been spun by angels. It had a softly rounded neckline and long tapered sleeves with tiny points of lace that fluttered at her wrists. The full skirt was gathered here and there with tiny bows, revealing a lace underskirt. She'd left her hair long and loose the way William loved it. In her hair she'd fastened sprigs of wildflowers. They were her only adornment.

William caught her hands in his. "You look so beautiful, you take my breath away."

"I'm glad." The smile she gave him rivaled the brilliant sunlight that played over her face. "I wanted to look beautiful for you." She gave him a long appraising look. "And I must say, you look dashing in your new coat and shirt."

"Thanks to my talented bride, I shall always look the height of fashion."

Molly dimpled. "Being driven to the church in Lord Kent's fine carriage was a delightful surprise."

William reached a hand into his breast pocket. "Then I hope you won't mind one more surprise."

He retrieved a strip of velvet cloth from his pocket and unrolled it to reveal a sparkling necklace of sapphires and diamonds set in rich gold. Without a word he fastened it around Molly's throat. At once the jewels began to pulse and gleam as though they were alive with fire. As they warmed to her skin they became so dazzling, they shot prisms of color against the walls of the chapel.

Molly touched a hand to the necklace and felt its heat. "I don't understand. How could you possibly come by something so fine, William?"

"Aye, my friend." Duncan looked equally puzzled. "Such a thing must be worth a king's ransom."

William held up a hand, silencing their questions. "These are all that are left to me of my heritage. This necklace of diamonds and sapphires has been in the Colton family since it was given to the first earl of Redbridge by Queen Elizabeth herself. Since then it has been given to every Colton bride. Our family believes these jewels to be enchanted. You see how they gleam and glow when they touch Molly's skin?"

The others nodded.

"Five years ago I was betrothed to a young woman, Katherine Mansfield, whose family would have added great wealth and prestige to that of my family. I thought I could go through with the marriage. But on the eve of our wedding, when I presented her with this necklace, the clasp refused to close, and the stones turned dim and murky against her skin. I knew it was a sign that we were about to make a terrible mistake, and so I called off our wedding. Because of that, my father disowned me, and told me I would be forever dead to him."

"Oh, my poor William."

He saw the look on Molly's face and touched a fingertip to her lips. "Don't grieve for me, Molly. Even though this is all I have left of that former life,

I know, by the way the stones have come alive against your throat, that I was right to wait for you."

"Oh, my darling." She touched a hand to his cheek, finally understanding the pain she had so often seen in his eyes. "My father once told me, after I returned alone and penniless to care for him, that each step in our lives brings us closer to whatever reward awaits us. Think of this. If you hadn't been forced to endure that humiliation, we could have never had this chance to wed. For the son of an earl would surely have never been permitted to love someone born of such humble parentage as mine."

They looked up as the vicar ascended the altar and stood waiting.

"Are you ready to begin your new life, my darling?"

Molly smiled as she placed her hand on William's arm. Together they approached the altar, with only old Duncan and Tyler to witness the exchange of vows.

As they spoke the final words that would make them one, they heard a commotion in the rear of the chapel. They turned to see a handsome, white-haired man and an elegantly attired woman starting toward them.

"Father? Mother? I don't understand." William blinked, unable to believe his eyes. "Why are you here?"

"It's true, then." The old man helped his wife along the aisle, keeping his hungry gaze fastened on the handsome man his son had become. "Your mother and I heard the rumors that you were to be wed."

As they paused, mere inches apart, William draped an arm around Molly's shoulders, holding her close. "We're already wed. This is my bride, Molly."

The old man reached out to take her hands in his. "You are, at long last, a bride worthy of the Colton name."

He lifted his gaze to the necklace at her throat, the stones glinting with fire. "The Colton necklace suits you, my dear. And from the way it gleams, I know my son has made the right choice."

He turned to his son. "I had no right to try to choose a bride for you. I know now that what you did all those years ago was not only right, but noble. For you were determined to uphold the Colton tradition, even though it meant facing public humiliation. I regret that I've wasted so many years. But I hope you will forgive a foolish old man and accept my apology, William. You were right and I was wrong to cut you out of my life. Your mother and I haven't known a single moment of happiness or peace since that terrible night when last I spoke to you in such a hateful manner and cast you out into the darkness. What's more, while I have watched from afar while you painstakingly cared for Lord Kent's estates, my own have been dwindling without your skill in overseeing them."

William saw the tears sparkling on his mother's lashes, and heard the way his father's voice trembled. It occurred to him that these two old people had paid a much dearer price than he. For while he'd grown up, they'd grown old. While he had discovered new strengths inside himself, his father had discovered his own weaknesses.

He touched a hand to his father's shoulder. "I long dreamed of this day. I spent many sleepless nights, imagining a loving reunion. And then, after more years, I'd given up hope of ever hearing such words from you. You'll never know what it means to me to know that I've earned back your love and respect."

"Then you'll bring your bride to live with us?" The old man's eyes lit with hope. "You'll take your rightful place as heir to my title and take over the care of our estates?"

William's tone gentled. "I'm not the man I was when I left, Father."

The old man took a step back, staring at the stranger who was his son. "I don't understand. What are you telling me, William?"

"Only this. Though I rejoice in your offer, Molly and I share a dream, Father. Of starting a new life in a new land. A land where a man is judged, not by his wealth or titles, but by the goodness in his heart. Where a man can succeed not because of his name, or the cut of his clothes, but by his willingness to work hard."

"You would turn your back on family for some...misadventure?"

William shook his head. "I'll always be proud to be called the son of the earl of Redbridge. But as for the title and the estate, I think they should rightfully go to my brother. I've learned to like being called simply Mr. Colton.'' He turned to his new bride. ''Do you still dream of going to the New World, Molly my love?''

Her eyes were wide with wonder. ''Would we take Duncan and Tyler with us?'' She glanced over at the old man and lad, who were wearing matching looks of amazement.

''Aye, for they're part of our family now. But only if they're willing to risk it.'' He looked over. ''What say you?''

The old man's eyes sparkled. ''I've heard grand things about the place called America.'' He nudged his grandson. ''Would you like to take part in an adventure, lad?''

''Aye, sir.'' The boy's eyes danced with excitement. ''How soon can we go?''

William turned to his parents, seeing the confusion and disappointment in their eyes. ''Someday soon, I think. But first I suggest we return to my childhood home and have the reunion we've all longed for. I'll look over my father's property, and do what I can to see it improved. For whatever time it takes, I'll put all my efforts into restoring not only my family's wealth, but their love as well.''

William caught Molly's hands in his and looked into her eyes. ''In the space of an hour you've become the bride of a titled gentleman, and you're being asked to risk a life of privilege and power for a dream.''

She touched a hand to his cheek in a gesture so endearing, he felt his heart overflow with love. ''Oh, my darling. As long as it's a dream we both share, we risk nothing."

He gathered her close, amazed at the feelings he had for this one small female. Because of her, his life had changed forever. He'd once believed that all that mattered was wealth and title, and a return to his former life. But now he'd found so much more. Laughter and love and a reason to live again. With Molly by his side, he truly believed he could have all that his heart desired.

He caught her hand and started down the aisle, with his beaming parents on either side of them, and his friends trailing happily behind.

What a strange twist of fate, he thought, that had brought them all together. Each of them had been stripped of all that had once mattered. And yet here they were, with shiny new hearts overflowing with love, rejoicing in the knowledge that they would soon embark on a journey to a new land.

But of all the fine adventures to come, William thought with a smile, marriage to Molly would surely prove to be the greatest one of all.

* * * * *

DESTINY'S BRIDE
by Carolyn Zane

To the authors of the entire Colton series,
whose e-mails kept me not only sane,
but laughing hysterically.
You are a classy bunch of dames.
Likewise, you wonderfully wacky editors
who put this project together. I'm baking
you all a delicious batch of Prozac cookies.

Thank you, Lord, for the valleys,
for therein lies the fertile ground for growth.

Chapter 1

Situated high on a cliff above northern California's spectacular sun-drenched coast, a medieval-looking Spanish-style church bustled with prewedding activity. Ocean breezes wafted through lacy palms and seagulls wheeled overhead, their constant cry a herald of sorts on this special occasion. The last of the wedding attendees were just now crowding through the massive mahogany doors and out onto the street as laughing groomsmen put furtive finishing touches on a black stretch limo.

Inside the church, her hand resting lightly in the crook of the tuxedo-clad usher's arm, Elizabeth Mansfield Sonderland waddled down the main aisle of the monolithic Prosperino Community Church's sanctuary. With a polite nod, the usher indicated an empty seat, second pew back on the bride's side—right smack in the center of the row.

Elizabeth hoped he took her grimace to be the smile she'd intended. Obviously, the handsome, yet unenlightened, young man had never been six months pregnant before. Behind her the church was standing room only, so this show would undoubtedly provide the prenuptial entertainment for the fidgeting throng.

She filled her lungs, then exhaled, hoping to somehow shrink, and proceeded to squeeze past pointy knees, tread on shiny shoes and with her belly, knock askew a hat in the front row.

"Sorry." Cheeks pink, she patted her tummy. "Baby on board."

Folks' smiles were indulgent. Finally, she squeezed in next to a grandmotherly type whose gaze flitted from her burgeoning midsection to the aisle to her bare ring finger. Though the woman schooled her face into a polite mask, Elizabeth knew she was searching for the baby's father.

She wanted to say, "He's not coming, as he finds marriage and babies distasteful," but figured that this was neither the time nor place. So, instead Elizabeth chirped an airy "Hello," and then, erecting a wall of serene maternal bliss between them, focused on the altar.

Her dear friend and boarding school roommate, Savannah Hamilton, was taking the plunge again, this beautiful late April afternoon, with the devastatingly handsome business tycoon, Harrison Colton. The couple had wed two weeks ago in Reno, so this wedding was for their family and friends. Though she was thrilled for her friend, Elizabeth couldn't help but harbor serious doubts about the institution of marriage.

Vows, even ones taken twice, weren't necessarily the stuff of happiness. Nor eternal bliss.

Then again, simply because her own marriage hadn't worked out didn't mean Savannah's wouldn't. Disgusted, Elizabeth ground her teeth and silently chided herself for allowing negative thoughts during this joyous occasion. Marshaling her concentration, she forced herself to shift out of her pessimistic mode. There would be time enough to nurse regrets for the rest of her life.

Today, she was here to celebrate.

After a bit, the tempo of the string quartet's music changed and the ushers escorted Harry's mother and grandmother to the front of the church. Once they were seated, the groom, followed by his brother and a plethora of groomsmen emerged onto the altar and turned to face the crowd. A little girl walked down the aisle, working the crowd, a bit of a dance skip in her step as she flung flower petals hither and yon. She was followed by a ring bearer and then a slow and steady parade of bridesmaids.

Had she not been pregnant Elizabeth would have been fitted for one of the beautiful deep purple satin bridesmaid gowns, but alas, it would never fit her generous curves. Savannah's cousin Brenda was wearing what would have been the dress now, as she was a perfect size eight and Elizabeth, well, Elizabeth was a perfect size Volkswagen bug.

The music stalled. The crowd inhaled collectively, then stood as pounding piano chords signaled the bride's arrival. Elizabeth struggled to her feet to watch Savannah glide down the aisle on the arm of her uncle. When at last the beautiful bride was standing next to her groom, the age-old "dearly beloved, we are gathered together to join this man and this woman in holy matrimony" caused Elizabeth's eyes to sting and her throat to burn.

The sweet expression on Harrison's face as he gazed at his bride was so touching. The lump in her throat grew and too late Elizabeth realized that she'd neglected to pack tissues in her purse. After a fruitless search, she dabbed at her cheeks with her wrists. Her gaze darted about for a scrap of something, anything, with which to blow her nose. She was about to use a welcome card tucked into the hymnal holder when the grandmotherly woman at her side loaned her a lacy handkerchief. Elizabeth cast her a grateful glance, then proceeded to blubber into it like a baby.

Hormones.

Had to be. She was usually never this sentimental. Blinking rapidly, she tried to forestall the tide and keep her mascara firmly on her lashes, but it was a losing battle.

As she fought for composure, the best man caught her eye and grinned. She answered with a watery smile and he winked. For a nanosecond, they shared a silent communication. A bond, of sorts, though they were virtual strangers. He inclined his head, ever so slightly, and Elizabeth felt as if they'd shared a lengthy conversation on the tenuous sanctity of love and new beginnings. In that moment, they were simply two people wanting the best for two other people.

Gracious, was he handsome.

Jason Colton. This much, she knew. He was the groom's drop-dead gorgeous brother.

Elizabeth had never shared more than a passing nod of acquaintance with Jason, but more than once Savannah had raved about her future brother-in-law, touting his upstanding moral character and his kind heart. Lips quivering, Elizabeth bit back a sob. He did seem very nice. She sniffed and scrubbed at her face with the inadequate wisp of lace. So very, very nice. At least from where she sat, back here in the second row. After all, he'd winked flirtatiously at her, and there was no disguising the fact that she was, at only six months, already great with child.

And, if the expression on his face was anything to go by, he appeared to be as struck, albeit dry-eyed, by the poignancy of this tender moment as she was. His Adam's apple bobbed above his bow tie, and the muscles in his jaw flexed. Legs spread for balance, hands clasped behind his back, he glanced at the floor, then to the ceiling. After seeming to study the ornate carvings overhead, he swallowed and looked back at his brother and Savannah with an expression that spoke of such love.

Of family ties.

And a yearning perhaps?

Elizabeth couldn't tear her eyes off him.

Savannah liked to say that her future brother-in-law was one of those rare birds who was as beautiful on the inside as he was handsome on the outside.

And he was single, she had confided, flabbergasted that as of yet, no one had reeled him in.

A ragged sigh hiccuped past Elizabeth's lips. Jason did seem like he'd make a nice groom. Too bad she hadn't married *him* four years ago instead of the handsome-on-the-outside-only Mike Sonderland. Not, of course, that it would have made a bit of difference in the long run. She gave her head a little shake. Daydreaming about Jason Colton was stupid, knowing what she knew about her family's dark history with the Coltons.

The ceremony passed in a blurry time warp and before Elizabeth could regroup and drag herself back to reality, Savannah and Harrison were married and striding, arm in arm, down the aisle to begin a new life together. The best man and the matron of honor were next and, as Jason passed her pew, he made a point of smiling directly at her. Elizabeth felt her cheeks flush, but persuaded herself it was only a prenatal hot flash of some kind.

Elizabeth turned to press the damp handkerchief back into her elderly seatmate's hand, but the woman patted her arm and said, "You keep it, honey. I have a feeling you're going to need it again."

Deciding to decipher the subtext later, Elizabeth nodded. "Thank you."

In the church's grand foyer, the wedding party had already formed a receiving line by the time Elizabeth had been swept back down the aisle by the crowd. Falling into place, she stood, waiting her turn to impart her best wishes.

Savannah squealed when she saw her.

"Elizabeth! I'm so glad you were here to share this moment with me!"

"Oh, honey, I wouldn't have missed it for the world. I'm so happy for you. It was a beautiful ceremony."

"It was, wasn't it? I can't believe we managed to put it together in two weeks. I'm just glad it's over!" Savannah laughed and her new husband swept Elizabeth into his embrace.

"Hey, beautiful."

"Harrison, you always know just what to say to a woman. Is it too late for us?" Elizabeth teased and reached up to lightly pat his cheek.

"Sad, but true." He winked at his wife and touched her hand as if afraid he might wake up from this dream and find her gone. "Savannah is my better half now, but I sure hate to let a dishy fish like you wiggle off the line. Maybe we could be in-laws someday." He grinned and jerked a thumb at Jason, who had just had his cheek smeared a coral pink by Elizabeth's grandmotherly seatmate. "My brother is available. And he likes kids. Don'cha, bro?"

"I like you, don't I?" Jason quipped.

"Oh, well, that's a must in this situation." Flustered, Elizabeth tried to keep the banter light, but embarrassment buzzed in her ears. Flirting with single men was certainly not part of her usual repartee. Especially given her condition.

"I don't believe we've formally met," Jason said,

grasping her hand and not seeming to take anything his brother said too seriously. "I'm Harrison's older brother, Jason, and you are my dear sister-in-law's partner in crime from the old boarding school days, I gather."

"Yes, I'm Elizabeth Sonderland. It's so nice to finally meet you. I've heard so much."

"All good, I expect. Well, don't believe a word of it." His sparkling whiskey-colored eyes and minxish grin were mesmerizing.

"Suddenly, I don't."

He continued to hold her hand, seeming not to have any intention of giving it up soon. Normally, Elizabeth would have become uncomfortable with this breach of her personal space, but not now. He had no motive, other than good-natured interest in Savannah's friend, she could just tell. His hand, so strong and warm, enveloped hers, infusing her with such a feeling of happiness. Of rightness.

Elizabeth took a mental snapshot. It was one of those moments in time when everything seemed simply perfect. The magic of the afternoon sun streamed into the foyer from a skylight above, backlighting this golden, soft-focus tableau, and the harp music that tinkled behind them was ethereal. Birds chirped outside, a fountain bubbled inside and all around them, people were smiling and hugging and filled with sublime joy.

Realizing that she was staring, Elizabeth blinked and a nervous giggle bubbled up from somewhere in the vicinity of the baby.

"When are you due?" Jason inquired, and folded

his other hand over the top of the hand he already held.

"End of July." She squared her shoulders, knowing that broad shoulders could reduce the appearance of the waistline, and then sagged. She could tell by his expression that it was a mug's game.

His chuckle was warm. "You're coming along nicely."

She sighed, knowing that this maternity getup did nothing to slenderize. "Thanks."

"Who's your OB?"

"Dr. Mhan."

"Ah. Good man. No pun intended."

"You know him?"

"We interned together over at Prosperino Medical Center about five years ago."

"You're an OB?" Good heavens. Elizabeth couldn't envision peeping over the end of the table and seeing that gorgeous face smiling up at her during a prenatal exam.

"No, I'm a GP. But I've delivered my share of babies."

"Really?"

"Mmm. I rank those moments among the highlights of my life. Right up there with today." His grin was so easy, so engaging, so sexy, that Elizabeth could almost believe that he was including her in this equation. "So, how have you been feeling?"

"Pretty terrific, actually. I know a lot of women hate being pregnant, but to be truthful, I've never felt better, physically speaking."

"You're one of the lucky ones."

"I guess."

"Getting plenty of exercise?"

"I do those prenatal water aerobics where a bunch of us get into the pool and bob around and pretend we're working." She eyed him with suspicion. "Why, do I need to lose a few?" Worry niggled at the back of her mind. She knew she shouldn't have eaten those brownies for breakfast.

"No, not at all. You look really fit. I was wondering what your secret was."

"Not to interrupt your client consult, brother, but there are some people here from Europe champing at the bit to say hello to you," Harrison interjected.

Elizabeth's heart fell. Time to move on.

With lingering regret—real or imagined on her part—Jason let her fingers slide from his own. "Take care," he murmured.

"I will," she answered, her tone equally intimate, much to her mortification. She cleared her throat. "Bye." The word came out a little more forcefully, a little more formally, than she'd intended, but, well, *que sera.*

"Jason!" a gnarled crone croaked. "Come here and let me smack you for making me wait to kiss you."

"Grandma Sybil!"

Jason folded his ancient grandmother in a tender embrace and the moment was over.

"So, sonny, when are you going to get it in gear and get yourself married?" Sybil demanded, squinting up at him as she fiddled with her hearing aid.

"Don't make me wait. I'm not into waiting these days." Her dry cackle was filled with good humor.

Jason cast a long-suffering glance at Elizabeth as she moved off to make small talk with cousin Brenda, the wearer of the divine gown that she was to have worn.

Elizabeth smiled. Yes, she thought with a sigh as the magic moment that had been hers too briefly, struck midnight, life continued to go on. The baby gave her a healthy kick and once again, she was a single pumpkin.

Finally, the multitude of guests were herded through the line and into the church's lush, beautifully landscaped wedding garden off the back of the sanctuary. Over a century old, the Spanish-style courtyard was secluded and romantic with its statues and fountains, yet large enough to host a sizable reception. Lavishly appointed tables for the sit-down dinner were scattered about under a number of huge, gauzy white tents, and a mouthwatering buffet was positioned up against a long, stucco wall. An orchestra played sweeping waltz music, encouraging the bride and groom to take to the floor for the traditional first dance.

In a blurry haze, Elizabeth peeped through her handkerchief and watched Savannah whirl across the worn-smooth cobblestone dance floor on the arm of her new husband. When Savannah's father cut in, Harrison turned to his mother. These two couples were joined by the best man and the matron of honor, and again, Elizabeth found her attention riveted to Jason Colton as he led his attractive partner around the floor.

What would it be like to dance with him? A bit like floating, perhaps. She glanced ruefully down to her tummy. Then again, perhaps not. She needed to find a seat. There was a stitch in her side that had been bothering her all morning.

Suddenly, she was starving and moved into the buffet line. When in doubt, eat. That had become her motto, of late. After filling her plate, she settled at a table and introduced herself to what had to be a dozen Coltons of various shapes and sizes, from seemingly all corners of the earth. Again, she used her married name, to keep from having to dredge up the unfortunate history between the Mansfields and the Coltons, and then skillfully erected her vacant wall to avoid small talk.

She trained her covert gaze on Jason and nibbled at her food and noticed that he seemed to make a point of catching her eye now and again. Probably out of a sense of medical duty, she supposed, but still, it was nice. He was definitely the belle of the ball, if a man could be such a thing. Women were practically lined up to dance with him, fawning and palavering. To Elizabeth he appeared to be the John-John of this giant Colton family. And, though he had his pick of the crop of single, young beauties, he chose to slowly whirl his decrepit Grandma Sybil around the dance floor, causing her cheeks to pinken and her eyes to sparkle.

Elizabeth took a moment to dab her cheeks and blow her nose. Savannah was right. He really and truly was very nice. Once the waltz had ended and Jason had escorted his grandmother back to her seat, he made a beeline toward Elizabeth.

At first, Elizabeth thought he might be heading to the buffet table directly behind her, as he hadn't had a chance to eat yet. But now, much to her consternation, she realized that he was heading straight for her. But why? Had he remembered that he needed to impart some prenatal advice regarding not overdoing at the wedding buffet? She glanced at her loaded plate. Well, he was too late for that.

Her heart seemed to pause in its pounding to allow her to hear his whispered words as he dipped low and brought his face even with hers.

"Care to dance?"

What? Yes! No, wait!

Dance? Here? Now? In her condition? Flustered, she glanced down at her navy-blue maternity dress and noticed that her napkin had shifted and she'd dripped a bit of salad dressing on her stomach. Figured.

The music started and she knew she had to give him an answer.

No. There was no way she was going to follow the best-looking man at this shindig to center stage and stumble all over his feet. Gathering her courage, she looked up into his liquidy, intoxicatingly beautiful brown eyes and felt herself go all mushy.

"Yes, I'd love to dance," she heard herself murmur and, taking his hand, rose to her feet and followed him through the endless sea of eyes.

His hands were gentle as he positioned one at

what was left of her waist and the other in her own hand. With seeming effortlessness, he guided her around the floor, and suddenly Elizabeth knew why his Grandma Sybil had looked sixty years younger in his arms.

"Do you make it a point of dancing with all the wallflowers?" She smiled up into his attractive face and watched the lines fork at the corners of his eyes.

"No. But I always make it a point to dance with the most interesting women in the group."

"And I'm interesting?"

"You tell me."

Oh, she was interesting all right. In an I-don't-care-to-talk-about-it kind of way. Months of practice made changing the subject easy. "Savannah was right about you, you know."

"Uh-oh."

"No uh-oh. She thinks you're very kindhearted."

"She hasn't seen the limo yet."

"What did you do?"

"Nothing much. Just a bit of shoe polish and shaving cream. A few cans, some balloons, streamers." He shrugged. "Naked blow-up dolls, lipstick prints on the mirrors, fancy underwear on the antenna, you know, the regular."

She laughed. "Naked blow-up dolls are the regular?"

"It's payback time for all the times he tortured me when we were kids. Besides, somebody has to drive."

Again, the mirth bubbled. "I can't wait to see this."

"You shouldn't have to. Won't be long now. Their plane takes off in two hours so they're going to have to toss the garter and the bouquet and high-tail it outta here."

As Jason swept her around the floor, Elizabeth laughed the carefree laughter of days gone by. Days filled with hope for the future. Her own wedding seemed like a lifetime ago. Something about Jason made her forget she wasn't innocent and slim and newly divorced. Something about Jason made her feel alive again.

The twisting pain in her stomach was killing her. Doubled over at the very top of the long cascade of steps that led from the front of the old church to the street, Elizabeth took a deep breath and cast frantic eyes about for a place to sit. This shouldn't be happening. It was too early. A scream rose in her throat and lodged there in frozen silence.

Everything seemed to turn to slow motion in Elizabeth's anguished mind. A cloud stole across the sun, casting a sudden chill over the landscape. The crowd's cheers and laughter roared in her ears and she felt suddenly light-headed. Disoriented. Panicky. Reaching out, she groped for a hand, hoping that someone might help her find a place to land, but there was no one.

Savannah was standing with Harrison at the church's enormous entrance doors. Lined up at the bottom of the long flight of concrete steps, single women flocked, eager to catch the bouquet. There was much movement and chaos as the flowers flew through the air and were caught by a squealing girl who did not look old enough to date, let alone marry.

Amid a shower of rice, Savannah and Harrison rushed down the church steps and were swept away in the gaudily decorated limo.

Still standing off on the sidelines, behind the waving crowd, Elizabeth clutched a low stone wall and sank to her knees as another pain bore down on her belly.

She was losing the baby.

On Savannah's wedding day, no less.

Tears, this time of terror, sprang to her eyes, and she fiddled in her pocket for the lacy handkerchief she'd been given earlier.

"Elizabeth?"

Jason's soothing voice seemed to come to her through the fog. Was she dreaming?

"Elizabeth, are you all right?"

"Oh, Jason," she cried, grasping his hand so tightly, she feared she might pull his thumb from the socket. "The baby. I think I'm losing the baby."

Chapter 2

Even six months' pregnant, Elizabeth was surprisingly light. With very little effort, Jason lifted her into his arms and, pushing the heavy mahogany door open with his foot, ignored the curious stares of friends and family. With a professional sense of purpose, he carried her back into the church, through the lobby and into the now eerily silent sanctuary. Her head was tucked against the crook of his neck, her silky brown hair tickling his chin, filling his senses with the scent of spring flowers. Low moans emanated from deep in her throat and he couldn't be sure if these were from the pain or fear.

Or both.

Taking great care, Jason lowered her to a pew in the back. He kept her gathered against his side as he found her wrist and took her pulse. With the exception of some giggling kids playing tag in the lobby, they were alone. When he spoke, his voice echoed off the high ceiling.

"Where is your husband?" He schooled his voice to reflect a calm confidence that he didn't really feel. There was something very special about this woman. A vulnerability she tried—without much success—to mask brought out the protective streak in him.

"Greener pastures."

"Is that a restaurant?"

"No. That's his new residence."

"Oh." Though he remained carefully neutral on the outside, inside the cogs were turning. So, this was why Savannah and Harrison had been teasing her about becoming an in-law. He'd thought it had been idle chitchat designed to get them all acquainted, so he'd played along. But it seemed that she and her baby had been abandoned. His gaze strayed to her bare ring finger and a muscle in his jaw jumped as he swallowed back his anger.

He switched his focus to the second hand on his watch and timed her pulse. Strong. A little fast. He touched her brow with his fingertips and then her cheeks with the back of his hand.

"He didn't want kids." Elizabeth lifted a limp hand to her mouth and valiantly fought the tears. "And now it looks like he's going to get his wish."

"Not necessarily. Try to relax."

"I can't," she moaned. "I'm terrified that I'm losing the baby."

"I know." While his hand was at her face, he tugged a stray strand of hair from her lips. He could tell that she knew as well as he did that having the baby now would present untold complications. "Tell me about the pains."

"Right here." She pressed the palm of her hand low against the side of her belly. "And here."

"Sharp or dull?" He followed her hands with his own, probing, palpating for the baby's position.

"Sharp. Not like a cramp, really, but more...I don't know. Like something tore."

"Here?"

"Yes."

"Mmm." He moved his hand to where the she'd indicated pain and prodded again. "Does this hurt?"

"Not really."

"Mmm."

"What, mmm?"

"Just mmm. No deeper medical nuances. Do you feel nauseated?"

"No."

"Mmm. Faint?"

"Not anymore."

"Are you on any medications?"

"No, just prenatal vitamins."

"Any spotting or bleeding?"

She blanched and looked to him for reassurance. "I don't think so."

"Okay, then. Where is your purse?"

"Uh..." She glanced around. "Out on the front steps, I think."

"Wait here, and I'll get it and then pull my car around and we'll go."

"Where?"

"To the hospital."

Alarm filled her eyes, filling her expression with dread. "The hospital? Jason, will my baby be all right?"

He took her slender fingers and twined them with his own. Gathering as much professional demeanor as he could muster, given the personal interest he was taking in her, he nodded and winked. "This is just a precaution. We want to make sure junior stays where he is, for a few more months anyway. Try not to worry. You'll be in good hands. There is an excellent chance the baby will be fine."

"Okay." Elizabeth sagged against his arm and nodded. Light streamed through the stained-glass impression of Jesus in the clouds, high in the apex of the nave behind the altar. Tears welling in her eyes, voice faltering, she whispered, "From your mouth to God's ears."

"What did they say?" Elizabeth pushed herself up on her elbows as Jason came into her hospital room, carrying a chart. She tried not to let her anxiety show, but it was becoming increasingly difficult. They'd been here in the maternity ward at Prosperino Medical Center for nearly an hour now and Elizabeth had been examined by everyone but the receptionist, it seemed.

The strong, steady beep of the fetal monitor had been the one lulling factor as she lay in bed, waiting for someone to return and tell her what all the tests and consultations indicated.

Jason's carriage was confident as he moved to her

bedside, and from her angle, he was all shoulders and broad chest and safety. He'd taken off his jacket and rolled up his sleeves, and against the white cotton of his dress shirt, good-size biceps strained.

"Dr. Mhan wants you to spend the night."

"Why?" She clutched the rails at the sides of her bed.

"Precautionary measure. Nothing more." He tapped her chart and smiled. "Right now he says there are no indications that this is a miscarriage."

"Oh, thank God!" Elizabeth fell back against her pillows and laughed with dozens of emotions that when combined, equaled blessed relief. "That's wonderful news."

Jason's pleased smile pushed creases into the corners of his eyes, and nudging her knee over, he settled at the edge of the mattress. "This calls for a celebration. How about I order us up a big old bowl of Jell-O?"

"Jell-O?" She could feel her face fall. "I was thinking more along the lines of a burger and fries. And a shake."

His pleasant laughter rumbled as he reached for her bedside buzzer and called the nurse on duty. "You are feeling better."

"Relieved. What was the problem, anyway?"

"Well, as near as we can tell, you were simply having a few growing pains. Since this is your first baby, your uterine muscles are tight. You are a small woman and junior seems to be on the big side. He was making some more room for himself in there and was probably a little more aggressive in his remolding than you were ready for."

"Oh." Elizabeth propped her elbows on her knees and eyed him, a small smile tugging at her mouth. "Why do you keep referring to the baby as 'him'?"

"You don't know the baby's sex?"

"Sounds like it's a boy."

"Do you want to know for sure?"

She sighed. "I guess. Although I was hoping for a girl. Thought it would be easier to raise a girl, without a father, you know."

She had no idea why she felt so inclined to confide in Jason. Other than it was easier to divulge private matters to a stranger than to an old friend sometimes. Especially a doctor stranger. A doctor stranger with sympathetic eyes the color of honey-soft leather.

He nodded. "Yes, I know. But not having a father can be hard on a girl, too."

"That's true. It was on me."

"I'm sorry." He folded her hand between his and gazed into her eyes, and Elizabeth knew a peace and comfort that transcended time. She felt as if she'd known him forever. It was strange.

"It's all right. He died a long time ago when I was very little."

"Do you remember him?"

"Some. Though most of my memories of him are sparked by pictures and stories my mother tells, I'm sure." Elizabeth fiddled with her covers with her free hand. "According to her, he was a paragon of virtue and a pillar of Prosperino society. Unfortunately, after his death, life was a bit of a downhill slide for the rest of us."

"That's rough."

"Mm-hmm. Mom had to take on extra jobs to keep me in the boarding school I attended with Savannah and I remember worrying about her a lot." Unconsciously, Elizabeth patted her baby. "I don't want my child to have those kinds of worries." She looked up at Jason's sympathetic expression and was compelled to continue. "Anyway, when Mike—an old friend of the family—proposed, Mom was relieved that I'd finally be taken care of and no longer her responsibility. I was never really head over heals for Mike. But mom seemed so happy, you know? So, like a good little girl, I got married."

"You married him more for her sake, than for yourself."

"Unfortunately." She heaved a noisy sigh and flopped back against the pillows. "But enough about me and my idiotic decisions. I don't know why I'm blathering on at you this way. Usually I'm much more reserved. Honest."

The light in his eyes turned playful. "I think your blather is interesting." Reluctantly, he patted and let go of her hand. "You know," he said, a slow grin transforming his handsome face, "boys might not be as interesting to dress, but they can be a lot of fun."

At his winsome expression, Elizabeth felt the laughter bubble up once again. Too bad Mike and she had never had such carefree conversations. Mike was always so uptight and controlling. When he was home.

"So," she said. "I take it it's a boy."

Jason nodded. "The ultrasound indicates that it's a big, healthy one. Those things have been known to be wrong now and again, but still, I wouldn't go painting the nursery pink. In any event, he needs to stay put for a while longer."

"Do you think he will?"

"Chances are good that you won't be back here for another three months."

"That's wonderful."

"Yep. Now. Is there anyone I can call for you? Let people know where you are and what you might need?"

Elizabeth pursed her lips and thought. "I'm sure there is... Let's see. Of course, Mike's parents are out of the question." Angling her head, she regarded him, still struck by the ease with which he inspired confidence. Must be a doctor thing. "His dad ran off when he was a baby."

"Like father, like son."

"Sadly we had the fatherless thing in common. And now, our baby..." She swallowed and blinked, then with a stoic breath, continued. "Anyway, his mother is in Florida, not that she would care anyway, as she's busy jet-setting and loath to become a granny."

Jason leaned toward her, his pose pensive. "I take it Mike is completely out of the question?"

"Completely. Our divorce was final two months ago, and he relinquished all parental rights to the baby. Made it clear he never wants anything to do with us again.''

Jason shook his head.

Elizabeth smiled resignedly. ''I know. Anyway, he's not even in California anymore. Last I heard, he was in Europe, looking for love in all the wrong places.''

''What about your family?''

''My mom lives up in Alaska with my sister and her husband. They run a really neat fishing resort up there. I'd call them, but I hate to worry them when there's nothing they can do from there. Besides, they're all planning on coming down in July to give me a hand, which will cost them a bundle since that's peak tourist season for them.''

''Friends?''

''Well, two of my best friends are on a singles cruise to Mexico, so they're out. I have a really nice neighbor, but she has three little kids and one compact car. Savannah is busy...''

Jason cocked a brow and shot her a sly look. ''But you know she's the type to drop everything and come running if she thinks you're in trouble.'' He reached for the phone.

Squealing, Elizabeth batted at his hand. ''Don't you dare call them on their wedding night!''

With mock disappointment, he set the phone back into the cradle. ''Spoilsport.''

''I think you've done quite enough to embarrass them for one day.''

''Oh, now come on. I saw you laughing during my toast to the bride and groom.''

"Yes, I'll admit, the rundown of his past loves was amusing. Especially the part about him dating the girl who modeled for gorilla cookies. You had to have made some of that up."

"Ninety percent, yes. Harrison was wild, but not *that* wild. He'll probably kill me when they get back."

A lovely young nurse entered the room as he was speaking.

"Hi, Dr. Colton." Her smile warm, she moved to the edge of the bed. "You rang?" She placed a light hand on his shoulder and Elizabeth hated herself for wondering how well they knew each other.

"Yep. Sherry, it seems our patient is ready for dinner. I don't suppose you could rustle us up a burger and fries?"

"Well, that's a good sign. Even so—" the nurse glanced at her wrist "—I don't think the cafeteria is grilling at this hour. How about a turkey club?"

"With chips and a chocolate shake?"

"For you, anything." She patted and rubbed his shoulder, then fingers trailing, disappeared to find them sustenance.

"Sherry is married to an oncologist whose clinic is across the street. He's a great golfer. We try to hit the links at least once a month."

Elizabeth did her best not to show her vast relief. "You golf?"

"I'm an addict."

"Me, too! But I'm horrible."

"I can imagine the little guy interferes with your swing."

"Yes. And no. I'm pretty much horrible all the time. But I love it! I play with my girlfriends whenever I can. They're all really bad too, but we don't care."

"We'll have to go someday. I can take a look at your swing."

"That would be fun," she agreed with much enthusiasm, then realized that she'd just accepted a date from Dr. Handsome. Ridiculous. She couldn't go golfing with him. She would have a baby and diapers and all manner of single-parent worries to deal with in a few months. He didn't want to go out with her. He was simply being nice.

Luckily, the conversation moved from golf to other sports and then to sports on TV, other kinds of TV shows, to movies, to books, to current events, and then, when Sherry returned with the food, to restaurants. By the time they were finished eating and the debris from their meal had been cleared away, Elizabeth had been subjected to another round of routine exams and it was getting late.

"You'll probably need to be getting home," Elizabeth mused, hoping against hope that he wouldn't. Something about Savannah's new brother-in-law made Elizabeth feel all tingly and alive and girlishly high school in ways that she never actually felt back in the stuffy, terminally strict all-girl boarding school.

He checked his watch. "It's only eight. Savannah would have my head if I left you and junior all alone just yet. Besides, I don't have anything waiting for me at home but a fridge full of TV dinners and a pile of work."

"Sounds like my life."

"It's up to you. Kick me out if you're tired. But I could stay for a while and we could play cards."

"I'm never too tired for a card game." Inside, Elizabeth was thrilled. Spending more time with Jason would certainly take, and keep, her mind off her troubles.

"Great." He stood and walked to the door. "I know the nurses keep some spare decks at their station. We can play double solitaire or something."

"So, you're a teacher."

"Mm-hmm. Although some days it feels more like a referee."

"What grade do you teach?"

"Sixth."

"Glutton for punishment?"

Elizabeth laughed as she dealt out the cards and the girlish flush on her cheeks was mesmerizing. She was such a little doll. Jason couldn't remember the last time he'd so enjoyed a woman's company. Her ex-husband had to be a first-class fool to give up such a jewel.

They'd been playing cards all evening, moving from pinochle to rummy to poker to old maid, but he couldn't begin to tell who'd won and who'd lost, as holding the cards had become an excuse for holding a conversation.

When she didn't think he was looking, Jason studied her features and lost himself in their exotic beauty. Her light, nearly sea-green eyes were large and almond shaped and as expressive as a tropical day in the South Pacific. They sparked and snapped with sunny warmth, though he'd noted the occasional storm clouds that spoke of her more sensitive side. Shoulder length and silky straight, except for where the ends waved under, her hair was the color of rich teakwood, threaded with gold. From personal experience, he knew it was as soft as it looked and smelled of wild meadow flowers. His covert gaze dipped to her mouth and quickly back to the cards she laid out on the rolling table that swung out over her lap. Her full-lipped, pearl-white smile was one within which he could be content to bask, in favor of the sun. Jason was drawn to her on a level that he'd never been to a patient before and he'd doctored his share of beauties.

There was definitely something different about Elizabeth.

She pushed herself up, warming to the topic of her career choice. "The sixth grade is tough in an I-could-kill-them-I-could-kiss-them kind of way."

He leaned back against the end of the bed and encouraged her to continue with his silence.

She raised and dropped a shoulder. "They can frustrate the heck out of me, yes, but they can be so funny, too. The girls can have lip gloss and a milk mustache at the same time."

Jason arched a brow. "Now there's a look."

Elizabeth's shoulders bobbed and her mirth rocketed up his spine, causing his own laughter to rise. "They're all very curious about my pregnancy and love to regale me with horror stories of childbirth that they have no doubt overheard from their own folks."

"It is a very dramatic age." Jason chuckled. "Don't take those stories too seriously. You're healthy, the baby is healthy, you'll have a beautiful birth experience. Do you have a labor coach?"

"No. Do I need one?"

"It might be a good idea to have someone there that you feel comfortable bossing around, for ice chips and such."

"Oh." Her eyes flitted about the room as if the subject embarrassed her. A long, weary sigh hissed past her lips. "I suppose I'll have to break down and ask somebody. I don't want to ask my mother, because she's so squeamish. My sister has a business to run, and I don't want to bother Savannah, her being a newlywed and all. I don't know. It's just another thing to do. To worry about."

"You're tired." He glanced at the clock. "And it's no wonder. How did it get to be nearly midnight already?" He swept the cards into a pile. "We can play again later. Right now, I'll get your blood pressure and temp and listen to the baby. Then it's off to dreamland for you, young lady."

"Okay." He could see that she was stifling her yawn for his benefit.

He pulled the blood pressure cuff off its hanger on the wall near her bed. Nudging the sleeve of her gown up, he slipped it on over the smooth muscle of her biceps and popped his stethoscope into his ears. The steady beat of her heart picked up in tempo, just slightly, as he laid her arm in his lap and pumped air into the cuff. Blood pressure was good. The nurse had left a digital ear thermometer, so he took her temperature and noted these readings on her chart.

Then he listened to the baby's heart rate, which was falling into a healthy normal range for a boy, and he smiled. If he had it to do all over again, he might go into obstetrics. Pregnant women were especially beautiful and there was nothing more magical and happy, usually, than childbirth.

"All very good." He pulled his stethoscope back down around his neck.

"Good," she breathed and leaned back against the pillows, limp with mental exhaustion.

"Any Braxton Hicks contractions?"

"You know..." Her yawn was a high, squeaky affair that made him want to crawl into bed and spoon her and whisper in the dark about all of those secrets that were too private for the fluorescent glare of reality. To really get to know each other in an accelerated fashion.

It shocked him, how badly he wanted to know her. All about her. Now.

She blinked up at him and his heart went into a free fall. "I've heard of those. What are they, anyway?"

He settled himself back to the edge of the bed where he'd spent the better part of his evening and let the chart drop to his lap. Noisily, he cleared his throat and donned his serious Dr. Colton expression. "Well, they vary in description from woman to woman, but usually it's a uterine contraction that radiates from the back around to about here.'' He laid his hand on her belly. ''It grips the baby and your tummy feels hard, like a basketball, for a minute or so, and then it relaxes. I guess you could say it's a rehearsal for the big event. You're a little early in the pregnancy for those.''

Eyes at half-mast, hair flowing over the pillowcase, she turned onto her side and, peering at him, asked, ''How do you remember all this stuff?''

''Just interested, I guess. I've always really liked babies.'' He grinned. ''And their mothers.''

''Oh.'' Her smile was as warm and alluring as morning light. ''That is...very sweet.''

He pulled the covers up under her chin and again she fought to stifle another yawn. Lashes fluttered against porcelain cheeks and her breathing became deep and regular, almost immediately.

''You get some rest,'' he whispered needlessly, for Elizabeth was already asleep.

Elizabeth woke to the feeling of someone slipping a blood-pressure cuff around her upper arm. She squinted through the shadows to make out the serene smile of nurse Sherry.

''I didn't want to wake you.'' Her voice was low and pleasant as she went efficiently through her routine and made notations on Elizabeth's chart. ''How are you feeling?''

''Very well, thank you.'' Except for the sinking realization that she'd fallen asleep on Dr. Wonderful and he was no doubt home and out of her life now.

She sighed, the empty chasm in her heart splitting just that much wider.

"I'll bet it doesn't hurt to have such a handsome guardian angel looking out after you." Sherry's smile was indulgent as she glanced over her shoulder.

Abruptly craning her neck out over the edge of the bed, Elizabeth followed the path of nurse Sherry's eyes with her own and her heart caught in her throat. For there, stretched out on a rolling recliner near the window, Jason lay, softly snoring. His arm dangled over the edge of the chair, and at some point, it appeared that Sherry had covered him with a blanket. The sight of his gentle expression filled Elizabeth with a poignant sense of security and happiness that she hadn't felt in far too long.

It was very quiet in the hospital at this hour. So quiet in fact that the early birds' twitters filtered through the reinforced glass. The cool morning rays of the sun were just prodding the shadows on their way, illuminating Jason's face. The beginnings of a beard darkened his jaw, and his hair fell over his forehead in a most appealing manner. She could learn to wake up to this picture every morning.

"He's still here?" Elizabeth was incredulous.

Sherry jotted more notes on her chart, then nodded at Jason. "He's been here all night."

"All night? What time is it?"

"Almost five. I get off in an hour and a half." The nurse donned a stethoscope and, planting it on Elizabeth's belly, listened. "I tried to convince him that I wouldn't forget you, but he wouldn't budge.

Said something about his sister-in-law murdering him in his bed if he didn't take good care of you." Sherry chuckled. "I think he's taking this new in-law thing pretty seriously."

"She thinks very highly of him."

"Everyone does."

"I can't figure out why he's not married."

Sherry removed her stethoscope and picked up her chart from where she'd left it on Elizabeth's belly. "He nearly was."

"What happened?"

Sherry shrugged and glanced over her shoulder. "He won't mind my telling. It's not like everyone around here doesn't already know." She sank to the edge of the bed and paused to scribble so intently on the chart, that Elizabeth feared Sherry might not finish the story. "Everything looks normal, which is excellent. You'll need to take it easy for a few days and monitor any unusual pains you might have. No lifting, strenuous exercise, kickboxing, that type of thing." Sherry grinned, and Elizabeth couldn't help but smile. Still, she wished Sherry would stick to the subject.

"If you have any questions, don't hesitate to call."

Elizabeth nodded. *Right, right, right.*

"I know he wouldn't care if you called him." Sherry flicked her wrist in Jason's direction. "He's a sucker for babies. Which, by the way, is why his engagement didn't last."

Finally, back on track.

"Really?" Elizabeth did her best to seem casual

and was glad the light was such that it disguised the bright spots of interest burning in her cheeks.

"Yeah," Sherry's voice was hushed and filled with tenderness. "In spite of his demanding career, his impressive pedigree and his to-die-for looks, he's a real family man at heart, I think."

"He seems to be very close to his brother."

"Yes, that whole Colton clan is thick as thieves." Sherry settled back against the footboard and squinted off into the past. "Last year he fell in love with a surgery nurse in the cardio department. Angelica Maldonado. Angie led him to believe that she wanted kids as much as he did. But a few days before the wedding all hell broke lose when he discovered that she had no intention of ever ruining her figure by having a baby and was only marrying him to get her hands on his money."

"How awful!" Elizabeth gasped, scandalized that anyone could treat such a sweet man so horribly.

"Oh, it was a mess all right. Invitations had been sent out, dresses bought, the works. Yesterday's deal must have been hard on him."

"Mmm," Elizabeth murmured in wordless agreement. Nearly as hard on him as it had been on her, it seemed. No wonder he'd been so reluctant to leave her last night. To return home to the echoes of regret held no appeal. She couldn't blame him for wanting to hang out with a pregnant woman and play cards. What safer place on earth could there be?

"Yeah." Sherry stood and moving to Jason's side, adjusted his covers and chuckled at his snorings as he shifted position. She crossed back to the bed and cocked a hip on the side rail. "Money can be a curse. You know, their family has a ton of money and more than their share of troubles."

"I've heard, yes." Elizabeth sighed. She knew a lot about the Colton family. Especially when it came to how much the Coltons despised the Mansfields.

"He doesn't have to work, but I think he does to give his life a sense of reality. And to give back to society. He's a real down-to-earth kind of guy."

"He is special." Too special for her, she decided, her heart heavy at the thought. Better for her to nip her crush in the bud. There were far too many insurmountable obstacles to overcome to ever dream that they could have a relationship.

Sherry gave Elizabeth's knee a pat before she stepped to the door. "You'll be released before my next shift, so if I don't see you again, good luck with your baby."

"Thank you."

Elizabeth snuggled down under her covers, watched Jason sleep and, against her better judgment, daydreamed that yesterday's wedding had been their own. Her eyes slid shut, and as she drifted off, the daydreams became real dreams. Dreams that she and Jason were awaiting the birth of the life they'd created from an undying sense of commitment and, most importantly, love.

I, Jason, take this woman to be my lawfully wedded wife. To have and to hold, to love and to cherish, from this day forward...

Oh, yes, it was a lovely dream. So warm and happy and real. So real in fact, she could almost swear she heard his sexy baritone murmuring her name as his lips touched her temple. Her ear. Her cheek.

Elizabeth. Elizabeth.

Chapter 3

"Elizabeth."

A warm, strong hand held hers, and she traced the knuckles with the pad of her thumb.

"Elizabeth?"

"Yes?" Lashes fluttering, Elizabeth struggled to surface from her dream. Jason's handsome face loomed before her, a mere whisper away, and she breathed deeply, smiling with sublime joy. It *was* real. He was here. Oh, this was paradise.

Elizabeth stretched the languid stretch of a cat napping in a sunny window seat. This was real and delicious and so very wonderful. His eyes sparkled, a reflection of what shone in hers, no doubt.

"Hey, sleepyhead, it's time to rock and roll."

"Hmm?" Her laughter was deep and throaty.

"It's nine o'clock. We've gotta check out of this

joint in less than an hour. Can you shower and do your beauty thing by then?''

''What?'' Elizabeth bolted upright in bed as reality came crashing down. With wide eyes she glanced at her surroundings and the details of yesterday's emergency suddenly came flooding back. Flopping forward, she drew up her knees, buried her head in her hands and groaned. She didn't even want to know what she looked like. Jason probably thought birds had been nesting in her hair, and her makeup and breath surely left something to be desired.

Though, why she cared so much what he thought now remained a mystery. It wasn't as if she were at her peppy best all day yesterday, what with the running mascara and shiny, red nose. But still, a girl—even a six-months-pregnant girl with smeared makeup and bad hair—had her pride.

And there he was, all minty fresh and looking *GQ* in his clean jeans and not too tight yet revealing just the same T-shirt. The stinker had even shaved and splashed on a dab of something lightly intoxicating on his jaw. He must have gone home to shower and come back already.

She yanked a sheet over her head. ''Mornin','' she mumbled.

''You feeling all right?''

She nodded, huddled against her knees, refusing to sit up and meet his eye.

''You sure?''

She nodded again.

His voice was leaden with humor. "Would you like me to leave?"

"No!" She could hear his laughter rumbling from deep within his fabulous granite chest, and it was contagious. Her laughter harmonized with his as she tugged off the sheet—her hair even worse now from the static—and pointed at him. "I think it's only fair to warn you that now that you've seen me looking like this, I'm going to have to kill you."

Jason hooted. "Listen, baby, I've seen interns who looked just like you for a solid year. And don't even get me started on some of my autopsy work. I think you look just fine. A little scruffy, maybe, but in a beautiful way. Besides, you can't kill me. At least not before I get your blood pressure."

She harrumphed. "Whatever it is, it's wrong."

"Let me be the judge of that," he said, his low laughter easy as he took her arm in his hands. After he'd run through the requisite tests, he snagged her chart from the end of the bed and began reading Sherry's notations. "Okay Ms.—" his eyes flicked from the chart to her face and back "—Mansfield? Wait a minute. I thought your name was Sonderland."

"It was." She peered at him for any sign of anger, but there was none. In fact, there didn't seem to be much reaction to the Mansfield name at all.

"Oh, reverting to your maiden name, huh?" He jotted numbers in various columns and then moved to the end of her bed and hung her chart.

"Yes." The word was a squeaky peep. Eyes scrunched closed, she waited for the other shoe to drop, but it didn't. Slowly, she opened her eyes and studied his serene expression. What was wrong with him? Didn't he know that he was supposed to be spurning her? Perhaps he was too preoccupied with her freaky-deeky hairdo to notice that he was in the presence of the enemy.

"Well, okay then, Ms. Mansfield. I'll go visit a few of my patients while you hop in the shower, and then we'll have Dr. Mhan discharge you and I'll take you home."

"Oh, you don't have to do that. I can call a cab. It's no big deal."

"Don't be absurd." He looked slightly wounded that she would even suggest such a thing. "Now go hop in the shower, or we'll be too late for pancakes at that little diner across the street."

"Pancakes?"

"You don't expect me to drive you home on an empty stomach, do you?"

Elizabeth tilted her head back and laughed at his comical expression. "No. But I insist on buying."

"You are mean."

"So some of my students tell me. Now, you are dismissed, sir. This little gown doesn't exactly protect my modesty."

"That's what I like about them." He grinned at the horrified look on her face. "I'll meet you back here in exactly one hour."

Elizabeth couldn't wait.

Slightly over an hour later, Jason was seated across from Elizabeth in a booth in Aunt Rose's

Old-Fashioned Diner. As he gazed at her over a healthy stack of pancakes, he knew in his heart that there was nowhere on this earth that he'd rather be.

And—what with his name and social standing being the stuff of legends—thc places that would be thrilled to welcome him into their folds at Sunday brunch that morning were numerous and elite.

But Jason never had cared much for the lifestyle of the rich and not so famous. He was a simple guy and found pleasure in simple things. He wanted a family someday. Several kids. A few dogs. Maybe a cat and a turtle or two. And a little place with a yard big enough for a trampoline and a tree fort and a cement driveway and a garage so he and his boys could shoot hoops.

In fact, the only thing wrong with this picture—considering that for the past few years, he'd honestly believed that he'd be sitting across the table eating breakfast with a pregnant woman by now—was that the woman should have been Angie, and the baby his.

Water under the bridge, he thought for the first time, without the ever-present pang that usually plagued him when he thought of Angie. Hmm. Must be healing. Maybe water did indeed flow under the bridge and on to bigger and better things.

Truth be told, he already felt connected to Elizabeth in a way that he never had to Angie, and he'd only known Elizabeth for a day. With Angie, it was clear that he'd been in love with being in love. With Elizabeth, he was beginning to think he could fall in love with life.

Again.

Yes, she'd had a profound effect on him, all right. He still couldn't believe that when he'd gone to wake her up this morning, he'd oh-so-lightly kissed her cheek and then inhaled the sweet scent at her temple. He'd have climbed over the rail and continued his journey right down her neck to her throat and back up to her mouth, had sanity not intervened in the form of Nurse Effie, Prosperino's version of Nurse Ratched.

As it was he'd had to trump up eyestrain as his reason for bringing his face so closely to Elizabeth's. The old biddy hadn't bought a bit of the eyestrain thing, and no doubt by the end of the day the nursing staff would be buzzing about his illegitimate baby. A small smile tugged at the corners of his mouth. Actually, the idea wasn't so terrible. He'd always wanted a son.

Plunging a hand through his hair, he attempted to drive this ridiculous train of thought from his brain. He was going around the bend in a big way. His gaze darted up to Elizabeth, and the drop of syrup that hovered on her full lower lip. Was it any wonder? He was sitting across the table from one of heaven's angels.

Yesterday's scare seemed to have no ill effects on Elizabeth's appetite, and she dug into her pancakes with gusto. Jason grinned. He loved a woman with a healthy appetite.

"I wonder what Savannah and Harrison are doing now," she mused as she took a break from eating long enough to dab her lips and then blow across her mug.

"I know what I'd be doing."

She stared at him for a moment, then burst out laughing. "Okay. Fine. I wonder what else they're doing."

"What else is there?"

"I can see you have a one-track mind."

"Not always. I can be persuaded to make civilized conversation. For example, it was a lovely wedding yesterday. Except for the part where you were stricken with pain."

"True, that was a bit of a downer. But I can't say I'm sorry it happened, being that I don't have to eat alone this morning."

"Ditto." His heart soared at her words. "They do seem perfect for each other," he ventured.

"Savannah and Harrison? Yes, they do." She emitted a somewhat strangled sound that he supposed she meant to be laughter. "Of course, I thought that Mike and I were perfect for each other four years ago. I couldn't have been more wrong."

"Did you date for a long time?"

"Yes. You'd think I'd have had a clue, huh?"

"Not always. Sometimes time doesn't have anything to do with whether or not two people are going to make it. I know. I dated a woman named Angie—"

"I know. Sherry filled me in."

Jason grinned and rolled his eyes. "I can always count on the nurses to take care of me. Anyway, where was I?"

"You were dating Angie?"

"Oh, yeah. As you probably know, I dated her for a year. More than once, people tried to talk some sense into me, when it came to her, but I didn't want to hear the truth."

Elizabeth commiserated. "Even though you know it's wrong, it's hard to walk away. I was raised to believe marriage is forever. I still want to believe that."

"Me, too."

"I'd been wrestling with leaving Mike for a long time, but could never bring myself to pack my bags, thinking that someday, somehow, I could love him enough that he would straighten up and fly right. We were married for three years, the last two of which were hell."

"That's too bad."

Elizabeth's shrug was philosophical. "He had a lot of problems. Childhood stuff that I couldn't seem to help him with. There was a big hole in his heart, the shape of his father, I think. He was always looking for the perfect love. At first, he thought he found it in me. But I couldn't undo all of his hurts."

Jason folded his hands on the table and leaned forward, listening intently. There was something about her experience that was so akin to his. Angie, too, had her share of problems stemming from a serious lack of self-esteem and he knew only too well what it was like to love a person who had more needs than it was possible to fill.

A long, heavy sigh blew past Elizabeth's lips. "Last October Mike came home after one of his philandering weekends on the town and begged my forgiveness and well, as you can see, I forgave him. But he was up to his old tricks within a week, and when he found out I was pregnant, that was the proverbial last straw. Which, in retrospect, is fine. Just saved me having to kick him out, down the road. He is not father material. Never wanted to be, so why force him and his lack of moral character on some poor little kid?"

"Sounds like you are recovering nicely."

"After several years of heartbreak, I really think I am moving beyond the pain. The baby is helping a lot. Giving me something to look forward to."

"You're lucky."

"It sounds like you're healing, too."

"You know, I think I am." He held up his mug and clinked it against hers. "Here's to better judgment in the future."

"And knowing when something is right."

Jason nodded, unsure as to what to say, for it had only been twenty-four hours and he was afraid he might already know.

Elizabeth's car was still at the church, so Jason dropped her there, and then insisted on following her home. As she navigated the streets to her little cottage at the edge of town, Elizabeth would occasionally glance into her rearview mirror and see him there, his rock-solid presence a comfort.

He'd been so amazing since the wedding. Completely above and beyond the call of duty. She needed to think of some way to show her gratitude.

Something special, but not so special that he got the wrong idea.

Or rather, she thought, casting a sheepish glance back at him, the right idea. She'd been somewhat remiss in battling her crush, it seemed, and now it had blown all out of proportion. If she didn't stop thinking of him as her gallant knight, and going all mushy every time he smiled, he was going to figure it out and run screaming.

Jason Colton was not here to fix her life. He was simply interested in her well-being from a physician's point of view. Surely, there were other women from his wealthy, privileged background standing in line to love him and marry him and give him sons. His sons.

She was just a friend of the family.

And given the hatred that characterized the history between their families, she wondered if she'd even be considered that.

Chapter 4

Jason parked his Jaguar behind Elizabeth's Toyota in a gravel driveway that flanked a small white cottage with black shutters. A smile that began in his belly worked its way to his mouth.

So, this was where she lived.

Instantly he loved her house and almost expected seven dwarfs to fling open the door in greeting. This was exactly the kind of storybook place he'd dreamed of living in with a wife and children someday. It oozed cozy warmth and love.

The front stoop was covered in one of the heaviest, most fragrant climbing rose bushes he'd ever encountered, and the flower beds that flanked the brick steps were loaded with the blooms of early spring. A picket fence, so cliché it could have come straight from happily-ever-after surrounded the post-age-stamp-size lawn, and a flagstone path led to the front door from the sidewalk.

All his life, Jason had been lost in the cool starkness of his family's massive mansion. And, though it had a regal sort of charm, he'd never really felt at home. No better was his empty condo, as, considering his lack of interest in all things decor, it was completely without any kind of homey ambiance.

Elizabeth fumbled with her key ring for the house key and noticed his look of amazement. "It's not much," she said, almost apologetically, "but it's all mine."

"It's wonderful." Jason touched her arm. "Really cute. I can see why you are happy here."

"Really?"

"Oh, yeah."

"Well, come in for the rest of the tour, then."

Beaming, she pushed open the front door and led him into a surprisingly spacious living room done in pastels and filled with airy Amish furniture, a comfy-looking couch, lots of books and quilts and a fireplace that was loaded with fresh-cut flowers. Off the living room lay a cheerful kitchen and dining room combo. Both rooms streamed with sunlight that filtered in from the many windows.

The hall that led to the back of the house brought them first to Elizabeth's room, where she stopped. After a quick peek into the comfortable room that lured him to come nap in a blissful haven of peace, she waved him on.

"Go ahead and check out the backyard and the

rest of the house while I change. There isn't all that much to see, but feel free to roam."

Jason took her at her word and moved first into the good-size bath complete with pedestal sink and claw-foot tub. A window looked out over a private patio garden and a backyard with space for a tree fort, a dog run, a trampoline and a basketball hoop on the side of the detached garage. Echoes of a young boy's laughter teased him in this reverie, and he could hear his own voice coaching a golf swing.

Realizing that he was spending an inordinate amount of time in the bathroom, he moved into the second bedroom, which he'd fully expected to see dolled up for the baby.

But he'd been wrong.

Surprisingly, the room was void of anything remotely nurseryesque. There were boxes, yet to be unpacked, of books and memorabilia and other miscellany, but nothing that would meet the myriad needs of a baby. Brows knit, he hung an arm on the door frame and stared absently at the piles of scrapbooks and desk contents.

The baby would be here in no time and she hadn't even begun to prepare. Not, of course, that he blamed her. It wasn't as if she didn't have a lot going on in her life. But still, the kid would need a place to sleep and to be rocked and to play....

Jason was so deep in thought that he didn't hear Elizabeth move up behind him until she poked her head under his arm and surveyed the room from his fresh perspective.

She cleared her throat and waved her hands, embarrassed. "I've been meaning to get some of that Beatrix Potter border paper and start combing the rummage sales for baby stuff, but time seems to have gotten away from me."

"You shouldn't be combing rummage sales and hanging wallpaper anyway." He peered down at her. She'd changed into jeans and an oversize sweatshirt that nearly hid the fact that she carried a little boy in her womb. She was like an answer to a fervent prayer. "Not in your condition."

"Jason, I'm pregnant. Not sick."

"Even so, this is a time to let yourself be pampered. Accept offers of help."

"I've had lots of offers, but the idea of a rambunctious bunch of paintbrush-wielding sixth graders running amuck in here gives me hives."

"What if I help? I'm not in sixth grade and, while I'm no Martha Stewart, I know the business end of a paintbrush."

Her eyes flitted to his, and then, as if she'd landed on a live wire, they took off for less heated territory. "You are very sweet, but I'm sure you have better things to do."

No. No he didn't. In fact, he couldn't think of a thing he'd rather do than help her put this room together.

"What time do you get off work on Friday nights?"

"Well, my contract states I have to stay until three thirty, but I usually stay until five or so to get my lesson plans done and to correct papers. Why?"

"Because we're going shopping."

"We are?"

"Yes. No ifs, ands or buts." With that, he leaned down, kissed her temple and showed himself the few steps it took to reach her front door. "I'll be here to pick you up at five fifteen, this Friday. Be ready."

Jaw slack, a slight smile twitching at the corners of her mouth, Elizabeth stared after him. And as she watched him go, she touched her temple with her fingertips and was reminded of her dream.

A steaming cup of herbal tea beside her, Elizabeth sat in the middle of what would someday be the baby's room and began to sort through the boxes she'd neglected to unpack since she'd moved into the cottage over four months ago. It was time to hold a rummage sale of her own, she thought with a sigh. Though she doubted her wedding album, filled with smiles that held promises now broken, would fetch much of a price.

She set it aside and dug through an assortment of high school yearbooks and some photo albums put together by her various sixth-grade classes and, after a quick skip down memory lane, set them together with her wedding album.

After more energetic rummaging, eventually Elizabeth came upon what she'd been looking for and dreading at the same time.

The book of genealogy and Mansfield family history.

Written by her father's grandmother, more than fifty years ago, this book was more a compilation of detailed journal entries and lineage diagrams than pictures, although there were a few tintypes of babies and other stern faces from the Mansfield family tree.

Cracked leather with an embossed *M* made up the cover which was held together by a length of black cord. A sketch of the Mansfield family coat of arms had been glued inside the cover, but the glue had dried up and the tattered brown paper fluttered loose and down to Elizabeth's lap. She studied it for a moment, then her gaze moved to the spidery handwriting of her great-grandmother's first journal entry, and Elizabeth was suddenly transported back in time as the tumultuous past between the Coltons and the Mansfields sprang to life.

As she relived the lengthy account of the arranged marriage between her distant relative, Katherine Mansfield, and William Colton back in Surrey, England, in 1750, her tea grew tepid, then cold. Dappled light patterns traveled from one end of the wall to the other as noon turned afternoon. Finally, eyes glazed over, Elizabeth had to stretch out her aching legs as they'd fallen asleep from sitting in one position for so long.

Poor Katherine, she mused, arching her back and yawning. Though the word picture portrayed by her great-grandmother of the indomitable Katherine was not the most flattering, still, having her intended tell her that he wanted out, on the eve of their wedding no less, had to sting. Especially considering that his reason had to do with how poorly a necklace had sparkled at her neck.

Although, Elizabeth had to wonder why twenty-four inches of sapphires and diamond's wouldn't sparkle...

An omen?

Elizabeth snorted and shook her head. She didn't believe in that kind of thing. William Colton had decided to take his necklace and head for greener pastures, pure and simple. And from the sound of it, he'd been smart to bug out while he'd had the chance. Still, she felt for Katherine. Watching the man you intended to spend the rest of your life with walk into the sunset without a backward glance was never easy, even if a guy was all wrong for a girl.

Elizabeth carefully opened and smoothed out an ancient rendering of her family tree, tracing the branches with her fingertips. She could see that Katherine's brother, Harold Mansfield, had indeed followed William Colton and his new bride, Molly Warner Colton, from Europe to America to avenge poor Katherine's fine name.

Elizabeth giggled as the absurd idea of her sister's husband running after Mike to avenge her honor flashed through her mind.

They did do things a tad differently back in Katherine's day.

Her fingers strayed to the lines that extended from Harold's name. It seemed that though good old Harold was bent on the brotherly duty of revenge, he was waylaid by love and, after marrying an American beauty for whom Elizabeth was named, had a family of his own. Harold Mansfield and his Elizabeth had many sons, all of whom feuded with the New England descendants of the Colton clan long past anyone could remember a solid reason for the fighting.

Eventually, factions of the two families feuded their way across the country. Revenge, competition and a desire to be the first to strike it rich in California fueled their travels, until two branches of each family settled in Prosperino and continued their ridiculous battle.

Like the Montagues and Capulets before them, the Coltons and the Mansfields seemed destined to be forever linked by petty jealousy, competition and, in some cases, downright hatred. At least until fifty or so years ago. There, the story ended abruptly with the death of Elizabeth's great-grandmother.

Elizabeth closed the journal and wondered who'd been fighting with whom—and where—in the years since. Having virtually grown up in boarding school, she hadn't heard of any great commotion during her adolescence, but those Mansfields and Coltons who may have been warring would hardly discuss their problems with her.

Elizabeth frowned. As far as she knew, her father was the last of the Prosperino Mansfields. Unless she counted herself and her sister.

Folding the family tree, Elizabeth carefully tucked it back into the leather-bound journal. Legend, she thought with a hearty sigh, was a powerful thing. Even an ancient legend, scarcely remembered, it seemed, by Jason Colton. She smiled. The fact that her name hadn't sparked any blinding aggression in him made her wonder just how much he knew or cared about the feud.

Even so, it cast an unfortunate pall on their friendship. Personally, Jason may not care, but surely, there were members of his wealthy and socially correct family who still detested any and all Mansfields and would be appalled to learn that he was fraternizing with her. Apparently Savannah hadn't mentioned her lineage to Harrison yet. Elizabeth couldn't help but wonder how that would affect their friendship.

Her eyes slid shut and her shoulders sagged. Though she had an innate sense that there could be something special brewing between herself and Jason, it was hopeless on so many fronts.

But still, pointing out that he shouldn't be keeping company with a Mansfield was hardly high on her to-do list. No. She couldn't risk losing him just yet. She needed him too much now. Just during this difficult phase in her life, of course, when the mere instructions to a crib or bicycle could reduce her to a blubbering idiot. Once she passed this pregnancy hurdle and its ensuing health problems and furniture assemblage issues, then she'd be too busy with the baby to be so needy and dependent on him anymore.

She grimaced. Gracious. Was she needy and dependent on him already?

Well, she'd just have to get over that. There could never be anything serious between them. And not just because she was pregnant and divorced. But because—even though the feud was ancient history—his family would never accept a Mansfield among their ranks, she was sure.

* * *

The following Friday evening, at precisely 5:10 Jason parked his Jaguar at the curb in front of Elizabeth's cottage. He was early. But he couldn't seem to help himself.

He'd been looking forward to this excursion since he'd left her last Sunday. In fact, he'd stayed up late that very night, combing the papers for bargains and the best places to find all the stuff junior would need once he made his entrance into the world.

At one point, just about midnight, Jason had stopped browsing the classifieds long enough to wonder if he was getting in just a tad over his head when it came to Elizabeth. If maybe the lines of their friendship weren't already becoming a little blurred. But after a moment's thought, he resumed his bargain hunting with renewed vigor. Nah. She needed help. He had time on his hands.

It was no big deal.

They were simply two souls in recovery. Healing from broken hearts. They had a lot in common that way, and other ways. Actually, all ways, as far as he could tell. He really liked her and he had a smug feeling that she really liked him, too.

And now, five long days later, at 5:11, as he bounded up her front steps, he touched his jacket pocket and felt for the bulge of the sales circulars as he rang her doorbell. He'd come prepared. Although, not quite prepared enough for the beauty that met him at the door.

The air whooshed from his lungs at her smile, and there was a curious, high-pitched ringing in his head.

For the most part, a bulky rose-colored sweater concealed the baby and she was dressed like a teenager in slim-fitting blue jeans, a loose ponytail and pair of white canvas shoes. He'd known she was beautiful, even when she was sobbing or sleeping, but when she was well rested and feeling up to par, she was a traffic stopper.

Again, he wondered about her ex-husband. Who was this idiot that could marry a goddess and then leave her for giving him a son?

"Hi," she chirped, and turned to retrieve her purse from the tiny hall table. "You said be ready. So I am."

"I see that. You look fantastic."

"Ugh."

"No, really. You're—" he gave his head a sharp shake "—you're beautiful."

A charming flush crawled from Elizabeth's slender neck and up into her cheeks. "Yeah, yeah, whatever. I know there's a secret conspiracy out there to keep up the spirits of us bloated preg-os. And, I'll give you exactly three hours to stop it."

Jason laughed as he led her to the car. "I came armed with circulars."

"You did? Cool." She trundled after him, down the flagstone path to the sidewalk and waited as he opened her door. "Me, too." She patted her purse, then laboriously settled into the passenger seat. "Where to?" she asked, once he'd started the engine and pulled out onto the street.

"Have you eaten?"

"No."

"Are you hungry?"

"Not yet."

"Good. Let's shop first. We'll do dinner later."

"Okay, but I'm buying."

Jason frowned. "Hey, it's my turn."

"So? You're driving."

"You really are bossy."

"I'm practicing the mom thing."

"Elizabeth?" Jason whispered. He stood behind her, his chest lightly pressing against her back. By the way he occasionally glanced over his shoulder, Elizabeth got the feeling he didn't want to be overheard by the aggressive salesperson that had been dogging them since they entered the BabyWorld Superstore earlier that evening. "What is this?"

"I think it's what they call a changing table," Elizabeth murmured. "At least that's what the sign says."

"Yeah, but what does it change into?"

"I...well, I think...actually, it...I don't really know. Hopefully something attractive, because it's sure ugly the way it is." She reached for the price tag and gasped. "Good heavens! At these prices, it should change into a car!"

Jason peered over her shoulder let out a low whistle. "Okay, don't panic. This is only one store."

"You can see why I've been putting this off." Elizabeth frowned and looked around at the gargantuan BabyWorld. "I have three months before the baby is here, and there's far more to this whole deal than I expected. And I'm on a limited budget."

"Look at it this way. People on your income do it every day. It's doable. You'll be fine."

The brassy-haired sales assistant took their puzzled looks as an opportunity to finally approach. She stepped between them, her Cheshire Catlike smile revealing a dash of red lipstick across her front teeth. Clouds of garlic escaped her lips as she held out a limp hand to Jason. "Hello. Can I help you today?"

Jason shook her hand and nodded pleasantly. "We're just looking, thank you."

"Well, if you have any questions, I'm Tamarra, your personal assistant at BabyWorld." With each breathy word, the acrid odor of garlic increased. "I couldn't help but notice you and your wife admiring our fantastic Dynamo Plus changing table."

Jason and Elizabeth exchanged amused glances but said nothing to correct her assumption that they were a married couple. In fact, Jason pulled Elizabeth more tightly against his chest, using her as a buffer of sorts, the way someone might use a cross or a silver bullet to stave off a vampire. "Yes, we were."

"It's beautiful, as well as functional, isn't?" Tamarra purred.

"We were just saying that ourselves, weren't we, darling?" Jason murmured into Elizabeth's hair and slid his arms around her shoulders, locking them loosely at her collarbone.

Elizabeth was suddenly glad that Jason knew CPR. Her heart beat arrhythmically. Her body tingled from toe to head, causing flames to ignite in her cheeks. Her mouth went dry and her tongue, numb. "Oh, uh, yes, uh, honey, uh, dear. Yes, we were."

She clutched his forearms, loving the steely strength he radiated. This was handy, too, considering that she felt so suddenly light-headed and breathy. Valiantly trying to appear as if she'd not just been mortally wounded by Cupid's arrow, she leaned against the steady beat of Jason's heart, and knew then and there she was a goner when it came to Dr. Jason Colton.

Their bodies were perfect together, curve for curve, plane for plane. They were exactly the right height for each other, too, his chin resting comfortably at her temple, her shoulder blades in the dip between his chest and abdomen. His masculine scent was familiar and alluring, and Elizabeth wished this moment would never end.

But even more, she wished it was reality, that she was married to Jason and the baby was his.

"And durable!" Tamarra's garlic laughter had them both blinking at each other. "This changing table is our most popular model, sturdily constructed of the finest materials for safety. We stock it in white and oak. If you want cherry or mahhhh—" Elizabeth buried her nose in Jason's sleeve and inhaled the fresh scent of his laundry soap "—hhhogany, we'll have to special order that. The mattress is extra."

"Okay. Thank you." Jason steered Elizabeth away from the hawkish rep. When they were out of sight, they sighed and still clutching each other, exchanged glances of relief. "I had to get you away from her. Toxic air pollution is bad for the baby."

Elizabeth filled her hands with the soft fabric of his shirt and laughed into its fragrant folds. "What on earth did she eat for dinner?"

"Whatever it was, I don't want it." He laughed with her and when they'd composed themselves, he took her hand, and fingers twined, they strolled down the diaper aisle together. "So, honey," he said, his sexy baritone sending shivers down her spine, "I wonder how much you would actually use a changing table?"

Elizabeth lifted a shoulder. "I'm still wondering what it is. And how is it different from a bassinet? And what, for heaven's sake, is a *bath*inet?"

"Well, she said something about a mattress, so maybe the changing table changes into a bed."

"Then what do you need a crib for? Which brings me to the next question, dear, do we want a regular crib, or a Portacrib? Stroller or buggy or jogger? Disposable diapers or cloth diapers? Pacifiers? Sippy cups? Bottles? And, if a onesie is a T-shirt, what is a twosie?"

"You're asking me? I feel like we've traveled to a foreign country. I don't speakie the lingie."

"Me, neither. Jason, am I paranoid, or is Tamarra following us?" Elizabeth grabbed Jason's arm and, ducking quickly down a new aisle, began to giggle. "Wait and see if I'm not right. Listen."

"Forget that, I can smell her. Run!" Jason whispered. "For the sake of the baby."

"Would you stop?" Elizabeth giggled. "We're gonna hurt her feelings."

"So? Hurry before she melts our eyes."

Elizabeth hooted and allowed herself to be tugged along. "Oh, wait, not that way. She'll head us off at high chairs. See, here she comes! Quick, turn here," she said and he yanked her down another row. They laughed and whispered and looked over their shoulders like truant school children. "Look! There she is again!"

"Yep. The old pretend to check on the stock while stalking the customer ploy. She's after us, all right."

The top of Tamarra's spiky copper head bobbed up over the next aisle from time to time as she darted after them.

"I wonder why she's so eager to help?"

"The commission on that changing table will probably put one of her kids in braces. That and the fact that she can probably tell we're both clueless as to the practical use for the stupid thing."

"We'll never get away. She knows I can't run in my condition."

Jason grinned and pulled her into his arms. "Maybe this'll drive her back," he murmured. Bending her slightly over, he pretended to ravish her.

Helpless in his arms, Elizabeth laughed herself silly.

"Darling," he said, loud enough for Tamarra to hear. "Let's make a baby."

Elizabeth squealed and batted at him. "We already did that, you goof."

"Let's make another one," he fairly shouted.

"Here?"

Jerking his head up, he looked around. "You're right. Let's head to the bedding department."

Elizabeth's face hurt from laughing. "Is she still here?"

"Nope. Scared her away. For now. Let's shop."

For the next hour, they explored, nudging each other with their elbows, teasing and murmuring and trying to make sense of the multitudinous choices, while at the same time actively avoiding Tamarra.

"What's this?"

Elizabeth shrugged. "Looks like some kind of a bouncy chair."

"No, I think it's a potty."

"Well, I guess you'd want to make sure, one way or another, before you encourage the kid to use it." She laughed. "What's it say on the box?"

"I don't read Cantonese."

"What kind of a doctor are you?"

"I've felt my IQ slipping since we walked in here, that's for sure." They rounded the corner, returning to the crib section.

"Jason, do you think I should get some bumper pads for the crib?"

"Bumper pads? Yes. And a set of boxing gloves. Never too early to start thinking about the ring."

"New rule. No contact sports."

"Aw, Mom."

"Don't aw-mom, me, sonny boy."

"You're good. Really. A natural."

"Thank you. I needed a little boost in confidence."

"Nah. You're gonna be great."

Elizabeth sighed. "What do you suppose bumper pads are for, anyway?"

"I don't know. I've never even baby-sat before." Jason frowned.

"Me, neither."

He darted a quick glance over his shoulder at Tamarra.

Smile broad, she rose to her toes and waved. Jason nodded and dipped his head to Elizabeth's.

"Honey," he spoke this endearment only to her and it sounded so natural, Elizabeth wondered if maybe he'd forgotten that they were only playing house, "we've been here for well over an hour and haven't made a single decision. Do you suppose we should break down and ask for some advice?"

"No!" The helpless look on his face sent her into another gale of laughter. "Oh, for crying out loud. I have a master's degree—in children's education, no less—and you're a *doctor,* for heaven's sake. Surely we can figure this out."

"Okay, so give me your best guess on this thing." From the shelf he grabbed a spiky, multicolored ball that, when set on the floor, flashed and rang and buzzed and vibrated and rolled spasmodically down the aisle.

Elizabeth stared at it, and then up at him. "We need help."

Jason nodded. "Big time."

* * *

"I was starving."

"Mmm. Me, too." Jason dug the last piece of pizza out of the box and offered it to Elizabeth. "Want this?"

"Ugh. No way. I'll pop."

"Okay, then, I guess I'll just have to eat it."

"You are ever gallant."

"Mmpfh."

They were sitting side by side on Elizabeth's living room floor, surrounded by all nature of baby paraphernalia and finishing up a pepperoni pizza they'd had delivered.

Elizabeth shifted to her hip, and slinging an arm over the couch cushion, lazily eyed him. He was so cute, eating pizza all sprawled out on her floor that way, his head propped up against the couch, his ankles casually crossed. He looked about as comfortable as if they'd known each other forever.

It felt as if they had anyway. It was the oddest sensation. On the one hand, there was the comfort of being with some kind of long lost soul mate, and on the other hand, the excitement of a brand-new relationship.

The attraction between them had been palpable from the outset. The moment he'd winked at her from the altar, a bond had been created.

Elizabeth filled her lungs, then slowly exhaled. She knew she shouldn't be thinking along these lines when it came to any man, never mind a Colton, but she had a sneaking suspicion she wasn't alone in her feelings.

Besides, he was a big boy. She guessed he could make up his mind if he wanted to hang around with a woman—a Mansfield no less.

He was smiling at her now, his lids at half-mast, his lip curled in a most sexy manner. It wouldn't be hard to lean ever so slightly forward and bring her mouth to his. To see if his lips were really as soft and seductive as they looked.

The adrenaline that suddenly pumped through her veins at the thought had reached her son and he let loose with a healthy kick.

"Ooo!" Elizabeth patted her belly. "You settle down in there."

"He kicking?" Jason pushed himself up on his elbows and rolling on his side, reached out and placed a hand high on her belly. "Where? Here?"

"How'd you know?"

"He's head down, so his legs would be up here, or maybe over here."

Elizabeth's head grew light under his familiar touch and again, her pounding heart invigorated the baby.

"Ah!" Jason's grin was ebullient. "I felt that!" He brought his head closer to her belly. "Do it again, buddy."

"If he does, it'll be a first. I can never get him to perform on command."

Ignoring her, Jason pushed at the baby's leg and the baby responded with another kick. Elizabeth watched with glee as Jason rolled on his back and laughed at the ceiling.

"This is a smart kid, Elizabeth. He's going to

keep you on your toes.'' He rose up on his elbow and to her belly he said, ''You be patient and stay where you are for a few more months, and then, when you get out, we'll try out those Fisher-Price golf clubs I got you today.''

Elizabeth felt tears of joy brim in her eyes as Jason continued to talk about the future, and her son, and how he was looking forward to meeting this little boy. As he spoke, he didn't seem to realize that he'd left his hand resting lightly, but oh so protectively, at the top of her belly.

Chapter 5

Two Saturdays later found Elizabeth and Jason standing on a tarp in the middle of her unborn son's nursery. They were both covered in splotches of pale-yellow paint and admiring the transformation their efforts had wrought on one of the four walls.

''He's gonna love it,'' Jason predicted.

''Think so?''

''Oh, yeah. It's warm and cheerful but not girly. I could happily live here myself.''

Elizabeth smiled. ''Your legs would hang over the edge of the crib.''

He pulled her to his side and rubbed at a dash of yellow on her cheek. ''Must you always be so pragmatic?''

A sunny giggle filled the air and, as her arm snaked around his waist, Jason felt his heart constrict with an emotion that he was not yet ready to name.

Her head bobbed beneath his fingertips. "I love it, too. I vote we paint the other three walls."

"You mean we're not done yet?"

She patted his cheek. "Hey, Martha, we still have border paper to hang and a crib to assemble. Don't fail me now."

Reluctantly, he stepped away from her, as he was becoming tempted to press his lips to her temple and, if she didn't protest, to the shadow of yellow on her cheek, and then on to her eyelids, her lips....

Back to work, he commanded himself and taking up a roller, dipped it into the paint pan.

In the past eight days, he'd battled moments such as this more than once. They'd spent every evening together, prowling home improvement depots, furniture marts, kiddie-lands and wallpaper huts, under the guise of preparing for the baby. But Jason knew, for his part anyway, the real reason was because of the instant and deep attraction he felt for the baby's mother. To him, the connection was so right, so intense, so perfect, it was almost as if their roots went back for generations.

"Jason." Elizabeth glanced up from the line of yellow she was cutting in around the window trim.

"Hmm?"

"Would you consider coming to my school next week and talking to my class? We are doing a series on career choices, and I know a doctor would be very interesting to my kids."

He smiled at the unconscious possession she took

of her sixth graders. "Sure. I did that once last year for a class at the junior high. Brought Morty, my skeleton. He was a real hit."

Delighted laughter bubbled from her lips and again, he fought the urge to throw down his roller and kiss her senseless.

"Oh, that sounds perfect! And maybe you could let them listen to their heartbeats with the stethoscope and try on the blood pressure cuff and take a temperature reading and all that kind of stuff."

He shrugged and, dipping his roller, reloaded it with paint. "Okay. And that reminds me. As soon as we're done, I want to have a listen to junior. Make sure he's coming along okay."

"Oh, he's coming along just fine." Elizabeth groaned. "I'm pretty sure he's going to be an athlete. He seems to think my bladder is a punching bag and this morning I could have sworn he bit me." She gave her stomach a wry pat.

Jason leaned against the wall and laughed. "That's my boy," he crowed and then, realizing his choice of words, glanced over at Elizabeth.

Their gazes collided like storm currents, and veritable bolts of lightning seemed to crash between them. For a long moment, neither of them moved. Not taking a step, he strained toward her, his eyes roving her face for a sign that he'd offended. But he found none.

Instead, he discovered a yearning that matched his own, and his heart expanded with a joy he hadn't felt in far too long.

However, having learned some of life's lessons

the hard way, there was a chink in the perfect veneer of the moment. His pragmatic and—thanks to Angie—somewhat jaded side couldn't help but wonder if this longing he felt coming from her was for him and the ever tightening bond that grew between them, or if she was simply looking for a way out of her single-parent predicament.

He'd fallen in love with a woman who wanted happily-ever-after for all the wrong reasons before. Was he doing it again?

Eyes flashing, he searched her face for the truth.

She was so beautiful. So vulnerable, yet there was a strength about her that drew him. He opened and closed his hands on the roller's handle and debated taking her into his arms and kissing her, as if in doing so, he could discover the true intention of her heart.

Outside, a siren faded into the distance. Inside, only the sound of his suddenly ragged breathing and the pounding of his pulse filled his ears.

There was no denying that something was happening between them. What to do with this knowledge remained a mystery.

For one thing, she was pregnant with another man's child. Not that it made a bit of difference to him, but what if it did to her?

For another, they'd only known each other for a short time.

But still, there was something else.

Something that he couldn't quite put his finger on. She was harboring a secret. He could see the signs haunting the sea green of her eyes whenever the conversation would approach the deep waters of her family history. She would hedge and avoid certain topics relating to her past, and didn't seem terribly interested in meeting his relatives.

It worried him.

He'd seen that same fear of discovery in Angie's eyes more than once. And though Elizabeth and Angie were two completely different women, the thought of any kind of lie unsettled him. Hopefully, Elizabeth would become comfortable enough with him to tell him what was bothering her, before they got in too deeply.

Because he could feel the tension between them growing and charging like thunderclouds on the horizon.

They had a date with destiny.

With her right brain, Elizabeth corrected spelling tests on a lap tray as she lay in bed later that same day. With her left brain, she talked on the phone with Savannah.

"Wow. Sounds like you had a pretty unforgettable honeymoon. So, now that you're back to boring old Prosperino, how's married life treating you?" Elizabeth red lined a misspelled word. "Are you pregnant yet?"

Savannah laughed. "It's only been two weeks. Give me a little time."

"That's plenty of time. Trust me," Elizabeth huffed.

"Speaking of being pregnant, what's this I hear about you swooning at my wedding? I heard that

Jason had to lug you back into the church. Sounds very romantic."

"Actually, it was. You are right about him, Savannah. He is a doll."

"Do I hear the beginnings of a teensy-weensy crush?"

"No. You hear the beginnings of a monster-wonster crush. And if you tell Harrison, I'll snatch you bald."

Savannah shrieked with glee. "Are you serious? You and Jason? An item? Tell me everything."

"Well, first of all, we're not an item. He's merely my dream come true. And you'd better not tell him, either."

"This is so juicy! Are you like, dating, or what?"

"I'd hardly call it dating. First of all, he gave me a ride to the hospital. Then he hung around to see if I'd be okay. Then he gave me a ride home. And then he helped me set up the nursery and today he took pity on me and flirted with me a little bit and that's about the size of it."

"I knew it!" Savannah nearly laughed herself silly. "I should have thought of it before! You two are perfect for each other! I bet you're going to fall in love and get married!"

"Hold on there, Mrs. Colton. You have forgotten one small problem."

"Elizabeth, the baby is not a problem. Jason loves kids. He'd be a great father for your child."

"I'm not talking about the baby."

"Then what?"

"I'm a Mansfield."

"Oh." There was a pregnant pause. "I'd forgotten about that. In fact, I probably shouldn't even be speaking to you, now that I'm a Colton." Her lilting voice dripped with playful sarcasm.

"I'm serious, Savannah. It was a big deal in the past. I'll bet Harrison's relatives wouldn't have liked you, if you were a Mansfield."

"Don't be silly. In-laws are in-laws. They're never going to like you."

"Would you be serious?"

"Can I be matron of honor at your wedding?"

Elizabeth sighed. "Yes."

And then, as they were wont to do when they were ten years old, they fell into fits of laughter and spent the next hour discussing the exact hue of Jason's and Harrison's eyes.

The following Monday, Jason—accompanied by Morty the skeleton—paid a visit to Elizabeth's sixth graders and was a smash hit. From the rear of the classroom, she watched his antics and was educated right along with the children. And, when she wasn't busy learning, she was loving.

He was simply wonderful with kids. A natural.

The back of her throat burned and her eyes stung with the bittersweet poignancy. He would make a funny, kind and understanding father. If she only could, Elizabeth would move heaven and earth to have met and married Jason first. To be carrying his baby.

Angie had been a fool.

The rest of that week Elizabeth spent her free evenings with Jason, prowling rummage sales for baby furniture that would fit her budget. After much rigorous searching, they found a slider rocker in excellent condition at an elderly woman's garage sale that Elizabeth planned to reupholster in a durable tapestry. At the Salvation Army they found a matching dresser and chest of drawers set that only needed a fresh coat of paint and some new knobs.

A woman who lived just down the street from Elizabeth offered her old changing table and even explained its various uses. And, though it had scribble marks and needed a new mattress pad, it would be perfect, once it was painted to match everything else.

Now and again, Jason would find an odd or an end at one sale or another that he'd decide he couldn't live without and he'd cart it off, eliciting a promise from Elizabeth that when they were done decorating the nursery, they'd tackle his place. Elizabeth was thrilled by this idea, as it would give her even more time with Jason.

At one point, when they were dragging the old wicker club chair that he'd found at a yard sale back to his place, Elizabeth had her first glimpse of his living space and had to agree that it desperately needed a woman's touch.

"How long have you lived here?" Elizabeth asked, as she entered his spacious oceanfront condo.

Jason came in behind her, carrying the wicker chair, which he dropped in front of his fireplace. With the exception of his unexceptional couch, it was the only piece of furniture in his living room.

He shrugged his shoulders. "A little over a year now, I guess."

"Over a *year?*"

"Yeah. Why?

"It looks like you haven't finished moving in yet."

Tilting his head, Jason bestowed her with a self-deprecating grin. "I know. Angie was going to decorate after we were married. When I called the wedding off, I couldn't figure out if I was going to stay or not and—" he threw his hands up in a helpless gesture "—since decorating isn't exactly my forte—"

"You haven't gotten around to moving *or* staying," she said, finishing his sentence.

He sighed. "Yep."

"It's a beautiful place."

"Not as nice as yours."

"Yeah, right."

Slowly, Elizabeth turned and allowed her gaze to drink in the panoramic view of the spectacular Pacific Ocean that lay outside his impressive expanse of windows. Just beyond his deck, a beach stretched out to meet the surf that, at this twilight evening hour, was reflecting gold and blue light. A dog chased a Frisbee off in the distance and some children struggled to get a kite off the ground without benefit of a breeze.

Inside the condo, his ceilings were high, the walls white and the floors a cherry hardwood. It was striking. And given the neighborhood, undoubtedly very expensive.

"No, really," Jason insisted. "I love your place. It's homey. Cozy. Filled with your personality. This place is...I don't know, it lacks something."

"Furniture," Elizabeth said, dryly.

Jason's laughter echoed in the room, and she reveled in the relaxed and happy sound.

"Come on." Taking her hand, he led her across the gleaming floor that cried for Turkish throw rugs and into the kitchen. His arm swept the state-of-the-art stainless steel appliances and the cherry-wood cabinetry. "This is the room where I never cook."

"Too bad," Elizabeth murmured. "Seems a terrible waste."

An island with a black marble countertop contained an elaborate grilling system that would have a gourmet cook drooling and, on the side that faced the ocean, a row of black-and-stainless-steel chairs invited guests to sit and visit.

"Tell you what. Help me get a bunch of kitchen gewgaws and cooking stuff, and I'll prepare you a meal you'll never forget."

She tossed him a saucy grin. "I hear ptomaine poisoning is unforgettable."

"True, but look at it this way." He arched a roguish brow. "I'm a doctor."

Elizabeth reached out to punch him and, grabbing her hand, Jason tugged her into the dining room.

"This is the room where I never eat."

"No wonder. You don't have a table."

"That's part of the reason. Remind me to have a table delivered before I cook you dinner."

"Chairs, too?"

"Right."

Elizabeth giggled. Lately, she noted, many of his plans seemed to include her. An indescribable feeling of happiness welled inside as she thought about helping him put his kitchen together. It had been so long since she'd felt included. Needed. Wanted. It was heady stuff, this feeling of belonging.

From the dining room, he led her to his office. "This is the office where I never work."

"Why?"

"Too quiet here. I can't think with all this silence. I do my paperwork in my office at the clinic." Next, Jason led Elizabeth down the hall toward the back of his apartment. "This is the guest bath and bedroom that no guests ever use."

Mouth quirked, Elizabeth eyeballed him.

"I know, I know, no bed. But I still don't see me entertaining overnight guests in here."

"Ah."

Jason took her by the shoulders and propelled her to his bedroom. A king-size bed was lost in the middle of the huge room. No pictures adorned the walls, no memorabilia, no plants. She sighed. It could be such a beautiful room. At night, the roar of the ocean had to be incredibly soothing.

He moved to the window, then turned to face her. "Actually, this is the only room I do use in this place."

"So this is the entertainment center." Elizabeth felt her face suddenly burst into flame and couldn't believe that she'd just blurted out what she'd been thinking. It had sounded like she was fishing for information. Or worse, like she was jealous. Or even worse yet, flirting. Trying to be snappy. Witty. Sexy.

She must look like a first-class idiot, a woman in her condition, making that kind of a comment to a man like him. She wished a wave would sweep into the house and drag her out to sea.

A slow smile stole across his face. "No, but I need one of those, too."

"Uh, oh, well..." Attempting to appear a sophisticated woman of the world, Elizabeth tossed him a bright smile then promptly backed into the wall as she groped for the door. "Check," she chirped then disappeared into the hall.

Since they still had some work to do in the nursery, Jason and Elizabeth spent that Saturday and the next at her place painting baby furniture various shades of cream and yellow. And now a couple of weeks after they'd begun, the room was a complete delight, all duckies and bunnies and toys for the tiny hands of one small boy. Once everything was dry and in place, it would be a showplace for sure.

They were dog tired and drowsy after a barbecue dinner of steak and salad out on her back patio.

Elizabeth followed her nose into the living room to find Jason already sprawled on her couch. Smiling, she moved to the entertainment center. "Thanks for making popcorn. It smells heavenly."

He tossed a piece into the air and caught it in his mouth. "You're welcome. And it is. Popcorn is one of my specialties. That and blueberry pancakes."

"You'll have to make those for me one day."

"I've been dying for you to ask," he teased. "How about if I make them for you first thing tomorrow morning? We could work up a sweat, swinging from the chandelier tonight."

"You're a regular laugh riot." Blushing, she changed the subject. "What on earth did you rent? This isn't exactly your usual Saturday night video." Elizabeth squinted at the title and then turned to eyeball Jason. *"The Wonder of Childbirth?"*

Jason grinned. "You're going to love it. Everyone who has ever seen it does. It shows all these people having babies and crying and stuff. We're gonna need this box of tissues. It's a real tearjerker. I don't think you can—no, I *know* you can't—watch it without getting all choked up."

"Let me guess. They're probably crying because it hurts like hell, and they just realized the pain has only just begun. Have you heard how much a college education goes for these days?" Elizabeth grumbled as she pushed the tape into the VCR and touched the play button.

"So, he'll get a job. Or a scholarship. Don't worry. That's a lifetime away." He patted the cushion beside him. "Come here, Mama. Take a load off. You worked hard today."

"It does look really cute, doesn't it?" she asked, referring to the nursery. Elizabeth hesitated by the TV, stalling.

"Way cool, thanks to my expertise with wallpaper paste."

"Yeah, right. You'd have glued yourself to the

wall if I hadn't been there to hose you off occasionally."

Jason laughed and wiggled a rakish brow. "Sit down, already."

"I'm comin'."

Elizabeth fiddled some more with the contrast and the volume knobs. Sitting next to Jason on the couch, sharing a bowl of popcorn was a dangerous thing, given her hormone-driven emotional state. Already she felt like crying and the darned video hadn't even started yet. He was so incredibly sweet, helping her this way. Being her friend when she was in such need.

Several times that afternoon she'd been tempted to come clean with him about the Mansfield-Colton thing. To clear the air and fill him in on the details that apparently his family had neglected to impart during his formative years. But the harmony had been so beautiful, she'd been reluctant to fool with perfection.

They'd laughed, they'd teased, they'd played, they'd done all the things that Elizabeth had never done with Mike. Her eyes strayed to a tiny framed photograph of herself and her ex-husband that still sat in a nook in the entertainment center. It was a picture taken during happier times, but none so happy as she'd had today. Sadly, she realized that if it hadn't been for this one photo she left out in the open, she would have a hard time remembering what Mike looked like.

He'd walked out on her only seven months ago.

But he'd left her two and a half years ago. She'd simply been too stubborn to admit it.

Again, Jason patted the cushion at his side. "Come on. It's starting. I have some tissues all picked out just for you." He plucked several from the box on the end table and waved them at her.

Unable to keep the smile from her face, she joined him on the couch and allowed him to pull her up against his side and poke a handful of popcorn into her mouth.

For the next hour, Elizabeth sat mesmerized, watching as the miracle of childbirth—from conception to labor—played out on the TV screen. As the program reached its climax and followed three separate women into the labor room, Elizabeth grasped Jason's fingers and let the tears flow.

It was so beautiful and natural, this having a baby. Much less scary than she'd originally thought. A lump the size of Vermont lodged in her throat, and for the first time since discovering she was pregnant, Elizabeth realized that she'd be leaving the hospital with a new member of her family in her arms. She would be somebody's mom.

Her nose ran, her lips trembled, her chest heaved, and in her peripheral vision, she could see Jason's Adam's apple bobbing. Occasionally, he'd rub his eyes. He was such an incredible man. So sweet. Tenderhearted. Caring.

And, as each grain of sand sifted through the hourglass, Elizabeth was becoming aware that she yearned for far more than a simple friendship with Jason Colton and she had since the moment she laid eyes on him. If she were to be completely honest, deep in her heart she'd already cast him in the role of her baby's father and her own future husband.

Elizabeth froze as an awful thought assailed her.

What if he viewed her as a good buddy? Or worse, a sister? Someone with whom to while away the hours until Ms. Right came along?

This man was tall, dark, handsome and rich. He could have his pick of women. Rich, beautiful, successful and skinny women. Why would he be spending so much time with her?

She blew her nose and dabbed at her eyes.

Couldn't be because he found her attractive. She directed a bleary eye toward her swollen midsection. After all, they'd known each other for a months now, and—much to her dismay—he'd been as respectful of her person as a monk. And could she possibly blame him? What with her swollen ankles and ugly outfits and indigestion, there was nothing sexy about her anymore, she lamented in silence.

Granted, they had a lot of laughs whenever they were together, and seemed to see eye to eye on just about everything. But what was in it for him? He had nothing to gain by spending his off hours with her.

Unless…

Nurse Sherry's words echoed in Elizabeth's mind. How his ex-fiancée's unwillingness to bear him a baby once they were married had been a deal breaker for Jason. Could the fact that he'd struck up a friendship with Elizabeth have more to do with his interest in her willingness to have a baby than in her as an individual?

The video finally dissolved to snow as it clicked into the rewind mode.

"Jason?"

"Hmm?"

Her heart started to pound and her palms grew clammy. No. Clamping a mental hand over her mouth, she knew she couldn't ask him about his desire to have a child of his own. Surely, it would bring back painful memories for him and they were having such a lovely evening. She simply couldn't bring herself to spoil this intimate moment.

Yet, she wished she knew exactly what was going on in his heart.

Blinking rapidly, she lowered her eyes. "I...thank you so much for being here for my baby." Intentionally, she left out any reference to herself.

The static from the TV seemed to fade away as he gently tipped up her chin and forced his penetrating gaze into hers with an intensity that had her heart suddenly thrumming.

Okay. This was not the look of a monk. A buddy. A pal. There was no brotherly interest in these eyes. Except for her shallow breathing, Elizabeth went completely still. Could it be that he viewed her as desirable?

Her pulse rocketed and she had to wonder about her blood pressure. Good thing he was a doctor.

Slowly, he slid up his hands to cup her face. "The baby is as good an excuse as any to be here with you." His voice was hoarse with emotion and there was great tenderness in his expression that assuaged her misgivings. His slight emphasis on the word *you* spoke volumes.

Before she could exhale her relief, he angled her mouth beneath his and kissed her with such slow, sweet, sensual longing it left no doubt in her mind as to his reasons for being there. This kiss was the real thing. It was the kind of kiss that altered physics and changed them from two empty, seeking individuals to one complete being. The kind of kiss that Elizabeth had never shared with Mike.

Never had Elizabeth experienced a kiss so exquisite. So incredibly soft and sexy and gentle, yet hot and needy at the same time. It was a dichotomy she'd never understand and didn't care to. All she knew at the moment was that she never wanted this kiss to end.

Together, their mouths moved of one accord, exploring, seeking, teasing. Elizabeth raised her arms and circled his neck. The baby's position prohibited her from pulling him too close and that frustrated her. Little legs pummeled her insides. She could feel Jason smile against her lips.

"He's trying to push me away."

Elizabeth nodded and laughed into his mouth. "I know. I can feel him."

"He's jealous. And I can't really blame him, as I want you all to myself right now."

"You do?"

"Oh, yeah."

Once again, Jason claimed her mouth with his own. He'd moved his hands so that one cradled the small of her back and one rested lightly at the side of her belly. And as he took possession of her soul with his kiss, Elizabeth knew that his interest in the baby was far different from his interest in her.

After he'd kissed her quite thoroughly, he abruptly released her and fell back against the couch.

"I've got to go." His voice was raw.

"Oh. Okay. I understand." He didn't want to fall for a ready-made family. Either that, or kissing a hugely pregnant woman was not all it was cracked up to be. Then again...

"No." He pulled her back into his arms and gave her another crushing kiss before he tore his mouth from hers.

Elizabeth sat dazed, bereft, at the absence of his mouth on hers.

"No, no no." Foreheads together, his words came out against her lips in a rush of heat. "You don't understand. I have to go. Because if I don't, I'll stay."

Chapter 6

"What are you wearing?" Elizabeth teased, cradling the phone between her shoulder and cheek.

"Isn't that my line?"

She looked down at the extra large T-shirt with the duck that cried I'm Quacking Up and the sweat socks with the hole in one toe and shrugged. "Sure. Okay. I'm wearing a teensy-weensy little teddy, fishnet stockings and spiky heels. Your turn."

Jason's laughter rumbled pleasantly into her ear. "I'm coming over."

"No way." She sighed. "It was hard enough saying goodbye tonight." She couldn't believe she'd just admitted that, but it was too late now. Besides, he knew it already.

They'd stood at the front door for at least a half hour after he'd prescribed beauty rest for her, holding each other and whispering their thank-yous and good-nights and other terms of endearment until, with a kiss that left her wanting more and wondering exactly what had just happened, Jason staggered to his Jaguar and drove back to his place.

Elizabeth didn't think he'd taken time to leave her driveway before he dialed her number and continued the sexy conversation where they'd left off.

And now, two hours later, they were still talking. Elizabeth was curled in her bed beneath the comforter, leaning her ear against the phone, allowing the soothing quality of his voice to lure her toward dreamland.

"Did you hear that?" she murmured, sleepily.

"Yeah."

"What was it?"

"Call waiting."

"Aren't you going to answer it?"

"No. Ignore it."

"But what if it's an emergency?"

"They'll call back."

"Jason!" She could tell he was teasing, but still...

His heavy sigh huffed across the line. The waiting call clicked again. "Okay, okay!"

Mirth at the frustration in his voice rose into her throat and passed her lips. "May I suggest that you put on your bedside manner?"

"Funny. I'll show you a bedside manner. Hang on a sec, okay?

"Okay."

"You'll be here when I get back?"

"Yes, of course."

"Promise?"

"Yes, now go, already!"

She laughed and could hear him clicking to the other line. While the phone line was silent, Elizabeth took the opportunity to turn over, which was much more labor intensive than it used to be, requiring that she prop her stomach with pillows and arrange her legs and back just so.

What a wonderful way to spend an evening, she mused languidly. Although she had to admit it would be far better if he were there beside her. But their future together was still in the fantasy stages, and Elizabeth forced herself not to count unhatched chickens. When she was finally resettled, she could hear more clickings on the line, and Jason's velvety voice filled her ear.

"Elizabeth?"

"Hi."

"Can I call you right back?"

"Sure. Is it an emergency?"

"Well, I guess you could call it that. It's my grandmother, Sybil. You remember her from the wedding?"

"Oh, yes. The one who cut in on us when we were dancing."

"Yep, well, she's calling from Europe," Jason sighed, "and she's not one to be put off. I'll call you again just as soon as she hangs up."

"Okay," she murmured, already looking forward to the telephone's ring.

* * *

"Hey, Gran, it's me again." Jason leaned back against his headboard and tightened the sash to his robe. This would take awhile. Conversations with Sybil always did.

"It's about time! It's not wise to keep me waiting. I might not be here when you get back," the elderly woman crabbed, as had been her habit for the last dozen or so years.

"What? You? No way. You're healthy as a horse. Especially now that you quit smoking. You did quit smoking, didn't you?"

"None of your damned business, sonny boy. Doctors. Bah."

He rolled his eyes and could hear the repeated click of her lighter.

"So, beautiful, why did you call?"

There was a long pause as Sybil took a drag off her cigarette. "Stop trying to get on my good side, boy. You're already in my will." There was a humor in her voice that softened her crotchety words.

Jason glanced at the clock, wondering how much longer Elizabeth would be awake. It was getting rather late. "What time is it in Paris, anyway?"

"It's morning over here, and I've spent the better part of it trying to raise someone who can answer a simple question for me, but every damned Colton in Prosperino is letting their damned machines talk to me. If I wanted to talk to a damned machine, I'd call my refrigerator!"

"So," Jason couldn't resist teasing, "I take it that I was not the first one on your list?"

"Of course not. Why would I call you? Unless I heard you were getting married. So." She wheezed for a moment and Jason could hear the telltale rattle of something worrisome in her lungs as she coughed.

"When was the last time you saw a doctor?" he asked.

"I'll go to the damned doctor when you propose marriage."

"Marry me," he teased.

"Not me, you ninny. A nice girl, from a good family."

Jason half expected this line of conversation, and instead of changing the subject as was his usual modes operandi since Angie and he split up, he paused and thought for a moment. "You might have to make that doctor appointment sooner than you think."

"Why? Because I'm dying or because you're getting married?"

"You're too mean to die, but I might be getting married. Someday."

"You're getting married?"

"I didn't say that. I'm not sure yet. I just met somebody really nice, and I'm taking it kind of slow."

"Don't take it too slow, boy. Neither of us is getting any younger."

"Duly noted. So, Gran, I'm dying of curiosity. Why did you call?"

"Changing the subject when I get on the marriage bandwagon, huh? Typical." She snuffled and muttered and finally remembered why she'd originally called. "I want to know if you've talked to Graham."

"Graham?" Jason and his uncle Graham were hardly buddies. Closing his eyes, he thought back and realized that the last time he'd seen Graham was at Harrison's wedding, and then it was only to shoot the breeze for a few minutes. "Why?"

"Because back when I was at the wedding, he told me that Meredith has *still* been acting as if her antenna isn't quite picking up all the channels, if you get my drift."

Meredith was Graham's sister-in-law, and as the wife of Sybil's nephew Joe Colton—the family's original oil baron—Meredith and her personality quirks had become one of Sybil's favorite harangues. Jason didn't spend all that much time over at Aunt Meredith and Uncle Joe's anymore. Not like he did when he was a kid. He remembered a sweet and loving Meredith who always handed out ice cream pops and let them ride their ponies on the lawn. She'd been the best.

But these days she was different. Edgier. Waspish. And these personality changes had come on suddenly about a decade ago. Too suddenly to be attributed to menopause or any other natural aging process. Without examining her himself, it was hard to say what was going on with Aunt Meredith.

"I don't know, Gran. I mean I've heard all the hubbub about Meredith acting strangely—"

"Strangely? Sonny, that woman is out of her damned mind. Why, that car accident she had ten years ago changed her from Pollyanna to one of Satan's minions. And she just keeps getting progressively more psycho. If you ask me…''

As Sybil nattered on, Jason leaned forward and cradled his head in his hands. More time had been spent dissecting Meredith's split personality than had ever been spent dissecting the atom, he was sure.

''I think you ought to get her into your office and run some tests on her. I wouldn't be surprised if you took a picture of her brain and found that aliens had stolen it!''

Jason hooted. Grandma Sybil was a one of a kind character, and he loved and respected her more than words could say. The tiny old woman was as fiercely protective of her family as a she-bear. And, that Sybil adored her nephew Joe was no secret to anybody.

''Okay, Gran. I'll send Aunt Meredith a notice that she's due for a checkup, and see if I can't figure out what's going on.''

''Good boy. You were always my favorite grandson. Don't tell Harrison.''

Jason snorted. She said the same thing to Harrison.

Sybil continued. ''If you pop the question to that girl you fancy, I want to be the first to know. Call me,'' she ordered, then abruptly hung up.

Jason groaned and flopped back against his pillow.

After church the next morning, Jason and Elizabeth went out to breakfast and then poked through antique shops for a lazy hour in Prosperino's trendy

Old Town section. A tourist Mecca, the warm Sunday in May had brought shoppers out in force to the delightful historic area. Everywhere, hanging flower baskets contained a colorful riot of blossoms, bright flags unfurled in the temperate breezes and large canvas umbrellas shaded tables that sat outside bistros for the best view of the sea.

On a whim, they'd ducked into a movie theater to catch a matinee. Elizabeth had been complaining that she needed to sit down and Jason didn't want a repeat of the episode at his brother's wedding. After the movie let out, they decided to shop for a while longer and, fingers laced, strolled down a shop-filled, tree-lined side street.

"I can't believe you didn't know that the girl who ran off with the drug dealer was really a man."

Elizabeth shrugged. "Okay, I had my suspicions, as she had a pretty healthy set of shoulders on her and practically no hips. But what really threw me was that part at the end, where you discover she's really a dead FBI agent, come back from heaven, to convince that drug dealer to give up a life of crime. And the drug dealer is really the mother of that one child who traveled back from the future to save that other guy—who the heck was he by the way—from finding out that he was really the child's biological father. I was so confused after the first ten minutes, I never caught up."

Jason chuckled and squeezed her hand. "Well, if you'd have stopped tugging on my arm and asking me who everyone was every five seconds, you might have figured it out."

"Oh, please. That movie was just an excuse to have a bunch of car chases and gunfire." She groaned. "I hated it. I really used to like those kinds of action things, but now, I don't know. This one scared me. I mean, do you really think the future is going to be like that? Is my son going to have to live in the basement of a burned-out building and fight to save the pitiful world from time-traveling, cross-dressing, gun-toting wackos like that gal with the pink hair?"

"Elizabeth, relax. It's just a movie."

Far from mollified, Elizabeth stopped in the middle of the sidewalk and looked up at him with real fear in her eyes. "Even so, Jason, it makes me realize how little I've done to prepare for my child's future."

"Elizabeth, we have just spent a month getting ready for him."

"But we haven't saved a single whale! And what about the rain forest? The shrinking ozone? Changing weather patterns, disease, pestilence, rising crime rates? Do you realize that I didn't recycle a single thing this week?" She gripped his forearm and her belly brushed his as she faced him. "Jason, I'm suddenly worried about the future of our world!"

"That's because you're a mommy now." He cupped her cheeks in his hands and kissed the tip of her nose. "You're supposed to worry."

She pulled her lower lip between her teeth. "You think so?"

"Isn't it kind of obvious? Your maternal instincts are kicking in."

"They are?" A small smile played at her lips.

"Mm-hmm. You're not the first mama I've ever seen freak out over the future of the planet. But listen. You're going to do your very best with this kid. And he will turn out fine. And it's not like I won't be there to help you defend him against the cruel world. You just say the word and I'll be only too happy to beat up the class bully."

"What if he *is* the class bully?"

"What do you get for the man who has everything?" Jason asked as they browsed through an antique shop that Elizabeth had been unable to resist.

"Who has everything?" she wondered, and held a bookend up to check the price tag.

"My uncle Joe. He's turning sixty next month and his wife, my aunt Meredith, is throwing a birthday bash for him that Prosperino won't soon forget."

"Well..." Elizabeth paused and thought. Men were always difficult to shop for. "What kinds of things does he like? What are his interests? Hobbies?" She was dying to know more about his family, but was always reticent to ask questions that might lead to her blurting out the truth about the stupid feud.

Jason shrugged. "His hobbies? Making money. Taking in foster kids."

"Hmm. Admirable hobbies, but a foster kid is hardly a birthday gift."

"See? I'm telling you, the guy is impossible to buy for."

"Don't panic. Tell me about his life and the perfect idea will present itself."

"For that, we need coffee."

"Are you going to eat the rest of that pie?"

Elizabeth cast a longing look at her plate. "I shouldn't."

"Pass it over here."

She obliged, even though she could have eaten a whole pie. They were seated on a deck outside a French bakery, just off Old Town's main street. A green canvas umbrella shaded them from the sun's slanting rays and a fresh breeze rolled off the ocean cooling the temperature to within a degree of perfect. Elizabeth held a cup of decaf coffee between her fingertips and listened as Jason regaled her with Colton family history. It was fascinating to hear about the family that made up the other half of the legendary feud. At least as far as this century went.

She looked on enviously as Jason wolfed down the rest of her pie. "Let's see," he mused, chewing thoughtfully. "Where was I?"

"Your grandmother."

"Oh, Sybil, right. Yep. You and she have something in common."

Elizabeth lifted her gaze from her coffee mug to Jason's face and tried to keep the skepticism from her expression. "We do?"

"Mm-hmm." He pointed his fork at her. "You are both single mothers of sons."

"Sybil was a single mom?"

"Among other adventures, yes." Jason settled back in his chair and tossed his napkin onto his plate. "Sybil was always a maverick. She was born here in America, but preferred Europe. She attended Bryn Mawr and became a journalist."

He tented his fingers beneath his chin as he described his grandmother. "She loves to tell about the times she visited salons and cafés in London, Madrid, Paris and Rome and rubbed elbows with the famous people of that era."

"Like who?"

"Well, let's see..." He closed his eyes and thought for a second. "Dropping names is her hobby, but with Sybil, you know she's telling the truth when she tells stories about Hemingway and Fitzgerald, Gertrude Stein and Virginia Woolf."

Elizabeth's jaw went slack. "Wow."

"Yeah. She a wow kind of gal. She's fluent in several languages and supported herself and her baby as a translator and reporter."

"She sounds like a fascinating woman," Elizabeth murmured, thinking that she also sounded intimidating.

"She is that. But she's the type of personality that you really have to know in order to understand. Sybil is not afraid to call the kettle black, and that has ruined a few relationships in her time. Especially with her brother, Teddy. And, don't quote me on this, but I have a feeling her fiery temper is the reason she never married my dad's father."

"She had a baby out of wedlock?" Sybil Colton?

Elizabeth stared at Jason and thought back to the regal dynamo at Savannah's wedding. She'd never have guessed in a million years.

"She did. Although she doesn't like to talk about it. She raised my dad, Frank, in a little village outside Paris and then he went to college here in the States where he met my mom, Shirley. They had me and Harrison when they were still pretty young. Together they built a business and today Harrison runs Colton Media Holdings. He seems to have inherited Uncle Joe's touch for making money."

"Ah. Uncle Joe. Family patriarch, oil magnate and the man who has everything."

"Very good! You've been paying attention." Elizabeth could tell he was genuinely pleased.

She tossed him an impudent look. "So, Sybil's brother Teddy is your uncle Joe's father?"

"Right." Jason leaned back to let the waiter freshen his coffee. "Joe is the oldest of two boys. Graham is his younger brother. But they weren't raised together. Joe was raised in a foster family."

"Why?"

"His mom and dad were killed in a car wreck."

"How awful."

"Mmm. That's a sad story." Jason squinted off toward the spot on the horizon where the Pacific melded with the California sky and then, seeming to remember the original subject, turned his attention back to her. "But even though Joe grew up without his biological father, he knew he was well loved by the people that took him in.

"You know," Jason said and his lazily hooded

gaze became dark. Penetrating. "I don't think it matters if the man who raises you is your biological father, or not, as long as he loves you as if you were his own flesh and blood."

Elizabeth stared at his lips and felt herself go limp with sudden—and nearly unbearable—gladness. She had the strangest feeling that Jason was talking about his feelings for her own baby. "Y-you don't?"

"Not at all. My uncle Joe is a prime example of how a man can teach a boy the art of being a man through love. His foster father loved him with all his heart, and Joe knew it. And because of that love, Joe has done great things for other children in need. He built the Hopechest Foundation for needy kids and fostered a bunch himself. Which just goes to prove that love really can conquer a lot."

"Yes." Elizabeth sighed, wondering if the love she felt for him could conquer the unfortunate past.

A slow, poignant smile tugged at Jason's mouth. "You'd love my Uncle Joe. He's definitely one of those inspiring rags-to-riches stories. He runs several major corporations and dabbles in oil now." He reached across the table and grasped her hand. "You ought to come to his birthday party with me."

"Oh, now that would create quite a little party icebreaker, you showing up with me and my pregnant belly."

Jason laughed. "I think it would be great! For once people would have something to talk about other than my wacky Aunt Meredith."

"Wacky Aunt Meredith?"

"That's another sad story."

Elizabeth squirmed in her seat and fiddled with the napkin beneath her cup. "I don't suppose you know anything about where your family came from, originally?"

Jason lifted and dropped a shoulder. "I'm not really up on the Colton genealogy beyond Sybil and Teddy. But Sybil would know. She's a real family history buff. She could give you the lowdown, if you're interested. She'll be at Uncle Joe's birthday party."

"Oh." She knew her smile was weak. "That would be…nice."

Chapter 7

The shrill ring of the phone roused Elizabeth from the light doze she was enjoying in Jason's new recliner. Another week had sped past, and it was Friday evening already. Her ankles and feet had been bothering her, so Jason had insisted on preparing dinner for them both in his newly decorated and outfitted kitchen.

The phone rang a second time and Elizabeth opened her eyes.

"Jason?"

She ran her hands over her face and listened. Silence.

"Jason?"

The phone rang a third time. Odd. It was then she noticed the note lying on the new end table next to her chair.

"E: Had to run to the store for ricotta cheese and salad dressing. I'll bring a chocolate ice cream for the baby. J."

Elizabeth smiled. She'd been craving ice cream, which was unusual as before her pregnancy she was indifferent to the stuff. Bending her knees, she pushed at the footrest and wrestled with the handle to the recliner. The baby was getting so big, the simple task of sitting up was becoming a major chore.

The phone rang again.

"I'm coming!" She flailed her way out of the chair and rushed to the kitchen just in time for the answering machine to pick up.

Muttering to herself, she searched for the off button, but recoiled and changed her mind about talking to the caller when she heard the unmistakable voice of Sybil Colton begin to crab after the tone had sounded.

"Jason, it's me. Where the hell are you? Why is no one ever there when I call? If you are there, pick up this instant. I don't have time to wait while you shilly-shally around doing whatever you freewheeling bachelors do with your evenings. Jason?"

Elizabeth's lips curved ruefully. Sybil Colton was such a character. There was a noisy exhalation and Elizabeth could almost smell the cigarette smoke.

"I'm beginning to get the feeling that people are avoiding me. Anyway, I've called to give you some advice about Meredith's mental state. I've been doing some reading and I want you to check her for a brain tumor when she comes to your office. According to the article I read, she is showing all of the classic symptoms. Get a picture of that brain and tell me if I'm not right."

The old woman fell silent for a moment and again, Elizabeth could hear Sybil suck on her cigarette and then exhale into the phone's mouthpiece, creating a crackling static.

"And I'm still waiting to hear some more details about this woman you're dating."

Elizabeth froze. Jason was dating someone? Her heart thrashed about inside her chest.

"So far, I only know that her name is Elizabeth, and that's not a whole lot to go on."

Elizabeth's hands flew to her mouth. Jason had told his grandmother about *her?* A curious mix of dread and elation curled around her heart. She leaned closer to the phone machine and fixed her gaze on the tiny speaker, as if this would help her better hear the old woman speak.

"I want details, boy! And please don't tell me that you've picked up another social misfit from the wrong side of the tracks. I could have told you that Angie woman was all wrong for you the minute I laid eyes on her."

Elizabeth glanced at her belly, then slid her fingertips into her temples and began to rub.

Sybil's voice seemed to grow crosser by the minute. "So, who is this Elizabeth woman's family?"

Uh-oh.

Tiny electrical pinpricks crawled across the flesh on Elizabeth's body. This was not good.

"Where are they from? What's their history? If

you're considering making this woman a member of our clan, I'm going to need more information!''

A member of the Colton clan?

Had Jason been discussing marriage with his grandmother? Elizabeth gripped the edge of the counter as Sybil gave in to another fit of wheezing and cursing.

''I hate these damned machines. Jason, call me as soon as you get back from wherever the hell you are. I have another question about Emily.''

Elizabeth closed her eyes. Emily? Who was Emily?

''I want to know if she's still having nightmares about that car accident she and Meredith were in. I heard she was dreaming that she wakes up in the car and sees *two* Merediths! One is an angel and one is the devil incarnate.'' Sybil cackled. ''That's no dream! I saw that movie about the woman with all those different personalities. The mean one would come out and raise hell until one of the nicer ones could come back and smooth things out. Jason, you bring the old Meredith back before any other batty personalities decide to escape her belfry.''

There was a clicking sound on the line that could have been the sounds of a call waiting.

''Jason? Hello? Damn this thing!'' Sybil swore roundly and crashed the phone's handset into its cradle.

Elizabeth stood and stared at the blinking light, paralyzed. So, this was a taste of Jason's family.

Sybil Colton hardly seemed the type to exude much compassion, when it came to a person's foibles. She patted her belly, then moved to one of the stainless steel stools and managed to sit down just before she fell down.

Jason had told his grandmother about her, but he hadn't, it appeared, told Sybil that she was a Mansfield.

"Hey, doll, I'm home," Jason called and kicked the door shut behind him. He found Elizabeth sitting at the kitchen island, staring at his answering machine. After he tossed his grocery bag on the counter, he came up behind her and playfully rested his chin on her shoulder. "You were sleeping so soundly, I didn't want to wake you."

"The phone woke me up."

There was an unusual note in her voice. Strain. Tension. Maybe worry.

"Oh?"

She nodded and waved distractedly at the answering machine. "It was your grandmother."

"Sybil called, huh? What did she want?" Something told him that he didn't want to know.

"She left a message."

Jason pressed the play button and listened. Sybil's noisy cacklings reminded him of a chicken attempting to lay an ostrich egg. His grin turned grimace as the familial skeletons came dancing out of the closet. Oh, well. Elizabeth would learn soon enough that his family was far from perfect.

Tuning out as Sybil attempted to diagnose Meredith's mental state, Jason stretched out across the cool marble of the island and took Elizabeth's warm hands into his own. Gut tight, he wondered why she was acting so aloof. He played with her fingers and waggled his brow, hoping to tease her out of her pensive mood.

Then, Sybil changed the subject.

"And, I'm still waiting to hear some more details about this woman you're dating."

Jason froze.

"So far, I only know that her name is Elizabeth, and that's not a whole lot to go on.... If you're considering making this woman a member of our clan, I'm going to need more information!

He cast a sheepish glance at Elizabeth for her reaction and noted that her face was fiery red. His heart lurched into his throat.

Busted.

Elizabeth knew he'd been talking to his family about her. Knew he'd informed them that they were dating. Knew that his interest in her had progressed beyond a mild interest in his sister-in-law's friend to a serious interest in the possibility of making her a member of the Colton clan.

After Sybil had slammed the phone down in disgust, the room was eerily silent.

Jason patted Elizabeth's hand and pushed himself off the island. Stepping to the freezer, he stuffed the gallon of chocolate ice cream inside and wondered what he should say now that the cat was out of the bag. After he shut the freezer door, he filled his lungs and pinched the bridge of his nose.

"I'm really sorry if she embarrassed you. I didn't

mean for you to find out how I felt about you this way."

Elizabeth swallowed. "How," she asked in a tiny voice, "do you feel about me?"

He moved around the island to stand at her side. A groan radiated from his gut. "I'm..." The word escaped on a long sigh. Slowly, he reached out and, cupping her cheek in his palm, stroked the high ridge of her cheekbone with his thumb. "I'm falling in love with you."

"You are?" She turned to face him and, eyes closed, slipped her arms around his waist. She rested her forehead against his chest.

"Mm-hum. I think I was a goner at my brother's wedding. The moment I laid eyes on you, all dripping and red-faced and trying to blow your nose on that welcome card, I thought to myself, that is the kind of woman I'd like to spend the rest of my life with. The kind of woman who shares my feelings about love and marriage and family. When I noticed that you were expecting a baby, I knew you were already taken and I felt..." He sighed and tipped her head back so that he could look into her eyes. "I felt cheated. Robbed."

"I've felt that, too."

"I know," he whispered before his mouth sought and found hers. As Elizabeth parted her lips and allowed him entrance to her mouth, Jason felt the strange and wonderful magic that came from discovering the secret to life's great mystery.

She was the one he'd been looking for all his life, he was suddenly sure. It didn't matter that she'd been married before. It didn't matter that she carried another man's child. Those were simply the circumstances of life. He'd had his own loves...and his own loses.

The past was simply that. Past. Gone. No longer an issue.

They'd both learned about what they did not want out of a partner. Out of life. And, Jason thought lazily, as he lost himself in the sweet sensuality of her kiss, they both knew that they did want love, marriage and family. No matter how that family came into being. His uncle Joe had taught him from the time he could remember that how a man became a father didn't matter in the least. What mattered was how a man loved and cared for that child.

Jason already felt hugely possessive of Elizabeth's baby. An ownership, of sorts, that didn't come from biology, but from love.

And he could tell, by the way Elizabeth was kissing him, she felt the same way.

"Jason..." Her breathing coming in labored puffs, her face pink from the abrasion of his five-o'clock shadow, Elizabeth twisted her mouth away from his and planted her palms on his chest. "Jason, I have to tell you something."

"Mmm." Jason nuzzled her neck and kissed his way back up her jawline and to her mouth. Her low moans of pleasure were music. "Tell me, tell me," he whispered into her mouth. She tasted so sweet and warm and feminine and...right.

Immediately the kiss grew frenzied. Hot. Their ragged breathing mingled with sounds of pleasure that emanated from their throats. Jason slid his hands from her face and around to the back of her head where he filled his hands with her thick, satiny brown hair.

When Jason kissed Elizabeth like this, nothing else mattered.

Again, Elizabeth broke free and, breathing as if she'd just run cross-country, gripped his biceps for support. "Jason." The word came out in a sob. "We have to stop."

"Why?"

"Because. I have something important to talk to you about. It concerns—" Her eyes darted about and she looked as if she were on the verge of tears. "I—"

Jason felt a sudden ember of dread flare and begin to burn in his belly. This thing she needed to talk to him about was serious. He sensed it was the secret she'd been harboring since they'd met, and he closed his eyes, steeling himself against the inevitable pain.

She was still in love with Mike.

Or Mike was coming for the baby.

Or Mike had suddenly come to his senses and decided that he'd been a moron to throw away a wonderful woman like Elizabeth.

As he stared down into her tortured face, old tapes from Angie's tearful last-minute confession played in his head. Elizabeth took a step back and raked her hair out of her eyes.

"Wait," he whispered, touching a finger to her

lips. "I have a feeling we need to be sitting down for this."

Elizabeth nodded.

He took her hand and led her over to his new couch. The couch that they had chosen together, just last week. He tugged her to his side and was on the verge of sitting down when his pager went off.

"Damn." He reached into his pocket and studied the number. "It's the hospital. I'll call and find out what's going on, and be back in a second."

"Okay," she whispered.

"Hey," he told her as they stood before the couch, "whatever you have to tell me, I—" he swallowed hard "—it'll be okay. I'm a big boy. I'll live."

Her head bobbed, but she didn't look convinced, and his heart plummeted. This was big. He was scared.

Jason had worked on people whose lives were hanging in the balance many times in his career, but never had he been as scared as he was now. Whatever she had to tell him was threatening their future.

Hands flexing with nervous energy, he strode across his expansive living room to the kitchen extension. He stabbed in the number to the hospital and as he waited to be connected from the switchboard to emergency, he watched Elizabeth.

Again, he was reminded of Angie's agony after he'd discovered she'd had a tubal ligation. Seemed she hadn't planned on telling him until after the wedding. Angie had made up her mind that she never wanted to have children, back when she was a very small child, and had had the surgery when she was still in her twenties. She'd had to leave the state to find a doctor willing to sterilize such a young woman.

Given Angie's abusive parents, Jason could understand her reasons for not wanting children of her own. What he could not understand were the elaborate lies she told him about all the children they would have once they were married. If he hadn't inadvertently overheard a conversation between Angie and an OBGYN nurse at the hospital one day, he'd still be laboring under the illusion that someday he'd become a father.

But Angie hadn't wanted a family. She'd wanted prestige, money, power and security. All of the things she'd missed out on, growing up with drug addict parents.

He clutched the phone as the hospital switchboard came on the line and prayed that he hadn't fallen in love with the wrong woman yet again.

"Karen? It's Dr. Colton. What's going on?"

Jason listened intently for a moment, his eyes never straying from Elizabeth. "Okay. Tell them I'm on my way. Five minutes or so. Thanks."

Slowly, he hung up the phone. Elizabeth's eyes were filled with misery, and he wondered if his heart was back in shape to take another beating so soon.

He cleared his throat. "One of my elderly patients has taken a pretty bad fall. Broken hip, among other problems. I have to go, but I shouldn't be gone too long." He lifted his keys from the hook on the wall above the phone table. "I promise to finish cooking dinner just as soon as I get back. And then we can talk.'' He cast her a smile he wasn't feeling.

Elizabeth nodded, her return smile equally weak.

Jason moved to the door, then changed his mind and quickly crossed back to the couch. Bending forward, he tipped her chin and settled his mouth firmly over hers. She arched toward him and slipped her arms up over his shoulders. Wordlessly, she pulled him closer and deepened the kiss.

A whimper filled her throat and her kiss communicated the desperation they were both feeling. Within moments, the passion had flared to a level they hadn't reached before now and Jason knew that he had to leave immediately. While he still could.

``You'll be here when I get back?'' he asked between ragged breaths. He could feel her nod as he devoured her jawline, her neck and then her collarbone with kisses.

``Yes,'' she gasped. ``I'll wait.''

``Don't move,'' he warned. ``I'll be back within an hour. I promise. Then we can pick up where we left off.''

``Okay.''

Elizabeth smiled up at him, which would have made him feel much better if it hadn't been for the tears that streamed down her cheeks.

Elizabeth stood at the kitchen counter, putting the lasagna together for Jason. She figured he wouldn't mind, as he would no doubt be hungry when he got home. It had been nearly an hour since he'd left, and she was feeling a little light-headed from hunger herself.

Then again, it could have been that kiss that left her a little woozy. She couldn't wait for him to come home. The sooner she came clean about this stupid feud and the wedge it placed between them, the sooner they could get on with their lives.

The phone rang as Elizabeth filled a dirty pot with soap and water. It was probably Jason, she surmised, glancing at the clock, calling to tell her when she could expect him home. She dried her hands on the towel that dangled from the refrigerator handle and picked up the phone on the second ring.

''Hello?'' Just the anticipation of hearing his voice left her breathless.

''Who is this?''

''Elizabeth.'' She frowned. This was not Jason. But the voice had a familiar quality.

''Elizabeth who?''

''Mansfield,'' she answered before she realized that the familiar voice on the other end of the line was none other than Sybil Colton.

Chapter 8

Sybil fell silent for so long, Elizabeth wondered if she was still on the line.

"Hello?" she ventured timidly.

"Mansfield? You say your name is...*Mansfield?*"

Elizabeth couldn't see switching to Sonderland now. Sybil would learn the truth sooner or later. "Yes. This is Elizabeth Mansfield."

The repeated click of the lighter, coupled with moans of extreme frustration, sounded across the lines.

"Ouch," Sybil mumbled. After apparent success and a deep breath of nicotine, the elderly live wire returned to the subject at hand. "You are the same Elizabeth that my Jason is dating?"

"Well, I guess you could—"

"I *knew* it!" Sybil shouted, causing Elizabeth to jump. "I knew it was too damned good to be true! For once in his pigheaded life the boy does what I want him to do, but then he has to go and screw the whole thing up by picking a damned *Mansfield!* I don't believe this! Why, I simply won't stand for it." She paused to puff furiously on a cigarette.

Legs weak, knees knocking, heart hammering, Elizabeth wobbled over to the breakfast nook and sank into a chair.

"What is he *thinking?*" Sybil demanded.

"Well, I—"

"I have half a mind to jump on my jet and run over there and smack some sense into that boy. But he never did listen to me. No way. I was the one who told him not to waste his time with medicine. He has a brilliant gift for business like his father and uncle before him. But would he listen? No! He has to save the world. But I'm sure you're familiar with his stubborn streak."

"Mmm-hmm." Elbows on the table, Elizabeth buried her head in her hands and pressed the phone to her ear with her shoulder.

"He can drive you mad. In a way, that boy reminds me of myself. I, too, was a rebel," Sybil announced, seeming to forget that she was fraternizing with the enemy. "Resented the hell out of my conservative upbringing. Lived an expatriate lifestyle during the war that caused a rift between my big brother Teddy and me, I tell you. That and the fact that I'm a dyed-in-the-wool feminist." Her voice took on a reminiscent quality. "Those were the good old days. I suppose Jason has told you about some of my times with Virginia Woolf and the gang. If he hasn't, ask him. Those were the good old days, I tell you."

Elizabeth held out the phone and stared at it. Where was this woman going with this? "Uh, Ms. Colton—"

"Call me, Sybil!" Sybil shouted, then wheezed and coughed at the exertion it caused.

"Okay, uh, Sybil," Elizabeth began, thinking that perhaps the old woman wasn't as opposed to the Mansfields as she liked to let on, "may I take a message for Jason?"

"Yes! You can tell that stinker for me that I forbid him to date a Mansfield!"

With a spring in his step, Jason bounded down the steps of his parents mansion and jogged across the parking area to his Jaguar. After spending an hour at the hospital with his patient, he'd stopped off here to talk to his mom and dad. He wanted to tell them about Elizabeth before Sybil burned up the phone lines with rumor.

As he sat in his car, he took a moment to once more look over the contents of the jewelry box he held. The sapphire-and-diamond choker was as beautiful as he remembered. According to his mother, the gems had been in the family for over three hundred years. The original necklace had been twenty-four inches, but recently, it had been skillfully fashioned into two chokers. Savannah owned one, and now…

The thought of all that history converging into his relationship with Elizabeth brought a lump to his throat. He ran his fingers over the cool stones.

Elizabeth would love it.

He couldn't wait to see her face when he presented her with this symbol of the feelings he held for her. This was the first time he'd ever held this piece in his possession. For some strange reason, it hadn't occurred to him to offer it to Angie before they were married. He watched the way the light danced and refracted off the precious stones in the California twilight. Something about this piece just screamed Elizabeth.

Whatever was bothering her, certainly they could overcome it together. She was worth whatever amount of emotional torment they'd have to work through when he got home. She would be there waiting for him, just as she'd promised. Unlike Angie, Jason knew that he could trust Elizabeth.

He tucked the box into his jacket pocket and slipped the key into the ignition. The Jaguar's engine roared to life and began to purr as he backed out of the driveway and headed for his apartment. From the glove compartment, Jason retrieved his cell phone and punched in his home number. It was such a warm feeling to know that Elizabeth waited there for him.

By the time the phone had rung for the fifth time, Jason began to grow alarmed. She should have answered by now. Even if she'd fallen back to sleep, surely she would have heard and answered the phone by now.

His answering machine picked up and he heard his voice invite the caller to leave a message at the tone.

"Elizabeth?"

There was no answer. "Elizabeth, honey, if you are there, pick up." He knew she was there. She'd said she was going to be there. "Elizabeth?" Myriad thoughts, all bad, flitted through his mind.

She'd gone into labor.

She'd fallen.

She'd fallen and then gone into labor.

His mind whirled with the possibilities. "Elizabeth," he said to the silent answering machine, "If you can hear me, don't worry. I'm on my way home." He tore through a yellow light and peeled around a corner. "I should be home in a few minutes. Hang on, sweetheart. No matter what the problem is, we can fix it."

Jason came to a screeching halt in front of his condo.

Sobbing, Elizabeth lay curled on the bed in her own bedroom, propped in a nest of pillows. So deep was her anguish, she wondered if she'd be able to go on living. Of course, for the sake of the baby, she'd stay alive, but to *live,* to really live, the way she had been with Jason… That just didn't seem to be in the cards for her.

Tissues wadded in both fists, she dabbed at the various streams that leaked from her eyes and lamented over future plans never to be fulfilled for the second time in less than a year. Face red, eyes puffy, she stifled a keening wail with her hands. Oh, Lord, why? Why me?

Sybil had been right, of course.

What had she been thinking? She should have known that Jason's family would never have accepted her. Not considering the history. There was far too much bad blood between the Mansfields and the Coltons.

And if the bad blood wasn't enough, surely pregnancy would kill the welcoming committee. The very idea that she'd come waltzing in, in this condition, and join the Colton clan was ludicrous. Protectively, Elizabeth patted the side of her belly.

"But that's okay," she murmured to her baby. "None of this is your fault, sweet potato." All over again, the tears squeezed from her lashes and rained down her cheeks. "It's just you and me, buddy. Just us against the mean old world."

Jason came tearing into his condo, fearing the worst. "Elizabeth?" he shouted, searching first the living room, and then the kitchen. The oven and all burners had been carefully turned off. Cold food had been stored in the refrigerator, the drainboard had been wiped down and the dishwasher loaded. Strange.

"Elizabeth?"

No answer. He blazed through the dining room, back through the living room and down the hall, frantically calling her name as he went. "Elizabeth! Answer me, honey! Where are you? Are you all right?"

Still no answer. After a thorough search that did not even yield her purse, Jason began to fear the worst. She'd had gone into labor and had somehow made it to the hospital. Yanking his cell phone from his pocket, he jabbed in the hospital's number and impatiently waited to be transferred to maternity.

Elizabeth was not there.

Nor was anyone answering to her description. Neither had any accident or emergency birth been reported to 911 or the local police department. None of Elizabeth's friends, including Savannah, had heard from her, either.

Slowly, Jason hung up and his natural fear turned to dread. She'd left, but not because of the baby. Deep down in his heart, he knew she'd left because of the secret she'd been harboring.

Old tapes of Angie's deception and multitudinous lies began to play in his head. Like mercury in the desert, Jason felt his blood pressure begin to rise, and his heart to throb in his ears. Slamming his front door behind him, he jumped into his Jaguar and, tires squealing, backed out of his driveway and into the street.

Once and for all, Jason knew it was time to get to the bottom of this secret. Then, when they'd had it out, they could forgive and forget and—in the grand style of Sybil Colton—get on with their damned lives.

Jason found Elizabeth curled in a nest of pillows on her bed. Tear tracks were evident on her cheeks, and her eyes, closed as she slumbered, were darkly shadowed against her pale skin. Slowly Jason eased onto the edge of her mattress and stroked tendrils of her silky brown hair away from her face.

She was such an angel.

Right then and there he vowed that no matter how terrible her secret was, he would learn to cope. His heart seized with love. He couldn't live without her, or the baby.

Elizabeth's eyes fluttered open, and she cried out when she saw him. "Oh, Jason." Throwing back the light comforter, she sat up and threw herself into his waiting arms.

Without words, they came together, an urgency to their kisses that left them both winded. After a bit, Jason pushed farther back onto the mattress and cradled Elizabeth in his lap. He nuzzled her hair, her cheeks, her neck and, rocking her gently, shushed her ragged hiccups.

She rubbed her face against his shirt and then clutching the placket in her fists, looked up at him through bleary eyes.

"I was so worried about you," he whispered, bringing his nose to hers. "Why did you leave?"

"B-because," she blubbered, "I was afraid."

"Afraid of what?"

"How you would react."

"To what?" He braced himself. This was it. He was on the verge of losing everything.

"To the fact that I'm a Mansfield."

"Right." That part he knew. He ran his hand from her shoulder, down her arm and then laced his fingers with hers. Lightly he kissed her knuckles and again waited for the other shoe to drop. "I know who you are, sweetheart. What I don't know is why you're so afraid."

"I'm afraid because I'm a Mansfield. Sybil was

so upset. I knew she would be. They will all be, when they find out.'' Fresh tears welled in her eyes. ''Oh, Jason, I'm so sorry I didn't tell you sooner. I should have, I know, but it's just that I'd gone and fallen in love with you, and I didn't want to rock the boat with something that I hoped didn't really matter anymore.''

''What doesn't matter anymore?'' Jason's confusion increased with her convoluted explanation.

''But it does matter, don't you see?''

''No, I don't see!''

''I was afraid of that.'' Her lips trembled as she beseeched him, ''Please forgive me.'' Her sobs began afresh.

Jason still didn't have a clue what she was talking about. His brow furrowed, he stared down into her red-rimmed eyes and wondered what the devil her maiden name—and his cranky grandmother—had to do with anything.

''I forgive you,'' he began, and tipped up her chin with his finger. ''But please explain to me, why does being a Mansfield have anything to do with us?''

''The feud! Katherine? William?''

Expression blank, Jason racked his brain for a clue to what she was talking about. He shrugged and Elizabeth continued her attempts to jog his memory.

''Three hundred years ago? William Colton dumped Katherine Mansfield?''

''Okay...''

Elizabeth grabbed his arm and gave it a shake. ''Surely you've heard about the great Colton-Mansfield feud.''

He shrugged a shoulder. "It vaguely rings a bell, but I fail to see what it has to do with you and me."

"You really don't know?" She sniffed and rubbed her eyes.

"No."

A slow smile began to push at her lips, and before he could figure out what had just transpired, she began to laugh. Or maybe she was crying with a smile on her face. It was hard to tell.

Jason peered into her face. Hopefully, this was a good sign. "Would you mind letting me in on the joke?"

She giggled and sobbed and sniffed and rubbed her face against his shirt. "Oh, Jason. It's such a long story, I—" She threw her hands up and sagged against him.

"Honey, I'm dying here. Could you give me the abridged version?"

She nodded and, arching against him, brushed her lips against his. "I'm sorry. Okay."

With a heavy sigh, Elizabeth plunged into the sordid history of the Mansfield-Colton families, hitting the highlights for the sake of expedience.

"And then, after you'd left for the hospital, Sybil called back and left a message for you."

Jason groaned. "What'd she say?"

"'That she forbids your fraternizing with a Mansfield and that she's going to get on her jet and come over here and smack you.'' Once again, Elizabeth's face crumpled. "Oh, Jason, she's right. Your family would never accept me."

He cupped her cheeks in his hands. "You think I'd give up you and the baby, because my grandmother is hung up on some ancient family feud?" He leaned back and gave vent to his laughter. "Oh, Elizabeth, who cares what happened three hundred years ago between two stubborn families in the midst of an idiotic grudge match? Listen. I happen to know that Sybil is the only one who cares about this stuff anymore."

"But how? How do you know?"

"I know because I just told my mom and dad that I'm going to ask a certain—and very pregnant—Elizabeth Mansfield to be my wife today."

"You *did?*" She stared at him, agog. "W-what did they say?"

"They told me to give you this." He kissed both her cheeks. "They will *all* love you, Sybil included, for who you are. The way I do."

"You love me?"

"I love you, with all my heart. And I want you and the baby and me to be a family. And I want this Mansfield—" he placed a firm hand on the baby "—to be born a Colton."

Fresh tears, this time of joy, brimmed in her eyes and threatened to spill over her lashes.

Jason stroked her cheek with the back of his hand. "Elizabeth, I want to do this right." He nudged her off his lap and fished in his pocket for a slim jewelry box.

"What's this?" Elizabeth whispered.

From the velvet-lined box, Jason withdrew a stunning necklace, all pillow-shaped sapphires, surrounded by diamonds and linked together to form a choker.

Elizabeth gasped at the beauty and felt tingles of

recognition race up and down her spine. There was something so familiar about this necklace.

Moving off the edge of the bed, Jason dropped to his knees and took her hand in his. "My great-great-great-great-great-great—" he stopped and counted on his fingers. "Was that seven greats? No, six, okay, great-grandfather gave this necklace to my great-times-seven grandmother."

"I know," Elizabeth whispered and grasped his wrists in her hands.

"You know?"

"Yes! Because this is the same exact necklace that he gave my ancestor, Katherine Mansfield, three hundred years ago!" At his puzzled expression, she continued. "My great-grandmother wrote all about it in a journal she kept, chronicling the feud between our families. Legend has it that on the eve of their wedding, William Colton put the necklace on Katherine's neck and the sapphires stopped sparkling. He took it as an omen and called off the wedding."

"He gave up a life with a dishy Mansfield babe? What a fool."

"Well, not really. From what I've heard, Katherine wasn't all that nice."

"Oh. And I guess there is the fact that if he'd gone through with that wedding, I wouldn't be standing here right now."

Elizabeth pouted. "That would be very, very sad indeed."

Jason clasped her hands. "Elizabeth Mansfield, say you'll marry me and put an end to this horrible, never-ending feud."

His expression was at the same time playful and hopeful, and Elizabeth had no intention of resisting.

"Hmm." She pretended to weigh his proposal. "I'll marry you only on the condition that I pass the acid test."

"Sybil will love you, once she gets to know you."

"Not her, silly. The necklace. Help me put it on, please."

His fingers shook as he locked the clasp at the back of her neck.

"Do they sparkle?" she whispered, for a moment wondering if the curse was still in effect.

Jason took a deep breath, and a slow smile pushed lines into the corners of his eyes. "Blindingly." He reached up and pushed her hair away from her face. "But they will never be able to compete with the emerald of your eyes. Elizabeth Mansfield, marry me."

Laughing, Elizabeth threw herself into his arms. "Yes, I'll marry you. But you'll have to deal with telling your grandmother that not only am I a Mansfield, but I'm pregnant." She giggled. "That ought to have her flying out here without benefit of a plane."

Jason's laughter mingled with hers. "Don't worry. Her bark is much worse than her bite. When she learns that you're about to make her a great-grandmother, she'll love you. Almost as much as I do."

* * * * *

Look for the first book in

THE COLTONS

series in June 2001:

BELOVED WOLF

by Kasey Michaels

Chapter 1

Joe Colton burst from the elevator before the doors had fully opened and raced down the corridor toward the nurses' station, his foster son, River James, right behind him. They'd flown from the family ranch in Prosperino, River at the controls, within an hour of the phone call from the San Francisco police, arriving shortly before dawn.

"My daughter—Sophie Colton," Joe demanded of the unit clerk, who was otherwise occupied in filing her nails. "What room is she in?"

The young woman looked up at him blankly. "Colton? I don't think we don't have a Colton." She swiveled in her chair, spoke to a nurse who'd just come into the station. "Mary, do we have a Colton?"

The nurse stepped forward, looking at Joe. "May I ask who you are, sir?"

"I'm her father, damn it!" Joe exploded, his large frame looking more menacing than paternal at the moment, his nearly sixty years having made small impact on him other than to dust some silver in his dark-brown hair.

River took off his worn cowboy hat, put a hand on his foster father's arm and smiled at the nurse. "Senator Colton is a little upset, ma'am," he said, being his most charming at the same time he emphasized the word *senator,* even if Joe had left national government office years earlier. "His daughter was mugged last evening. Colton. Sophie Colton."

It might have been the dropping of Joe Colton's title, or it might have been River's lazy smile, but Mary quickly stepped out from behind the desk, asking the two men to follow her down the corridor.

"I'm sorry, Senator," Mary said as they walked, "but your daughter was the victim of a crime. We can't be too careful. She came back from surgery a little over an hour ago, and is probably sleeping, but I can tell you that she made it through the surgery without incident. Have you been apprised of her injuries?"

"Oh, God." Joe stopped, put a hand to his mouth, turned away from the nurse. Obviously the long night had taken its toll. That, River thought, and the fact that Meredith Colton, Sophie's mother, hadn't seen any reason to accompany her husband to San Francisco.

"Yes, we have, but we'd like to hear a recap from you, if you don't mind," River said, stepping up, taking over for this so very strong man who had already buried one child. River knew he couldn't understand all that Joe must have been going through since the call about Sophie had come in to the ranch, but he had a pretty good idea that the man had been living in his own special hell; reliving the call about Michael, fearing the worst for his daughter.

River, however, had been more mad than frightened, once he'd spoken to the patient liaison at the hospital, who had assured him that Sophie's injuries, although extensive, were not life threatening. While Joe Colton had sat in the back of the small private jet, praying for his daughter, River had been at the controls, wishing himself in San Francisco so that he could knock down Chet Wallace. Then pick him up, knock him down again. And again.

Joe collected himself, motioned for the nurse to continue down the hallway.

"She suffered a mild concussion, Senator," Mary told them, stopping in front of Room 305, her hand on the metal door plate. "I want to prepare you for that, as she may be confused for a while once she wakes. Plus, she's got lots of scrapes and bruises, from her contact with a brick wall, as I understand it, and the gravel in the alley—those have been cleaned up, of course. And there are some fairly deep scratches on her...on her chest. They'll be painful, but aren't serious, and we've already begun treatment with antibiotics. We can't be too careful with human bites or scratches. I—I'm sorry."

The bastard had *bitten* her? River hadn't known that part, wished Joe didn't have to know that part.

Joe moaned low in his throat. River squeezed his work-hard hands into fists.

Mary continued, "The orthopods put her knee back together—torn Medial meniscus, which is fairly common—but she's in a J-brace and on crutches for at least five or six weeks, and then will need some pretty extensive rehab. And," she added, sighing, "Dr. Hardy, chief of reconstructive surgery, sewed up the knife gash on her face. She'll need follow-up surgery, at least that's what's on Dr. Hardy's post-op notes, but at least she's been put back together. It's a miracle the knife didn't hit any large blood vessels or nerves. Still, even though the cut wasn't dangerously deep, it took over one hundred stitches to close her up again."

"Oh, God," Joe said, pleaded. "My baby. My beautiful, beautiful baby."

River clenched his teeth until his jaw hurt. Sophie. Beautiful, beautiful Sophie. Dragged into an alley. Mauled, beaten, cut, damn near killed. And for no reason, no reason at all. Just because a bastard high on drugs had gone berserk. Just because she'd been in the wrong place at the wrong time. Now her entire life had been altered, changed forever.

"I think we're prepared to see her now, ma'am," River said, motioning for the nurse to step back so that he and Joe could enter Sophie's room. "We promise not to disturb her."

"Certainly, sir—Senator," Mary agreed, then walked past them, back to the nurses' station.

''Ready, Joe?'' River asked, a hand on his foster father's back.

''No,'' Joe told him, his voice so low River had to lean close to hear him. ''A parent is never ready to see his child lying in a hospital bed.'' He lifted his head, took a deep breath. ''But let's do it.''

River pushed open the door, let Joe precede him into the room, then followed after him. He didn't want to see Sophie this way, injured, helpless. That's not how he had seen her when he'd first come to live at the ranch and she'd chased after him until he'd let down his guard, let her into his life. His Sophie, four years his junior—which had been such a huge gap when they were younger. The angry young man and the awkward, braces-on-her-teeth, skinned-knees, pigtailed, hero-worshiping kid.

She'd driven him crazy, made him angry. Gotten under his skin. Wormed her way into his bruised, battered and wary heart.

And then she'd grown up.

Oh, God, she'd grown up.

Escape to a place where a kiss is still a kiss...
Feel the breathless connection...
Fall in love as though it were the very first time...
Experience the power of love!

Come to where favorite authors—such as Diana Palmer, Stella Bagwell, Marie Ferrarella and many more—deliver heart-warming romance and genuine emotion, time after time after time....

Silhouette Romance—
stories straight from the heart!

Visit Silhouette at www.eHarlequin.com. SRDIR1

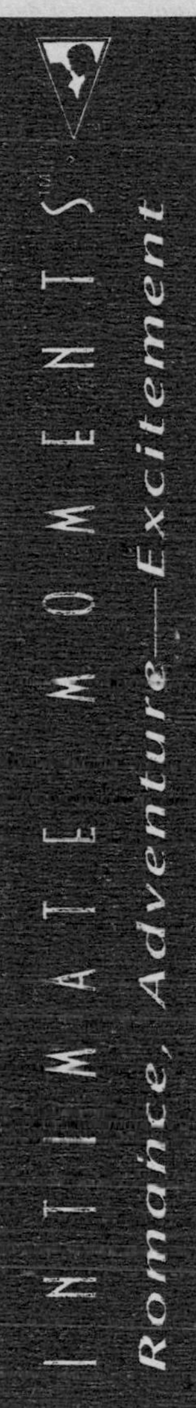

IF YOU'VE GOT THE TIME... WE'VE GOT THE INTIMATE MOMENTS

Passion. Suspense. Desire. Drama.
Enter a world that's larger than life, where men and women overcome life's greatest odds for the ultimate prize: love. Nonstop excitement is closer than you think...in Silhouette Intimate Moments!

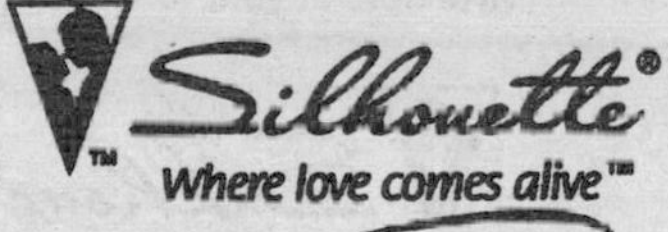

Visit Silhouette at www.eHarlequin.com

SIMDIR1

passionate powerful provocative love stories that fulfill your every desire

Silhouette Desire delivers strong heroes, spirited heroines and stellar love stories.

Desire features your favorite authors, including

Diana Palmer, Annette Broadrick, Ann Major, Anne MacAllister and Cait London.

Passionate, powerful and provocative romances *guaranteed!*

For superlative authors, sensual stories and sexy heroes, choose Silhouette Desire.

Available at your favorite retail outlet.

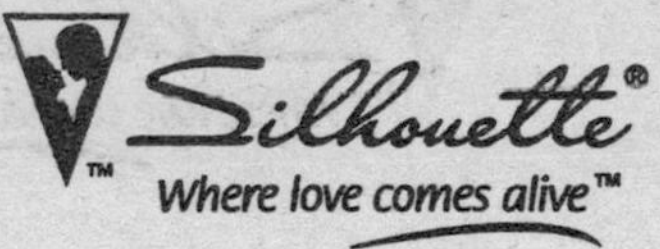

passionate powerful provocative love stories that fulfill your every desire

Visit us at www.eHarlequin.com

SDGEN00

Silhouette®

SPECIAL EDITION™

Emotional, compelling stories that capture the intensity of living, loving and creating a family in today's world.

Special Edition features bestselling authors such as Nora Roberts, Diana Palmer, Sherryl Woods, Lindsay McKenna, Joan Elliott Pickart—and many more!

For a romantic, complex and emotional read, choose Silhouette Special Edition.

Available at your favorite retail outlet.

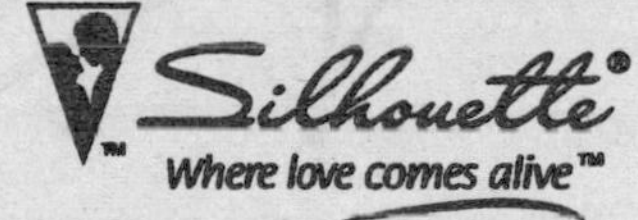

Visit Silhouette at www.eHarlequin.com

SSEGEN00

Silhouette
SPECIAL EDITION™
Emotional, compelling stories that capture the intensity of living, loving and creating a family in today's world.
Silhouette®
Desire
A highly passionate, emotionally powerful and always provocative read.
Silhouette®
Where love comes alive™
Silhouette
INTIMATE MOMENTS™
A roller-coaster read that delivers romantic thrills in a world of suspense, adventure and more.
SILHOUETTE Romance
From first love to forever, these love stories are for today's woman with traditional values.
Visit Silhouette at www.eHarlequin.com
SILGENINT

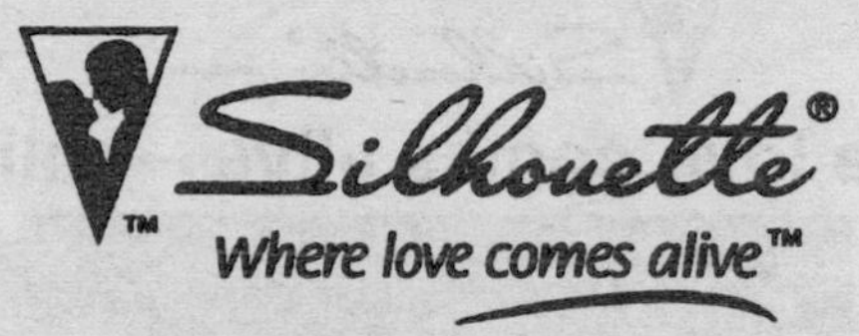

From first love to forever, these love stories are for today's woman with traditional values.

A highly passionate, emotionally powerful and always provocative read.

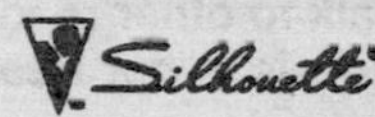

SPECIAL EDITION™

Emotional, compelling stories that capture the intensity of living, loving and creating a family in today's world.

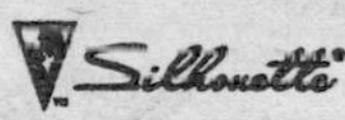

INTIMATE MOMENTS™

A roller-coaster read that delivers romantic thrills in a world of suspense, adventure and more.

Visit Silhouette at www.eHarlequin.com

SDIR2

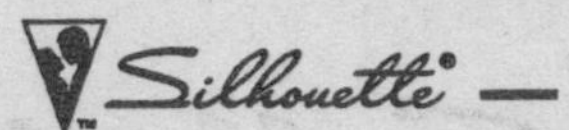

where love comes alive—online...

eHARLEQUIN.com

shop eHarlequin

- Find all the new Silhouette releases at everyday great discounts.
- Try before you buy! Read an excerpt from the latest Silhouette novels.
- Write an online review and share your thoughts with others.

reading room

- Read our Internet exclusive daily and weekly online serials, or vote in our interactive novel.
- Talk to other readers about your favorite novels in our Reading Groups.
- Take our Choose-a-Book quiz to find the series that matches you!

authors' alcove

- Find out interesting tidbits and details about your favorite authors' lives, interests and writing habits.
- Ever dreamed of being an author? Enter our Writing Round Robin. The Winning Chapter will be published online! Or review our writing guidelines for submitting your novel.

All this and more available at
www.eHarlequin.com
on Women.com Networks

SINTB1R